Author's Books

MOMMY...WHAT WAS WAR?

Pending

OUR DESTINY
if we want it
**A GLOBAL
COMMONWEALTH
OF COMPASSION**

WE HAVE TO
Stop the World
MAKE SENSE
I Want to Get Off!
OF THIS WORLD

**ON WINGS TO
THE SPIRITUAL CENTER
OF THE WORLD**

HE PUT THE FLAVOR
Most of All
IN THE SOUP
He Taught Me Christ
OF THE WORLD

**MY HEART:
A MANGER**
*A Christmas Eve
Reflection*

Also

AND A GENERATION WILL YET ARISE
TO SING '*HOW MAJESTIC THE VISION!*'
rousing lyrics for symphony & mixed chorus

Thanksgiving 2008

To Tony + Maria D'Urso

MOMMY...
WHAT WAS WAR?

BE FILLED
WITH HOPE !

You are loved –

TED Conlin

Ted Conlin

TRAFFORD
Bloomington, Indiana

Order this book online at www.trafford.com
or email orders@trafford.com

Most Trafford titles are also available at major online book retailers.

Note for Librarians: A cataloguing record for this book is available from Library and Archives Canada at www.collectionscanada.ca/amicus/index-e.html

Printed in Victoria, BC, Canada.

ISBN: 978-1-4269-1068-5 (Soft)
ISBN: 978-1-4269-1139-2 (Hard)
ISBN: 978-1-4269-1181-1 (e-book)

Our mission is to efficiently provide the world's finest, most comprehensive book publishing service, enabling every author to experience success. To find out how to publish your book, your way, and have it available worldwide, visit us online at www.trafford.com

Trafford rev. 9/24/2009

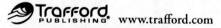

www.trafford.com

North America & international
toll-free: 1 888 232 4444 (USA & Canada)
phone: 250 383 6864 • fax: 812 355 4082

WITH ENORMOUS GRATITUDE
I salute my dearly beloved
spouse of more than half a century
ADELLA KRAFT CONLIN
whose boundless love,
constancy of unwavering
and unselfish support,
has made possible
this volume.

**Without her
there'd be no book.**

**** Please View Acknowledgements at Back of Book ****
They Are Worth the Read...You Won't Be Disappointed

~ GIFT & LEGACY ~

We are all fruit from the same tree of life and
stand on the same shoulders of those who came before us.
Thus it is with enormous gratitude and affection that
I present this volume as gift and legacy to my children:

Judy Adella, Amy Marie, Peter Timothy,
and Cathy Paul (in Heaven),
cherished and held in awe, each one.

Too, to my awesome birth family
of nieces and nephews...
brother Walter's children:
Joseph, Thomas, Maria *Ria*, Paul.
brother Leonard's children:
Leonard, John, Jane, Walter *Joseph* (in Heaven),
Timothy, Elizabeth, James *Jimmy*, Mary.

We are blessed, so we pray:
Together, in solidarity, as family,
through every kind of struggle and challenge...

With affection...in life that is a journey, a voyage,
a pilgrimage not without meaning and purpose,
let us each be a candle for the others
as though a splendid torch...

Wanting to make it burn as brightly
as possible before handing it on
to future generations. Amen.

We are blessed!

~ DEDICATION ~

THE image of the suffering child is one of the most potent images of the past century. The child in distress is often used as a visual symbol of far larger issues: war, famine, pestilence, catastrophe, poverty, economic crisis. War and its child victims is the focus of this volume.

"Mommy...What Was War?" is dedicated to the many tens of millions of children made victims of war during my own lifetime, but given little more than a footnote in the forest of books written about war and peace.

It's as if they, the children, don't matter or don't have an important place in the say of things.

But they *do* matter. Their contribution to world peace has been through their pain, suffering, betrayal, anguish, despair... All of which God has taken and allowed "little pencils" such as myself to rise from the ashes of conflict and war to help in the task of making war obsolete.

It is *not* an unrealizable dream!

We Will Remember
We Shall Never Forget

20th Century dictatorial governments have killed more of their own people - more than three times as many - than have been killed in all 20th Century civil and international wars put together. The century's death toll from government killing reached 119,94,000 people by 1985. The overwhelming majority of the victims - 115,423,000 - were killed by governments in nonfree countries. (Governments in partly free countries, killed 3,140,000; in free cuntries, 831,000).

Over the same period, the victims of international and civil wars totaled 35,654,000. In other words, governments have killed more people in cold blood than in the heat of battle. And these figures are only approximations — the real numbers are probably much higher.

By studying the most lethal democides of the 20th Century, it's been found that 143,166,000 men, women and children (have been) shot, beaten, tortured, knifed, burned, starved, frozen, crushed or worked to death; or buried alive, drowned, hung, bombed, or any other of the myriad ways these governments have inflicted death on helpless citizens or foreigners.

To repeat: These were victims of deliberate violence by governments other than victims of wars, civil or international. The seven most lethal democides were:

> Soviet: 61,911,000
> Chinese Communist: 38,702,000
> Chinese Nationalist: 10,214,000
> Nazi: (including 5,291,000 Jews) 20,946,000
> Japanese in World War II: 5,890,000
> Yugoslav: (1941-87): 2,640,000
> Armenian: 1,000,000
> Rwandan: 1,000,000

The final version of this listing of death by governments in the 20th Century will include three more democides: Vietnam, Cambodia and the one committed by Pakistan in Bangladesh. No doubt it will also include the democides of Idi Amin and Milton Obote of ill-fated Uganda and the democide of Saddam Hussein against the Kurds.

The public's consciousness is not yet open to the idea of peace not being an impossible dream, of war not being an inevitable reality. The idea might be there, but it has not entered sufficiently to have taken root. The doors of perception are not yet opened. . . . But when they do open - *our task being to help hasten that day* - then women might give birth to children able to ask, "Mommy... what was war?"

- *Ted Conlin*
from his book
WAR ON TRIAL
1995

Ted Conlin at his home away from home, a Trappist monastery, St. Joseph's Abbey, in the rolling hills of Spencer, Massachusetts — year 2007.

~~ TABLE of CONTENTS ~~

SALUTE
DEDICATION
GIFT & LEGACY

ACKNOWLEDGEMENTS
(please find at end of book)

FOREWORD
PREFACE

PART I
A SOLITARY EXPLORER'S
EXPEDITION FOR WORLD PEACE

INTRODUCTION
The Religion of An Explorer

EINSTEIN AS A TORCH BEARER
FOR A "SANE" WORLD

BORN BURDENED BY
A GROTESQUE CENTURY

THIRTY YEARS IN THE WILDERNESS
AND WASTELANDS OF WAR

"OUTSIDE THE BOX"

A HINGE BETWEEN TWO AGES
New Kinds of Dictatorship
A New Kind of War

THE QUESTIONS NOW ARE
DIFFERENT...THAN BEFORE

IF ONLY FOR THE CHILDREN OF WAR,
I *HAD* TO DO THIS THING —
There Was No Turning Back!

THE "PATMOS" EXPERIENCE

PART II
THE PRIVILEGED
TIME WE LIVE IN

CHOOSING TO BE CHOSEN
AND THEN GOING THROUGH
SOME SACRED DOORWAYS

As My Exploration
Pushed Forward
THE PROJECT DIDN'T SEEM
NEARLY SO FUTILE OR FOOLISH

REVISITING MY BOOK
"WAR ON TRIAL"

"PLUS ULTRA"

A WONDERFUL ADVENTURE

PART III
BEYOND WAR

The Unexpected Leadership of
Poland's Karol Wojtyla
THE SYNCHRONICITY OF
THE TWO EVENTS
The Unexpected Cosmic
Drama at Medjugorje

A WELLSPRING
AMID THE MOUNTAINS
MEDICAL SCIENCE STUDIES

MY ONGOING WITNESS
TO THE 'MIRACLE OF THE SUN'

THE GOSPA'S VISITS AT MEDJUGORJE
DICTATED BY THE CIRCUMSTANCES
IN WHICH PEOPLE TODAY LIVE

"PROTECT MEDJUGORJE"
SAID JOHN PAUL II

AN ARRANGEMENT MADE
IN HEAVEN AND SEALED ON EARTH

THE WOMAN WITH A BROOM

ENDNOTES

~ FOREWORD ~

Ted Conlin's *Mommy...What Was War?* is an amazing account of the long journey undertaken by the author in his indefatigable quest for a solution to the gravest problem that has beset humanity since times immemorial – war. Like an explorer of the seas, Conlin has seen in the distance the mountaintops of distant continents where peace and love, not war and hatred, reign supreme. As if in a dream, he envisions a time when a child might ask his mother that most strange of questions, "Mommy, what *was* war?"

It is not difficult to appreciate the strangeness of the question because war is and has always been the most pervasive and entrenched condition in which humanity has lived. The twentieth century and the first few years of the present century give ample testimony of the reality of war.

A review of the recorded history of all nations, even among the most sophisticated, reveals a tragic spectacle – war. Perhaps, as the ancient Greek philosopher Heraclitus observed, war, which he called the father of all things, is ingrained in human nature and is that which ultimately engenders change and revitalization. Those who promote war, for whom war is what renders their lives meaningful and thus a prerequisite for change, would gladly agree with him when he noted that those who seek and pray for peace do not know what they are searching. For in advocating peace they are only hoping for death, that is, an end-state where there exists no possibility for change and progress.

There are and have been some, however, who would not stand in agreement with Heraclitus. For them, peace is attainable or is, at least, a goal toward which we are morally obliged to travel. Immanuel Kant, the great German philosopher of the eighteenth century, held this conviction. For him, the prospect of a world at peace, a world in which nations actualize the possibility of living peacefully with one another, is realizable. He outlined without hesitation the conditions under which it would become a reality, and it was his outline that centuries later would give birth to international institutions such as the League of Nations and the United Nations. Such and similar institutions, however, have failed to actualize the Kantian plan. Yet, why?

Ted Conlin, like Kant and many other utopian visionaries, also envisions a time when war will be a historical curiosity, a grotesque aberration, an embarrassing condition that has been responsible for incalculable suffering. Unlike Kant and other optimistic philosophers, for whom a heavy injection of rationality in human behavior would be the effective antidote to the ravages of war, Conlin envisions a spiritual revolution. In his own words, "we must effect a major shift in the world, a shift of the kind that would have us move toward [a] completely spiritual culture."

Conlin undertakes a detailed description of numerous instances in which war has wrought immense calamities on nations and communities, with emphasis made on the war that plagued former Yugoslavia. His capacity to describe and assess such calamities is engaging and challenging, and the fervor with which he captures human suffering is extraordinary. The reader is compelled to feel the pain and anguish of those afflicted by war. Conlin's call for a permanent truce and for a lasting cessation of atrocities is so intense and sensible that the attentive reader cannot but choose to join him in his campaign for peace.

The approach taken by Conlin, a thoroughly spiritual approach, may not be welcomed by some, but will surely be taken seriously by many. Two decades before the end of the twentieth century, so far the bloodiest of all centuries, reports began to emerge from Medjugorje, an obscure village in what was once Yugoslavia. A lady appeared to children, bringing to them and through them to the whole world a message of peace. The children called her Gospa, which in Croatian means Our Lady, that is, the Virgin Mary. Her reported words were: "Peace, peace, you must seek peace. There must be peace on earth. You must be reconciled with God and with each other." Such was her message, a message that has been continuously repeated since that time.

Our Lady's message could not have come at a more appropriate time, a time when war was everywhere and when the flickering moments of peace were only the result of mutual fear among nations. For it is indeed a historical fact that lasting peace has not been achieved since times immemorial. It is as if the warring instinct had been embedded in human nature in so profound a way that nothing can be effective to counterbalance it. War is and has been an endemic human condition.

Conlin's book recognizes this disheartening reality. Yet, he is convinced that a reversal of this unfortunate condition is possible and moved by a remarkable conviction, born out of a profound and consistent faith, Conlin envisions a time when children will ask their parents what indeed was war.

In the future, if humanity embraces the message of Our Lady of Medjugorje, and if the repeated calls from philosophers to infuse human behavior with a heavy dose of rationality are heeded, perhaps the need for war among nations and peoples would become an aberration of remote past times.

Perhaps, too, Plato's pessimistic statement that "only the dead have seen the end of war" would have proven to be mistaken. Conlin's well documented and thoroughly enthralling book deserves to be read with an open and sympathetic mind.

Luis E. Navia Ph.D.
Professor of Philosophy
New York Institute of Technology

~ PREFACE ~

THIS book, perhaps the most improbable of books anyone has ever dared to imagine or hope for, begins with my religion as an explorer. It *the book* is based upon an unshakable conviction that peace is not an unrealizable dream, nor is war an inevitable reality.

From the very outset my mission has been to help in the task of hastening the day when the world's children will look back on war as an 'inconceivable aberration' of their forefathers... when mothers might have children knowing they'll be able to ask the question: *Mommy, what was war?*

But this is not just a book. It is a report distilled from forty years of journaling my experience as a solo explorer searching for a solution to the problem that is war and threat of war.

Others have written on war and peace, such as Tolstoy and Einstein. And before them there'd been the ancient Greek philosophers. In the canceled preface to one of Tolstoy's later drafts of *War And Peace*, he says that what he wrote would not fit into any category, "whether novel, short story, poem, or history." The same holds true for *Mommy, What Was War?* It does not fit into any category.

More than a book *Mommy...What Was War?* is this 80-years-old explorer's summarized report of a life-long quest that had as its genesis the question, "How can we discover the sources of wholeness, healing and hope amidst a broken and suffering world?"

This report references my earlier book *WAR ON TRIAL* and my current work in progress, *BEYOND WAR*. The latter proposes a worldwide commitment to the creation of a "Global Commonwealth of Compassion." It invites going through some sacred doorways.

It invites going "outside the box" of traditional conversations about war and peace; outside the box of given perceptions of human existence and destiny; outside the box of science and its limitations; outside the box of how a history of conflict and war between some religions can cloud, make dark, how one perceives religion in general.

Indeed, one of the more important things I've learned during my years of experience as an explorer is the importance of stepping back now and then, stepping outside the box, and then to view the world from the perspective of an astronomer or an archaeologist . . . to relocate oneself in time, in place, in the flow of evolution . . . and then to look at everything with the eyes of a child.

It was a lesson I took seriously. More, I adopted it as my own as I struggled with the realization that the public's consciousness is far from being open to the idea of peace not being an unrealizable dream, of war not being an inevitable reality.

I saw that although the idea might be there, it has not entered sufficiently to have taken root. Had the situation been otherwise, then my quest might have appeared less foolish in the eyes of many who've seen it as folly.

Then came a night in June of 1981, at one in the morning, when a storm of Homeric force split the sky over two tiny mountain-villages in a region of the world known for its centuries-long history of little love lost between the two hamlets. The night before had been sticky-hot and oppressive, heavy with menace. "It's like the Day of Judgement out there," shouted one peasant as she shook her sleeping husband. It had a fine, crashing, orchestral overture, well-suited to this region of violent contrasts and untamed emotions.

Going back a thousand years personal feuds and vendettas lay deep in their bloodstream; never had they known the meaning of the word peace. And now everything seemed to be on fire. Smoke was belching out of the pine trees. The firemen were having a hard job coping with all the fires.

Later that same day a calm tranquility settled over the area. It was the beginning of a drama, a cosmic drama, the likes of which has never been seen before; and twenty-eight years later continues to play itself out, is still unfolding. In fact, it would prove to be the heralding of the most privileged age above all others.

Only by having already taken my quest "outside the box" was I fortunate enough to have found, early on in this drama, that here is where I would find the solution to the problem that is war and threat of war. I have not been disappointed. This book explains why.

May our Lord God bless, guide and protect you.

The AUTHOR

~~ PART ONE ~~

A SOLITARY EXPLORER'S
EXPEDITION FOR WORLD PEACE

INTRODUCTION
THE RELIGION OF AN EXPLORER

Since Auschwitz we know what man is capable of.
Since Hiroshima we know what is at stake.
Since the Unimaginable of 9.11.01
we know we must come up with a solution
to the problem that is war and threat of war
— and thus my quest.

IN the darkest days of the Nazi occupation of France, quiet heroes emerged as the forces of the Resistance. Heroism then, as now, arose from the small things. A generation after the Allies liberated Paris, I could see that the story of resistance to Inhumanity with its quiet heroes was still alive, still well and still desperately needed. A Czech poet stood up to totalitarianism… and won! A middle-aged woman took on the Marcos regime in the Philippines… and succeeded!

Over the years I'd marvel at how more great things have been wrought, come about, by one person than by all the great armies of history. At the same time the centuries-old problem that is war and threat of war, a broken world, invited a certain distress. While I knew that I was not the one person who could put an end to war and threat of war, I very much wanted to live as though I were that one person.

Because of this and the many, many millions of children killed, wounded and traumatized by war, I undertook to commit all of my talents, resources and energy to that end. In a world constantly honing its skills of total destruction, in a century of times gone mad and why it's known as a "Century of Tears," I asked only that

God's grace guide and sustain me in the effort. I believed, I trusted, I felt called.

My quest began with a simple question that had but one aim: to help hasten the day when children will be able to look back on war as an 'inconceivable aberration' of their forefathers. The question was this:

> "How can we discover the sources of wholeness,
> healing and hope amidst a broken
> and suffering world?"

With this one question began my search for a solution to the problem that is war and threat of war.

A solution!

Inspired in part by the quiet heroes in places all over the world working for peace, going to jail for peace, giving their lives for peace, very ordinary people, some of whom were my friends, I simply wanted to lend my support in a world where people still matter. The story behind what led to this quest - an odyssey that began with what I describe as an 'Exploration into God' - must remain for another time except to borrow from Christopher Fry, contemporary poet, when saying:

> Dark and cold we may be, but this
> Is no Winter now. The Frozen misery
> Of centuries breaks, cracks, begins to move;
> The thunder is the thunder of the floes
> The thaw, the flood, the upstart Spring.
> Thank God our time is now when wrong
> Comes up to face us everywhere,
> Never to leave us till we take
> The longest stride of soul men ever took.
> Affairs are now soul size,
> The enterprise
> Is exploration into God.

IT is a noble thing you are doing, said some, this quest for a solution to the problem that is war; but also it is a waste of your life. What you are seeking is impossible; it doesn't exist, not now, not ever.

Peace is *not* an unrealizable dream.
War is *not* an inevitable reality.

Where is the promise? You are foolish! But all such protestations fell before my perceived essence of what it means to be a person, a human being.

It means that we are people through other people. We cannot be fully human alone. Why? Because we are connected, we are made for interdependence — my humanity is caught up, bound up, inextricably, with yours. We are made for family — caring about others, going the extra mile for the sake of others. Initially my having gone the extra mile was made for the sake of the children victims of war, and then later the women victims; the innocents and the blameless. War that is always a dehumanizing experience no matter the thought justification. When I dehumanize you, I inexorably dehumanize myself.

So the solitary human being is a contradiction in terms. Therefore we work for the common good, go the extra mile, because our humanity comes into its own in belonging. Thus we embrace others, we are generous, compassionate, kind ... this is our Creator's dream. It is the power behind the Rev. Martin Luther King Jr.'s call for a Beloved Community or what I've come to envision as an evolving Global Commonwealth of Compassion. My calling card looks like this:

Welcome Mary House
PEACE ABBEY
...because the children of war beg for hope...

At the top it says: 'Ted Conlin, Author / Explorer for World Peace'. At the bottom: 'Peace Is *Not* An Unrealizable Dream, War Is *Not* An Inevitable Reality. Our mission is to help hasten the day when the world's children will be able to look back on war as an inconceivable aberration of their forefathers.'

The abbey is actually my family homestead. Its primary concern is with the mutilated dreams and visions of the many millions of children who, in just the space of my own lifetime, have been made

Peace is *not* an unrealizable dream.
War is *not* an inevitable reality.

innocent victims of war. What have we done to their future, I ask? What have we done to help God's human enterprise make peace its most urgent and noble aspiration? Violence is not the answer to human suffering, and terrorism is the most dangerous of answers! I'm quick to add that there is nothing new about terrorism. What is new since 9.11.01 is the chilling realization that the terrorist threat we thought we had contained within tolerable boundaries was not contained at all, menacing our well-being as a people, even our survival as a nation if not civilization itself.

My "Dream" is for a world without war or threat of war—war of any kind. There are upwards of two-hundred million reasons driving that dream. For nearly that many in number have been killed by war in just the very tiny fraction of time since my own mom and dad themselves were children. It is a mind boggling, heart shattering, statistic that has made my quest for a solution to the problem that is war and threat of war not so foolish at all.

No one may speak for the dead children, no one may interpret their mutilated dreams and visions. Yet I sense their presence. For I myself was once a child; from personal experience I know something about how war can take over such dreams and leave one's self shattered, broken, a mere shadow of one's former self. It is not something I talk about.

Decades later, while watching the news from Iraq where today's global War on Terrorism is most visible and kidnappings and beheadings as a tactic of war are on constant display, I find myself asking the question, "Can this be true? This is now the 21st century, not the Middle Ages!" And yet it is true, it is happening. Young men with explosives strapped to their bodies but concealed by outerwear go into crowds of unsuspecting others be it in a bus, at a wedding or funeral, in a marketplace, wherever, only to detonate and destroy both themselves and those others. Here the old ways of the ancient world prevail, a dark and obscure world. I pray and labor for the day when "Mommy…what was war?" will be a question like music to a world's ears.

Peace is *not* an unrealizable dream.
War is *not* an inevitable reality.

FROM early years in my childhood, ideas of exploration filled my mind. I go all the way back in memory to 23 August 1938 when I'd been certified as qualified for The Open Road Pioneers Club; the certificate signed by Deepriver Jim, the Campfire Chief, still claims a cherished place on my desk even though a whole lifetime and new century later. Interestingly, it happened that just two years earlier *The Atlantic Monthly* - in its December 1936 issue - ran an English explorer's item entitled An Explorer's Religion; his name was Francis Younghusband (1863-1942).

But it would not be until many years later before I'd chance upon Younghusband's account and here find a spiritual kinship. Especially in the very first paragraph did I sense that kinship where this Englishman makes note of the "conventional type of religion" in which he'd been brought up "did not long satisfy" him. It recalled for me my "Exploration into God" experience of earlier years, my first venture as a serious explorer when looking for God's hand in the universe and an answer to the question: "Can science and religion comfortably coexist?" Now the English explorer's story:

> From both parents, from generations back, I inherited a religious disposition and I was brought up in religious surroundings. I was, therefore, as naturally disposed to religion as others are to art or science. But the conventional type of religion in which I had been brought up did not long satisfy me. As I went out into the world I had to form my religion for myself, as I believe everyone should if religion is to be of any depth and service in life.

> At nineteen years of age I joined a cavalry regiment in India. Two years later I went for a joyous scramble through the lower ranges of the Himalaya, and it was here that my whole being began to expand. Ideas of exploration incessantly seethed in my mind. In 1887, with one Chinese servant, I set off alone from Peking on a further exploration across the

Peace is *not* an unrealizable dream.
War is *not* an inevitable reality.

Gobi Desert and the length of Chinese Turkestan and over the Himalaya to India. In the very midst of the Himalaya I read of how even these stupendous mountains had been raised from the bed of the sea. 1 learned of the titanic forces at work, of the colossal age of the earth, of its being only a droplet of the sun, of the sun being only one of millions of other stars, of us men and of all the multitudinous variety of animal and vegetable life on this planet having evolved from a single microscopic animalcule a thousand million years ago. My conception of the universe grew and grew and I marveled at the wonders which science revealed. But science did not destroy my religion; rather did science expand it. The more science taught, the keener did I become on religion.

On the day I left, I went alone up on to the mountain in the holy calm of eventide. Suddenly, as I sat there among the mountains, bathed in the glow of sunset, there came upon me what was far more than elation or exhilaration; I was beside myself with an intensity of joy and with this indescribable and almost unbearable joy came a revelation of the essential goodness of the world. I was convinced past all refutation that men at heart were good, that the evil in them was the superficial. Though since then I have seen much evil, my faith in the essential goodness of things has never faltered.

Thus for me the world is no mere mechanism. We form one vast community influencing and influenced by each other and all imbued with the same World Spirit. Clearly, therefore, our part is unceasingly to seek after higher and higher perfection both in ourselves and in the various communities to which we belong. We will regard ourselves as among the myriad agents through which the universe as a

Peace is *not* an unrealizable dream.
War is *not* an inevitable reality.

whole is working to better life on this planet. We will therefore by prayer and meditation, by study and emulation, fill ourselves as far as we can with the essential spirit of the world, and then put that spirit in all we do. We will carefully select that line of activity along which we feel we can be of most service. It may be in the service of our country,

It may be as an artist or writer in creating more beauty, it may be in combating some crying evil, or in creating some beneficial business, or in making a home - whatever it may be, into what we will put the very best of ourselves. We will align ourselves with the Great Purpose of the universe.

So, as the sum of it all, the religion which I have made for myself — the religion of an explorer — is a very simple religion. I have found it to work in practice. And my one longing now is to make it of service to my fellows.

Peace is *not* an unrealizable dream.
War is *not* an inevitable reality.

EINSTEIN AS A TORCH BEARER
FOR A "SANE" WORLD

> To know that what is impenetrable to us
> really exists, manifesting itself as the highest
> wisdom and the most radiant beauty, which
> our dull faculties can comprehend only in their
> primitive forms — this knowledge, this feeling,
> is at the center of true religion.
>
> Albert Einstein, *The Merging of Spirit and Science*

IT is important that I acknowledge Albert Einstein's role in why I have prepared this report. All along, as this scientist probed the mysteries of the universe, his quest had been to see achieved a 'sane' world, a world without war or threat of war.

It was tragic that the great scientific discoveries in which Einstein had so prominent a part, were in his time primarily used not for the improvement of human working and living conditions ... but for magnifying the means of terror and destruction. In fact, he regretted his part — had he been able to turn back the clock, this saddened scientist would have settled for being a "locksmith."

Except for his devotion to science, no cause was more important or closer to Einstein's heart than the determination that the institution of war be forever abolished.

A few days before his death, Albert Einstein affixed the last signature of his life to a statement of nine scientists, in which the world was warned it would run the risk of universal annihilation unless the institution of war was abolished in the near future.

IN my own career of searching for a solution to the problem that is war and threat of war, forty years of quest before finalizing my findings as detailed in this report *Mommy...What Was War?* — I'd been heartened by a felt spiritual kinship with this deeply religious man, a religious believer, as he once called himself...

...A man who revered nature with profound humility, who looked again and again in awe at the trees in front of his study, reflecting upon the richness and beauty of their branches and leaves and upon the minuscule understanding which man had acquired of the laws of nature in thousands of years of research and observation.

Einstein fought for the abolition of war not merely because he hated brutality and considered it unconscionable to seek solutions to international conflicts through killing of human beings ... he was convinced that, as long as war existed as an accepted institution, the intellectual freedom of the individual - *which he considered to be the foundation of human society* - could not be realized.

When in the summer of 1914 he rebelled against (what would be) the first world war as "something unbelievable," when he lamented his belonging to the "rotten" species of man, one suspects he must have felt that man's actions in war violated the sublime laws of the universe, that the willful killing of millions interfered with nature's course for which he, the scientist, had the deepest reverence.

It would seem that precisely because, as a scientist, he was engaged in the most abstract work of attempting to increase human understanding of nature, he felt the compelling need to convince his fellow human beings not to flout nature's will... and decided to devote himself to the most concrete, even if at times visionary, objective of fighting for human survival and creative fulfillment.

The production of the atomic bomb and its use over Japanese cities in 1945 made Einstein less tolerant than ever of token gestures toward peace. He was convinced that a nation could not arm and disarm at the same time. He felt this even more strongly when, after

Peace is *not* an unrealizable dream.
War is *not* an inevitable reality.

1945, the possibility of nuclear war threatened the annihilation of the human race.

MANY documents exist that reveal Einstein as a man with a driving urge to help in what he himself called *"The greatest of all causes: good will among men and peace on earth."*

Einstein, as possibly no other man of his generation, enjoyed a singular reputation throughout the world. He was respected, admired, revered and loved. His name had an undefinable meaning for the mighty and the humble, partly because it had become a symbol of a scientific discovery of momentous significance, but possibly even more because of Einstein's innate humanity which communicated itself at all levels and in all streams of human life.

There'd been the warmth and charm of his personality. The disarming informality with which he would greet friend and stranger alike. The utter lack of any air of superiority, so characteristic of the mighty and famous, the candor of his conversation. The manner of his speech, clothing and food, the furniture in his study... all reflected the complete simplicity which characterized him and which is difficult of adequate description.

Einstein had no use for anything that was not necessary or essential to human existence. He had organized his own life with great economy in matter and time, avoiding the superfluous and concentrating on what seemed important, enriching or enjoyable. Simplicity characterized even his emotional life as far as he allowed it to become known. Except for rare occasions there was, despite his warmth, an almost unbridgeable distance between him and the world outside.

He was very much like a monk. Because my home away from home is a Trappist monastery in the rolling hills of New England, I know something about the ways of monastic life. Einstein qualified.

Einstein knew of the reverence in which he was held, but could not explain it to himself and thought it was undeserved. However embarrassed he felt about it, he nonetheless recognized that his

Peace is *not* an unrealizable dream.
War is *not* an inevitable reality.

unique position in the community and the world offered him exceptional opportunities for action in behalf of individuals and society as a whole.

He felt a deep responsibility to lend his efforts and influence whenever he hoped they might prove effective. He was ready, at any hour, to interrupt his scientific work, which mentally absorbed him even when he was otherwise occupied, to devote time and energy to individuals or public causes.

But as the years wore on, nothing became more compelling to Einstein than the struggle to abolish war. I know the experience.

LESS than forty years after Albert Einstein's death in 1955, while the Balkans were on fire as war ravaged Croatia and Bosnia-Hercegovina, inspired by Einstein's devotion to the cause of a "saner" world, I undertook the Herculean task of prosecuting war, all war, and called it WAR ON TRIAL. Less than a decade later, on a blue sky Tuesday morning in 2001, jet-fuel laden airplanes filled with passengers slammed into the Twin Towers of Manhattan's World Trade Center not far from my home here on Long Island. Later, I would write in my journal:

> After the assault of 9.11.01, as the missing moved to lists of the dead, a geography of that Tuesday's terrorism emerged in communities all over Long Island. Terror that traveled from Lower Manhattan exited grimly in our suburbs, filling quiet pockets with grief. In communities across Long Island and beyond, the terrorism took its toll with the randomness of a tornado that splinters one house and ignores the one next door. Nine of its dead were nearby neighbors, firemen among them, members of my parish, here in wonderful Westbury... where I live and have my home.

At some point in the window of having penned *War On Trial* and then experiencing the "Unimaginable" that was 9.11.01 in my own backyard, I came to know something of why Einstein was a

Peace is *not* an unrealizable dream.
War is *not* an inevitable reality.

lonely man who suffered from his loneliness and whose often sad eyes seemed to have a forlorn, faraway look, as if they wanted to pierce the mysteries of the universe. He was very conscious of the fact that, in an ironical way, the world had made his life lonely also in a physical sense. His unique reputation and universally known countenance had made him a virtual prisoner in his own house and immediate surroundings; inconvenienced by the attention that was paid him everywhere. He could not live an everyday life as lived by millions, go where he might have liked to go, do what might have pleased him or mingle with whoever might have appeared congenial or interesting.

But it was the Einstein as a lonely man who suffered from his loneliness and whose often sad eyes seemed to have a forlorn, faraway look, as if they wanted to pierce the mysteries of the universe, that I mostly identified with in coming to know something of his having been lonely and his loneliness. Living in the archives of the hidden horrors and sins of war, while others view your quest as futile and foolish, folly-like, can do that to a person. Yes.

My career *indeed my vocation* as an activist in lending a hand to the task of healing a sad and broken world had begun with the question:

How can we discover the sources of wholeness,
healing and hope amidst a broken
and suffering world?

The first step involved what I called an *"Exploration Into God"* and about which I kept journals. In one entry I made note of the Russian born Fyodor Dostoevsky, a profound writer noted for his vast body of works. In them he depicted the depth and complexity of the human soul with remarkable insight. More than a century ago, at a moment when Christians were for the first time asking such questions about doubt and faith, Fyodor Dostoevsky wrote from his Siberian prison:

"I am a child of disbelief and doubt, to this very
hour and even, I am sure, to my last breath. How

Peace is *not* an unrealizable dream.
War is *not* an inevitable reality.

great are the sufferings I have had to endure from this thirst to believe, which only grows stronger in my soul with the growth in me of arguments to the contrary." Yet Dostoevsky goes on to insist that in his eyes, "There is nothing more beautiful, more profound, more congenial, more reasonable more virile, more perfect than Christ. And not only there is nothing, but with a jealous love I say that there can be nothing. Still more, if someone were to demonstrate to me that Christ is outside of truth, and that truth really lies outside of Christ, I would rather stay with Christ than with truth." When Dostoevsky suggests that the non-believer coexists in him with the believer, the "no" with the "Yes," his passionate love for Christ still remains undiminished. Child of doubt and disbelief, he nevertheless hears Christ's "Do you love me?" and returns, day after day, to the journey from doubt towards believing.

After years of exploration into God it would also be my summation and conclusion. At the same time the centuries-old problem that is war and threat of war invited a certain distress. While I knew that I was not the one person who could put an end to war and threat of war, I very much wanted to live as though I were that one person. Einstein as a Torch Bearer for a humanity in harmony with both itself and with nature became an icon, an inspiration, for me.

Because of this and the many, many millions of children killed, wounded and traumatized by war, displaced by war, orphaned by war, I undertook to commit all of my talents, resources and energy to that end. In a world constantly honing its skills of total destruction, in a century of times gone mad and why it was known as a "Century of Tears," I asked only that God's grace guide and sustain me in the effort. I believed, I trusted, I felt called.

Peace is *not* an unrealizable dream.
War is *not* an inevitable reality.

BORN BURDENED BY
A GROTESQUE CENTURY

The real art of life consists in finding out
what is the question to be solved

and the person who can find out
what problem is to be solved
is the man, the woman,
who really makes
contributions to life.

EACH succeeding generation doesn't know, doesn't remember, all
that the preceding generation went through. In my case it was the
Second World War, global and total. It happened on the ground,
in the air, on the seas, under the waves. The fighting was terribly
mobile; no front stayed fixed for long. The German word for a war
that would strike like lightning, Blitzkrieg, entered the world's
language once German forces burst into Poland in September
1939.

Soon came advances in Norway and Denmark (April 1940),
Holland, Luxembourg, Belgium (mid-May 1940), France (Paris fell
14 June 1940), North Africa (March 1941), and Russia (June 1941).
Lightning war seemed invincible. When Germany's ally Japan
devastated the American fleet in a surprise attack on Pearl Harbor
in December 1941, Blitzkrieg looked an impressively exportable
strategy.

It had indeed been total war. No-one in Europe or many other
places was immune from its horrors. Distinctions between soldiers

and civilians were obliterated; you were as likely to die in bed as on the battlefield. More than 40 million lost their lives: over twenty million in the Soviet Union, three million Germans, three and a half million Japanese, some 300,000 Britons, the same number of Americans.

In the ruthless Hitler-inspired war of extermination, asylums were emptied as their populations of the mentally ill, the mentally deficient, the emotionally disordered, were among the first to perish. The Action T4 program systematically killed upwards of 250,000 people with intellectual or physical disabilities, mass murder in the name of "racial hygiene." Then the six million Jews, and gypsies, homosexuals and other Untermenschen, who perished in ghettos, prisons and extermination camps. Entire communities could be wiped out; massacres were not uncommon. Oh the bitterness, the folly, the pain!

The War involved ordinary people as never before. Total war touched all corners of life. What united lives on both sides of the War was a shared sense of civilian existence disrupted by unimagined and unsought horrors. As one young Russian orderly who had to drag men to safety under fire, wrote: "Whoever says war is not horrible, knows nothing about war! Nothing!!" Like when on 10 June 1944 at Oradoursur-Glanes near Limoges, German soldiers shot 402 men and burned alive 240 women and children locked in a church. That kind of "nothing" - it was just one of many such insanities in that war.

THE Second World War ended in 1945 with a changed geo-political order, and an international crisis of conscience. In the last stages of the war in Europe, the fate of Jewish and other prisoners held in extermination camps like Buchenwald and Auschwitz made the genocidal nature of the Third Reich clear. Six million Jews had perished in the Holocaust. Then in the last days of the war against Japan in the Pacific, American planes dropped atomic bombs on Hiroshima and Nagasaki, and the "nuclear age," with its potential for global annihilation, began:

Peace is *not* an unrealizable dream.
War is *not* an inevitable reality.

It was a warm, clear morning on 6 August 1945 when the Enola Gay appeared in the sky over Hiroshima, Japan. Out of her belly fell the most awesome force the world has ever seen. In a flash, almost 100,000 people were cremated and a whole city obliterated. The heat of the firestorm that swept Hiroshima left the imprint of human shadows on stone as memorials of that dreadful day, and perhaps as a foretaste of what might be ahead.

By October 1945, some fifty countries, meeting in San Francisco, combined to found the United Nations, with the aim of bringing peace, security, democracy and prosperity to the world. The unease, horror and anxiety were not allayed. The United States and Russia emerged as the two dominant Superpowers, effectively dividing world influence between them, and confronting each other with nuclear weapons in the 45-year Cold War that followed. For writers the crisis of war and its bitter ideological aftermath sometimes made writing seem almost impossible. Post-war literature took on a very different character from the modern movement that went before.

But I am not a writer, I am an explorer; therefore I scout and keep journals, make commentary. Exploring is my first profession, searching for a solution to the problem that is war and threat of war. If perchance I've become a writer because of that experience, then it has had to have been in God's Will that this be my destiny in life. It is said that for every writer there is a territory and a time.

My "territory" is the problem that is war and threat of war. My "time" is the grotesque century I'd been born into and then the 'Unimaginable' of the next century. The Unimaginable that was 9.11.01 when, from my family homestead here on Long Island, I could see the billowing smoke of Manhattan Island's Twin Towers of the World Trade Center — a day that shook the world and left thousands dead in the WTC, at the Pentagon, and in the Pennsylvaina countryside. Later, I would write in my journal:

Peace is *not* an unrealizable dream.
War is *not* an inevitable reality.

After the assault of 9.11.01, as the missing moved to lists of the dead, a geography of that Tuesday's terrorism emerged in communities all over Long Island. Terror that traveled from Lower Manhattan exited grimly in our suburbs, filling quiet pockets with grief. In communities across Long Island and beyond, the terrorism took its toll with the randomness of a tornado that splinters one house and ignores the one next door. It was like Pearl Harbor all over again.

Peace is *not* an unrealizable dream.
War is *not* an inevitable reality.

THIRTY YEARS IN THE WILDERNESS
AND WASTELANDS OF WAR

IT was into the wilderness and wastelands of war where Law is silent and Lie prevails where, ever since the Vietnam Nightmare of a long 35 years ago, I've all but kept myself embedded. Fast-speed forward now past the "killing fields" of Cambodia, the "ethnic cleansing" of Bosnia, the "genocide" in Rwanda, to today's failed efforts to stop the slaughter, the genocide, in Sudan's Darfur province, in Africa; the killing of black African Muslims by black Arab Muslims and the widespread use of rape as a weapon in that war. It was Carl Sandburg who wrote, "Little girl . . . Sometime they'll give a war and nobody will come."

Others have written on war and peace, Tolstoy and Einstein come to mind. Long before them there were the ancient Greek philosophers. In the canceled preface to one of Tolstoy's later drafts of War And Peace, he says that what he wrote would not fit into any category, "whether novel, short story, poem, or history." What Tolstoy wrote in his canceled preface reflects precisely what I say about two of my own proposed book-manuscripts, War On Trial and Beyond War — "other than as 'nonfiction' they do not fit into any category" thus having made it difficult to find a publishing outlet.

However...a former long-time editorial associate of the Journal of Critical Analysis has written this about War On Trial in which I prosecute war as being a male sickness: ". . . Ted Conlin's proposed book makes a wonderful, indeed important contribution to making this planet at long last what it was always meant to be: the Planet of God... a world without war.

"It combines in an effective manner various aspects which would be essential in creating a powerful document: the most impeccable scholarship, a wealth of information, a perceptive understanding of the issues, and a solution to the problem (war and threat of war) . . . I have agreed to write a foreword."

But because it did not fit into any category, and after months of unsuccessful effort to bridge the moat around the castle that is the publishing industry, I decided to back off and give full attention to my Beyond War project. For many years as an explorer for world peace my sole purpose has been to help in the task of hastening the day when mothers might give birth to children who will ask, "Mommy, what was war?"

Thus, while family, friends and neighbors slept, I would toil upward in the night for long years, decades, working on my dream. At one point, because of urgent need for a more functional home-office in place of little pathways through piles of work-related materials, I took several months leave from all engagements in order to construct pretty much by my own design and labor an exterior annex we call Mary's Cottage. It's used solely as an archives and for storing some of those quest related materials.

One sunny day, while nailing in rafters for the roof, I'd been given to puzzle over this question: "If I should be asked if I knew the response to Auschwitz and Dachau or to the Rape Camps of Bosnia, what would I say, how would I answer?" I remember sitting high astride the open ridge, my legs dangling, thinking, "Not only do I not know it. But I don't even know if tragedies of this magnitude have a response.

"But what I do know is that there is 'response' in responsibility. Responsibility therefore is the key word (it would be my conclusion)."

In having assumed some of that responsibility in my already long quest for a solution to the problem of war, I'd pushed and even forced myself. No matter how futile or foolish as some did suggest. No matter how unsettling, sickening, my forays into the most brutal massacres in the long annals of wartime barbarity. I

Peace is *not* an unrealizable dream.
War is *not* an inevitable reality.

was doing it for the children victims of war, but also for the youth of today, for the children who will be born tomorrow. I did not want my past to become their future.

But too I was doing it out of fear. Fear that the terrifying disrespect for Life, for death and dying
(reference The Rape of Nanking by Iris Chang,
the darkest chapter that stained Japan's history;
reference also the Yale Divinity School Library)
brought on by the bestial machinery of war throughout all of the 20th century would be reduced to a mere footnote in history. I feared this reversion in human social evolution might be treated like a harmless glitch in a computer program that might or might not again cause a problem, unless someone or ones forced the world to remember it.

I recalled Helen Keller deaf, blind and mute since 18 months of age and something she'd once said: "I AM only one, but still I am one. I cannot do everything, but still I can do something. I will not refuse to do the something I can do." Nor would I refuse.

It is ironical that in an age when we have prided ourselves on our progress in the intelligent care and teaching of children, we have at the same time put them at the mercy of new and most terrible weapons of destruction. What's done to children, they will do to society. Men for years now have been talking about war and peace. But now, no longer can we just talk about it. It is no longer a choice between violence and non-violence in this world, it's non-violence or non-existence.

"Man is stumbling blindly through a spiritual darkness while toying with the precarious secrets of life and death," said U. S. General Omar Bradley of World War II distinction. "The world has achieved brilliance without wisdom, power without conscience. We know more about war than we know about peace, more about killing than we know about living." About war, we know that all war is Deception.

I carry in my wallet these words of Oscar Romero, the Salvadoran archbishop assassinated in 1980 while celebrating Mass in his war-torn homeland: "One must not love oneself so much as to avoid

Peace is *not* an unrealizable dream.
War is *not* an inevitable reality.

getting involved in the risks of life that history demands of us… Let us do what we can."

During my exploration for world peace, a world without war or threat of war, I've had the help of an imaginary Circle of Advisers; some are among the living while others have transitioned, passed on. All serve or once served as lamplighters in a dark and troubled world, a war-weary existence. In my decision to be a scout, an explorer for world peace, in the eyes of some a seemingly unrewarding if not futile pursuit, I needed all the help I could get.

After all, it was not until fairly recently that man had even undertaken the study of himself. Previously, in earlier times, in Greece or the Middle Ages, the human animal took himself for granted as unique. The world was made for him and except for supernatural forces he was the center of the universe, shaped in his own image, which set an ideal pattern for his life.

From this self-centered position, human beings were able to admire each other, enslave each other, write poetry about each other, deplore each other's sins, threaten each other with divine punishment and conclude they deserved immortality.

Then the discovery that the sun did not revolve around the earth changed things, was the turning point; from then on human pride was reduced. But now as we move into the third millennium, and though we've gotten to know a lot about ourselves as human beings, we find ourselves still operating from that same old self-centered position as though pride had never been reduced at all.

'King of the Mountain' — it was a game kids played when I was a youngster, growing up in the country. Find a hill of earth somewhere, race to see who could be first on top and then battle away to keep from being pushed or pulled off. The one able to stay on top without losing his place the longest would then, with an outward display of gleeful triumph, thump his chest and shout as though for all the world to hear, "Me, me, me-e-e-e!!! I'm the king! Me, I'm the king, king of the mountain!"

Peace is *not* an unrealizable dream.
War is *not* an inevitable reality.

Years later, I would come to see the world - going all the way back to the great kingdoms of the early days - pretty much as a global "King of the Mountain" playground for grown men and creating an ongoing Hell right here on Earth. Going back into history we see Babylon, Egypt, Rome, with Attila and the barbarians overrunning it. We see Alexander plundering the world. We see Genghis Khan. And then, for a time perhaps, we keep seeing ruins of all those kingdoms and empires. Ruin upon ruin upon ruin. Each of the plunderers having claimed a 'hill of earth' as his mountain, and its people—his subjects.

Today in what is a new world of weaponry and everything else, it is still a world plagued by adult 'King of the Mountain' games: a world of who can wrest the most land, plunder the most wealth, hold the highest office, boast the biggest war machine. Humanity is still stuck, but now deeply mired, in the jungle of an endlessly warring world. War that is like bush-clearing—the moment you stop, the jungle comes back even thicker, but for a little while you can plant and grow a crop in the ground you have won at such terrible cost. During the past century, most notable for its absence of peace, those "little whiles" were few and far between.

They still are … major wars and civil conflicts during the mid-1990s in Liberia, Angola, Sierra Leone, Congo, Nigeria, Rwanda, Burundi, and Zimbabwe took MILLIONS of lives.

Our newest players in this global "King of the Mountain playground" are today's terrorist networks each with their own command and control centers, bent on taking over the world and, failing that, destroying the world. The world is still a wilderness but now with new kinds of dinosaurs: tribes, ethnic groups, nations, corporations, cartels, crime syndicates, and, yes, religions or belief systems, each wanting to be King Dinosaur of their respective realms.

In the economic sphere, witness how Western societies have recently turned the person into an economic animal. Witness America and the impossibility of maintaining a robust democracy alongside an economic oligarchy in which the financial wealth of

Peace is *not* an unrealizable dream.
War is *not* an inevitable reality.

the 'Top One Percent' of Americans now exceeds the combined net worth of the 'Bottom 95 Percent' according to a New York University economist . . . . obliquely speaking, a tacit reminder perhaps of an America as described by George Bernard Shaw who said that it was "the only country which had gone from barbarism to decadence without once passing through civilization." It is a new dinosauric age that we live in.

The extinct dinosaur, gigantic and hopelessly outmoded and unwieldy, has risen from the Ashes of the Ages to roam no less outmoded and unwieldy in a new kind of wilderness, a jungle of wars that are unprecedented crimes against Peace, Humanity, Earth — Earth that is the only "Biospiritual" planet* we know (and the subject for a whole other volume or two from my journals).

> * Space explorers marveled at the astounding beauty of our planet from 17,000 miles away while gazing at earth sailing through space; they realized in a deeply profound way the power of its being home for all dwelling there. From their exceptional journeys, they all came back with the revelation of beauty.... They all emphasize that our planet is one, that boundaries are artificial, that humankind is one single community on board spaceship Earth. After returning to earth, they sensed anew that the air we breathe is the air that has circled the globe and been drawn in and out of people, creatures and vegetation in lands and seas far away.
>
> They experienced a deepened awareness of the fact that each one of us is part of a vast and marvelous dance that goes on unceasingly at every moment in the most minute particles of the universe — these tiny parts of matter are always moving and intermingling with everything around them. The dance of the stone, the dance of the soil, the dance of the worm, the dance of the wolf cannot be contained. They dance with everything else that is.

Peace is *not* an unrealizable dream.
War is *not* an inevitable reality.

Our ecosystems are key reminders of this ballet of interaction — what a marvel, to think that each cell of our bodies is part of an intricate interweaving of the dynamic of creation! The creation of one Great Being who enlivens the dance of our beautiful planet and everything that exists. The darkness of outer space, the greenness of our land and the blue of our seas, the breath of every human and creature, all are intimately united in a cosmic dance of oneness with the Creator's breath of love.

What this oneness of the cosmic dance tells us is that we simply cannot live apart from one another. We need each other. More...we are meant to live in peace with each other and to care for our planet now bleeding and wounded by how we exploit its resources and make war upon it.

Peace is *not* an unrealizable dream.
War is *not* an inevitable reality.

"OUTSIDE THE BOX"

AND so now it was time for me to take my expedition outside the box, to get away from the "blah blah blah" of politics and diplomacy, to flee from the "scribble scribble scribble" of the academics. Among the things I'd learned during my years as a scout, as an explorer, is the importance of stepping back now and then to view the world from the perspective of an astronomer or an archaeologist—to relocate oneself in time, in place, in the flow of evolution.

There is a saying: The real voyage of discovery consists not in seeking new landscapes, but in having new eyes. Soon after taking my expedition "outside the box" I experienced two awakenings each of which took me into two previously unexplored realms. In the first experience and taken from a journal entry, there'd been the troubling realization of: "How easy it is to dupe ourselves and others with exaggerated intelligence. How deep, so very deep is the dungeon that we're digging and building for ourselves as we turn our backs to God. What a lot of undirected-propelling through cloudy-space there is in too many college classrooms today. Indeed, it is one of the reasons why our brains are so foggy, why the world is foggy — perhaps even mad. If not mad, lost."

I'd prefaced this telling entry by noting that "today's changed Perception of the Human Brain has important implications for education...but also for addressing the problem that is war and threat of war." This is explained in my Endnotes at the end of this volume.

In the second experience, also from a journal entry, I found that: "The time has come to begin quite humbly the journey back to God, back to the Mystical, back to the Transcendent on which all life depends and which science by its own admission cannot penetrate. Science that is not in conflict with religion but, say its experts, we have to recognize the limits of where we are, and appreciate that Something, Someone, is responsible for all the inescapable harmony and beauty we see throughout all of Creation" . . . more on this, the details, will come in later chapters. The time has come where we need to make a complete break with the patterns of history. We need to recover the sense of a transcendent reality.

The illusion or pretense that the world of the senses, which is the object of science, is the only reality is being unmasked as we move now into the 21st century. No longer is the world viewed as independent of God, however one defines that undefinable word. The deification of man/woman is now nearly universally viewed as the product of ignorance, spiritual blindness, or simply being out of touch with actual reality.

So I turned to John Paul II and his vision for a world without war: a Civilization of Love. John Paul II, brilliant and mystical, whose years in Krakow, Poland, both as a university and then 'underground' seminary student from the nearby small town of Wadowice, were spent crushed in the vise-like grip between Hitler's invading occupiers from the West and Stalin's invading occupiers from the East. Later as Pope he would find his papacy caught up in a hinge between two Ages: one civilization was passing, the dawn of the next loomed before him and with it a new millennium. There's a whole wealth of book in that one sentence.

He was a wonderfully brilliant leader who taught the world how to live, how to suffer, how to die. He was the most trusted, most believable, of all the world's leaders, friends and foes alike — he was universally trusted, universally believable. Witness how they all came and sat together for his funeral, even though some at the time were at war with each other. So very remarkable!

In Maurice West's novel, The Shoes of the Fisherman, Pope Cyril says: "I hope and pray for a great movement. A great man, who will shake us and bring us back to life, for example a man like Francis of Assisi. What does he stand for? For a complete break

Peace is *not* an unrealizable dream.
War is *not* an inevitable reality.

with the pattern of history, a sudden and inexplicable renewal of the primitive Christian spirit." I saw in John Paul II - he who would reach beyond religious boundaries to become one of the most beloved and influential religious leaders the world has ever known - the makings of just such a man.

What in John Paul's life left a lasting impression on me was his humanity, his authentic humanism, his desire if not efforts to effect a bonding of Humanity and Divinity in a way uniquely transdenominational. He managed to embody for a quarter of a century the conviction that Christian faith - *faith that isn't abstraction but ground to walk on* - is the greatest of all human adventures, that it deepens our humanity.

He managed to embody the conviction that power can be used in a different way from how the world demonstrates power . . . and he would go on toward the spiritual. He embodied such convictions in an era that was basically a time of Pope John Paul II versus the Displacement of Divinity gang.

Of no little note here, his first doctorate was in mystical theology — something that has been all but stripped from modern seminaries. More than an intellectual, he was a mystic. Indeed, his heart belonged to mysticism; he was aflame with mystical passion, like Saint John of the Cross.

I never think of that era without revisiting Russian born Fyodor Dostoevsky, a profound writer noted for his vast body of works; in them he depicted the depth and complexity of the human soul with remarkable insight. More than a century ago, at a moment when Christians were for the first time asking such questions about doubt and faith, Fyodor Dostoevsky wrote from his Siberian prison:

"I am a child of disbelief and doubt, to this very hour and even, I am sure, to my last breath. How great are the sufferings I have had to endure from this thirst to believe, which only grows stronger in my soul with the growth in me of arguments to the contrary." Yet Dostoevsky goes on to insist that in his eyes, "There is nothing more beautiful, more profound, more congenial, more reasonable, more virile, more perfect than Christ. And not only there is nothing, but

Peace is *not* an unrealizable dream.
War is *not* an inevitable reality.

with a jealous love I say that there can be nothing. Still more, if someone were to demonstrate to me that Christ is outside of truth, and that truth really lies outside of Christ, I would rather stay with Christ than with truth." When Dostoevsky suggests that the non-believer coexists in him with the believer, the "no" with the "Yes", his passionate love for Christ still remains undiminished. Child of doubt and disbelief, he nevertheless hears Christ's "Do you love me?" and returns, day after day, to the journey from doubt towards believing.

In the wake of John Paul II's demise one could see that the world had not quite caught on as yet to where he was leading us, taking us. "This was not a pope from Poland," I'm given to say, "this was a pope from Galilee."

He went out among the people, this pope of passionate humanism." For some it was obvious that John Paul was too far ahead in history, too far ahead of what history could bear at the moment.

But I caught on, I saw, I embraced this pope whose work of unity, peace, mutual respect, and understanding, was never directed at anyone or any particular group. It was never "against," but "for": for construction, for renewal, so that everyone might take part more fully [and] consider one's self a promoter of creativity, work, duty, [and] joy in the construction of the common good.

This was so very clear, for example, when through Solidarity he struggled with the Poles to reclaim their self-esteem after centuries of subjugation.

Peace is *not* an unrealizable dream.
War is *not* an inevitable reality.

A HINGE BETWEEN TWO AGES
New Kinds of Dictatorship
A New Kind of War

FROM the very beginning my exploration for world peace has been based on the premise that it is our broken covenant with one another which must be restored. In a century that had become the canyon of our great human divide, a century of war on top of war, everything now depended on our reconciliation. The old spiritual "The Welcome Table" – and the original title of my book *War On Trial* – imagines a great banquet where there is plenty of room, a place, for everybody.

"The Welcome Table," one of the famous African American spirituals is based on the gospel story parable of the kingdom. The words go like this:

> We're gonna sit at the welcome table,
> We're gonna sit at the welcome table one of these days,
> Hallelujah! . . .
> All God's children around that table. . .
> No more fightin or grabbin at that table. . .
> I'm gonna walk the streets of glory. . .
> I'm gonna get my civil rights. . .
> We're gonna sit at the welcome table one of these days.

I never fail to connect this image with a true story from my archives which speaks volumes on the side of hope for the ultimate restoration of that broken covenant and thus an end to the "King of the Mountain" game in world affairs:

> The date was 24 December 1914; the place, the trenchlines of Northern France. The story has been told time and time again by the soldiers who occupied the western front that Christmas. A few

photographs still exist, providing proof that this extraordinary event did, in fact, take place.

A message came from the British Headquarters of Sir John French on the morning of 24 December warning his units in France and Flanders to expect a German attack on Christmas. Any semblance of peace should be interpreted cautiously.

German soldiers dragged Christmas trees into their trenches that year, decorating them with parts of their parapet. Lt. Johannes Niemann of the 133rd Royal Saxon Regiment claims that some soldiers tied small candles to the trees, reminiscent of Christmas back home. British troops, seeing the lights and remaining mindful of the warning from headquarters, suspected an attack and began firing. No fire was returned and things seemed to settle down late that evening.

Somewhere in the early hours of Christmas the Germans began to bury their dead as they sang "Stille Nacht." The British returned the sentiment with a round of "God Rest Ye Merry Gentlemen." A request for a ceasefire was shouted out and soon, the unimaginable happened. Soldiers from both sides began to crawl out of the trenches and into their foe's line of fire. They met in No Man's Land where weapons were laid to rest and open hands extended by both sides. They called a truce and traded cigarettes. The Germans brought out a barrel of beer, and the English put plum pudding into the hands of their enemies. They exchanged photographs from home, eyes tinged with tears brought about by longing, but explained by the bitter cold.

There are tales told of a football match that took place on the 50 yards of frozen ground that had served to separate the troops. Each side claimed

Peace is *not* an unrealizable dream.
War is *not* an inevitable reality.

victory, but perhaps the true victory belongs to faith, a belief that the coming of the Christ child instilled in all humankind a desire for peace that outweighs one man's desire for power over another. The Christmas ceasefire stands as a shining example of sanity in the midst of madness. The tale told by the soldiers, the last of whom died quite recently (2005) remind us that we are, in our essence, one in God, united powerfully by the Incarnation.

As Christmas night folded over the fields of France, soldiers returned to their trenches, and the next morning, they returned to war. Both armies tore chunks out of the other, ripping apart the same hearts that had been changed by Christmas cheer. The sound of repeating rifles replaced the sound of Christ's peace and thousands upon thousands of men perished in the years that followed that Christmas Day.

The men who held that miracle in their memories often said that once they had met their enemy up close, they discovered that he wasn't what the politicians and papers said he was. On both sides of the rifles were fathers and sons, brothers and boys who lived next door. Only language and loyalty to kings and countries kept them at odds.

An officer's written account of that day was sent home to his mother, who brought it to the papers for publication. Shortly thereafter, she received news of her son's death. His obituary appeared beside his letter, a contrast that uncovered the true toll and, yes, the truly utter "stupidity" of war which always represents a great defeat for humanity.

For me, the idea of coming up with a solution to the problem that is war and threat of war actually had its onset some years ago when men shook the bonds of planet Earth and landed on the

Peace is *not* an unrealizable dream.
War is *not* an inevitable reality.

moon, fulfilling an ancient human dream as they stepped for the first time onto another celestial world. On 20 July 1969, Apollo 11 astronauts Neil Armstrong and Edwin "Buzz" Aldrin raced their lunar lander across the desolate moonscape, searching for a soft landing spot. Moments after the spacecraft built just several miles down the road from our family homestead here on Long Island touched down, Armstrong radioed home: "Houston, Tranquility Base here. The Eagle has landed."

For one crowning moment we were creatures of the cosmic ocean. Hailed as humankind's greatest technological achievement, the moon landing was to have been the stepping stone to the colonization of space.

It was the dream of John Fitzgerald Kennedy who occupied the White House during the Camelot years, an idyllic period named after the legendary seat of King Arthur's palace in England. It was he who had opened the decade with a challenge to Americans to commit themselves to public service and seek new frontiers; without skipping a beat, he then challenged our nation's scientists to land a man on the moon and—gave them ten years to do it in.

"The moon project," he said, "may hold the key to our future on earth."

They did it in eight!

They did it in eight even though it had been the most turbulent decade in our history, including JFK's assassination just three years later, in 1963, as he rode in a motorcade in Dallas. "The torch has been passed to a new generation of Americans," he'd said. Some listeners imagined he compared himself to the departing Eisenhower, nearly a generation older than he. But Kennedy meant more: "And so my fellow Americans, ask not what your country can do for you—ask what you can do for your country."

Three days earlier, Eisenhower, in his farewell speech to the nation, this former Supreme Commander of Allied Forces in the European Theater of Operations during World War II, had warned our nation against a growing "military-industrial complex." Many

Peace is *not* an unrealizable dream.
War is *not* an inevitable reality.

listeners were surprised that an old soldier would bite the hand that feeds him.

In fact, Ike cautioned against the military's potential for wrongdoing without reference to its past record: "The potential for the disastrous rise of misplaced power exists and will persist." I've always considered myself privileged to have served as one in an honor guard along the route of this then-general's triumphal return to Washington after Germany's surrender. With him, in a scene of tears and cheers from onlookers, were forty soldiers who'd just flown in with him from what only hours earlier had been the front lines of battle, but now standing tall and beaming from inside each one's own personal jeep. It was a moment I'll never ever forget.

> While "beware the military-industrial complex" went over the heads of most citizens, for the socalled "hippies" of that era's cultural revolution it became the mantra of their call for an end to war, all war. "BEWARE THE MILITARY-INDUSTRIAL COMPLEX" was seen on protest signs and banners in cities and on college campuses everywhere. But because most people had never taken the hippies seriously it'd be dismissed as merely a hippie thing. Not until Iraq, a full generation and billions of war-spent-dollars later, did Eisenhower get acknowledged, get credit, for that warning. Earlier, in a speech of 15 January 1946, he'd said this: "I hate war as only a soldier who has lived it can, only as one who has seen its brutality, its futility —*its stupidity!*"

Three decades later, Bosnia and Rwanda shocked the world because of the madness of genocidal slaughtering having taken over and decimated those two countries; one in Europe, the other in Africa. Just ten years later, on a Tuesday morning in my own little corner of the world, the entire world found itself shocked anew by a third unimaginable: the horrible events of 9.11.01. It was like the Gates of Hell what I saw just several days later when at "Ground Zero" in downtown Manhattan.

Peace is *not* an unrealizable dream.
War is *not* an inevitable reality.

We were at war!

A new kind of war had begun.

With tears rolling down my cheeks my thoughts raced back to what it's architect once said about his creation now just a massive quantity of debris: "The World Trade Center should ... become a living representation of man's belief in humanity, his need for individual dignity, his belief in the cooperation of men, and through this cooperation his ability to find greatness." But now this!

Just as baby-boomers will never forget the day President Kennedy was shot, this generation will always remember September 11th 2001. In the wake of the terror attacks on that day there was one question from the children that we heard many, many times: "Will we ever be safe again?" This one question served to put new resolve into my commitment to coming up with a solution to the problem that is war and threat of war.

I'D been born into an era during which time Hitler was out to control the world; Communism was out to enslave the world; and now, if a perversion of Islamic belief has its way, its extremist leaders are out to destroy the world. The latter involves a clash of cultures, perhaps even a clash of civilizations. At the time it had the makings of a Third World War—or worse. To pretend that a militant Islamic fundamentalism is not a major piece of the eschatological puzzle is a stubborn refusal to understand the time.

Today, the threat of Islamic fundamentalism, with its clout to sponsor international terrorism, is the latest if not most disquieting, threatening player in the continuous destabilization of world affairs by grown men - the male of our species - who just never ever seem to tire of playing "King of the Mountain" games.

ABOUT the growth of Islamic fundamentalism and the rise of al-Qaeda, it is both telling and warning that the leaders of this most successful terrorist group in history, Osama bin Laden and Ayman al-Zawahiri, are transformations of formerly incompetent and idealistic soldiers in Afghanistan.

Peace is *not* an unrealizable dream.
War is *not* an inevitable reality.

But not so incompetent as to evolve a philosophy so compelling that they and their cohorts small in number would willingly - eagerly - sacrifice their lives for it. In the process they wanted to kill as many people as possible.

The story of al-Qaeda had really begun in America, not so long ago. The most frightening aspect of this new threat, however, was the fact that almost no one took it seriously. It was too bizarre, too primitive and exotic. Up against the confidence that Americans placed in modernity and technology and their own ideals to protect them from the savage pageant of history, the defiant gestures of bin Laden and his followers seemed absurd and even pathetic. And yet al-Qaeda was not a mere artifact of seventh-century Arabia. It had learned to use modern tools and modern ideas.

No less threatening in today's Western world is the "Dictatorship of Relativism" which, in having overtaken large segments (moral, religious and ethical) of the European and American societies, invites unimaginable consequences of widespread and tragic nature.

Relativism teaches that anything goes, there are no absolutes, no values. It does not recognize anything as certain, and allows one to rationalize truth to suit one's own ego and desires.

In fact, it is the ultimate recipe for a society's self-destruction, the aborting of its destiny and reason for existence.

THE human race during the past century has just passed through one of the darkest periods of its history. The darkness of conflict penetrated into the remotest corners of the world and its unprecedented violence destroyed whatever illusions we might have had as to the solidity and permanence of the civilization humankind was so proud of.

The rapid developments of the material side of civilization had aroused the interest of men and kept them in a kind of breathless expectation of the next day's miracle. Little time was left for the solving of the true problems: the human problems.

Peace is *not* an unrealizable dream.
War is *not* an inevitable reality.

Men - anesthetized by the mechanical progress of the preceding fifty years - were hypnotized by the incredibly brilliant display of the new inventions following one another almost without interruption from 1880 on. And like children were so fascinated by their first view of a three-ring circus they even forget to eat or drink.

This prodigious spectacle became the symbol of reality. And true values, dimmed by the glitter of the new star, were relegated to second place. The shift was easy and painless because philosophers and scientists of 19th century had already prepared the minds of the thinking public by setting up question marks without answers.

Many people had a presentiment of the danger and gave the alarm, but it remained unheeded. It remained unheeded because a strange new idol had been born and a true fetishism, the cult of novelty, had taken hold of the masses. On the other hand the wise ones, the discerning minds, in a world changing every day, replacing yesterday's garb by a more brilliant and unexpected one, fought only with venerable but outworn arguments.

The wise ones, the discerning ones, in a world where dazzled children opened wide their eyes in an admiring ecstasy which insensibly turned into a true faith in the unlimited power of science and invention, found their words stripped of the prestige once honored by youth.

Compulsory education had opened up new paths, highways, and lanes in the intelligence of the young; particularly in men because, unlike today, access to higher education favored the male of our species.

But without becoming much more intelligent, the male learned to employ the tricks of rational thought. An infinitely seductive tool, a new toy had been put in their hands and they all had the illusion that they knew how to use it.

This tool had obtained sensational results which gradually transformed their material life and raised unlimited hopes.

Peace is *not* an unrealizable dream.
War is *not* an inevitable reality.

Ultimately it would lead to what is today's dictatorships of greed and relativism; also to an era when serious attempts are being made to build the human community absolutely without God.

To make clear the point: Europe already has developed a culture that, in a way not previously unknown to humanity (as we saw in the Soviet Union and China), excludes God from the public consciousness. This has been accomplished either by denying the Divine altogether or by judging that its existence cannot be demonstrated, is uncertain and, therefore, somewhat irrelevant to public life.

It is likewise true here in America where we experience the rejection of reference to God as an expression of the desire to see God banished definitively from humanity's public life, and driven into the subjective realm of residual cultures of the past.

The starting point of this view is "Relativism" which has become a dogmatism that believes it is in possession of the definitive knowledge of reason, and with the right to regard all the rest as a stage of humanity, which has basically been surpassed, and which can be suitably relativized. John Paul spoke of Relativism as the "third dictatorship" of his time on earth. The first two were Fascism and Communism.

The "Dictatorship of Relativism" is the new foe no less dangerous in the long term than were Fascism and Communism.

But also there is such a thing as the Dictatorship of Absolutism. We see this in the Vatican, for example, when on occasion the absolute values its Catholic Christianity teaches are so badly practiced in its institutional alliances, politicking and business affairs ... that it invites disillusionment, erosion of faith, loss of hope among the waiting faithful.

Wait without hope, indeed! Without hope we not only cannot wait, we cannot even put one foot in front of the other — and thus the Western world's drift to Relativism with its anything goes philosophy and reducing a future society's minds to value-free mush.

Peace is *not* an unrealizable dream.
War is *not* an inevitable reality.

Then there is the Dictatorship of Greed in what one might say is the ultimate in adult 'King of the Mountain' games. Witness the epidemic of greed that's swept through the top layers of American business in recent years. Witness the rogues' gallery of the nation's wealthiest criminals some of whom were the highest paid executives in the world but caught in crimes of alleged deception and accounting. Witness our government's role in crime richly rewarded in an increasingly winner-take-all system that it vindicated in spades the long years of warning by John Paul II about America's "unbridled" and yes "savage" capitalism.

Witness Enron, Tyco, WorldCom. Witness that some of America's richest men could turn to crime and bring on such massive corruption as to shake if not fracture the very foundation of our nation's economic structure.

As in no other time, money talked and what it said was that one's worth has a numerical value, and that the greatest of society's Who's Who were millionaires if not billionaires. Sign the tab in certain midtown Manhattan eateries and your fellow diners' eyes would slide over. Is that a $48,000 Michel Perchin pen? What's on your wrist – a $300,000 Breguet watch?

The level of personal wealth - of hoarding - was extraordinary, and worse, much of it was from the mere manipulation of paper value as opposed to any real production.

Also, much of it was made in processes that caused pollution, stripped forests, and depleted other resources, perhaps even adding to the problems with the climate.

Man thinks he can make arbitrary use of the earth, subjecting it without restraint to his will, as though it did not have its own requisites and a prior God-given purpose, which man can indeed develop but must not betray.

Instead of carrying out his role as a cooperator with God in the work of creation, man sets himself in place of God and thus ends up provoking a rebellion on the part of nature, which is more tyrannized than governed by him.

Peace is *not* an unrealizable dream.
War is *not* an inevitable reality.

I purposely use the word "man" because it's been the male of our species who not only promotes, plans and executes war, but it's the male who's been responsible for provoking a rebellion on the part of nature by his exploitation of its resources and destruction of natural habitats.

In just one of many examples of greed destroying what God has made, in Indonesia, a huge gold-mining firm spread almost a billion tons of waste directly into a jungle river in what had been one of the world's last untouched landscapes. Selfishness, greed and corruption are devastating both humanity and nature in what now is a lacerated world. Oh, the creatures, the furry forest mammals, the birds that were proving to be far smarter than scientists thought, the whales that lovingly nudged rescuers, the dolphins that saved drowning humans: they were beaching themselves or dead at roadside or scrambling to find shelter where shelter no longer exists.

And then it happened. America's banking and investment industry collapsed in a meltdown the story of which TIME magazine's cover of 9.29.08 said it all: HOW WALL STREET SOLD OUT AMERICA. Inside under the caption "The Price of Greed" it said that "for years the financial markets roared along as if there were nothing to fear. Now its payback time—and all of us will be feeling the pain."

TIME magazine's main story began by saying: "If you are having a little trouble coping with what seems to be the complete unraveling of the world's financial system, you needn't feel bad about yourself. It's horribly confusing, not to say terrifying; even people like us, with a combined 65 years of writing about business, have never seen anything like what's going on. Every day brings another financial horror show. Some of the smartest, savviest people we know—like the people running the U.S. Treasury and the Federal Reserve Board—find themselves reacting to problems rather than getting ahead of them. It's terra incognita, a place no one expected to visit." Utterly remarkable!

Peace is *not* an unrealizable dream.
War is *not* an inevitable reality.

The headlines of every major newspaper in America screamed about

THE PIRATES OF WALL STREET
THE SHAMELESS GREED OF WALL STREET
THE LORDS OF WALL STREET
WALL STREET RECKLESSNESS
WALL STREET CORRUPTION
WALL STREET ARROGANCE
WALL STREET: A TERRIBLE TREASON
WALL STREET: THE SELLING
OUT OF AMERICA

America, the preeminent financial capital of the world, ambushed by arrogance and greed. Within days what we came to see as a shamelessly "rigged" system orchestrated by "greed" resulted in headlines from London to Tokyo screaming: A GLOBAL FINANCIAL TSUNAMI! GLOBAL FINANCIAL MELTDOWN NEVER SEEN BEFORE! Not only had greed like a terrible treason sold out our country, paralyzed our nation, but quickly proved catastrophic for the entire world's economy.

This all happened in September 2008; seven years earlier in that same month is when the Twin Towers of the World Trade Center at Wall Street itself suffered its own meltdown in a collapse so tragic as to stun and bring the whole world to a halt. In that terrorist attack of 9.11.01 there'd been three targets: Wall Street as the icon of America's financial power; the Pentagon as the icon of America's military power; and Washington itself as representing America's political power in the world. It changed the world forever.

But later when the financial tsunami of recent days swept through our economy and paralyzed our country, all one could think was there are enemies out there in the world. It is a fact — as made clear on that blue-sky Tuesday morning in September of 2001 and, for a long while, the dominant thing that we had to deal with was the grief, the sorrow, and the sense of loss, not only of the lives lost but also of our lost innocence. But now the attack had come from inside our country; its pirates and lords were the very

Peace is *not* an unrealizable dream.
War is *not* an inevitable reality.

pillars of society. They were fellow citizens, neighbors. They wore the American flag on their lapels.

Prior to 9.11.01 we had been perched up on this high catbird seat of our own special privilege, wealth and safety since the Second World War—even during that war. But, as the Buddha reminds us, life is suffering. Most human beings live in daily danger, with wars and rumor of wars, with refugee problems. We thought that we were just about to enter into the alabaster city undimmed by human tears. But with the assault of that Tuesday on 9.11 now we were suddenly jolted into reality, and from then on we were going to be living with a sense of danger.

According to the mass mind, all we knew is that we had been hit by somebody. We didn't know who they were. We didn't know where they came from. We didn't know why and we didn't know when they would strike again. All we knew is that everything was different.

Now once again, outraged and grief-stricken by the screaming headlines about Wall Street, all we knew was that we had been hit. We didn't know who the pirates were. All we knew is we'd been hit and that everything was different. What made us uncertain was we didn't know what kind of world this act was calling us into.

Just like back in 2001 when it wasn't hard to feel the agony of having loved ones ripped from one's side so that a handful of fools could make a point, so too now it hasn't been hard to feel the agony of millions of Americans without jobs, homes and savings because of that culture of fool pirates of Wall Street whose greed took down Main Street.

They, the fool pirates, no less fools than those who flew planes loaded with fuel and passengers into the Twin Towers and the Pentagon, are extremists... extremists dangerous in their own way of scheming and plotting for their own greedy reasons. Their actions albeit on paper were no less calculated, no less with coldness executed, than the actions of Osama bin Laden and his extremist hit-men.

Peace is *not* an unrealizable dream.
War is *not* an inevitable reality.

IN THOSE years of warning - a hinge between 'Two Ages' - John Paul II would prophetically proclaim that communism is no more a danger to the world than is "excessive" capitalism, meaning America's "Empire of Greed." America, the "Empire of More." Greed without restraint in American society had become an undemocratic force creating divisions which now approach a kind of wealth apartheid. This is an immensely wealthy society but it is not a humane society.

Witness our many tens of millions of senior citizens for whom medical care and needed medications are out of reach, denied, because they simply can't afford it. Yet, just hours ago, the newspapers reported that the CEO of a major national health plan insurer just received a "bonus" in stock options worth One-Billion, Four-Hundred Million Dollars. You figure!

But it gets worse. Some historians estimate that the gap between the wealthiest and the poorest in America - with its "winner takes all" King of the Mountain system of economics - has become greater than at any time since Imperial plutocratic Rome.

Bring into this picture the vastly wealthy American transnational corporations, some of which have now grown gigantic, actually becoming global forces with more power and resources than some countries. They derive power not only from wealth but because they can fluidly migrate to whichever nation offers the least legal restraints, the cheapest labor, the most amenable economies and the friendliest politics. In this sense they float above the world's constraints.

In the universe of corporations everything focuses on the acquisition of resources, labor, and markets. These are the sources of power. Inside these corporations 'Equality' hides her face.

In ancient Rome when "bread and circuses" were introduced to distract its subjugated people, for like reason today's conglomerates swallow up newspapers, magazines, publishing houses, and networks - particularly television. In the television industry news bureaus have been moved over into the "entertainment" divisions .. . and walls of resistance in the print media have kept good reporters

Peace is *not* an unrealizable dream.
War is *not* an inevitable reality.

and editors from trying to place serious and informative reports over which they have long labored. One wishes that journalists in general would show more interest in uncovering the dangerous linkages thwarting our democracy. It is not for lack of honest and courageous individuals who would risk their careers to speak truth to power — a modest risk compared to those of some journalists in authoritarian countries who have been jailed or murdered for the identical "crime." But our journalists are not in control of the instruments they play.

Corporations are not elected, so they are concerned with nobody's approval. Aside from occasional shareholder meetings, they never ask the public for ideas or permission. Nor do the workers elect their leaders. Inside, most business corporations are steeply hierarchical structures, in which employees' freedom to do what they want is openly bought for the wage. They are not responsive to the will of those they employ; some have inner dynamics that are feudal; some of their hierarchies are also jungles of dysfunction.

In democratic America most corporations are iridescent examples of autocracy, thriving on soil where the Constitution guarantees everybody's freedom and equality although producing the greatest good - wealth - for the smallest number.

If wealth is the only standard we use to judge, then we have to admit corporations are staggering successes and everything to venerate. They absorb people's lives. We consume their products daily, use their services hourly, rely on them for information. We are dependent. We compete to work in them. What protects them is that we are taught the system is rational. We are also taught that the goodness of a society depends on how well its topmost members are doing, so the higher our topmost members, the more they are discussed with awe.

The natural foe of corporations is government. But international corporations are so wealthy they slide over governments. They have become like tourists in their own country. As they lose national loyalties, they come close to becoming powers without obligation.

Peace is *not* an unrealizable dream.
War is *not* an inevitable reality.

As the largest transnational corporations grow, they become sovereign and untouchable.

Large scale competition among these massive corporations — many of which are an integral part of the "Military-Industrial Complex" Eisenhower warned about in his Farewell Speech — is what upgrades greed from whimsical excess to lethal force...to war!

It recalls the old saying: sooner or later every war of trade becomes a war of blood. We see this today in Iraq where the Oil and Munition industries are big parts of the reason for the horrific war going on in that part of the world.

In the race to exploit the notion of competition, competition itself a good thing, there's been lost in this culture of greed the idea of cooperation. Consider the priority of place we've given to competition over the civility and culture of solidarity, of caring cooperation.

Perhaps the greed monsters could learn a lesson from a group of Canadian Indian children. If a prize is offered to the first to answer a question in this group, they all work out the answer together and shout it out at the same time. They couldn't bear one to win, leaving the rest of them losers. The winner would be separated from their brothers and sisters; he or she would have won the prize but lost solidarity.

I'M thinking now of a scene created by Cecil B. DeMille that's not likely we can ever forget. It's from Moses coming down from Mount Sinai with the Ten Commandments ready to give the Israelies hell for making and worshipping a graven image—the golden calf. De'Mille's whole scene seems so primitive and unsophisticated. Imagine: a golden calf that people bend their knees before.

But—is it really so far fetched? Idolatry is still the prime sin of society. We have become classier in our idolatries, it's true. Instead of the molten golden calf, we choose idols that are called by other names like power, success, prestige, control, self-righteousness, religion, lust and materialism. Oh, it's true we don't dance around these idols and bend our knees before them. All we do is devote our

Peace is *not* an unrealizable dream.
War is *not* an inevitable reality.

whole lives to them while we neglect the One True Lord God who cannot and will not share center stage with any lesser gods.

In the financial tsunami of recent weeks that has swept through our economic system of things, the god of Greed is what has brought down that system and paralyzed our nation's economy. (I'm reminded here of Dorothy Day of the Catholic Worker whose movement beginning in the depression, flourishing through hot war and cold war, was given to declare that the only cure for humanity is a Christian revolution, the only revolution that's never been tried. And then Gandhi when asked why he'd never converted to being a Christian replied: "I would have, but I've never met one." Profound!)

While millions have lost their jobs, homes and life savings and pensions because of greed-driven deceit, the villains have raked in zillions of dollars in so-called "executive bonuses." I would call such behavior a crime against humanity.

Too I'm thinking treason and what means the word traitor.

Like boring termites which make rot of barns and homes, the worm of viral greed when given the opportunity can take down entire industries as it did banking and investment along with the giant auto industry. Had it not been for taxpayer monies from our national treasury used to bail out these places all would have been lost. Indeed, the only reason the offending executives even have a job (despite bonuses that in the words of one senator reward incompetence) is because of the taxpayers.

When reading the initials for one of the offending institutions, AIG, one of the world's largest insurance and financial groups, one is more likely to think *Arrogance Ignorance Greed* than *American Insurance Group* whose roots go back to 1872 with the founding of its flagship company.

AND so today we have new kinds of dictatorship, a new kind of war: global terrorism. But too now we have war that is capitalism with its gloves off; greed upgraded from whimsical excess to lethal force. Also we have war that is assault on Nature with its not forever natural resources and habitats. Ours is a hinge between two ages.

Peace is *not* an unrealizable dream.
War is *not* an inevitable reality.

THE QUESTIONS NOW ARE DIFFERENT—THAN BEFORE

BOSNIA, Rwanda, Cambodia and Iraq for us has generated an endless stream of questions, from the very simple to the most profound. Which has been all for the good, because spirituality starts with such questions; also because spirituality represents the deepest questions.

The answers of course have varied greatly during human history. Thousands of religions (with or without God, e.g., Buddhism, Jainism and Sikhism), coupled with philosophies and spiritual practices, have offered humans their manifold insights and beliefs. Most of them thought they had the ultimate, total truth or universal principle, and they were all too often prone to fight each other to assert their belief.

But the questions now are different than before because now they come wrapped in a latter day mourning and misery. In my first proposed book-document, War On Trial, I speak of war-time Bosnia as a "crucible of social conflict that serves as the world's laboratory for the study of hate and its anatomy. Too, it serves as a laboratory of absolutely providential moment for the study of evil that is as real a power in the world today as the sun or the wind."

Bosnia, for purposes of my quest, my exploration, was a world laboratory set on a global stage for all the world to see and learn, not only about the anguish of humanity and its felt helplessness, but about the perplexity of the individual — especially the war lord, the barbarian, the thug, the sniper, the slaughterer, the rapist, the butcher, the mutilator, the weapons maker, the munitions manufacturer — and the need of Divine guidance.

Most remarkable of all in this picture, as I tell it, is that historically Bosnia was the first and only laboratory of its kind, out in the wide open for all the world to see and know, to probe and ask questions about. It was a grand opportunity there for the taking. As though a God-like microscope able to see and take everything in, recent technological advances and the opening of instantaneous global communication channels had brought our planet to an unprecedented state of awareness . . . making it impossible for a country or a people to live in secret or in isolation. It was a "perfect" school for the study of such matters as hate and evil, ancient quarrels and aggression, politics and diplomacy, crimes against humanity and crimes against peace.

Such are these crimes that they raise fundamental questions about the psychology of those responsible for war and those who conduct war . . . one thinks here of the infamous Montenegron psychiatrist (Radovan Karadzic) "indicted' by the Hague War Tribunal for crimes against humanity and crimes against peace during the recent "ethnic cleansing" of Bosnia: where women's bodies became a favored tactic and battleground of war; and children, if not entire civilian populations, its intended targets.

> Amazingly, just now as I write comes news that after nearly a 13-year manhunt, Karadzic, accused architect of massacres and making madness visible, making him one of the world's top war crimes fugitives, has been arrested. A doctor and psychiatrist who received training in the United States, he is the suspected mastermind of mass killings the UN war crimes tribunal describe as "scenes from hell, written on the darkest pages of human history." They include the three-year deadly siege of Sarajevo and 1995 massacre of 8,000 Muslim men and boys in Srebrenica, Europe's worst slaughter since World War II. As the "intellectual leader" psychiatrist Karadzic stands responsible for the deaths of 300,000 people, because without him there would have been no war or genocide. The charges against him as outlined by

Peace is *not* an unrealizable dream.
War is *not* an inevitable reality.

the International Criminal Tribunal are genocide, extermination, murder, willful killing, deportation, inhumane acts and other crimes committed against Bosnian Muslim, Bosnian Croat and other non-Serb civilians in Bosnia and Hercegovina during the 1992-1995 war.

When speaking of the insanity that the politics of war creates, I am always reminded of a Croatian woman who during the 1990's war in then-Yugoslavia told this story: "I have a friend from Novisatch, and she is Serbian," she said slowly. "The direct telephone lines are cut now, but whenever she goes to Hungary, or I go to Italy, we call one another. And what we do is, we cry. She cries and I cry. Because we can hardly stand that kind of politics, you know. But what can we do?" And tears well up in my eyes; every time. I know too many such stories. Too, too many.

For me, Bosnia, more than anything else perhaps, has been the engine driving my expedition for world peace. What fuels that engine is the great legion of child victims of war born in my own lifetime. Tears! Consternation! More tears! Thus I never tire of working for the day, praying for the day, when women will give birth to children who will be able to ask, "Mommy, what was war? I've made their lives the work of my life.

I recall how, in a voice both innocent and wise, touchingly reminiscent of Anne Frank's, ten-year-old Zlata Filipovic's wartime diary awoke the conscience of the world. It was penned during that war of recent times in Bosnia. On television she had seen the bombs falling on Dubrovnik and, though repelled by the sight, couldn't conceive of the same thing happening in Sarajevo, cosmopolitan city of the then recent Olympic Winter Games and where she lived. When it did, the whole tone of her diary changed.

Early on, she starts an entry to "Dear Mimmy" (named after her dead goldfish): "SLAUGHTER-HOUSE! MASSACRE! HORROR! CRIMES! BLOOD! SCREAMS! DESPAIR!" I could see in her pained entries the world of a child increasingly circumscribed by the violence around her, its danger steadily invading her life. No more

Peace is *not* an unrealizable dream.
War is *not* an inevitable reality.

school. Living without water or electricity. Food in short supply. The on-slaught that destroyed the places she loved, killed or injured her friends, visibly aged her parents. In one entry Zlata cries out, "War has nothing to do with humanity. War is something inhuman." In another entry, now at age 12, she thinks about killing herself. Not until after two years of persevering and enduring while guns from the surrounding hills pounded the beleaguered city, were UN peacekeeping forces able to cross the siege lines and evacuate her.

On one page of her diary Zlata said, "What is this war doing to my parents? They don't look like my Mommy and Daddy any more." On another page, "I will try to get through all this, with your support, Mimmy, hoping that it will all pass and…that I will be a child again, living my childhood in peace."

But in fact she was among the more fortunate of young girls during that war, for there were thousands of child and teenage victims of the Siege of Sarajevo. Meanwhile, in the public squares of villages outside the siege lines, young girls everywhere were being assaulted and raped, humiliated and shamed, in full view of parents and neighbors who'd been forced to stand and watch or else be shot and killed. In my archives I have a war-time press photo, taken in Tuzia, Bosnia, that shows fifteen of those girls kneeling while their mothers stand behind them. They'd agreed to be photographed and quoted for…"the world to know our story."

Peace is *not* an unrealizable dream.
War is *not* an inevitable reality.

IF ONLY FOR THE
CHILDREN OF WAR
I *HAD* TO DO THIS THING

There Was No Turning Back!

FROM my own growing up years in the pine barrens of Long Island with miles of sand-duned shores shaped by tides and storms of the Atlantic, I have many stories. In one of them I recall us kids joking about how 'the cow jumped over the moon' and speculating that 'the moon is made of cheese.' Any thought of actually planting a flag and then walking on the moon would have been absolutely unimaginable, pure fantasy, hilarious.

And yet when President Kennedy made it our goal, when as a nation we realized that it could hold the key to our future on earth, and made a commitment, had the will, set a deadline, the unimaginable suddenly became the doable. And...we did it!

I recall with no little pride that its Lunar Landing Module was built by fellow Long Islanders - neighbors - at the Grumman Aircraft plant just several miles down the road from my home. In that same decade however, and I recall this with a certain shame, the American Negro still counted as "two-thirds" a human being even though long ago emancipated and having fought in his country's wars only to return home not yet fully free, still suffering the economic and social consequences of segregation.

For this reason Martin Luther King had his own dream. Although Black Americans were Americans, yet they still subsisted as aliens in the only land they knew. That Americans of African origin once wore the chains of chattels remained alive in the memory of both

51

races and continued to haunt and separate them, America's own apartheid rooted in the historical fact of slavery and its aftermath, was its own nightmare. King wanted to end that nightmare.

For too long this inherited stigma had exerted an inhibiting effect on the extent to which African Americans could realize their full human potential. King wanted to end that stigma. So…in what was the largest protest of its kind in the history of the capital, few of us alive at the time will ever forget his stirring, now famous "I Have A Dream" speech. He delivered it as several hundred thousand gathered at the Lincoln Memorial to demand passage of Civil Rights Legislation. I'd been a board member of the Long Island Coordinating Committee for Civil Rights responsible for sending trainloads of Islanders to that event.

America at that time was as though two nations, between whom there was no recourse and no sympathy; who were as ignorant of each other's habits, thought, and feeling, as if they were dwellers in different zones, or inhabitants of different planets. Although like Kennedy, King too would be assassinated, like Kennedy his dream also was destined to come true…and why we celebrate every January 15th as a national holiday in his honor.

There is implicit in all human tragedy a waste, a pointlessness. Tragedy unobserved is even more pointless. But tragedy unremembered surely must rank with profound sin. I well remember paths crossed with each of the three Kennedy brothers and how Jack not only was the President, he looked it. Young, confident, clean-cut—"vigah" wasn't just a joke, he really exuded it when you saw him in person—a happy, healthy symbol of the might and the invulnerability of his nation.

The Kennedys had a special sense of identification for young America. Jack was 46, the war hero who had fought in the ranks with millions of others in World War II, the young skipper of PT 109 who had swum all night pulling an injured shipmate to safety. Then came that Friday in 1963 when, while smiling broadly in a Dallas, Texas, motorcade, he'd probably never heard the shot or

Peace is *not* an unrealizable dream.
War is *not* an inevitable reality.

knew what hit him…something terrible, terrible went wrong. And he would never smile again.

Then there was the Rev. Dr. Martin Luther King, Jr., soul of the Civil Rights struggle. Just several nights before his slaying, I was on stage with King where together we'd been promoting the upcoming "Poor Peoples March On Washington." Until then the Civil Rights Movement in which I'd long been active had been organized pretty much as a campaign for Social Democracy. Meanwhile a grassroots momentum had been building for Economic Democracy as well. On that wintry evening in March of 1968 King's listeners bonded resolutely, because he showed them how they were all related to one another and that we shared the same demons and the same divines. "We go farther, faster, when we go together," he said. He cemented the bonding by his own example of including all of us, no matter our color, status or age, into his dream of a fair and workable future.

This poor people's march we were girding up for would not be a black march or a white march. This would be the poor people's march. He urged that we stay in Washington, our nation's capital, until legislation was passed that would reduce the poverty in this rich country. We may have to build tent cities, he said, and if so, he wanted to be able to do that.

Just several days later, a day before he was fatally shot (in Memphis, Tennessee) sending shock waves throughout the nation, King, in his second now most-famous speech and upon whom hung the dreams of millions, said this: "I just want to do God's will. And he's allowed me to go up to the mountain. And I've looked over. And I've seen the promised land. I may not get there with you. But I want you to know tonight that we as a people will get to the promised land. And I'm happy tonight, I'm not worried about anything. I'm not fearing any man. Mine eyes have seen the glory of the coming of the Lord."

Sitting alongside the Rev. King on that evening, his chief aide Reverend Ralph Abernathy also on stage, I couldn't help but recall these words of President Dwight D. Eisenhower in his farewell

Peace is *not* an unrealizable dream.
War is *not* an inevitable reality.

message: "Every gun that is fired, every warship that is launched, every rocket fired, signifies in the final sense, a theft from those who hunger and are not fed, those who are cold, and are not clothed. The world in arms is not spending money alone. It is spending the sweat of its laborers, the genius of its scientists, and the hopes of its children."

But now we were involved in Vietnam playing the role of the Ugly American in the worst possible sense. It's what gave the situation its persistent nightmarish quality. Confucius said, "A man who knows he has made a mistake and has not corrected it makes another mistake." Thus now, a generation later, we find our country at war in Iraq with its own persistent nightmarish quality.

King was an admirer and student of Gandhi's non-violent way of bringing about peace and justice. In a land torn and tortured by fear and hatred, Gandhi had discovered in South Africa, infamous for its apartheid (strict racial segregation), that love is an active revolt. The fruits of his discovery were his Satyagraha movement, based upon love and respect for his enemies. Britain and India had learned much from one another through his satyagrah movement. But Gandhi was shot, just as Socrates was poisoned by his own people.

The message of all of them to all who had come from all over the world in search of peace seemed to be first, before all practical questions, a need for those who would be prepared to give themselves to the uttermost in the service of peace and the methods of peace.

Only an army of the trained, disciplined, efficient, and of those wholly consumed by a love which is unearthly and universal, having no reservations, no racial or other barriers, but dedicating themselves through selfless action to the creative purpose in human history, could save the world.

The two assassinations – Kennedy and King – won't be washed away. And the long night remains, not a bad dream, but without divine intervention a reality to haunt us all the days of our lives. I pray with the hope, in the hope, that those who come after us will

Peace is *not* an unrealizable dream.
War is *not* an inevitable reality.

find an insight, a wisdom and a workable moral out of these events which so far elude us who lived them.

For those in the future who may learn from the past, my own dream and what I strive for is that someday our planet will be a Spiritual Democracy, a Global Commonwealth of Compassion. Today's international community is only an assemblage of powers. How the governors came to power is seldom questioned. At this stage of history, all one can hope for is peace, restraint and cooperation among the tenants of power.

But at some point in our evolution the question of the proper representation of the people in the management of our globe will certainly pose itself, as will the spiritual quest for our proper place in the universe and in the eternal stream of time. There is urgent need to determine the cosmic or divine laws which must rule our behavior on earth.

For such is the abyss of darkness that surrounds the earth's atmosphere — the result of millennia of human brutality, violence, malice, indifference, and injustice — that we are at a crossroads from where we either go in the direction of a completely spiritual culture on earth, a global commonwealth of compassion, or we face many horrific things happening in the years ahead.

"Ask not what your country can do for you," Kennedy had urged, "ask what you can do for your country?" After considering the question, in an inspired leap of faith I would make what for me would be an irreversible decision to become a scout, an explorer, for world peace. Futile, cried some; foolish, said others. But more than a decision it was a response to an impulse, as though a call from beyond myself. What did it mean, what might it entail, I had no idea. But so mystically compelling was the impulse, to have ignored its call was completely out of the question.

There'd been absolutely nothing supporting the idea of such a project other than the haunting echoes of local pioneer aviators when teasing Igor Sikorsky as being "crazy" thinking he could invent an aircraft that could take off vertically rather than horizontally. He was making plans for that aircraft while boarding

Peace is *not* an unrealizable dream.
War is *not* an inevitable reality.

in a home directly behind where I now live and have an office. "But Igor," they'd chide, "you are defying the laws of aerodynamics in attempting such a project." He'd respond simply by saying, "Yes, but what great practical application should I succeed!" The account of this Russian immigrant's success is now one of the aeronautical world's great achievement stories.

More than anything it was the determined character of Igor Sikorsky that fascinated me. His story is the story of a Russian boy obsessed with the idea of building a plane that could fly vertically as well as horizontally. Against all odds he kept working on the project. After the Bolshevik Revolution in 1917, seeing that many czarist pilots were being executed, Sikorsky fled Russia and eventually made it to the United States.

Here, with incredible tenacity and will power, he developed and built one of the largest helicopter industries in the world. If I could be half as determined in realizing my vocation as Igor was in realizing his dream — as a young boy he actually had a dream in which he saw his helicopter — then for sure I'd be able to help in hastening the day when children will look back on war as an incomprehensible aberration of their forefathers. In my dream I saw that war is not an inevitable reality. I saw that peace is not an unrealizable dream.

> Whenever I'm tempted to give up on my exploration for world peace, I look out my office window to where Sikorsky struggled with his said "crazy" project and take heart, feel strengthened. Looking a little further I see the nearby telephone lines which Lindbergh's Spirit of St. Louis barely cleared (because of its extra fuel tanks) as it lifted from the ground for the first solo non-stop flight across the Atlantic. Then looking East several miles down the road, there are the buildings that once housed the Grumman Aircraft Corporation where locals, my neighbors, built the Lunar Land Module for the Apollo 11 moon mission.

Peace is *not* an unrealizable dream.
War is *not* an inevitable reality.

It was as though I was living at the heart of an energy center of kind where the said-impossible in our dreams for world peace could be made possible if only we'd put our imagination to work; imagination, where there is vision and adventure and the discovery of new worlds. The above projects - Lindbergh, Sikorsky, Apollo 11 - all began in the imagination, a God-given device which allows us to expand and enrich the world in which we live. Said our great poet Carl Sandburg: "Nothing happens unless first the dream."

So...unlike Lewis and Clark who'd not only been commissioned but resourced in their search for a path to the Pacific, I'd embarked on my search as a "solitary" explorer with the most "meager" of resources, knowing only this was something I just had to do. If only for the children of war, I had to do this thing. The pictures these children paint and their own words in sessions especially created to help them with their memories of war, tell us that we have betrayed them. In their pictures and words, the children shout out their terrible fear and grief; they rebuke us and plead with us to spare them. And in that awful shouting they reveal the health, vitality, natural grace, and artistry of childhood. Who better than children to sum up, without artifice or sentimentality, the monumental stupidity of war!

I will never forget Nemanja, eleven years old, who during the recent Balkan Wars cried out: "I do not want to grow old while still just a child." Nor the children of a sixth-grade class who asked: "Like Anne Frank fifty years ago, we wait for peace. She didn't live to see it. Will we?" Some of them didn't. Of those who did survive, one, a displaced child, said this: "A grenade had landed on our shelter. We had to climb over the dead bodies to get out. Meanwhile the snipers kept shooting at us." If for no other reason than the children of war, I had to be an explorer, a scout for world peace. I couldn't let down or give up on them by not accepting the call. I just couldn't.

BUT then in the middle of the war in Iraq I suffered a disabling medical disorder that involved my inner-ear and brain domain which baffled doctors as well as research scientists of several countries.

Peace is *not* an unrealizable dream.
War is *not* an inevitable reality.

Overwhelmed by the grim picture of things, especially the medical prognosis, I despaired. I was devastated, felt betrayed, and yes shed tears. But not for overly long. In my way of thinking it was an unacceptable conclusion; along with prayer I became proactive. There had to be a solution and my mission had to continue.

Ultimately it did, even though not right away; it took all of several years. Years earlier, one Sunday morning, a police ambulance had sped me to the local hospital because of a sudden, complete loss of vision in one eye. It had been a frightening moment; there'd been the thought possibility of losing sight in the other eye as well because of sympathetic ophthalmia, which I knew some-times attacks the good eye of a person whose other eye has stopped functioning. How possibly could I go on with my research and outreach for a solution to the problem that is war and threat of war? What will happen with all of my decadeslong accumulation of work? The first doctor talked surgery at which my intuitive nature balked. The second doctor, who'd authored the World Eye Manual for Emergency Eye Care and Eye Surgery, put me on a noninvasive path whereby sight was fully restored by the end of twelve months.

More recently, just as I was nearing completion on the manuscript for this volume, I got ambushed by emergency open-heart surgery. Providentially it happened that follow*in*g my insurance company's denial for an angiogram, a way was made clear for that procedure to take place—but immediately. Several hours later my wife was aghast when the cardiologist phoned to say I wouldn't be going home, that I had need of triple bypass surgery—within 24 hours. At six o'clock the next morning, on Thanksgiving Day, now a patient in one of America's best known heart hospitals right here on Long Island, I was on the table ready to go. Later the doctor reported that if I hadn't had the bypass and if there'd been need for an emergency operation, I wouldn't have survived the surgery. He happily refers to me as his "miracle" - Cheers! - and justifiably so; I'm so very, very grateful. However, the trauma of this intrusion triggered a significantly elevated hemi-diaphragm which invited windedness, a gasping for breath when climbing small hills or stairs at home. Thus I'd been benched once again; post-surgery arrhythmia didn't

Peace is *not* an unrealizable dream.
War is *not* an inevitable reality.

help matters. Earlier, there'd been other surgeries as well; and, too, a neurological impairment in my right arm which radiated pain into the small of my upper back when using the keyboard at my computer, an important tool in my work; it's why I all but quit playing the piano.

But something Dag Hammarskjold former secretary-general of the United Nations once said helped me through the several crises: "You have not done enough, you have never done enough so long as it is still possible that you have something to contribute."

I'd be tempted to think, "But I have done enough, I have . . ." There'd been the mind-bending libraries of wartime atrocities such as the archives of Dachau and the other gas ovens where millions of ourselves were murdered by millions of ourselves. There'd been the swelling ranks of child soldiers, children as killers, many thousands of them. And the horrific cruelties of rape camps in Bosnia; the shelling of hospitals and bombing of cemeteries in Croatia.

All of this crazed conduct takes a toll on one's psyche and emotions when tracking the actual realities and hidden sins of war . . . war that is the vilest thing on earth. There'd been scene after scene of skulls piled up and the blood pooled; of live captives being used as targets for bayonet practice; of other captives used for medical experiments. At times I'd felt as though I couldn't carry it anymore ... the child in me would rebel ... I'd weep ... the world was simply unbearable, too dark a burden. What hope was there for my children, my grandchildren, my great-grandchildren and their children to come? Would there even be a world?

How does one even begin to explain to one's children no matter their age that the main goal of the German Einsatzgruppen during World War II was to turn the Jews in the Soviet Union into landfill? Which in large measure, they did.

Having raced in behind the invading German Army in June 1941, these mobile killing squads proceeded to fill ravines, quarries, trenches, ditches and pits in Russia, Belarus, Ukraine, Lithuania, Latvia and Estonia with the bodies of more than 1.3 million Jewish men, women—and children.

Peace is *not* an unrealizable dream.
War is *not* an inevitable reality.

When most of us think of the Holocaust we think of Auschwitz. But the industrialized, largely hands-off method of killing Jews at Auschwitz and the five other gassing centers in Poland was developed to a great extent because of what the German leadership saw as the too hands-on experience of the Einsatzgruppen in the Soviet Union — individual bullets shot into individual Jews by individual Germans, or by the local police they oversaw. In Babi Yar, a ravine in Kiev, the Einsatzgruppen shot 33,771 Jews in just two days. The work was bloody and sometimes even for these hardened killers, demoralizing. Auschwitz was the final solution to the Final Solution.

Fifty years later, in Yugoslavia, Serb politicians and academicians in their pursuit and plans for a "Greater Serbia" launched an internecine bloodbath that shocked most of the world. For the survivors the pain of that war's politics was excruciating. I remember a Croatian woman saying, "I have a friend from Novisatch, and she is Serbian. The direct telephone lines are cut now, but whenever she goes to Hungary, or I go to Italy, we call one another. And what we do is, we cry. She cries and I cry. Because we can hardly stand that kind of politics, you know. But what can we do?"

So…medical ordeals and all else not withstanding, it happened that in every instance of moments unbearable a certain enthusiasm a felt urgency for my project would prevail and keep me going. "Nothing great has ever been achieved without enthusiasm," said Ralph Waldo Emerson. Enthusiasm for me meant a deep satisfaction in what I was doing plus the added element of a goal or a vision that I was working toward. I would feel like an arrow that was moving toward the target—and rejuvenated by the journey.

However, what persisted in all of this making things even more annoying and thus burdensome for me was the troubling disorder of my inner-ear/brain-stem/brain domain, an intrusive malady, which continued to baffle doctors as well as research scientists of several countries. Often I'd find myself exhausted, overwhelmed, sick with despair, lost. Were it not for the legions of innocent children and blameless women victims of war, I just might have

Peace is *not* an unrealizable dream.
War is *not* an inevitable reality.

quit my quest for a solution to the problem that is war and threat of war long years ago.

But it would have given the ongoing scoffers of my quest asking why waste my talents like this, asking what prompted such a quixotic enterprise, a chance to wag a finger in my face and say we told you so! But I would have none of that. Years of deliberation had culminated in a hidden fixed resolve to go to war against war, to search for a solution to the problem that is war. Certain images kept surfacing from my pool of wartime memories that kept me from doing and dwelling on that.

From Yugoslavia, for instance, there'd been the soldiers throwing babies and children up in the air and catching them on their swords. The young boy who, while walking across a bridge minding his own business, only to have his arm grabbed by one in a small group of passing enemy soldiers and flung into the rock-strewn waters of the river far below. There'd been the men who'd been captured like animals; they were slaughtered, murdered; living men were thrown off cliffs. A train took six carloads of mothers, young girls and children; after reaching a certain point and now off the train, they were led up the mountains and…thrown alive off the precipices. Brutality and fanaticism went had in hand. An entire community of monks was taken outside their monastery and buried alive.

Warfare is always bitter and ruthless, always a nightmare descent into pure barbarism. Remarkably, it's been the single image of that young boy who, while walking across a bridge, was grabbed and flung into the rocky river below…that has most moved me to stay the course in my quest, and thus not to quit. I carry that image, as though on a banner, in all that I think and do. Spiritually I've adopted him. Although I do not know his name, I dedicate this volume to him so that war doesn't have the last word in the story of his brief life here on earth. It is my intention that with this book his life will live on, have meaning, be forever honored. Dag Hammarskjold was right…it's still possible that I have something to contribute.

Peace is *not* an unrealizable dream.
War is *not* an inevitable reality.

Along with such images from my enormous pool of the insanities of war that kept me from quitting my quest, I'd kept myself focused and my spirits afloat from the threats and challenges of my medical issues by thinking of Lewis and Clark . . . who as they searched for a path to the Pacific and then succeeded had not been without their own kinds of ongoing disappointment, hardship and sickness. Two-hundred years ago William Clark carved his name on a rock formation along the Yellowstone River. That spot, known as Pompey's Pillar, is one of the few marked places along the Lewis and Clark Trail where you can be certain that one of these explorers actually stood.

One can easily stand at Pompey's Pillar and see one's life as rather dull compared to Clark's. What is left for the modern-day adventurer when others have already reached nearly every place on earth? But when considering it more deeply, one might realize that the purpose of exploration isn't simply to get there first. It's to learn something new, to break fresh ground, to return home with something worth sharing. And perhaps even to feel something of William Clark's words on seeing the Pacific Ocean: "Oh! The joy!"

Peace is *not* an unrealizable dream.
War is *not* an inevitable reality.

THE 'PATMOS' EXPERIENCE

LEWIS and Clark's spirit of "keepin' on keepin' on" despite all the grueling hardships of their expedition has long been a motivating influence in my own search. Although "keepin' on" at the task of hastening the day when the world's children will look back on war as an 'inconceivable aberration' of their forefathers has had its own risks, hazards and disappointments different from those of the Lewis and Clark experience, they've been no less real, the work no less tough, no less grinding and gritty. Indeed, it is what has determined the architecture of my life.

God's amazing grace has helped me to override my concerns for self by my concerns for the children and women victims of war.

I think here of that seven-year-old boy who was hit in the face by a sniper's bullet in the middle of Sarajevo during that citiy's one-thousand days of siege and solitude, holding on to his mother's hand as they ran past a U.N. armored personnel carrier. As the boy lay dying, his face was turned toward the asphalt, his left hand raised to his head, soaked in his blood. His name was Nermin Divovic. He wasn't killed by surprise, by a shell. He was sought after by a Serb sniper who waited, got him into his telescopic sights, looked at his face and then pulled the trigger. Then the same sniper shot Nermin's mother in the stomach so she would not die immediately, but would watch her son die first.

I find strength, comfort, solidarity, courage, in knowing that I am part of a universal manifestation of persons dead and alive who have said "yes" to Life and Peace, and "no" to Death and War. They are the large coterie of people in each generation who refuse to be silent when confronted with Death-dealing. I experience a spiritual attachment, a community of faith with these people. I am with them. And they are with me, in ways that may appear shadowy but are very real. Not only is there this tremendous, magnificent, welcoming host of folks who are prepared to welcome me into the Light beyond this life, but also they are available to me now on this side of death.

In the midst of everything that seems so overwhelming, they are saying to me, to us: "We are with you," and there is a way through; there is a way to stand; there is a way to move; there is a way to hope; there is a way to believe. Don't give up. Be not afraid. To know that this cloud of witnesses is present is to know that regardless of how alone we feel sometimes in our peacemaking efforts, when risking arrest at protests perhaps and even going to prison, we are never alone. We are never alone; nowhere, no how, in nothing. Never.

I find light and a new kind of consciousness in the exiled apostle John who found himself on the island of Patmos for adhering to God's word and the testimony of Jesus. He was isolated because he was true to God's word, but that isolation brought revelation. He couldn't see any future for himself on a lonely island, and yet he'd been given to see the whole future of humankind (the downfall of the empires of the world); shut off from men, he'd been open to God's vision for humanity.

I connected with this story when realizing that John was not only on an island; he was in a desert on that island — within the isolation there'd been barrenness. Well…there have been moments in my history of struggle with health issues while toiling as an explorer for world peace where I myself came to know this "desert on an island" experience… with its own barrenness of kind that can bring one close to depression if not to the death that is despair.

Unlike Lewis and Clark who'd been commissioned and resourced in their search for a path to the Pacific, I'd embarked upon my quest as a solitary explorer with the most meager of resources knowing only this was something I had to do. Never in all of my forty years of quest have my resources not been meager. Indeed, had it not been

Peace is *not* an unrealizable dream.
War is *not* an inevitable reality.

for the "children of war" and its "women victims" all so innocent and blameless, it's very likely I couldn't and wouldn't have stayed with this mission, so seemingly futile and folly-like the experience, so arduous and draining of personal reserve and monies; there is no money at all to be made by such an undertaking. What would make it a matter of compelling imperative that I not quit, however, was the utter reality of an amazing Divine Intervention experience extended over a period of time on the side of my staying the course. Ultimately it would take me to the 'Mountaintop'. For anyone who has the courage to enter our human sorrows deeply, there is a revelation of Joy, hidden like a precious stone in the wall of a dark cave.

Peace is *not* an unrealizable dream.
War is *not* an inevitable reality.

~~ PART TWO ~~

THE PRIVILEGED TIME

WE LIVE IN

CHOOSING TO BE CHOSEN
AND THEN GOING THROUGH
SOME SACRED DOORWAYS

The public's consciousness is not yet open to the idea of peace not being an impossible dream, of war not being an inevitable reality. The idea might be there, but it has not entered sufficiently to have taken root. The doors of perception are not yet opened —

When we look at the world, it is hard for most of us to believe that love, not force, not chance, made it. But the time will come when it will be quite natural for us to think that love made the world. Even now it is a belief that the human race is moving toward. Love...we sense that this is the way human beings are intended to live.

MY exploration for a solution to the problem that is war is not a project of academia nor has it ever been funded by grants of any kind. It is solely the project of the Welcome Mary House, a peace abbey; locally it is more generally recognized as the Conlin family homestead. Here is where Adella brought into the world our three very delightful, cherished children: Judy, Amy and Peter. A fourth child, Cathy Paul, about whom we'd been so very excited went to heaven before birth; but with loving affection very much remains in heart and memory as well as in our daily prayer life, never not to be included in all we are and do.

As I write we have nine beautiful grandchildren and twelve great-grandchildren. All along it's been my beloved Adella who has been the heart and linchpin of all we are and do as a family. With her life Adella has taught that love isn't something you do, but who you are.

It is said that God at times writes straight with a crooked line. Certainly this has been true in how my life has unfolded and evolved. Although I started out in the New York State College of Agriculture at Cornell University with visions of being a farmer, sowing seed so that others might eat and be nourished, destiny it seems had other plans. Before being able to complete my studies in agricultural engineering at Cornell in the beautiful Finger Lakes region of upstate New York, a series of innumerable unforeseeable experiences grew and fashioned in me in a more superior way an education not to be found anywhere in all of academia.

And from this evolved a compelling commitment to help in the task of building a world without war and threat of war, a world without slavery—of any kind. In this commitment I'd be sowing seeds of another kind, seeds of world peace. Peace on Earth as it is in Heaven. Peace that is a Global Commonwealth of Compassion. A Civilization of Love – love that bridges all divisions and heals all wounds.

While acknowledging the origins and causes of war, for purpose of this report I make it a point to keep brief my comments. And while acknowledging the hatreds that go back a thousand years as in the case of some Balkan ethnic groups or the thirteen-hundred years between the Shias and Sunnis of today's Iraq, I keep my reins drawn, say little.

Instead, I focus on the privileged time we live in. A time I'm given to say that is awesome, incredible, unlike any other in history. Despite all the horror of the past one-hundred years and counting, or maybe because of it, destiny and evidence seem to be saying we today are a chosen people, a people called.

Indeed, the time is nearing when it will be quite natural for us to think that Love made the world. Even now it is a belief that the

Peace is *not* an unrealizable dream.
War is *not* an inevitable reality.

human race is moving toward. In fact, the whole content of human history, I say, is nearing that moment when it will find its meaning and its fulfillment — and it seems we in our time have been chosen to announce just that! Not only to announce, but to help make straight the path to that fulfillment by becoming light enough for that meaning to be seen and grasped.

But we can't become light and help make straight the path without first breaking out of the centuries-long cycles of aloofness and denial about God and his Plan for the Human Enterprise. We can't do it without choosing to be chosen, and then going through some sacred doorways.

Without looking back, are we willing to accept a new vision of reality? Just as a fish in the ocean can't analyze the ocean he is in, neither can most social or political commentators grasp the meaning of their society and culture they are part of it. They see their own sections of ocean as the whole and interpret life accordingly. But it isn't the whole.

Today's ongoing cosmic drama at Medjugorje (about which I will report shortly) makes it abundantly clear that the person — Christian, Jew, Muslim, whatever — is a person of two worlds; there is perspective in that. To be in the world, yet not of the world, is more than theological talk. It is a very real perspective that is larger than any human viewpoint. It is a God-given view.

There is a way given; it is a marked road that gives an ability to look around, to see, to participate in - but not to be absorbed by - the world in which we live. We live in our world, but it does not control our thinking. At least it shouldn't.

A lot of secular fish are swimming around in this world-ocean. They reinforce each other in what they already believe about life. To each we want to say, "Little fish, can't you see? You could see so much if you belonged to the One who created all fish and the ocean in which the fish live, and who knows how he intends the two to fit together."

Peace is *not* an unrealizable dream.
War is *not* an inevitable reality.

What if human beings had been born blind. We would be able to feel the earth, the wind, the sun on our face. We would know they existed and we'd probably be able to invent devices to measure them and study them. But what about the distant, pale stars? Would a race of blind people ever think to search the heavens for stars?

No, it doesn't seem likely. An entire universe would escape our knowledge unless someone came to give us a clue of its existence.

THE world today is in dire need of replenishing its stock of faith. It is perhaps at the very heart of my journaling as an explorer, this discovered need for humanity's spiritual maturity if the world is to know peace: worthwhile peace, holy peace, enduring peace.

For it is clear that peace is neither the absence of war nor something diplomatically contrived, but the effort to surrender to our Creator—from the heart. It is also the effort to remain in a state of forgiveness. Forgiveness means accepting the core of every human being as the same as yourself and giving them the gift of not judging them.

It bears repeating: Forgiveness means accepting the core of every human being as the same as yourself and giving them the gift of not judging them.

And here the point: The time has come to begin quite humbly the journey back to God, back to the Mystical, back to the Transcendent on which all life depends and which science by its own admission cannot penetrate. Science that is not in conflict with religion but, say its experts, we have to recognize the limits of where we are, and appreciate that Something, Someone, is responsible for all the inescapable harmony and beauty we see throughout all of Creation.

Our Creator, who even today diagnoses the world's sickness and points us to his Purpose for our existence, calls on us to take him seriously and not to stubbornly choose our own course...as though making a way out of nowhere in an existence that has no plan. And he does this most compellingly, indeed dramatically, from the theater of a tiny, obscure mountain-village in the Balkans

Peace is *not* an unrealizable dream.
War is *not* an inevitable reality.

where the Virgin Mary, his special messenger down through the centuries, has been making daily visits since June 1981, twenty-eight long years ago.

It was here, between the chain of Dalmatian mountains in the west – which still further west plunge headlong into the sea – and the turbulent Neretva river in the east that has carved ravines and gorges as well as creating fertile valleys, that my exploration for world peace took a leap into a realm that I could never have imagined except possibly in my fantasy life, so profoundly out of the ordinary were the phenomena I found taking place there.

Here I would find the solution - Solution!!! - to the problem that is war and threat of war. More, I would find miraculous confirmation for what I'd been saying for years, that there is now incontrovertible evidence that humanity has now entered upon the greatest period of change the world has ever known. Something is happening to the whole structure of human consciousness—in which a fresh kind of life is starting.

We are being called to rise to a whole new realm or dimension of existence, a whole new domain, and no one can remain indifferent. No matter the history books, no matter what reactions we may have to current events, no matter the counsel of the world's cynics, we ought first to reaffirm a robust faith in the mystical destiny of our Creator's Human Enterprise.

In fact, my most recent journalings, Beyond War, a set of two volumes, begins with that very thought. It begins with my leap into a realm I might never have imagined. So utterly profound were the unique phenomena, indeed a cosmic drama, I found taking place in that remote mountain-hamlet with a funny sounding name to most Western ears. The name Medjugorje is of Slav origin and means the region between two mountains (medu – between, gora – mountain). More details on the Medjugorje event and its years of mystical phenomena in subsequent chapters.

AS an explorer, I am first of all a recorder, a keeper of journals, and only then a reporter. If and when there is commentary in

Peace is *not* an unrealizable dream.
War is *not* an inevitable reality.

my journals, in frequent instances it is Inspired, which means through the Holy Spirit. For in the end it is only the Spirit who can answer our questions. Spirituality and mysticism are areas of experience that are peculiarly human. It compels our interest, demands our attention, when mystics assure us that to compare scientific knowledge with mystical wisdom is like comparing a tiny candle with the noonday sun. Mystics are like windows to the universe; their souls gaze backwards to the Source and they smile that encounter to us. Like all good poets, the late great John Paul II was a true mystic.

For this reason I readily acknowledge John Paul II's contribution to my exploration. John Paul whose spirituality deeply rooted as it was in the Mystical, and in the mystery of the Cruel Cross, is what kept me on track all during these long and oft-times difficult if not grueling years of quest. Whole decades in search of a way to shake the iron tyranny of war that is a male sickness.

A tyranny that for most of the 20th century, and now in the 21st century, has held whole portions of humanity in fetters as war here, there and nearly everywhere goes about doing its dirty, awful business.

Although increasingly aware of being well into the autumn years of my now long life, I'm enormously grateful for the many years I've had and, despite questionable health along the way, for having remained faithful, run the race, kept my promise to the child victims of war — a big part of the reason I'd been born, I am wont to say.

It is time, and indeed the main message of this report, that the global consciousness of all people and peoples be made open, receptive, to the idea of peace not being an unrealizable dream, of war not being an inevitable reality. The idea might be there, but it has not entered sufficiently to have taken root. The doors of perception are not yet open. My purpose, my goal, in writing *Mommy…What Was War?* is that it will help to open wide those doors. My purpose in part is to provoke a discussion about war and

Peace is *not* an unrealizable dream.
War is *not* an inevitable reality.

peace that acknowledges peace as not being an unrealizable dream and thus war not an inevitable reality. It is time.

As My Exploration Pushed Forward
THE PROJECT DIDN'T SEEM
NEARLY SO FUTILE OR FOOLISH

A hundred years ago when Friedrich Nietzsche made his famous declaration that God is dead, he was not so much suggesting that God had died in the heavens as he was saying that God no longer really mattered in day-to-day life, save as a hangover, a shadow. Generally speaking, this is still the picture. Our world has lost its sense of God, its sense of spirituality, its soul – the Beyond. It has sold out to the actual forces of Darkness. Generally speaking, we live at the poverty level when it comes to spirituality — spirituality that unlike religiosity is a proactive consciousness of the Mystical, the Transcendent, the Sacred. Consequently, civilization is like a ship that has lost its moorings in the deep of a stormy and everswelling sea.

EARLIER in this report I told how I'd begun my exploration for world peace on the premise that it is our broken covenant with one another which must be restored. Given all of humanity's brokenness, separations and divisions, war after war, war on top of war, it is why everything now depends on our reconciliation — especially in the area of religious rivalries.

I am thinking now of the song of the humpback whale, one of the strangest in nature. It is a weird combination of high- and low-pitched groanings. Those who have studied the humpback whale say their songs are noteworthy because these giants of the deep are continually changing them. New patterns are added and old ones eliminated so that over a period of time the whale actually sings a new song.

Peace is *not* an unrealizable dream.
War is *not* an inevitable reality.

From one of my perceptions of the Medjugorje story I see that the religions or major belief systems in the world also are being called to sing a new song. They too are being called to an "elimination" of their old "patterns" — so as to evolve new patterns in how they perceive and relate to one another. How? By coalescing and continually composing new praise around the fresh mercies of God; mercies that are not meant for any one religion or belief system in particular.

It is you - the Christians, the Jews, the Muslims, the Others - who are divided on earth, says the Virgin Mary at Medjugorje; it is not this way in Heaven. A woman pilgrim once asked the visionary Mirjana, "What does God say about us Americans?" Mirjana smiled and good-naturedly replied, "Oh, she thinks you Americans are the greatest!" Then added, "And she thinks the Muslims are the greatest. And the Russians." The pilgrims knew then that Mirjana was having fun with them.

She clarified, "Our Lady does not identify specific groups. She calls all 'her children.'" Unfortunately, many of us and our religions just keep on singing "the same old song." So very clearly, the world's religions need a whole new song around which, together, they can gather, coalesce, and with God's mercies make new the face of the earth.

A whole new song! It was John Paul II's dream, his vision – John Paul whose legacy is forgiveness – when twice he gathered leaders of the world's major religions at Assisi, in Italy, to pray, each in their own Way, for world peace, holy peace. Both of the two events, without precedent, were remarkable for their success. The gathering itself was a very public expression of the idea that there can be unity in diversity, and diversity in unity.

SOME years ago, the great Spanish philosopher Ortega y Gasset expressed the thought that engineers must realize that to be an engineer, it is not enough to be an engineer. While they are going about their business, history is pulling the ground out from under their feet. None of us needs to be reminded today that there is a shaking of the foundations . . . that we, the people of the Earth, having crossed the threshold and standing now in the Third

Peace is *not* an unrealizable dream.
War is *not* an inevitable reality.

Millennium, stand also in the midst of one of the most chaotic and crucial if not most dangerous periods of history for all of humanity.

In fact, we are striving frantically to keep the winds of dissension and the waves of destruction from capsizing the frail ship of civilization in whose hold we cower. We are searching desperately to chart a course for the journey ahead to lead us into calmer waters and a safe harbor.

Former astronaut, Joseph Allen, from his view is credited with this statement: "With all the argument, pro and con, for going to the moon, no one suggested that we should do it to look at Earth. But that may, in fact, have been the most important reason of all."

From my view of the world scene I submit that our one hope today is to grasp the garment of God that is so clearly rustling through the events of our time. And nowhere is that garment rustling more clearly than in the unfolding drama at Medjugorje. It's a cosmic drama that's been twenty-eight years continuing of New Bethlehem and Second Pentecost. It's a celestial event that inspires us to believe that, Yes, we can hope to achieve greater spiritual maturity, greater moral and ethical stature, in the world today. There is cause for optimism.

Medjugorje, some say, is the edge of Heaven. It is a drama that leads not only to the idea of God, but to the certainty of God, and to the impulse that we should attempt to put our secular superstructure back on religious foundations, but not of the "old time" kind. For religion is the serious business of the human race and thus must not bear any taint of arrogance that is an overbearing and oppressive sense that everything one's belief system does is right. For Christians, Jesus is God spelling himself out in language that humans, even children, can understand.

It was 24 June 1981 twenty-eight years ago that two teenagers from the church parish of Medjugorje in rural Yugoslavia spotted the shimmering image of a woman - the Blessed Mother - while walking aimlessly along a rocky, thorn-covered hill called Podbrdo.

Peace is *not* an unrealizable dream.
War is *not* an inevitable reality.

Since then some 25 to 30 million believers from every continent have carried their curiosity and belief (in Our Lady there) to the village, making the world just a little more a single village under a single God.

It is a special grace and gift from God, this continuing "drama" of Our Lady's visits with the visionaries of Medjugorje. I know of no one who has been to Medjugorje without bringing something positive back home with him or her. And as a source of spiritual power, Medjugorje has become something inclusive of the entire world — not the Catholic world only.

Cheers!

Too, these visitations have had a special significance for the world as extraordinary signs of God's love for his Human Enterprise. For even though the self-communication of God has attained its high point and completion with Christ, such a display of His loving power — coming as it does by way of the Blessed Virgin, the Bride of the Holy Spirit — can only mean: God cares for us in a way that is both paternal and maternal.

One aspect of that care manifests in how Medjugorje has roused up our disturbingly secularized West; "the West," says Our Lady, "(which) has made civilization progress, but without God, as if they were their own creators." And, too, how it has roused up the Church, which has become torn apart in many ways, preoccupied with itself, too often captive of the Vatican's "frozen chosen," divorced from Christian mysticism, poor fishers of men, of human creatures. "My children don't you see that the faith begins to extinguish itself, and that it is necessary to awaken the faith among people" — faith that gives answers which reason cannot know.

It bears repeating...faith that gives answers which reason cannot know.

A second aspect of that care manifests in how Medjugorje has come to be an idea of what means "pilgrim," of how one can and must make his or her way back to faith, faith that isn't abstraction but ground to walk on, back to Lord God. That is why Medjugorje is here: as a call to discover in ourselves our original self, the self

Peace is *not* an unrealizable dream.
War is *not* an inevitable reality.

that is the image of God written into our genes, into our character, into our nature — and to live it and to bring it to light!

Very clearly, whether we care to recognize and accept it or not, the Mother of God, in Medjugorje, is here to start a new era, a new time. She is opening a path so that prayer can begin to rule in the whole world. She is here to influence every tribe, nation, ethnic group, every culture and creed — indeed, it is already happening. Our Lady is here to raise up great saints. This too is happening.

In this time of being crowded by the Adversary; in this time when large blocks of commercial television through their programming are in the business of marketing evil; in this time when Lie reigns; in this time when distractions and the intellect conspire to make us deaf to the Voice that speaks out of Silence, the Blessed Mother comes to encourage and guide the innumerable good people of this planet who want to live in peace, friendship, freedom, justice. The good people who want to enjoy the miracle of life under the generous rays of our sun, under the good guidance of the Lord God of the universe.

Too, Our Lady, whose very Presence is a message we cannot dismiss, is here to help us heal the antiquated quarrels, divisions, and insanity that is rush to bloody revenge of those who refuse to recognize the oneness of our planetary home and of the human family.

Our Lady has visited on other occasions throughout history, especially since the mid-19th century; and with the passing of time, far from losing relevance and significance, her visits have gained in urgency and value. The obvious fact is that since her visits on the Rue du Bac, Paris, France, 1830, and then in Fatima, Portugal, 1917, with still other appearances between these two dates, the international scene has been one of constant unrest and warfare.

More, it's comparable to what Hobbes described as the bellum omnium contra omnes (war of war against everybody) carried to degrees of overwhelming intensity by our technological advances. Thomas Hobbes is the English philosopher and political theorist best known for his book, Leviathan (1651).

Peace is *not* an unrealizable dream.
War is *not* an inevitable reality.

For the locals in Medjugorje, what I've come to see as a mission station of Heaven, Our Lady is called the Gospa; it's the Croatian word for Mother of God, Mother of us all. In this volume Our Lady's various titles are used interchangeably but for no particular reason.

WE are still living in biblical times, an era that did not pass with Christ's crucifixion on the cruel Cross. We are still living in the time of Job and Noah. Our Lady, on the other hand, from outside the construct of time and space, sees, as does God, all the nonsense of the world's advocates of violence who, *either in the realm of speculation or in their own thought practical activity,* have exalted war as the necessary condition of human existence which guarantees progress and growth. They argue that universal reason demands, so to speak, war as a prerequisite of change. By far, unfortunately, this view has prevailed, and the efforts of peace societies and advocates of peace have merely served to counterbalance in just a minimal way the ever-growing, ever-expanding, militarism of our national states.

Some philosophers, despite their opposing philosophies when addressing the questions of war and peace, with dismal pessimism agree on the "natural depravity of men whose egotistical rabble has not the slightest inclination by nature to maintain any form of constitution or to observe any laws." For both, "the human being is malicious and untrustworthy, war is a natural human condition, and only by fear alone can we be guaranteed a lasting state of security."

The Blessed Mother at Medjugorje comes to dispose of all such pessimism… pessimism which serves only to justify and vindicate the advocates of militarism and conflict; the majesty of militarism which binds and commands with implacable rigor like an unforgiving judge.

But fear alone cannot be sufficient, simply because fear presupposes a feared object, a supreme judge, an enforcer of the law. On the international level, however, there is no law, no judge, no object of fear, as long as one's nation has even the slightest

Peace is *not* an unrealizable dream.
War is *not* an inevitable reality.

advantage over the others. Here, then, war becomes the ultimate trial, the decisive judging force. How are we, then, to find a lasting peace.

At Medjugorje one finds out how. It is my purpose to see happen by asking "Mommy...What Was War?" that a more optimistic perception of things might come to prevail regarding the attainment of world peace. In my acknowledgements at the end of this report I cite the distinguished Robert Muller who served as an undersecretary for UN Secretary-Generals Dag Hammarskjold, U Thant, and Kurt Waldheim. Muller was known as the resident philosopher of the United Nations and its prophet of hope, believing the world can—and will—become a better place to live.

Muller, in conversation with me on several occasions, told of how his many years at the UN served to convince him that there is a growing movement, even in the seemingly endless conflict between nations, toward a brotherhood, sisterhood, of all peoples. Hidden perhaps, but happening. He contended that the nations of the world are, sometimes in spite of themselves, overcoming their narrowness and working together for true peace and respect among all peoples. He held a vision of an everevolving humanity, reaching toward fulfillment and happiness.

Even though from this highest of stations in world affairs where he'd long been privy to the worst-case scenarios of projected human conflict, and now my point in sharing this story, still he was able to share heartening evidence that beneath the worst jingoist bluster, lie the natural impulses of fraternity and understanding.

> Muller - a devout man - believed that the more we learn about our planet, its life forms and our place in the universe, the more we discover that each human life is a true miracle. In each of us, there is a spark of divinity. We are a microcosm of the universe, of all past, present and future, a convergence of infinity and eternity. The exercise of the miracle of life by each individual and by societies is a spiritual

Peace is *not* an unrealizable dream.
War is *not* an inevitable reality.

function, deeply anchored in the mystery of time and space.

With voice and text his was the appeal to the world's religions that they redouble their efforts to educate their followers to the true birthright of us all—unconditional love for each human being, a reverence and awe for the miracle of life, and an attitude of life marked by gratitude and joy, the right to live in peace. The Gospa, the Blessed Mother at Medjugorje, is on the same track, but as the special messenger of God. Let me be your mother and your tie to God, she is saying.

Today's primary motive for world peace is fear of extinction, devastation, poverty, death, and a final catastrophe. Wrong! If our primary motive does not stem from forgiveness, the legacy left to us by John Paul II and one of Our Lady's main messages at Medjugorje, then there will be no peace, no peace at all. "Reconcile, reconcile, reconcile!"

Our Lady at Medjugorje, in her school of prayer, school of heart, school of love, school of peace, and thus a college for our times, our generation, has given us the paradigm of change so that we might make significant advances if not great leaps toward world peace. Difficult, but not impossible! If it must be done, it can be done! Peace is not an unrealizable dream, war is not an inevitable reality.

Our mission, the mission for all of us, is to help in the task of hastening the day when the world's children will be able to look back on war as an 'inconceivable aberration' of their forefathers. If we must, we can! Our Lady at Medjugorje is here to take us to where she can show us how.

She has come to give us a new world, to show that Earth and Heaven are parts of the same entirety. In Medjugorje, heaven has opened up and we can touch it as never before...never before has the veil been so parted!

For this reason Medjugorje is not meant to be explained or debated, but experienced. Medjugorje is a school of love. Once we

Peace is *not* an unrealizable dream.
War is *not* an inevitable reality.

have come to the deep inner knowledge – a knowledge more of the heart than of the mind – that we are born out of Love and will die into Love, that every part of our being is deeply rooted in Love and that this love is our true father and mother ... then all forms of evil, violence, war, illness and death lose their power over us and become painful but also helpful reminders of our true divine childhood.

Medjugorje is a call, it is not a shrine. It is a place of key lessons for a world order that, in Graham Green's words, is "the disputed and ravaged territory between the two eternities (heaven and hell)." Thus the realization as noted in one of my journals that God, as usual and out of his great love for us, "is taking extraordinary measures to lead us to Himself. Thus no one can say God has not intervened in our time...no one! If all this isn't God hitting each of us on the head with a baseball bat, then I really don't know what's going on."

Peace is *not* an unrealizable dream.
War is *not* an inevitable reality.

REVISITING MY BOOK
"WAR ON TRIAL"

shaking the iron tyranny of war
- war that is a male sickness

WAR ON TRIAL & The Celestial Messenger in my experience of authoring that volume, actually a tome, was not so much a work of journalistic or collegiate scholarship as a leap into an invisible dimension. But I will leave it for Dr. Luis Navia's covering letter to his general assessment and critical review of that proposed book's manuscript, to say more:

"I have just finished reading Mr. Ted Conlin's manuscript for a book entitled WAR ON TRIAL & The Celestial Messenger. I am greatly impressed by the content and style of this most timely work. I am sure that once it is published, it will appeal to a wide audience and will make a significant impact not only on our understanding of the crisis which has affected former Yugoslavia for the last ten years but, more profoundly and to the point, through that understanding, a wonderful, indeed important contribution to making this planet at long last what it was always meant to be: the Planet of God... a world without war. Ted Conlin's proposed book combines in an effective manner various aspects which would be essential in creating a powerful document: the most impeccable scholarship, a wealth of information, a perceptive understanding of the issues, and a solution to the problem. I am enclosing a one-page assessment of the work. I have also agreed to write a foreword. Sincerely, L. E.

Navia Ph.D." Professor of Philosophy, New York
Institute of Technology."

WHAT follows is Dr. Navia's assessment of the volume. He also
provided critical reviews for each of the book's five sections:

"Ted Conlin, in prosecuting war that has made of
the 20th century a world bleeding and tortured, a
Century of Tears, has made a remarkable case for
abolishing war, all war. And he has chosen to do
it by focusing on the conflict that has affected and
is affecting former Yugoslavia. Other books on the
subject have been written from a variety of points
of view, covering, as it seems, every aspect of this
brutal conflict.

"But what is outstanding about Conlin's work
is its successful attempt to embrace two apparently
disjointed events which have taken place in former
Yugoslavia in the last decade: the genocidal war -
indeed, as Conlin observes, probably one of the most
devastating and savage military events of recent
times - and the apparitions of the Virgin Mary in
the village of Medjugorje.

"As if in a paradoxical and baffling coincidence,
hell and heaven, war and peace, despair and hope,
hatred and love, have come together in one and the
same place. Against the background of the sound of
canons and guns, the voice of the celestial messenger
announces its message of peace to the world.

"The extraordinary merit of Conlin's work is
not only its impeccable scholarship, its breadth, its
photographic descriptiveness, its impassioned appeal
for peace - the peace which emanates abundantly
from Medjugorje, but its ability to decipher the
enigma of the events in Medjugorje in both the
context of the Serbian atrocities in Bosnia and in

Peace is *not* an unrealizable dream.
War is *not* an inevitable reality.

the broader context of a world that has been at war with itself in increasingly Apocalyptical ways for the past one hundred years.

"Conlin understands the meaning of those events and succeeds in clarifying them for the reader. He ties them together in a way that is difficult to forget and impossible to refute. . . . Conlin's work is among many other things a devotional call for planetary conversion. But the profound religiosity which pervades all its pages does not detract in any way from its serious import as a thoroughly documented and scholarly examination of the political and social conditions which have eventually led to the Serbian-Bosnian conflict.

"In fact, a non-religious reader is bound to find the book highly instructive and fascinating in its analyses and descriptions of that conflict and that conflict's root-connectedness, its points of connection, with all war. Those who share even a small drop of Conlin's authentic faith will surely profit immensely from a reflective reading of his monumental work.

"It is simply impossible to read this work without feeling compelled to re-examine one's own position vis-a-vis what appears to be the most brutal human confrontation of our times, and vis-a-vis the message of Medjugorje, a message that comes to us as if it were a last urgent appeal to become engaged in a universal campaign for lasting peace."

Next I present Dr. Navia's critical review of the book's first chapter entitled A Sort of Introduction:

"This introductory chapter of Ted Conlin's WAR ON TRIAL, beginning with the Prosecution's Opening Statement, outlines in an effective and clear manner

Peace is *not* an unrealizable dream.
War is *not* an inevitable reality.

the contents and purpose of his work. In the former Yugoslavia (as a case example for prosecuting war, all war), a land beset by the ravages of a brutal war in which the most savage and criminal instincts of human beings have suddenly come to the surface in order to immerse thousands of innocent people in suffering and pain.... war in which, as Conlin graphically describes it, the forces of evil appear to be unrestrained and willing to commit every imaginable excess.... war in which our closing twentieth century is witnessing the most horrible degradation of human dignity.... a door of hope and reconciliation has been opened. As if to invite the killers and their victims to enter into another world.

"Conlin provides for us in this introductory chapter an unforgettable picture of contrasts: on the one hand, the war and its outrages, and on the other the presence of the Virgin Mary as she made herself visible to children in the tiny Yugoslavian village of Medjugorje, which the author rightly refers to as an oasis of peace..... Here we have the two poles of the human reality: the bestiality of the worst aspects of our human nature and the possibility of redemption through a commitment to peace and love.

"What the author proposes to do in his eloquent and moving work, and what he summarizes with mastery and precision in the introduction, is through the devastating reality of the moment in former Yugoslavia to raise our awareness of the devastating reality of all war, and to set this reality against the background of the messages of the Virgin Mary as these have been communicated to visionaries in Medjugorje ... almost as if he were forcing us to make a choice between the two conditions, the actual one in which humanity in this century appears to have descended to the lowest level of inhumanity,

Peace is *not* an unrealizable dream.
War is *not* an inevitable reality.

and the possible one in which a possibility is given unto us to raise ourselves to a higher plane of human existence.

"Even those who may remain skeptical concerning the apparitions of Medjugorje may find this introductory chapter challenging and thought provoking. Conlin remains faithful to the facts of the war, and describes them in great detail. His account of the apparitions is scholarly and sensitive. And, above all, his success in establishing a sharp contrast between the former and the latter constitutes a compelling introduction to his work. Undoubtedly, a reading of this chapter will assure a reading of the entire work."

BECAUSE space allows for just a brief revisit to my large book War On Trial, a tome, I've chosen pared-down extracts from just two chapters - Lysistrata and The Male: A Child of the Weapon - for inclusion in this report. I've selected the latter because it is an image that serves a useful purpose. I selected Lysistrata because of its poignancy of message in support of my prosecution of war—all war.

LYSISTRATA
"What Have We Done To Greece?"

FOR those of us who are the survivors of the past century — where literally Hundreds of Millions were slain by the insanities of war — most of them blameless women, innocent children, the frightened and the fleeing — there is the imperative that we acknowledge a responsibility which can be neither denied nor shirked. We have a responsibility to use our every resource and opportunity to helping in the task of hastening the day when children will be able to look back on war as an 'inconceivable aberration' of their forefathers.

This is at once the burden, the challenge, the cross we carry with us into the third millennium. The "us" refers mostly to the

Peace is *not* an unrealizable dream.
War is *not* an inevitable reality.

male of our species because it is the men who display most the fine line between the monster in the person and the hero or the martyr. Witness during the past century, and indeed the thousand years before that, how it's been a history of this "monster" thing taking over, enslaving, raping, terrorizing, slaughtering. A thousand years of subjecting his opposite in gender to sexual conquest and slavery, many of them left mutilated, wasted, in need of vaginal repair. Then because shamed and shunned went into the forest, found a tree—and hanged themselves. While still others walked into the sea and did it that way.

"Lysistrata," the classic Greek play, is based on its observation that throughout history men have had a passion for fighting and copulating in pretty much equal proportions:

> In this play the women of Athens, led by Lysistrata and supported by other delegates from the other states of Hellas, determined to force the men to stop an ongoing war, went on strike, threatening no more love-making until the men stopped the wars. They met in solemn conclave, and Lysistrata shared her scheme, the rigorous application to husbands and lovers of a self-denying ordinance—"we must refrain from the male altogether."
>
> Every wife and mistress is to refuse all sexual favors whatsoever, until the men have come to terms of peace. In cases where the women must yield 'par force majeure,' then it is to be passive, with ill grace and in such a way as to afford the minimum of gratification to their partner. By these means Lysistrata assures them they will very soon gain their end. "If we sit indoors prettily dressed out in our best transparent silks and prettiest gewgaws, and all nicely depilated, they will be able to deny us nothing." Such was the burden of her advice. Thus the motto was sexual solidarity. . . .

Peace is *not* an unrealizable dream.
War is *not* an inevitable reality.

After an agony of frustration, the men gave in, the women prevailed, and there was peace. The play has lasted 2,500 years, but macho man still goes on killing while he ignores the common sense of women. Towards the end of the play, the Athenians and Spartans held a quarrelsome peace conference which was almost overwhelmed by the pain of erections that the delegates were suffering. Lysistrata called on the goddess Harmony to persuade the foolish men to negotiate. Harmony succeeded in getting the enemies to the conference table by leading them by their tumescent members. . . .

Once there, she placated them with a striptease when they began carving up Greece between them. But when the map of Greece had been torn into tiny pieces, Harmony abdicated in tears... and the enemies, at last horrified at what they had done, held up the pieces of the map and said, "What have we done to Greece?"

Today, 2,500 years later, little has changed. In Europe, during the wars of the 1990's in former Yugoslavia, as adversaries sat around the Peace Talks conference tables in Geneva and London, we saw how maps were being redrawn on bodies en masse of women raped and wasted. The only thing different was that, unlike the Greece experience, there'd been no expressions of "horror' by the enemies at what they were doing. No one was holding up pieces of the map saying, "What are we doing to Bosnia-Hercegovina?"

Bosnia-Hercegovina and the horrors inflicted upon its young girls and women shows how much we live today as though in the time of Lysistrata - 2,500 years ago - with the male instinct for conquest and war still humanity's central problem. War that is "an adventure with no return." War that is always a catastrophe both spiritually and materially. War that because it's a license to kill, is an invitation to every kind of moral insanity, every kind of outrageous incivility. War, finally, that is always an assault on God and his self-giving love.

Peace is *not* an unrealizable dream.
War is *not* an inevitable reality.

THE MALE: A CHILD OF THE WEAPON
(an image that serves a useful purpose)

Space allows for only an extract from this chapter:

IT almost seems that if, in using our own creative imagination, we were to extrapolate with unrestrained imaginative abandon from the data of recent century, we would discover that the male is a child of the weapon. That is to say, it was a weapon that fathered the male of our species. Not only that, but instead of man developing weapons for himself, he was in some way developed by biology to be a user of weapons. In another way of saying it, the male is a biological invention here to suit the purposes of the weapon. . . . Fantasy? Of course. To suppose that instead of weapons being developed for man, man was developed for weapons is carrying alienation pretty far! But it does image for us, thus serving a useful purpose, a world-view in which aggression, barbarism, murder, and every form of violence seem bound to prevail. It's a view to which many are committed, and the reason for today's public cynicism regarding the probability of peace ever reigning on earth. . . . It is a cynicism that is used in a cruel, contemptuous manner to describe what is said to be the human descent. And alas, in the name of 'realism' it is increasingly being accepted by people who have become disenchanted and distrustful toward their world and themselves. . . . It is just such a world-view as this that lends support to the pomp and circumstance of military build-up and might, the construction and evolution of the war machine, the marriage of the military and industrial and about which President Eisenhower, in his farewell speech to the nation, warned: "Beware! Beware of the military-industrial complex!" END

Peace is *not* an unrealizable dream.
War is *not* an inevitable reality.

THUS the civilizing process, the evolution toward world peace, if Bosnia and later other such scenes of unmitigated horrors are any gauge, Afghanistan and Iraq come to mind, still has a long way to go. Getting out in front of the issue of war and what's been a thousand years of rape and carnage, will not happen by itself. We all have a role; we can each make a contribution. For some reason, we want to hinder or ridicule, instead of wanting to help and encourage the peace dreamers, the peace visionaries, the peace activists. It is said about them that they are "crazy" or "romantics" or "fantasists" or some other fool thing.

The problem is that in all such hubris we are very much "like crabs in a bucket" — when one tries to get out, the others hang on to him and pull him back down. We can get only so far out with our dream before getting pulled back down. Nothing would be more damaging to human peace and ascent than to believe that it cannot be done, that holy peace, true justice and the survival of our species are unlikely or impossible.

It bears repeating: Nothing would be more damaging than to believe that it cannot be done.

Recall if you will the face of the most terrorized and warred upon person you have seen in picture or person — and then ask yourself if the next step you contemplate is going to be of any use to that person. If you can't think of any such person, then think about the conditions into which children are born today and the kind of future which is being prepared for them —think about Irma:

> Irma Hadzimuratovic is 5 years old, and she is one of thousands in Sarajevo alone who have been struck by artillery shells. In August 1993 she laid naked on a bloodstained bedsheet in that city's old military hospital, moaning quietly, and doctors saying her only hope of survival was evacuation to a hospital abroad.
>
> A committee of four foreign doctors under a cumbersome system of screening patients must approve every evacuation aboard a United Nations

Peace is *not* an unrealizable dream.
War is *not* an inevitable reality.

plane. Each of the four are from different UN organizations and are rarely in Sarajevo. Two of the committee members are based outside Bosnia. They had no immediate plans to meet.

One afternoon, one of the team of doctors caring for Irma, pulled nervously on a cigarette outside the intensive care unit where Irma laid. For five days running, he said, he had made the journey of several miles to the United Nations Building, only to be told that there was no hope of finding a place for Irma on any one of the 20 United Nations aircraft that left there each day, most of them empty, after delivering relief supplies (this being a besieged city, a military front line) and shuttling officials (this being a city zoned as under UN protection... that is to say, to the extent that this is possible in a war of such craziness and surreal twists, indeed a war where mutilated kids are forced to endure surgery under primitive conditions).

"I have had hundreds of different answers," the doctor said. "They've told me she can't go because she doesn't have the proper papers, because they haven't a hospital for her to go to, and because they don't have a properly-equipped evacuation aircraft. Some of the excuses are just stupid, such as, 'Who will take care of her body if she dies?'"

When the mortar fired by Serbian nationalist troops on a street near Irma's home at the end of July, killing two people, including Irma's mother, Elvira, 30, and wounding 12 children, a mortar fragment entered Irma's back, compressing her spine and rupturing her intestines.

Although the spinal injury did not cause paralysis, Irma's doctors were puzzled by symptoms that suggested she was suffering from either a

Peace is *not* an unrealizable dream.
War is *not* an inevitable reality.

brain injury from her head hitting the ground or from meningitis resulting from infection of the spinal cord. They said that an accurate diagnosis would require a CAT scan, an impossible task in a city where there is no main electricity and where hospital generators provide insufficient power for the complex machines.

"If she stays in this hospital, she will die, that is certain," the doctor said, gesturing to the bed where Irma lay, eyes open, with her body heavily bandaged and laced about with tubes. "We would not be asking the United Nations to evacuate a patient that we thought would die anyway. She can die here as well as anywhere. But we think she can be saved, at almost any hospital in Europe or elsewhere that is operating under normal conditions. All we ask is the chance to get her there."

This story, together with a picture of Irma lying in a Sarajevo hospital with a puncture near her spine and ointment on her lips, her mouth and eyes wide open in a look no child should have, made for a media blitz that shredded international red tape, thus allowing this little Sarajevan girl, critically injured by Serbian artillery fire, to be evacuated to Britain for advanced medical treatment.

The evacuation - aboard an air ambulance to London's Great Ormond Street Children's Hospital - got global news coverage, shaming other governments (British Prime Minister John Major, after tearful pleas from his people, had ordered personally the evacuation of Irma) into action to save other civilians wounded in the then 16-month-old conflict. Too, Irma's story - that of a five-year-old girl with severe spinal, abdominal and head wounds - focused world attention on young casualties of the war in Bosnia, and on the plight of Sarajevo's hospitals - battered

Peace is *not* an unrealizable dream.
War is *not* an inevitable reality.

by months of shelling - whose patients sometimes with life-threatening wounds or illnesses, cannot be treated because they lack equipment, running water and electricity.

Irma's Bosnian surgeon had lobbied reporters in the besieged Bosnian capital of Sarajevo to publicize her plight. "This child was not evacuated for humanitarian reasons, but because of the pressure from the public and the press," he said. "For this child it's probably too late," he added, his voice choking with emotion. "It may already be too late to save her. I am afraid her chances are not very good today. If she had been evacuated when we asked, her chances would have been better."

Doctors in Sarajevo had two hours notice to prepare Irma for her journey. Bundled in blankets, her head twisted back by the shrapnel embedded in her spine, she was placed in an armored UN ambulance. For one long moment, she was alone in the hulking as rain swept through its open windows.

All that could be seen was a hump of blankets and a small hand stretched towards three dolls. Several people at the hospital's battle-scarred entrance wept in silence. Others stood stoically as if they had seen too much agony to pass judgment on Irma's journey. She was driven down Sarajevo's "sniper alley" and placed in a Hercules transport aircraft. Its pilot said weather conditions had been "horrendous" and that any other flight would have been canceled. "But, given the circumstances, we knew we just had to give it a go." The flight lieutenant has two daughters of his own. After landing in Ancona, Italy, Irma, accompanied by her father and two-year-old sister, was transferred to the ambulance plane and flown to Heathrow.

Peace is *not* an unrealizable dream.
War is *not* an inevitable reality.

The doctor who examined her at Ancona said: "She is unconscious and gravely ill (in her first morning in London, Irma lapsed in and out of consciousness, her tiny body seized with convulsions). Working by candlelight, doctors in Sarajevo have worked wonders." Indeed! Doctors in Sarajevo managed to revive Irma from clinical death immediately after the attack that so terribly wounded her and killed her mom.

Irma's flight came only a day after the first media reports of her story and within hours of tearful demands that Mr. Major should intervene. Operation Irma is what the mercy mission was dubbed... a mercy mission... hope for the wounded in a city where 1,100 children have been killed in recent months, and 15,000 wounded, by sniper fire, mortars and by stepping on land mines.

Thus began what was to become Britain's airlift of wounded from the Bosnian conflict. It opened the floodgates for others to follow. Indeed, fifteen countries offered nearly 800 hospital beds for Sarajevo siege victims. Italy set the ball rolling by promising to take all 454 on the UN's list of people seeking evacuation, an offer soon followed by others across Europe, America, Australia and the Gulf. Offers also came from individuals wanting to pay for treatment and from private clinics. Thus with the UN flooded with offers of help, Britain's airlift (earlier said by some to be nothing more than "gesture politics") was put on temporary hold.

And Italy, after hearing complaints that the West had made a "media circus" out of the airlift, said it preferred to set up a Red Cross field hospital in Sarajevo itself. Indeed a UN spokesman in Zagreb said he was appalled at articles in the British press which claimed that wounded soldiers had taken the

Peace is *not* an unrealizable dream.
War is *not* an inevitable reality.

place of children when 21 Bosnians were flown to Britain and Ireland for treatment the previous day.

Thus the scramble to help coincided with controversy over Operation Irma and the selection of evacuees, some claiming that soldiers bribed their way onto the flights... soldier-patients bribing doctors to recommend them for evacuation. "You find yourself thinking, simplistically," says one-on-the-scene observer, "that children deserve priority in evacuations in this increasingly shambolicly organized public relations exercise with a media circus, photo opportunities, and allegations of soldiers being rescued."

One official of the U. N. High Commission for Refugees said that some doctors were threatened at gunpoint to add names to patient dossiers given to the UN medical evacuation team overseeing the airlift. And that corruption is widespread as families use the tactics of desperation to save relatives. Indeed, the intimidation of local doctors is so widespread that the UNHCR is supplying guards. "This is total war and people are out to survive," said the official. "There are 400,000 people all desperate to get out of Sarajevo. There are diabetics without insulin and their relatives will do anything to help them."

And then London revealed its own interest in the evacuation. "The British said they needed more children," said the UNHCR's coordinator for evacuation. Their stated aim, he said, was to "please British public opinion" (manifested in wide-spread anger and tearful pleas). He said one British doctor of distinguished rank went around wards as if it were a supermarket. "I'll take this one. He's a good case," he quoted the doctor as saying. Commented the coordinator, "It's disgusting." He's the same doctor who set up the cumbersome system

Peace is *not* an unrealizable dream.
War is *not* an inevitable reality.

of screening patients that requires accord by four doctors from different UN organizations who are rarely in Sarajevo and meet once a month.

THE large document War On Trial (nearly a thousand pages) that began with me launching out on a quest for world peace, for a solution to the problem that is war and threat of war, soon evolved a proposal for a major conference at Hofstra University here on Long Island. It would look at the then Balkan Wars of the early 1990's as a Laboratory for the Study of War at the end of a century that had known nothing but war.

(Historical note: A decade earlier, in 1982, Hofstra had launched a series of presidential conferences that evolved into what today is Hofstra's prestigious Center for Presidential Studies, one of the few institutions in the country to focus on U.S. presidencies. What I would have liked, and indeed envisioned, was a Center for Peace Studies. It never happened. Had it happened it would have been a first here in America. Since then such centers have been established at Notre Dame and Columbia Universities.)

After all, the thinking went, Bosnia-Hercegovina — with its well-earned sobriquet as the Powderkeg of Europe — was a wide open event. It was there for all the world to have a look, poke, probe and try to understand. Too, there was Medjugorje, a tiny mountain-village in Hercegovina where, since 1981, the Virgin Mary as God's special messenger had been appearing, reportedly on a daily basis, to six peasant children with messages of reconciliation, peace, conversion, for the world. Thus it too was a wide open event, not only because of the apparitions but because of how it had grown steadily in reputation as a veritable oasis of peace, holy peace, even though surrounded by years (1991-1995) of bestial war to which no nation or collection of nations could put a stop.

Bosnia (Bosnia-Hercegovina abbreviated by the world press) is the place where for three years of a four-year war the world witnessed the shameless slaughter, heinous deeds, the blood-soaked mania of a Serb Aggressor who in then Yugoslavia sowed the seeds of panic, destruction and death. And the world unable or, even more troubling, unwilling perhaps to stop it.

Peace is *not* an unrealizable dream.
War is *not* an inevitable reality.

Miraculously, from Medjugorje, at the heart of that heinous war, sprang a potent wellspring of maternal water of life. It's been an event that humbles the intellect, or endeavors to be superior to, but which can never equal reason. Yes, the form taken by this issuing was the Virgin Mary, making of Medjugorje a place of Apparitions, Peace, Hope. A place today where nothing seems to have happened but where, in fact, everything wears the tangible and eradicable aura of its events.

Given the over thousand year history of the region, a history that has meant an immense amount of human pain, arranged in an unbroken continuity, thus a land of fear; and given enemies without and rulers within; and given a region known for its prisons, its torture and violent death, thus peace a stranger, it is almost as if Medjugorje and its Apparitions had to happen.

It had to happen so that we could finally see this region and its people in its true colors. This was a people seemingly of slow movement and calm resignation, as if in a state of forlorn indolence. But who with their constant expectation of a miracle — a miracle not as something sensational but rather as the positive intervention of a beneficent God in an otherwise desolate destiny — gave to their otherwise unremarkable countryside an almost human warmth inconsistent with its barren appearance.

To really know that history, then one understands without need of explanation or convincing that Our Lady not only could, but just had to appear somewhere around here. For indeed the people of these parts have, since time beyond remembering, epitomized the suffering at Golgatha, on Calvary, and Mary's suffering at the foot of the cruel Cross.

In a time when the world itself is in agony, in travail — and at the end of a century which because of its unprecedented record of man-made misery, and despite all its advances and overcomings, has gone down in history as the "Century of Shame" — it is easy to see why of all places in today's world, the celestial messenger chose Medjugorje, in the crucible that is Bosnia-Hercegovina, as the best place from which to speak to that world.

Peace is *not* an unrealizable dream.
War is *not* an inevitable reality.

One has to understand that Bosnia at the time was a place where a portion of its people had lost its humanity, its reason, and become dark. And that as long as the people there used history as an excuse for the inexcusable, there would be the stink of what is demented if not demonic in the air. And, that Medjugorje was a place where what was happening wasn't some sort of passing fancy, no, but an event that was critical things happening for all humanity, for the entire Human Enterprise!

Given the violent and oft'times hate-filled centuries-long history of that part of the world, unlike in significant ways that of any other part, coupled with the Medjugorje event, the Mother of God drawn by her Motherhood and the trouble in which these people found themselves, the idea of the Balkans as a classroom for the study of War and Peace had a genuine appeal. Especially because of the wide-openness of these events, both the human and the divine, each with a 'show and tell' in abundance, there for all the world to study as though through a microscope.

Unfortunately the intended conference never came off because of scheduling conflicts with the university. In the Lord's own scheme of planning and scheduling things; however, there grew an opportunity for that proposal to take on a life of its own, in the process allowing me to pen WAR ON TRIAL & The Celestial Messenger.

MEANWHILE, I'd found myself appalled when discovering that rape in time of war was not a felony, not a war crime, not a crime against humanity. I was especially chagrined when finding that rape was an "official policy" of that war's Serb leaders, the aggressors, in Belgrade. I campaigned, petitioned, lobbied to change things and ultimately as others did likewise I was able to make the following report in my journal of Year 2006:

> Mass rape and sexual enslavement in time of war will for the first time be regarded as a crime against humanity, a charge second in gravity only to Genocide, after a 2006 landmark ruling from the Yugoslav war crimes tribunal in the Hague which

Peace is *not* an unrealizable dream.
War is *not* an inevitable reality.

sentenced three Bosnian Serbs to a combined tariff of 60 years in jail.

In a judgment that is likely to have far-reaching implications for war crimes trials in Rwanda, Kosovo and East Timor, the tribunal elevated systematic rape from being a mere violation of the customs of war to one of the most heinous war crimes of all - a Crime Against Humanity.

The court ruled that the three veterans of the 1992-95 Bosnian war were guilty of the systematic and savage rape, torture and enslavement of Muslim women in 1992 in the town of Foca in southeastern Bosnia.

"This is the first case where sexual slavery has been charged," the UN prosecutor said. "What sets this apart is that this is a case in which we have a large 'rape camp' organization. This is the first case of sexual enslavement and the only one with sexual assaults and no murders."

In the past, international courts such as the tribunals set up in Nuremberg and Tokyo after the second world war have been reluctant to class wartime rape as a serious crime of war but the Hague tribunal took a much tougher line on the issue. The judgment has given hope to thousands of surviving "comfort women" used as sex slaves by Japanese soldiers during the second world war who have been fighting in vain for recognition and compensation from the Japanese government.

The presiding judge described in graphic detail how the three Bosnian Serbs had in the summer of 1992 abducted girls as young as 12 and subjected them to "appalling sexual torture in sports halls and a variety of rape houses." She told the court: "Rape was used by members of the Bosnian Serb armed

Peace is *not* an unrealizable dream.
War is *not* an inevitable reality.

forces as an instrument of terror. The three accused are not ordinary soldiers whose morals were merely loosened by the hardships of war. They thrived in the dark atmosphere of the dehumanization of those believed to be enemies."

She said to the defendants, "You abused and ravaged Muslim women because of their ethnicity and from among their number you picked whomsoever you fancied. You have shown the most glaring disrespect for the women's dignity and their fundamental human rights on a scale that far surpasses even what one might call the average seriousness of rapes during wartime." Human rights groups estimate that "tens of thousands" of Muslim women and girls were systematically raped during that war.

The International Criminal Court, which hears its first case (against the Democratic Republic of Congo) in 2007, will be crucial in spreading that message globally. The court will recognize a broad spectrum of sexual-violence crimes — including rape, enforced prostitution, forced pregnancy and enforced sterilization — as crimes against humanity or as war crimes. But the court will step in only when national governments are unable or unwilling to prosecute.

Because the use of rape as a weapon of war is escalating all over the world, women's bodies a battleground over which opposing forces struggle, it can be said that every war is a war on women. Women and their children are on the front lines. Every war ends the lives of so many women, so many children!

And while we may long for the luxury of believing that the systematic rapes in Bosnia and Rwanda

Peace is *not* an unrealizable dream.
War is *not* an inevitable reality.

were inhuman events, outside the range of everyday experience, such crimes are growing in numbers in countries such as Cambodia, Uganda, the Congo, Sudan and Colombia. Colombia's civil war has claimed more than 40,000 lives in the past decade while two million people have been forced from their homes, the majority of them women and children. Today, 80 percent of the civilian casualties of war are women; 80 percent of the world's refugees are women and children.

Amnesty International says that during the 1994 genocide in Rwanda, 250,000 to 500,000 women were raped, one-third of them gang-raped. After the conflict ended, the victims were often ostracized by family and friends; 80 per cent of survivors were found to be "severely traumatized." The world was horrified, but a decade later, it says, nothing has changed.

Women and girls are still the unacknowledged casualties of the world's conflicts, currently raging in 35 countries from Iraq and Chechnya to Colombia and Sudan. This, despite various United Nations declarations, treaties and promises that underscore the gravity of violence against women and children caught in these conflicts.

Amnesty field workers report that in the year-long crisis in the Darfur region of Sudan, thousands of women have been systematically raped or mutilated by pro-government militiamen known as "Janjaweed," or "men on horseback . . . girls as young as eight have been abducted and forced to stay with the Janjaweed in military camps," says the report. "Several testimonies collected contain clear cases of sexual slavery. Some record women's and girls' legs and arms being deliberately broken to prevent them from escaping."

Peace is *not* an unrealizable dream.
War is *not* an inevitable reality.

All of which is to report that women and girls are still the unacknowledged casualties of the world's conflicts. In many cases, women have been publicly assaulted, in front of their husbands or wider community; (the same thing has happened to young teenage girls, in front of their families or in the village square). Pregnant women have not been spared; those who resist have been beaten, stabbed or killed. Patterns of sexual violence don't "just happen" in the rage and fog of war, Amnesty says. "They are ordered, condoned or tolerated as a result of political calculations. Furthermore, they are committed by individuals who know they will not be punished."

The report documents how, earlier this year, a group of women put an end to the military atrocities being committed in the Imphal region of India. After a woman was arrested, mutilated and killed by security forces on suspicion of belonging to an armed group, the group stripped naked and publicly dared the soldiers to rape them.

Word spread and mass protests erupted all over the region. The action led the central Indian government to end the categorization of the region as a "disturbed area," and to stop the use of military "special powers" there.

Peace is *not* an unrealizable dream.
War is *not* an inevitable reality.

"PLUS ULTRA"

Before moving on to Part III of this Report, it is of relevant interest that I add some closing thoughts to what's been said so far.

IF in William James' words the greatest discovery of his generation was that human beings can alter their lives by altering their attitudes, then the greatest discovery of today's generation has been this: Although the doors of perception are not yet open to the idea of world peace not being an impossible dream, non-the-less they are opening. In the public's consciousness the idea might be there, but it has not entered sufficiently to have taken root.

Yet the doors are opening. The great project today is to open wide those doors so that it - the "idea" - can take root. It is the purpose of this report.

"Every person takes the limits of (their) own field of vision for the limits of the world," wrote Arnold Schopenhauer . . . perhaps it is why Thoreau opined that "most men live lives of quiet despair." But in Valladolid, Spain, there stands a monument commemorating the great discoverer Christopher Columbus who died in 1506.

An interesting feature of the memorial is a statue of a lion destroying one of the Latin words that had been part of Spain's motto for centuries. Before Columbus made his voyages, the Spaniards thought they had reached the outer limits of earth. Thus, their motto was "Ne Plus Ultra," which means: "No more Beyond." The word being torn away by the lion was "Ne" or "No," making it read "Plus Ultra." Columbus had proved that there was indeed "more beyond."

Plus Ultra, the more beyond that is the time when children will be able to look back on war as an 'inconceivable aberration' of their forefathers…is what I have devoted my life to, given my resources, my everything. All done willingly, knowingly, humbly; one might justly say a complete sacrifice. "The greatest use of life is to spend it for something that will outlast it," wrote James; said Winston Churchill, "We make a living by what we get, but we make a life by what we give." In exchange for giving myself to this quest, I have been blest to find myself. And who I found — who I am — is who we all are: the walking, talking embodiments of love. I've been able to give myself so completely because Adella my beloved spouse has been willing to walk alongside me for all this time, for more than half a century. Thus, despite my litany of diverse medical issues inclusive of the aforementioned "baffling" disorder, I've been able to give myself away totally. Despite eye surgery and then skin cancer alongside that same eye, I stayed the course. I've never forgotten the words of Dag Hammarskjold, former secretary-general of the United Nations, when saying: "You have not done enough, you have never done enough so long as it is still possible that you have something to contribute."

The baffling disorder was the one challenge in all my years of quest when I'd been made to believe I'd have to quit, bail out, abandon the project. Although I knew I still had "something to contribute" it didn't seem possible that I could continue. I was inconsolable; I grieved for the children of war who beg for hope and to whom I had long decades ago made this commitment of quest. I felt ambushed by a malady for which there was no cure and no mercy. During the first couple of months it even precluded sleep, made sleep impossible.

Until the end of the 20th century this disorder (not a disease) had been but a mere footnote in most medical textbooks and not treated very well by our doctors. Nor did it have the interest of our medical research community of scientists. Thought to be just an "ear thing" there'd been little treatment and no felt imperative for coming up with a cure. Commonly known as Tinnitus in its little more than an annoyance form . . . in its most acute form and what was an absolute torture for me, it is known as Intrusive Tinnitus. Intrusive Tinnitus is a devastating disorder involving not only the inner ear but, also, the brain stem and the brain itself inclusive of the limbic system which is concerned with emotion and learning . . . also activated is the autonomic nervous system. Thus…it is not just an ear thing! It can take one to the edge. Scary.

Thus I had reason to be terribly fearful of what might happen with my project and the problem that is war. But things got even more complicated and frightening when Hyperacusis a second disorder also of baffling kind occasionally seen in patients with Intrusive Tinnitus took me to a place from where I saw no exit, no way by which to climb up and out. Interiorly I cried out: Who if anyone is out there to carry on my mission with the same passion; with the same sense of mission; with the same conviction that peace is not an unrealizable dream, with the same burning certainty that war is not an inevitable reality?

For three long years my life, my quest, indeed my everything, remained as though hijacked by ceaseless struggle with this disorder; it wreaked absolute havoc with my limbic system. Its center is a group of interconnected deep brain structures involved in olfaction, emotion, motivation, behavior, and various autonomic functions, such as the nervous system. It was hell. Beyond hell.

Six years later, in 2009, Gary P. Reul, Ed.D. and Chief Executive Officer of the American Tinnitus Association at the Oregon Health & Science University in Portland, in a TINNITUS TODAY, COMMITTED TO A CURE publication, offered this advice in a report: "Don't let tinnitus control your life, because it will if you let it. For some, tinnitus violates every waking moment with an intrusive sound in their ears and/or head. I personally went through tremendous changes in my life when my tinnitus and hyperacusis began. It took me a number of years to feel that I could choose my destiny, not these conditions. I hope you have or will take action sooner than I did."

Although I never before could have imagined anything more anxiety producing than being trapped by deadly tornado, or all-consuming fire, or crazed race-riot, all three of which had been my experience at different times, the absolute tyranny over any

Peace is *not* an unrealizable dream.
War is *not* an inevitable reality.

sense of well-being posed by intrusive tinnitus and the equally intrusive hyperacusis...gave me to know anxiety in a new and unprecedented way. It had taken over the me that is me. I was in for a tough battle.

I found it difficult to explain or understand. The great adventure called my life had begun without my active cooperation, and I'd known it would not be achieved without me. But that me had now been taken over by a tyranny I could neither see or know. It was a humbling time, a learning time, and required the strength of my faith to get through it. Indeed I had to get through it because I'd made a commitment to the children of war who beg for hope.

I couldn't, wouldn't, let them down.

At some point I took to investing myself in proactive efforts to overcome the twin disorders. I began by immersing myself in the then newly evolving tinnitus research work going on in Germany, England, Australia as well as here in the United States. Interestingly, I even became a "Test Site" for a newly engineered "relief device" by a company eager to market the product. After several years the brain habituated to it (the disorder), albeit not fully; but to a place where with enormous gratitude I was able to dig in and continue with my Quest. Meanwhile the hyperacusis had quit, not of its own accord, but because of things I'd learned in my proactive efforts. It is said that knowledge is power; in this case it proved to be healing power.

One of the things I learned, but slow to come upon, was that my intrusive tinnitus (and the hyperacusis as well) were disorders of kind that can be exacerbated by stress. That is to say, although they are not disorders created by stress, in certain cases they can become stress-driven. What doesn't help matters at all here is that the annoying head-sounds created by tinnitus brings on its own kind of stress.

For me, in my case, it was a major revelation . . . and in the long run of enormous importance in helping me get through the ordeal and back to work on the problem that is war and threat of war, back to the children of war, back to we must conquer war or war

Peace is *not* an unrealizable dream.
War is *not* an inevitable reality.

will conquer us. The challenge here for me would be to keep the stresses generated not only by the intrusiveness of the tinnitus, but by war and my own investment of self in the quest for a solution, from overtaking my own sensitivities. "Journey Without Maps" is the title of my account detailing that struggle. Already a malady of the 21st century, the Walter Reed Army Medical Center reports this disorder as the Number 1 service-connected disability among veterans returning from Iraq and Afghanistan.

It is my intended purpose and prayer that all this reference to my struggle with tinnitus will somehow, in some way, provide added impetus to the need within the medical research community — already at work albeit too little on the problem — for coming up with a cure.

Meanwhile, if ever I was to get some of my journaled reports published there'd been an ongoing struggle to get by the protocols of the "hard and harsh world" of the publishing industry and its gatekeepers. Talk about stress! My experience had not prepared me at all for this; clearly it would be tough going if I was to succeed.

I'd have to cut a path through a thick undergrowth of Publishing House process and House politics before even understanding the system, and without ever being able to identify the ground over which I'd be moving. Not that I didn't try. And not that it didn't create its own unique stress, long and drawn out, because it did. But...Paul was right in Romans 8: "All things work together for good for those who love God."

Unfortunately, while working on the final draft of this volume is when there'd been the need for a triple by-pass because of several blocked arteries. But it had left me with a significantly diminished capacity of my right lung function; there'd been an injured phrenic nerve occasioned by the surgery. This is the nerve that innervates the diaphragm which is the major muscle required for ventilation. Because of the necessity for spending several months in cardiac rehabilitation and then more weeks in pulmonary rehab, but interrupted by a knee injury from a fall down some stairs *rupturing the quadriceps and tearing a tendon, thus requiring orthopedic rehab,*

Peace is *not* an unrealizable dream.
War is *not* an inevitable reality.

stress again came into the picture of things serving to reactivate the tinnitus…albeit much less troublesome.

> From Romans 8:28 I learned in all of this that although the "slings and arrows of life" may knock us down, none will ever penetrate so deeply that we will be overcome and destroyed. The verse (powerful but one of the toughest to pray) simply states: "All things work together for good, for those who love God and are called according to his purpose." If out of the hellish darkness of the Crucifixion God brought the miraculous light of the Resurrection, He can certainly take the bad things that happen to us in our lives and bring some kind of blessing out of them.

Also I've learned what Jesus in Scripture does when He cures the sick man. He gives him a job: "Pick up your mat and walk." All too often we miss the point of our own healings. Jesus doesn't forgive us or heal us just to make us feel better. Rather, when He heals us He gives us a job. The job is always to give away the gift He's given us to another who needs it.

For example when Jesus gives the gift of sobriety to the alcoholic, He expects that person to help bring someone else to sobriety. When Jesus forgives us He expects us to give forgiveness to someone who has hurt us. When Jesus restores hope in my life, gives my life purpose, He expects me to give hope and purpose to those who live in despair or without meaningful purpose.

It is one of the reasons that I do what I do with my life. In a war weary world my job is to bring hope and purpose to those who despair of harmony and peace ever reigning over our human enterprise.

OF all my health related issues for which I'd been sidelined and had to mount comebacks, intrusive tinnitus challenged me the most. But then there was another kind of challenge; the challenge of wanting to quit when my explorations took me into the "hidden"

Peace is *not* an unrealizable dream.
War is *not* an inevitable reality.

horrors and "hidden" sins of war, and asking "Why am I doing this to myself?"

There'd been the incredible attempts to dehumanize the person at the concentration camps of Auschwitz, Dachau, Treblinka and other such sites. There'd been Japan's militaristic culture that, in fostering in its soldiers a total disregard for human life, actually served to launch the "Rape of Nanking" – one of the worst atrocities in world history. One of the most damning aspects of war is that it is never confined to the legions of young men who spill their blood in battle. Invariably it boils over to effect civilians. One-fifth of those killed in World War I were civilians; in World War II, this figure rose to one-half. In the wars since then, it has been 90 percent. Making matters darker, the extremes in cruelty have increased in no less proportion.

I could share here something about the "hidden" horrors and "hidden" sins of war, but it's best not to go anywhere near that kind of thing, there's a poison there that can infect. At some point in all of this a question other than "Why am I doing this to myself?" came to beset me: "Has all this suffering, all this dying around us, all this cruelty, all this insanity, a meaning?"

For, if not, then ultimately there is no meaning to survival; for a life whose meaning depends upon whether one escapes or not the events of war....ultimately would not be worth living at all. The civilian victims of war, especially the children and the women, what they suffered, how they died, is what was making my life worth living as I struggled over long decades, dark years, so that what they suffered, what they endured, not be in vain.

So I never quit, I stayed with the mission. From the very beginning there'd been in me an intuition with flame so bright with promise of a solution to the problem that is war and threat of war that I simply could not ignore it. It begged a response. I gave it my all. Because it is not the purpose of this report, perhaps at another time I'll tell the story of my spiritual journey while engaged in this quest; what I lived, what I learned,

Peace is *not* an unrealizable dream.
War is *not* an inevitable reality.

So…just as Lewis and Clark had challenges unique to their search in their expedition, so too have I had challenges unique albeit quite different in mission but no less unique in the struggle to endure and persevere despite all the many disappointments and obstacles.

Often I've been asked, in all of this haven't you ever felt discouraged, known despair, felt foolish? Yes, of course; oftentimes I've felt discouraged and known the death that is despair. But never, ever, have I felt foolish.

How could one feel foolish in the face of standing up to war that is always hell, war that is slavery, war that is vomit on God's Creation?

How could one feel foolish in the face of the "killing fields" of Cambodia with its everywhere horrifying clusters of corpses and skeletal remains of the 2 million (of 7 million) people slain during that country's murderous reign of Khmer Rouge revolutionaries (1979); many if indeed not most of those victims executed simply for showing signs of intellect or Western influence?

How could one feel foolish in the face of a century dominated by war, a century best known for its absence of peace?

But then they'd press: How did you manage your despair? Where did you find your strength? How did you persevere? I can best explain with one or two little stories.

Ignace Jan Paderewski, the famous composer pianist, was scheduled to perform at a great concert hall here in the States. It was an evening to remember—black tuxedos and long evening dresses, a high-society extravaganza. Present in the audience were a mother with her fidgety nine-year-old son. She had hoped her boy would be encouraged to practice the piano if he could just hear the immortal Paderewski at the keyboard. So—against his wishes—he had come.

As she turned to talk with friends, but the boy weary of waiting - and strangely drawn to the ebony concert grand Steinway and its leather tufted stool on the huge stage flooded with blinding

Peace is *not* an unrealizable dream.
War is *not* an inevitable reality.

lights - slipped away from her side. Without much notice from the sophisticated audience, the boy sat down at the stool, staring wide-eyed at the black-and-white keys. He placed his small, trembling fingers in the right location and began to play "Chopsticks."

The roar of the crowd was hushed as hundreds of frowning faces turned in his direction. Irritated and embarrassed, they began to shout: "Get that boy away from there!" "Where's his mother?" "Who'd bring a kid that young in here?" "Somebody stop him!"

Backstage, the master, overhearing the sounds out front, quickly understood what was happening. Hurriedly, he grabbed his coat and rushed toward the stage. Without one word of announcement, he stooped over behind the boy, reached around both sides, and began to improvise a counter-melody to harmonize with and enhance "Chopsticks." As the two of them played together, Paderewski kept whispering in the boy's ear, "Keep going. Don't quit, son. Keep on playing. Don't stop. Don't quit."

And so it was with me. Every time I felt ready to give up on my quest for a world without war and threat of war about which others thought foolish and impractical, saying somebody stop him, along came the Master, who'd lean over and whisper, "Now keep going. Don't quit. Keep on. Don't stop. Don't quit" as He provided just the right touch at just the right moment. This happened so often as not to be easily dismissed. Meaning that I could not...not persevere. It was an imperative.

In a second story I've long had a fascination with bridges. The Brooklyn Bridge that spans the river tying Manhattan Island to Brooklyn here on Long Island is truly a miracle bridge. Every time I drive or walk across this masterpiece of bridge design and construction, I think of John Roebling. In 1883, this creative engineer was inspired by an idea for this spectacular bridge. However, bridge-building experts throughout the world told him to forget it; it could not be done.

Roebling convinced his son, Washington, who was a young up-and-coming engineer, that the bridge could be built. The two of them developed the concepts of how it could be accomplished and

Peace is *not* an unrealizable dream.
War is *not* an inevitable reality.

how the obstacles could be overcome. With unharnessed excitement and inspiration, they hired their crew and began to build their dream bridge . . . a bridge that on that horribly tragic Tuesday morning of 9.11.01 was destined to be a welcome sight for the tens of thousands of fear-driven folks fleeing the roiling clouds – towering and thick with gray ash – racing through the canyons of Downtown Manhattan. Our nation's darkest day, our finest hour.

The project was only a few months under construction when a tragic accident on the site took the life of John Roebling and severely injured his son, Washington. Washington was left with permanent brain damage and was unable to talk or walk. Everyone felt that the project would have to be scrapped since the Roeblings were the only ones who knew how the bridge could be built.

Even though Washington was unable to move or talk, his mind was as sharp as ever, and he still had a burning desire to complete the bridge. An idea hit him as he lay in his hospital bed, and he developed a code for communication. All he could move was one finger, so he touched the arm of his wife with that finger, tapping out the code to communicate to her what to tell the engineers who were building the bridge.

For thirteen years, Washington tapped out his instructions with his finger until the spectacular Brooklyn Bridge was finally completed. And so again, especially with this in mind, I could not...not persevere.

I who could walk, talk and write, keep a journal. How could I not persevere in the wake of this man who, despite his own catastrophic condition, devised and executed a means, a way, to do what he did? A man whose tenacity of spirit and will is memorialized forever by a bridge whose structural design is a marvel of the ages; awesome in the eyes of bridge builders everywhere and of every succeeding generation.

Lastly, how did I manage my despair? How did I find the strength? In the early years of my quest for a solution to the problem that is war, my study of wartime atrocities had had the effect of axing my innocence at its deepest roots. It'd been a horrible

Peace is *not* an unrealizable dream.
War is *not* an inevitable reality.

awakening; it stirred doubt about the veracity of my mission, the reality of my quest; and left me desperate for the said "bliss" that is ignorance. War is hell, absolute hell; I had no need to know more. The uncovered hidden horrors of war had left me tortured by a terrible despair.

In despair for my children, their children and the children to come, I turned to a dear friend, Walter J. Ciszek, a Jesuit priest now in heaven. Born in Shenandoah, Pennsylvania, he was destined to spend 23 years behind the Iron Curtain of the Soviet Union. In 1940 he entered Russia, but was arrested by the Secret Police a year later and sentenced to fifteen years hard labor. After spending five years in solitary confinement, in an execution cell, in the infamous Lubianka Prison, in Moscow, he was sent to the Siberian slave-labor camp above the Arctic Circle.

Father Ciszek was declared "legally dead" in 1947 here in the U.S.A. In 1963, he, along with another American, was exchanged for a Russian couple held for espionage in this country. He is now a candidate for Sainthood; I have provided witness testimony in the Canonization process.

Meanwhile, I carry in my wallet hard-earned words of Father Walter Ciszek whose own experience with despair has helped me to embrace and endure my own despair regarding the horrors - especially the "hidden" horrors - of war.

Horrors of kind that drove George Washington to announce, "My first wish is to see this plague of mankind banished from the earth;" and Dwight D. Eisenhower to warn: "People want peace so much that governments had better get out of their way and let them have it."

When despair threatens to overwhelm me, get the best of me in my quest, I reach for my wallet and Father Walter's words:

"Of course there were doubts, at one time there was near despair. It was not reason that sustained me then but faith. Only by faith could I find God present in every circumstance, only by faith could I penetrate the mystery of his saving grace, not by questioning it

Peace is *not* an unrealizable dream.
War is *not* an inevitable reality.

in any way, but by fully co-operating with it in exactly the way be asked. It was then, in differing measures and with varying degrees of success, that the glimpses of his providence ruling all things would work to dispel the doubts and the fears that were constantly on the edges of the mind.

"So I learned by trial and error that if I wanted to preserve my interior peace and joy I had to have constant recourse to prayer, to the eyes of faith, to a humility that could make me aware of how little my own efforts meant and how dependent I was upon God's grace even for prayer and faith itself.

"None of this came easily, for I was not a disembodied spirit. Hunger could distract me, the interrogators could confuse me, a body aching in every joint and worn down by a long arctic day of grueling work could leave me totally exhausted and very much discouraged.

"It is much easier to see the redemptive role of pain and suffering in God's plan if you are not actually undergoing pain and suffering. It was only by struggling with such feelings, however, that growth occurred.

"Each victory over discouragement gave an increase in spiritual courage; every success, however fleeting, in finding the hand of God behind all things, made it easier to recapture the sense of his purpose in a new day of seemingly senseless work and hardship and suffering.

"Day by day, I learned to experience in some measure the power of God as manifested in the mystery of the passion. Pain and suffering comprised the sacrifice needed in the passion for saving souls. A similar sacrifice had to be undertaken by all those called to the apostolate. And yet the suffering and sacrifice were touched by deep spiritual joy, be-

Peace is *not* an unrealizable dream.
War is *not* an inevitable reality.

cause in them one saw God's will accomplished in an otherwise frustrating life, the great work of salvation promoted.

"If you look upon sacrifice and suffering only through the eyes of reason alone, your tendency will be to avoid as much of it as you can, for pain in itself is never pleasant. But if you can learn to see the role of pain and suffering in relation to God's redemptive plan for the universe and each individual soul, your attitude must change.

"You don't shun it when it comes upon you, but bear it in the measure grace is given you. You see in it a putting on of Christ in the true sense of the word. Out of this insight comes joy, and an increase of hope; out of it, too, grows compassion for others and a hope that they also may be helped to understand the true meaning of life and its trials, its joys and its sufferings.

"Fired with this enthusiasm, the soul constantly yearned to communicate the wonders of God's grace to everyone. This desire, this zeal, knew no bounds, set no limits for its activity. Through its attainment in reality was something that surpassed human effort, the soul on fire with this understanding paid little attention to concrete results. The most important thing was to keep the flame of zeal burning.

"Hence the constant need of daily prayer, the constant efforts to see in the pain and suffering of each day a true work of redemption, a true sharing in the saving acts of Christ."

Shortly before Fr. Ciszek's death, I received this penned note from my dear friend: Dear Ted and Adele, P.C. (Peace of Christ) . . . Your Christmas card and letter from Boston were received. You still have the physical energy Ted and mental stamina to confront the evils and wrongs of social and political life and try to express

Peace is *not* an unrealizable dream.
War is *not* an inevitable reality.

the truth for the sake of common good. It's a worthwhile work you are doing. It's not always appreciated, but that does not matter. To be a witness of what is right and acceptable for the general good of community is worth every effort. I'm trying to do what is in my power and at a pace proper to my age. It's rewarding and revealing, because the concept of the all perfect God becomes a more and more convincing reality above all else.

Love and prayers....Fr. Walter

Somewhere in all of this struggle I wrote:

**When God wants to make a man
He puts him into some storm.**

**He puts him out into the surge of storm
where he is shook and beat down upon
- like the oak planted by the sea or
on the cliff of some mountainside.**

**And like the oak become king of the forest
in the midnight battle with the elements,
man too, taken and broken in storm,
wins his rugged fibre
by how he's made in battle.**

**Made to become a hero of life!
Equipped, by God, for service
- to his fellow human beings,
to his environment and to the Pattern and
Will of God who exists in him and in all of us.**

IMPORTANT to include in this report is some reference to my working involvement in health issues not at all so dramatic or destructive as the insanity that is war: war that is a disease, war that is a continuation of politics by other means, war that once had me thinking of myself as an alien on some strange planet.

Peace is *not* an unrealizable dream.
War is *not* an inevitable reality.

Beginning with my simple question of some forty years ago, "How can we discover the sources of wholeness, healing and hope amidst a broken and suffering world?" my life evolved in such a way that I matured to mix with a wide and varied cross-section of society. They ranged from the marginalized and outcasts to the very successful and well-off, from the able to the not so able, from the sickly to the well; there'd been no exclusions. No stranger to suffering, my own and that of others, I'd become sensitized to what I came to perceive as a broken world; a world in need of healing.

I learned something about things which most individuals who survive and remain sane can take for granted most of the time. About God, I learned that he exists and has never revealed Himself except in terms of love; indeed, God cannot love but totally, 100 percent. About hope, I learned that without hope we cannot put one foot in front of the other. About faith, I learned that as the essence of courage is to stake one's life on a possibility, so the essence of faith is to believe that the possibility exists.

I'd become sensitized to the massiveness of ignorance and evil, of Lie, that keeps us from living in a peaceful world; and of humanity's need to rediscover a felt presence of God. We say we believe in God, but we live our lives as if God doesn't exist. Jesus came to shatter our image of God and, from its ruins, invites us to live in a new wonder.

Apart from the health issue that is war, there were the other kinds of diseases and disorders that begged attention, remedy, cure. Most notable among them was mental illness and an asylum industry reminiscent of 17th century pesthouses: dungeons of despair. "Never doubt that a small group of thoughtful, committed citizens can change the world," preached Margaret Mead, noted anthropologist with whom I once spent a most delightful afternoon. "Indeed, it's the only thing that ever has." I'd been part of a collection of such groups responsible for dismantling that industry. Also, I'd been a working member of a small select committee responsible for revising New York State's "Bill of Rights" to include the mentally ill. Later I would have a seat on the Mental Health Panel of the United Way of Long Island.

Peace is *not* an unrealizable dream.
War is *not* an inevitable reality.

Subsequently, as a representative of consumers of health services, I would hold a seat on each of a half-dozen regional health planning councils including the Long Island Health & Hospital Planning Council; here I was active on its Long Term Care Committee.

Still later, and now in my seventies, I would find myself as an active "Pastoral Care" member of the Association of Christian Therapists. ACT is a unique Roman Catholic international organization consisting of Christian health care professionals of all denominations and of all specialties in total health care...inclusive of lay apostolates with the recognized gift of healing. The vision of ACT is to consecrate and integrate the healing professions under the Lordship of Jesus Christ - the Risen Christ - a free healer who came to heal all that is divided, disordered, and diseased throughout all of humanity.

The language of God, the mysteries of healing, the world's need for authentic hope, all had had my rapt attention in a life, my life, that was not without plan. It took many years before I'd learn that God writes straight with a crooked line. In a life not always healthy, not always peaceful, not always successful, sometimes sinful, God was at work on why I'd been born: to help in the task of bringing healing and hope of genuine or authentic kind to a world desperate for healing, desperate for hope, desperate for faith. This then would be my destiny, my legacy.

Just as war has taught me a lot about peace, so too have personal health issues taught me a lot about healing. Both have taught me a lot about hope and truth, but most of all about compassion. It is why I have used my own sicknesses and sufferings to allow me to understand the sufferings and struggles of other people.

SUCH were my experiences as a youth growing up in the years of the worldwide Great Depression and then a second World War that my destiny was irrevocably cast. Healing, hope, harmony, spirituality, compassion, peace, reverence for life, were words and concepts seeded into the very ground of my being, without any help or invitation on my part. It just happened that way, or maybe not. Perhaps it was my then sensitivities at work in some ordained or

Peace is *not* an unrealizable dream.
War is *not* an inevitable reality.

providential way that made my ground ready, receptive, a growing place for the cultivation and pursuit of such ideas as these.

And so evolved in me as did happen in Francis Younghusband's account of his early life the "religion of an explorer"…with a longing to make it of service to my fellow human beings. I spoke of this English explorer and our spiritual kinship early in this volume.

So too evolved my wide culture. In part this involved decades of dealing with the human condition of brokenness and despair — in prisons, in safe-houses for battered women, in the nursing home industry, in the asylum industry, in the substance abuse culture, in shelters and safe-houses, in war relief work. Then there were my international involvements with Taize, l'Arche, and Olympics for the physically challenged; each of which deserve if space allowed chapters of their own.

Worthy of note also there'd been the legendary Harrison Salisbury, former Moscow Bureau Chief for The New York Times (1949-1954) who, in 1967, in an already distinguished career as one of America's leading journalists, covered the entire periphery of China … travelling more than 25,000 miles along that country's frontiers, from the jungles of Southeast Asia to the bristling Siberian-Chinese border, working on his narrative ORBIT OF CHINA the heart of which were the epic questions of the day: war or peace between China and America, the struggle of India and China for Asian leadership, the dangerous conflict of the Soviet Union and China. Of his numerous volumes about Russia and China this was the most thoroughly researched and thought likely to be the most lasting.

But then in 1985 he wrote THE LONG MARCH, the untold story of that epic march of fifty years earlier when the Red Army of China's Communists scurried for their lives in the face of Chiang Kai-shek's formidable legions. A year later, heroically, remarkably, they had created the legend of the Long March of 25,000 li, 6,000 miles. They had survived and begun the movement that was to bring Mao Zedong and his comrades to power in the world's largest nation. The story of that epic march had never been told…and never could be until then.

Peace is *not* an unrealizable dream.
War is *not* an inevitable reality.

Salisbury traveled 7,400 miles over the backroads of China, crossing the fiercest rivers, the jagged peaks of the Snowy Mountain range and the formidable wastes of the Great Grasslands, following almost every mile of the Red Army's track. He and I were good friends; during one period, together we played a lot of bridge and volley ball, mostly bridge; he encouraged me with my early writing projects. It was he an extraordinary piece of work who early on set the bar for my own explorations, especially my quest for a solution to the problem that is war and threat of war.

Eighteen years earlier, in 1967, in a distinguished career as one of America's leading journalists, Salisbury penned ORBIT OF CHINA. Assigned by The New York Times to cover the entire periphery of China, this multilingual reporter traveled more than 25,000 miles along frontiers from the jungles of Southeast Asia to the bristling Siberian-Chinese border. Wherever he went— remote Himalayan villages or glittering Hong Kong—Salisbury sought from peasants and princes the story of China—her explosive impact on Asia and the world.

But what struck me most in his narrative of personal experience and penetrating analysis had nothing at all to do with China but, rather, about Ernie Pyle's take on war. Pyle was the most celebrated war correspondent of World War II. Killed by the Japanese, he is remembered as having been a humble correspondent who artfully and ardently told the story of a war from the foxholes. He wanted people to see and understand the sacrifices that soldiers had to make.

Now to Salisbury's story about Pyle. The road to Lo Wu begins at Kennedy Airport 8,657 miles away. It crosses the continent, soars over the Pacific and touches down in Honolulu, just long enough for a drive up the quiet crater of the Punchbowl where fourteen thousand graves of World War II lie, row on row, beside a smaller field of Korean War dead. In the hot morning sunshine, the Punchbowl seemed incredibly neat, the big monument standing solid up against the shoulder of the old volcano rim and the pleasant driveway curving past the geometric rows.

Peace is *not* an unrealizable dream.
War is *not* an inevitable reality.

A tractor was working in the western quadrant, and the raw red of new-turned Hawaiian earth was bleeding onto the green lawn.

"We're getting them in from Vietnam now," the attendant said, hitching up his chinos. "Not like Korea, of course. But they're coming in now. Almost every day. The planes bring them in."

The taxi crawled forward a hundred yards and stopped. There was Ernie Pyle's stone, convenient to the road for those who still remembered Iwo Jima—and Ernie. I remembered Ernie very clearly. Sitting on a cot at the Aletti Hotel in Algiers, the mosquito netting pushed back, his face lined and tired and thin, the bottle of whiskey, a full quart bottle of Teacher's, in his hand. He had just flown in from leave in the States, the long way, across the Atlantic to Dakar and up the coast. He was going back to the front and the GI's and he didn't like it and he wished he never had to see another front, never had to write another GI story, never again had to sweat out the early-morning jump-off, the crawling forward from the lines, the lonely jeep ride into nowhere.

"Ob, God," Ernie said, "I wish I didn't have to go back to the war. I wish to Christ I never had to talk to another GI. I wish to God there never was another GI or a war or ..."

"1 don't know how to say this," he went on. "But in Tunisia, the last time I was at the front I was talking to a kid. All he said, over and over again, was 'Fuck my shit. . . . Fuck my shit. . . .' Those three words. That's all. Somehow it got me."

We listened to him silently. On the boulevard outside the Aletti you could hear the rumble of trucks, a convoy or something going by.

"Oh, hell," he went on. "Don't mind me. I've had my war and now I've got to go back again and really what's there to say about it that the kid didn't say?"

He went back, of course, and if the shrapnel hadn't come his way at Iwo he might have been standing there in the hot sunshine smelling the faint fragrance of frangipani, following another road... the road to Lo Wu.

Peace is *not* an unrealizable dream.
War is *not* an inevitable reality.

Continues Salisbury, I thought of Pyle and of the war, the endless wars of our time, as the plane flew westward over the Pacific, misty and almost invisible 37,000 feet below. Ernie Pyle's war was a long time back. Then there was, or seemed to be, a simplicity about the world that no longer existed. It hadn't really been true, of course, but I thought then that I could tell the Good Guy from the Bad Guys. It seemed black and white, good and evil. I knew that Good would triumph and Evil go down to defeat.

Now there was another war and nothing was simple about it — nothing at all. There was no agreement, no easy, recognizable consensus of Good, only terrible portents of Evil. The young GI's were dying again, in dirt and filth and agony, Ernie Pyle's words on their lips. Napalm was ravaging the villages, searing brown bodies along with the white, the young with the old, women and their babies, those who knew they were dying and those who did not know there was a war going on.

Over the whole world there were alarm and fear lest the contagion spread, lest the engines of destruction, so much more mighty, so much more efficient, (the highest kill ratio in the world, sir!), might be unloosed in ever widening-circles, fanning out from Asia and beyond.

It was this which had put me on the road to La Wu, set me off on a mission to the most distant ends of the earth. I was not going to the battle front. Not Vietnam. I was going beyond the fighting lines. I would by-pass the confused, sweating jungles of Indochina and try to make my way to the edge of China, climbing the high Himalayas, skirting the black deserts of Central Asia and the wilderness of Siberia, seeking the sources of torment and the tragedy—if, indeed, they were to be found.

ULTIMATELY…this ever-widening culture of relationships and experiences such as Salisbury's accounts would evolve in me as though a natural sense of duty to humanity a giving of myself totally to the cause of Global Peace and Harmony.

Peace is *not* an unrealizable dream.
War is *not* an inevitable reality.

In a world desperate to create a new dawn in human consciousness, every impulse in me would be as though reflecting a sense of the old human story and dream that is humanity's eternal quest. . .

> . . .the old quest for a moral and spiritual order on this planet; for the attainment of the highest form of life; for the fullest possible consciousness of all.

It is the message of the Bible, the Koran, the Talmud, the Hindu philosophy, U Thant's Buddhism without God, the red Indian's worship of nature, Mother Teresa of Calcutta's poignant love, the beloved John XXIII's encyclical Pacem In Terris.

IN a world grown to know more about killing than living, more about disease and disorder than harmony, we have jettisoned truth in favor of Lie. Thus on the larger stage we've settled for barbarism, war and inhumanity; while in our own individual lives we've settled for a medicine that might extend our lives but in neglecting the spiritual dimension fails to reclaim our health...body, mind, emotions, spirit.

My first real hope in all of this, the something that pulled me out of the misery of life, was my awareness of an enormous truth taking place in Medjugorje. The enormity of God was present there in that little hamlet and little church between the mountains. "If this is true," I asked myself, "then what on earth have you been believing important up to now?"

In making myself conversant with the story up until that point, and some of the controversy about its authenticity, I recalled Arnold Schopenhauer as having said, "All truth passes through three stages. First, it is ridiculed. Second, it is violently opposed. Third, it is accepted as being self-evident." Amazingly, I'd been filled with a feeling of something great and huge, something awesome, a truth that lifted me. I didn't know how or what, but I knew my life would be different. I learned and grew. Previously, I had felt such despair because even though I had invested my whole self and resources to

Peace is *not* an unrealizable dream.
War is *not* an inevitable reality.

help make a better world, a healthier populace, yet I'd felt no joy in what I'd been doing. It all seemed so futile.

But now I began to realize that if I gave my life to God, with no reservations or exceptions, and unimportant though my life seemed, I was doing everything to change the world. Because although I could do nothing, God could do everything by using my life according to His will.

In this world, we, like every creature, do not exist for ourselves. We do not have the reason for our existence in ourselves. We exist as creatures because of God. It is good to dwell on this profound truth of our existence. It is the most forgotten truth of our time. Instead, we look at the surface and forget the essential. The Essential! One will probably say that this is a terrible truth, a terrible dependence, that it reduces us to the condition of slavery.

But no, it is not slavery. The Creator does not create for Himself. He does not need His creation. It is a gratuitous gift. He creates humankind not as we make products that we control, but as an autonomous creature, whom He "hands over into the hand of his own counsel," or as Scripture says, He hands over to humankind, freedom. With man/woman (as with the angels) made to His image, God does not create dependence but freedom.

Such is the difference between God and human beings. We can only build robots. God is capable of creating free and autonomous beings, masters of their own destiny, partners.

One could probably say that it is a dangerous gift since freedom allows one to choose evil as well as good. It could make humankind capable of forgetting God, revolting against Him, and fighting Him. Does God then want to destroy His creature or revoke the freedom of His creature? No, even despite everything. He continues to allow us to be free that we may turn toward Him, or toward nothingness—we are free to choose for Him or against Him.

At times, humankind becomes intoxicated with this negative power; the intoxication of Prometheus defying God. God alone is the primary cause of everything that exists. Humankind is never the

Peace is *not* an unrealizable dream.
War is *not* an inevitable reality.

primary cause of any being, but only the secondary cause, shaping it. But we can be the primary cause in the order of nothingness, destruction. We can be an anti-creator, one who destroys what is best in creation—its order, equilibrium, beautiful growth. And this disturbing power can result in an intoxication that is self-destructive and destroys others. This was the intoxication of Hitler, which led to his sad end in a bunker.

Peace is *not* an unrealizable dream.
War is *not* an inevitable reality.

A WONDERFUL
ADVENTURE

EARLY in this report I briefly touched on the story behind what led to my quest for a solution to the problem that is war - an odyssey that began with what had been for me an 'Exploration into God'. From that experience evolved in me a passion for coming up with a solution to the problem that is war and threat of war...and I consecrated myself to that passion. From the crucible of all the many challenges and suffering invited by living out that passion, an amazing thing happened: another consecration, a consecration of divine kind, presented itself. Actually it was a years-long gradual thing, the idea of consecrating myself to the marvelous love of God, Creator of all things, including my own liberty, but he creates it truly free.

What a wonderful adventure I thought to offer oneself to God, to give oneself completely to God Who has given us everything. Intuitively, it was the logical next step for me to take in my search for a solution to the problem that is war and threat of war. More, there is nothing more logical than to ratify the gift of God, with a gift of ourselves in a definitive alliance. It is not to alienate us; it is to find again in God (in its fullness) our roots and the very sap of our life. That should also be as simple and as natural as the innate love of an infant for his mother, to whom he owes, humanly speaking, almost everything.

I had come to realize that God does not do anything in us, without us. I'd come to see at some deeper level than before that love is reciprocity; thus God could not realize this consecration without an impetus, a gift on my part. He arouses it in us...if we so desire it, because love is free. God does not force us. That would no longer be love. In this love which exceeds us, reciprocity itself is a gift of God, for God is Creator of all things. From this I saw the importance of prayer of the heart!

The pilgrimage of our deification (which is what consecration invites) is more extraordinary than that of the caterpillar in its cocoon which becomes a butterfly, without knowing full well what is happening to it. We need splendid doses of faith and of clarity, in order to understand the great adventure of the love of God to which we are called. Love that is reciprocity. It may appear a foolish adventure. . .but according to the folly of God of which St. Paul speaks: a folly of love which Jesus carried as far as the cross.

Also. before moving on to Part III of this report, I must say this. In us, among us, there is a life force that drives us beyond ourselves. It is God's energizing presence, his holy Spirit, that whispers us into the great quest within, that makes life alive with a purpose not seen but deeply, consciously, stubbornly felt even in the midst of chaos, even at the edge of despair...here sounds the truth in us that we are more than we seem to be. Often in my struggles of Quest and health issues, I've had the experience.

Life does not begin and end with us.

There is more than we know, there is an electric charge animating the world at very level and, most of all, within.

Holy Spirit suffuses all of life, calls us into the mystery that is God, reminds us of the model that is Jesus, brings us to the fullness of ourselves.

Holy Spirit is the great anti-gravitational force that calls us out of somewhere into everywhere, that keeps us moving toward, through, the black holes of life, certain that on the other side of them is light, waiting and wishing us on.

Do I believe in the Holy Spirit? You bet I do.

Peace is *not* an unrealizable dream.
War is *not* an inevitable reality.

ANCIENT RIVERS IN ME

Ancient rivers of my people
    flowing in me.
I hear their voices, and know
    what it means:
I am to be a witness to
    their truth and power,
pressed forward by the force
    of their being,
by their faith and the
    integrity of their struggle,
by the silent graces
    they earned for me
and by the roaring
    of their voices.

The voice of all has entered
    so profoundly into me
that I am song of their song,
    hope of their hope.
Their daring and risk are part of me.
I'm unwilling, unable
    to be detached from their
    struggle, sacrifice, suffering.

Their voice is a calling in me
    to be man, hope and promise
    for tomorrow;
a calling to be son, strength and
    solace, breaker of bonds
    that enslave;
a calling to be father, rock and
    reconciler, builder of bridges
    that connect —
bridges between persons and nations,
    bridges between the
    world and Lord God.

Ted Conlin
Trois Riviere
Province of Quebec Canada

Peace is *not* an unrealizable dream.
War is *not* an inevitable reality.

~~ PART THREE ~~

BEYOND WAR

The Unexpected Leadership of Poland's Karol Wojtyla
The Unexpected Cosmic Drama at Medjugorje

THE SYNCHRONICITY OF
THE TWO EVENTS

AS my years of monitoring the events at Medjugorje wore on, I began making links between the unexpected leadership of Poland's Karol Wojtyla on the world stage as Pope and, during the same period, the unexpected visitations of the Virgin Mary beginning just three years after Karol Cardinal Wojtyla was elected Pope — a surprise to all and shaking the Vatican.

Such was the synchronicity of the two events that I'd had no problem concluding this was no mere coincidence. Nor could it be chance. This was the Will of God at work, God who has his own logic. God who is infinitely loving, but infinitely discreet and merciful. It made sense, my conclusion.

"If the Synchronicity has little meaning or interest for the world of tribes, ethnic groups and nations, then it should," says one of my journal entries of that period. Why? Because it has huge meaning. Because it is a Great Mercy at a point in history when Humanity, as though having cast off its moorings, now finds itself wildly adrift in the heaving swells of an unknown sea.

"When a moment (a summons from the beyond) knocks on the door of your life," wrote the Russian novelist and poet, Boris Pasternak, "it is often no louder than the beating of your heart, and it is very easy to miss." For me who'd known just such a knock when first called to be a scout, an explorer for world peace, it was not all that easy to "miss" because of a certain felt-urgency from behind that knock ...whatever its source. And in that source, a plan. For me it was a moment of higher identity and knowing, a knowing crowned with an awareness of absolute possibility for a world without war and threat of war.

With this extremely commanding "synchronicity of the Two Events" there is a summons of historic magnitude knocking on the door of all Humanity: all tribes, all ethnic groups, all nations and nation-states. We cannot deny it. Neither must we ignore it. The winds of grace are always blowing, but to catch them we have to raise our sails. History is not merely cyclical, but is going somewhere and, indeed, has been struggling all along toward higher ends.

Helping to keep my own sails raised has been the Moscow 1944 miracle as told by Yevgeny Yevtushenko, one of the most loved modern Russian poets. He is especially notable for his description of transforming moments.

Had he lived in Jesus' time and spent time around him, he would have left us descriptive accounts, marvelously drawn, of Jesus constantly involved in transforming things: water into wine, bread and wine into Himself; withered limbs to working limbs; blind eyes to seeing eyes; guilt into forgiveness; dead bodies into living bodies; crucifixion into resurrection; sorrow into joy.

Such moments, for Yevtushenko, sometimes have to do with compassion taking the place of hatred, hostility, bitterness, vindictiveness. It is a remarkable theme when one begins to understand that Russians of his generation experienced both Stalin and Hitler. Because it is a theme central to his writing, one is left wondering why. In the following story from his autobiography, we begin to understand why.

In 1944 Yevtushenko's mother took him from Siberia to Moscow, where they witnessed 20,000 German war prisoners being marched through the streets:

"The pavements swarmed with onlookers, cordoned off by soldiers and police. The crowd was mostly women... Russian women

Peace is *not* an unrealizable dream.
War is *not* an inevitable reality.

with hands roughened by hard work, lips untouched by lipstick, and with thin hunched shoulders which had borne half of the burden of the war. Every one of them must have had a father or a husband, a brother or a son killed by the Germans. They gazed with hatred in the direction from which the column was to appear.

"At last we saw it. The generals marched at the head, massive chins stuck out, lips folded disdainfully, their whole demeanor meant to show superiority over their plebeian victors.

"'They smell of perfume, the bastards,' someone in the crowd said with hatred. The women were clenching their fists. The soldiers and police officers had all they could do to hold them back.

"All at once something happened to them. They saw German soldiers, thin, unshaven, wearing dirty, blood-stained bandages, hobbling on crutches or leaning on the shoulders of their comrades; the soldiers walked with their heads down. The street became dead silent... the only sound was the shuffling of boots and the thumping of crutches.

"Then I saw an elderly woman in broken-down boots push herself forward and touch a police officer's shoulder, saying, 'Let me through.' There must have been something about her that made him step aside. She went up to the column, took from inside her coat something wrapped in a colored handkerchief, and unfolded it. It was a crust of black bread. She pushed it awkwardly into the pocket of a soldier, so exhausted that he was tottering on his feet. And now from every side women were running to the soldiers, pushing into their hands bread, cigarettes, whatever they had. The soldiers were no longer enemies. They were people."

It was a Cana-like miracle, except it was not water but vinegar that was changed to wine. It was war shown for what it really is, a male sickness and a main theme of my WAR ON TRIAL book-document. For if it hadn't been for the women, there wouldn't have been the wine. The women whose gesture of compassion showed just how simple a thing reconciliation can really be when the heart is right. In this story, it was simply "a crust of black bread." That's all it was.

Peace is *not* an unrealizable dream.
War is *not* an inevitable reality.

But it was enough. It started the others running, with their bread and whatever else they had. It couldn't have been much, perhaps all they had, because of the war. But it was enough. In the act of giving the bread, was revealed the hidden things of the spirit to the spirit. Something mightier than hate and hostility took over. Love was born. There was no need to judge and condemn. Instead, there was a new awareness, a new understanding. There was a certain contentment, a new freedom. God's Love, always present, was at work.

When I first heard this story I filed it away in my memory bank as a story worth keeping. But years later there came a moment when I would hear it again, as though for the first time…and when I did, I wept. It happened during a period when I'd been researching the atrocities of 20th century wars . . . the gripping and meticulously researched accounts of the rape of Nanking - the forgotten holocaust of World War II; the ovens of Auschwitz; the cultural genocide of Tibet and its traditions by Communist China; the 'ethnic cleansing' of Bosnia; the killing fields of Cambodia; the genocide in Rwanda; the so many, many places where war, the blood-swollen god, had forced men collectively to commit acts which individually they would revolt with their whole being.

I'd learned and seen things, heard things, that would take years to wash from inside my head. I saw that everything, everything in war is barbaric, bestial, making the victor stupid and the vanquished revengeful. I saw that war is a disease; it is like typhus, it is a male disease, a universal perversion. I'd been given to see how the afflictions of humanity flow from the male's ineradicable aggressiveness, his destructiveness, his persistent malevolence. And so I wept when hearing the story of the Cana-like miracle in Moscow.

I wept because in today's world of the five continents become a global village, all persons have become neighbors to one another; but torn by our diversities and tensions, our history of hatreds and greed, centuries of war, rape and plunder, we do no yet know how to live together.

Peace is *not* an unrealizable dream.
War is *not* an inevitable reality.

"If my soldiers began to think," said Frederick the Great, an efficient and just ruler in the spirit of the Enlightenment, and a patron of the arts, "not one would remain in the ranks."

But I also wept because this great Moscow 1944 Cana-like miracle, as told by Yevtushenko, so beautifully if not poignantly served to confirm for me what the aforementioned explorer Francis Younghusband in The Atlantic Monthly of years earlier had captured when saying this:

> On the day I left, I went alone up on to the mountain in the holy calm of eventide. Suddenly, as I sat there among the mountains, bathed in the glow of sunset, there came upon me what was far more than elation or exhilaration; I was beside myself with an intensity of joy and with this indescribable and almost unbearable joy came a revelation of the essential goodness of the world. I was convinced past all refutation that men at heart were good, that the evil in them was the superficial. Though since then I have seen much evil, my faith in the essential goodness of things has never faltered.

THE Moscow miracle and how it buttressed my own long held conviction that men at heart are good and the evil in them is superficial, helped a lot to keep my spirits up in what most folks told me was an impossible dream. Yet for me, to dream the impossible dream, but even more to strive for the impossible goal, is necessary to the human soul which would rise above drabness and bondage, war and destruction.

Dom Helder Camara, Catholic Archbishop in Brazil, was of like mind; he, an acclaimed saint of our time, was an explorer in ways not unlike Younghusband and myself. Like Don Quixote, like Christ himself, this recently deceased servant of the poor and the oppressed was a reformer who wished to establish the knight errant's 'Golden Age'—the kingdom of God on earth. It was his great quest.

Peace is *not* an unrealizable dream.
War is *not* an inevitable reality.

I once spent a day with Dom Helder at the United Nations Plaza headquarters of the World Conference on Religion and Peace. Author of Race Against Time, The Impossible Dream, and Sister Earth, he spoke to all he met, from crowds of anonymous poor to journalists and government officials, with the simplicity of a child—yet it was obvious to me that, as I'd already heard, Dom Helder did indeed give politicians sleepless nights. "I'm very fond of Don Quixote," he once said. "He is much more realistic than is generally believed." For me the message of both men was clear, it was ennobling, it spoke to the heart. Indeed everyone, but everyone bar none, understood him. I liked that.

In his strong belief in humankind Dom Helder saw himself as a Don Quixote, and perhaps this comparison best illustrates what kind of person he was. His passion for the possible — and the impossible — making him refuse to rest content with the "scandal of sub-men, sub-women, stuck in a subhuman life, trapped by subhuman work," served to reinforce my own passion. Inspired, I felt an immediate kinship with this man of like passion and belief. But I'd been surprised, somewhat stunned, to discover that like Mother Teresa of Calcutta, another "giant" in how people thought of them, that he too was "tiny" in actual physical stature - that is to say short in height. So tiny that I quite nearly embarrassed myself upon meeting him by an impulse that had me just short of making a move to pick him up so I could hug him; instead we just shook hands. It was that kind of moment.

Dom Helder was not naïve. He knew there is a price for the splendor of truth. That price is the agony that mystics feel in the face of anything that blocks or impedes the splendor. He made no attempt to psychologize evil or to pretend that willed ignorance of evil will somehow make it disappear. Grounded in the true western way, he moved into prophetic confrontation with evil by naming it. He named the blasphemy of tampering with human life through abortion (the greatest atrocity in human history as though human beings are soulless bipedal apes). He named the blasphemy of biocide: the destruction of life forms and whole species of life

Peace is *not* an unrealizable dream.
War is *not* an inevitable reality.

forms for superficial and greedy purposes. He named the two-headed blasphemy of war, both "conventional" and nuclear.

My dream all along had been that I'd live to see the day when children would be able to look back on war as an 'incomprehensible aberration' of their forefathers. It is why I undertook to be a scout, an explorer, in a quest to come up with a solution to the problem that is war and threat of war. I'd never seen myself as a Don Quixote as did Dom Helder, but I did have Helder's passion for the possible - and for the impossible - making me refuse to rest content with the scandal of war that reduces my fellow brothers and sisters to sub-men, sub-women, stuck in the subhuman life of incessant warfare, the men trapped by the subhuman work of being paid killers, the women trapped by their bodies used as battlefields.

Then it happened that on one night, on the far side of the world where the night before had been sticky-hot and oppressive, heavy with menace, a storm of Homeric force split the sky. It woke the wife of a peasant farmer in Medjugorje, and she rushed outside to see what was happening, then back inside to shake her husband awake. "It's like the Day of Judgement out there," she shouted. Everything seemed to be on fire and the thunder was crashing around the sky.

In that very instant began what would be an ongoing story signaling the death knell for the centuries-old curse that civilization, no matter how advanced, is always on the edge of a return to barbarism. That civilization, once achieved, does not automatically perpetuate itself. That we are always on the brink of a fear, in imminent danger of relapsing into barbarism.

Peace is *not* an unrealizable dream.
War is *not* an inevitable reality.

A WELLSPRING
AMID THE MOUNTAINS

For twenty-eight years (continuing), since June of 1981,
in an obscure corner of the world, sprang a potent
wellspring of maternal water-of-life, an event that
humbles the intellect, or endeavors to be
superior to, but which can never equal reason.

IT was a drama which was to shake local villages to the roots. It
began on Wednesday, 24th June 1981, the Feast of St. John the
Baptist. And it had a fine, crashing overture, well-suited to this
region of violent contrasts and untamed emotions going back a
thousand years. In all that time the people here had never known
the meaning of the word peace. No, there was only fear, there were
enemies without, rulers within, there was prison, there was torture,
there was violent death.

The night before, at one in the morning, with a storm of
forebodingly fierce force breaking the sky, the wife of that peasant
farmer shook her husband, Pero, awake. "It's like the Day of
Judgement out there," she shouted. Everything seemed to be on
fire giving the firemen a hard job coping with all the fires.

Later, that same day, in the atmosphere of calm tranquility that
followed the storm, on the hill Podbrdo in nearby Bijakovici there
appeared a luminous shape, the shadowy, shimmering figure of a
young woman, apparently hovering some way off the ground. Two
young peasant girls out walking, Ivanka and Mirjana, in seeing the

figure, became frightened and raced back to the village as quickly as they knew how.

Later in the day, when seeing the mysterious figure again, but this time along with another girl by the name of Milka, what all three saw was a young woman in gray, holding something in her hand which she seemed to be protecting.

It was the opening scene of a cosmic drama that twenty-eight years later is still unfolding. I would soon learn of this unusual phenomenon precisely because of what the woman had come to say. By this time it was the following day, four other children (Vicka, Marija, Ivan, Jakov) were gathered with Ivanka and Mirjana – (Milka was tending her mother's sheep), when again this luminous figure of a woman appeared. She, the luminous figure, explained her presence with these words: "Peace, peace, you must seek peace. There must be peace on earth, you must be reconciled with God and with each other. Peace, peace, peace."

Whatever it was they were seeing would quickly prove to be a supreme authority for them. It would enable them to bear whatever was in store for them and yet remain serene. They'd feel no enmity towards those who would persecute them and never encourage others to feel enmity. They would always and only ask for peace, reconciliation and prayer.

She had come to say "God exists." Says Marija, "She had come to inspire all of us to search for peace: peace in our own hearts, peace within our families, peace in the world." She had come to inspire all of us to search for peace! In our own hearts! Within our families! In the world!

This was the essence of her words to the Six children on that second day. In fact, it was a desperate plea for peace that would go echoing 'round a world which, in that summer of 1981, seemed to hover on the brink of self-destruction. Relations between the superpowers were at their lowest ebb, and there were real fears of a Soviet invasion of Poland — they had invaded Afghanistan the previous year — that might engulf the world in nuclear war. In those dark days, few people would have rated the chances for peace

Peace is *not* an unrealizable dream.
War is *not* an inevitable reality.

as being very high. Though the very idea chilled the blood, the time for building fall-out shelters seemed to be at hand.

I first learned something about the horrors of war, the toll it takes, the weeping it invites, when as a young teenager I'd stand outside the fence of Mitchell Field, the East Coast Command Center of the Army Air Force, and watch the hospital-planes fly in from D-Day in Europe. Every fifteen minutes around-the-clock for long months on end one of those planes would come in for a landing, flying low over my home, bringing back troops who'd been wounded in battle. I would watch as stretcher after stretcher of the bandaged and broken were carefully lifted from the aircraft, placed in waiting ambulances, then taken to the base or area military hospitals.

As I watched, I lost tears knowing that some of the wounded very well might be from the ranks of soldiers who just months earlier, in miles-long convoys from places like Kentucky and Tennessee, had passed by my home, sometimes stopping for a leg-stretch and chat with the locals, on their way to a nearby bivouac area before shipping out to England in preparation for the invasion of Europe's mainland. Many never made it back home again, not even to be buried.

> From my own little village of Westbury during this war that would span two oceans, 42 men were killed, many were wounded, others had become prisoners of war or reported as missing in action. In proportion to its population Westbury is ranked as having been one of this nation's hardest hit communities.

Those who cannot remember the past - the ten-thousand who died on the beaches of Normandy many of whom never got to use their guns - are condemned to repeat it. Today I wear a T-shirt of my own design stenciled with the words, I SURVIVED THE 20th CENTURY. On the back are words of General William Tecumseh Sherman from a speech at the Michigan Military Academy: "I am sick and tired of war. Its glory is all moonshine. It is only those who have neither fired a shot nor heard the shrieks and groans

Peace is *not* an unrealizable dream.
War is *not* an inevitable reality.

of the wounded who cry aloud for blood, more vengeance, more desolation. War is hell!"

As I did with any new information, impulse or sighting of possibility for a path that might lead to world peace, enduring peace, holy peace, my antenna went straight up when learning about that shimmering shining-figure. She who'd been seen hovering above a hill in the remote, tiny mountain-village of Bijakovici in the Balkans. Because it's one of five clustered villages in the parish of Medjugorje, Medjugorje itself being one of the five, the hill Podbrdo is commonly said to be in Medjugorje.

I decided to monitor the situation, to wait and see what if anything more than what I already knew developed or came of it. Meanwhile, my once tiny village had grown since the days of World War II and some of our newer neighbors had come from living amidst a terrible civil war in Central America's El Salvador, where they awoke to find the dead bodies of their neighbors, friends and relatives lying in the streets outside their homes; others were beaten, tortured and frequently threatened. But then, ten years later, in 1991, in territories all around Medjugorje one of the most bestial wars of the century broke out setting the Balkans on fire. Then in another ten years, in 2001, the tragic events of that Tuesday in September - September 11th - shook the world and left thousands dead in New York City's World Trade Center; at the Pentagon just outside Washington, D.C. and in the Pennsylvania countryside a short distance from Pittsburgh. Like a knife blade, that date severed past from future; it was a moment that changed the world.

Meanwhile, in deepest Africa, in Kibeho, in the mountainous farm region of Rwanda, strange sights could be seen in the skies, the sun spinning and pulsating or splitting into two separate suns. This was in November of 1981, just four months after the onset of an apparitional woman appearing to the children in Medjugorje where, too, the sun had been seen pulsating and spinning.

In Kibeho there were seven children, six girls and a boy, who, at the very same time as the children in Medjugorje were being visited by a luminous woman figure, were also encountering a luminous

Peace is *not* an unrealizable dream.
War is *not* an inevitable reality.

woman figure. She is "a woman of incomparable beauty," reported Alphonsine Mumureke, the first who saw her.

The essence of the apparitional woman's message here was that the world wasn't just indifferent, but had turned against God. And that the greatest suffering that could ever befall us would be the total absence of God. Ten years later, in 1991, the year when war broke out in the Balkans 3,000 miles to the north, war broke out here too, in Rwanda: a half-million slaughtered by machetes, knives and nail-studded clubs in just the first three months of conflict.

All of this - especially Bosnia and Rwanda - I thought to be particularly remarkable coming as they did in the wake of the luminous lady urging "peace, peace, peace" at a time when there'd already been peace in both of those two places. I saw the events of 9.11.01 as though an "I told you so!" to world leaders as well as to a glacial-moving Church for not having taken seriously enough the plea for "Peace, peace, you must seek peace."

I'd long before concluded that waging peace just wasn't enough, wouldn't do it, wouldn't get us to a world without war or threat of war. I saw that we live in a time when all solutions to the problem of war — other than that of Jesus' simple exhortation to love our enemies — have brought the world to the brink of destruction. Long ago Ralph Waldo Emerson in Miscellanies had written, "War, to sane men at the present day (this was in 1884), begins to look like an epidemic insanity, breaking out here and there like the cholera or influenza, infecting men's brains instead of their bowels."

The 20th century, with its endless wars and ending as it did with the Bosnia and Rwanda shockers; and then, just as the world was greeting the dawn of a new century, the "Unimaginable" attacks on America that brought comparisons with the 1941 "Infamous" Japanese assault on Pearl Harbor, confirmed Emerson's diagnosis of war as a disease, as an insanity, as epidemic. Had it not been for Dad's last minute decision just three months before the attack not to relocate the family to Hickam Field (the USA Air Force Base at Pearl Harbor) on a construction assignment where he'd be project manager, I might not be here to tell the awful story.

Peace is *not* an unrealizable dream.
War is *not* an inevitable reality.

On that day, December 7th, some 360 Japanese warplanes reached the Hawaiian Islands and pulverized the American military base at Pearl Harbor; within two hours of unremitting attack, the Japanese planes had sunk or seriously damaged eight U.S. battleships and obliterated 200 aircraft; thousands died or were wounded — Tokyo's forces escaped the dramatic raid virtually unscathed. Months later Dad, a highly esteemed civil engineer and dear friend of Rear Admiral Ben Moreell, founder of the Navy's celebrated Construction Battalions (Seabees) during World War II would again turn down a proposed assignment ... this time to share in the management of the newly specially-created city of Oak Ridge, in Tennessee.

Oak Ridge is where the "top secret" Manhattan Project that would develop the A-Bomb to be dropped on Hiroshima was scheduled to be based. So secret was this project that not even Congress knew about it. Dad always long-prayed on bended knees before making a decision of any kind; thus it happened that he didn't accept the Oak Ridge offer about which in months ahead we'd have reason to be enormously grateful.

For on 6 August 1945 the uranium 235 bomb fell above Hiroshima and exploded. People exposed within a half-mile of the fireball were seared to bundles of smoking black char in a fraction of a second as their internal organs boiled away. In the testimony of the survivors, they described ghastly scenes of people whose skin hung from them "like a kimona" and plunged themselves into the rivers, shrieking in pain. . . .

Three days later, on 9 August, 1945, a more powerful plutonium bomb went plummeting down onto Nagasaki, Japan's city of two hundred thousand souls of whom more than seventy thousand would immediately die — many without a trace, incinerated. "We have done the devil's work," exclaimed Robert Oppenheimer, Director of the Manhattan Project, soon afterwards.

And so, as someone once said, God has put a limit to man's intelligence, but apparently no limit to his folly! Albert Einstein himself, the theoretical physicist without whom the A-Bomb

Peace is *not* an unrealizable dream.
War is *not* an inevitable reality.

might never have been conceived, cried out, "If only I'd stayed a locksmith!"

I'd come to see wars, conflict, as all business. One murder makes a villain. Millions a hero. Numbers sanctity. I used to wonder where war lived, what it was that made it so vile. And then one day I came to realize, to know, where it lives: it is inside ourselves. "The only devils in this world are those running around in our hearts," I'd recalled Gandhi as having said, "and that is where all our battles should be fought."

In that moment I said to myself, either man is obsolete or war is. It was then, as I reflected on what I had said, that my exploration, my quest for a solution to the problem that is war, took a turn inward. I thought about war, everything about war, as being barbaric. But that the worst barbarity of war is that it forces men (the male of our species) collectively to commit acts which individually they would revolt with their whole being.

I agreed with William James who, in The Varieties of Religious Experience (1902), wrote: "What we now need to discover in the social realm is the moral equivalent of war. Something heroic that will speak to men as universally as war does, and yet will be as compatible with their spiritual selves as war has proved itself to be incompatible."

The moral equivalent of war of course is peace. But, I asked, what is there about peace that is heroic, what is there about peace that will speak to men as universally as war does? While asking this question I couldn't get Medjugorje off my mind. In the beginning, at the outset, I'd had an instinctive, instant sense that, Yes, this luminous, shimmering woman on the hill Podbrdo really was the Virgin Mary, God's celestial messenger to earth. I had no doubt which in itself was quite remarkable, I thought. It would not be the first time she's come.

All along as a scout, an explorer, on a quest for world peace, my very best tools had been my intuition; my ability to think outside the box; and my spirituality of looking at everything as though with the eyes of a child. It's how I'd studied the origins and causes

Peace is *not* an unrealizable dream.
War is *not* an inevitable reality.

of war, the pornography of war, the disease that is war, war that I'd been born into in a century saturated by the blood of wars that spanned both oceans.

This time, regarding Medjugorje, as my instinct kicked in it would be no different. With something burning inside of me and thinking outside the box, I recalled the first time I'd heard the story: the night when a storm of Homeric force split the sky over Medjugorje.

Later, that same day, in the atmosphere of calm and tranquility that followed the storm, there'd been the appearance of a luminous shape, the shadowy, shimmering figure of a young woman, hovering above ground on the hill Podbrdo. There'd been the two peasant girls, Ivanka and Mirjana, one of whom had seen her, but in fright both raced back to the village. But not before Ivanka had exclaimed in excitement, Mirjana, look there, it's the Gospa (the Croatian word for Mother of God, Mother of us all).

She would later say, "I don't know how I knew, but somehow I just did." Mirjana, though seeing that Ivanka's face had gone pale from fright, refused to look where her friend was pointing. "Don't be an idiot," she retorted, "why on earth would the Gospa appear to us?" But the sight of Ivanka's face had scared her and it was then that both girls ran back to the village

Later that afternoon the two girls along with a third, Milka, were heading home after letting Milka's sheep out of the pen. The time was about six-fifteen. When they reached the spot where Ivanka had looked up and seen the mysterious figure, the girl again cried, "Look, there she is." Mirjana and Milka, following her pointed finder to a distance of 200 meters or so, saw a young woman in gray, holding something in her hand which see seemed to be protecting.

"She was a long way away," says Ivanka. "We couldn't see her close up, just the outline of her body." We couldn't see her face," confirms Mirjana, "and anyway, we didn't know what the Gospa would really look like! But something inside us insisted it was the

Peace is *not* an unrealizable dream.
War is *not* an inevitable reality.

Gospa. We knew it was her, but we felt confused, and just stood there looking at her."

Ivanka, agrees: "We didn't know what to do, where to put ourselves. We felt a mixture of joy and fear. So much joy, yet so much fear, it's impossible to describe it." By Friday, two days later, there were seven children who had seen the Gospa one of whom, Milka, never saw her again after that first day. It was on that Friday when the Gospa, weeping, cried, "Peace, peace, you must seek peace."

After the war that had set the Balkans on fire, war that was four years of shells destroying churches, schools, hospitals and cultural landmarks, war that was death camps, rape camps and a campaign of 'ethnic cleansing' in which entire villages were wiped out while specific forms of assault were developed to inspire terror, it was observed that throughout all those years of horror Medjugorje had remained as a veritable "oasis of peace" — despite all its surrounding villages having been torched and destroyed, despite the nearby ancient city of Mostar reduced to rubble.

Mostar - once home to the three ethnic groups of Catholics, Muslims and Orthodox - lay in tatters, its beautiful buildings razed. The four-hundred years old Mosque and the venerable church of Sts. Peter and Paul alike, merely rubble. The proud arched bridge linking the Turkish quarter gone forever. The Catholic Bishop's palace a burned-out shell. The leafy people's park now a graveyard, because there was no room left anywhere else to bury the dead. Death and destruction and a terrible devastation everywhere — except in Medjugorje. Remarkable!

Just twelve miles from the ravaged city of Mostar and surrounded by villages that had suffered the bombs of war, Medjugorje had remained an oasis of peace in the midst of terrible and heinous conflict, bestial cruelty.

Had it been divinely protected, as so many of its people believe? Was it the outpouring of prayer that cast the gray cloud over it, reported by the Serbian pilot sent to bomb the valley, but who inexplicably could not find it?

Peace is *not* an unrealizable dream.
War is *not* an inevitable reality.

Or was it simply, as the cynics claim, just too tucked away to have come to the attention of the warring forces? Six bombs were dropped on the valley. Two exploded on the outskirts lightly damaging an outside wall of a house and killing a few animals. The other four rockets simply did not detonate on impact.

And Medjugorje, the valley where the Mother of God continued to appear to the visionaries daily, became a safe haven for thousands of refugees. From a war that had left three million people displaced, half a million children orphaned or abandoned, an estimated twenty-five thousand women the victims of rape and perhaps three thousand unwanted, unloved babies born of these terrible happenings.

This too, all of this, I would see as remarkable. What can be said of such a place as Medjugorje, which survives the all-destroying wrath of war? Only that it stands out starkly as miraculous in itself. A true oasis of peace. Peace, in the sense of Medjugorje, that is not an interlude between wars but a peace that is a lasting state, come what may.

Yes, so remarkable was all of this that I began to see all other events in today's world as secondary in importance to Medjugorje.

There's nothing comparable in history.

In a world that seems to have taken an ax to the root that connects us to God, one suspects that Mary, the Gospa, saw Medjugorje as the very best place from which to speak to that world. In that place, where East meets West, its people going back a thousand years have never known the meaning of the word "Peace" — only conflict, violence, war.

What seemed clear to me in all of this is that at Medjugorje, in an embattled world, the Mother of God had come to challenge us; we must become as little children. It is an absolute imperative!

I present now a composite picture of Mary in her apparitions, as given by the Six visionaries seeing her: Our Lady's appearance is preceded by a flash of light, in the early days by three flashes. She is tri-dimensional as any living human being. Her beauty is beyond

Peace is *not* an unrealizable dream.
War is *not* an inevitable reality.

anything in our world. She wears a beautiful luminous gray gown, but not completely gray, somewhat like coffee, but not like coffee. On feast days her gown is bright gold. Her veil is brilliant white. She has a crown of stars around her head. She appears on a small bright cloud.

She appears as a young woman, perhaps 19-20 years of age, thin, and of medium height. Her face is white with rosy cheeks. She has black hair. somewhat curled and hanging on the left side. Her eyes are blue. She has a gentle look and beautiful smile. She has been seen with her Infant in her arms. She has also been seen in tears and has shown her Son with bleeding wounds and a crown of thorns. She ends her appearances with "Go in the peace of God," and disappears into the same light from which she emerged at the beginning.

It's been reported that in an interview the visonary Vicka has described Mary with these words: "The appariion we see is of a real person, not some mist-like vision. Our Lady has a real body, a real personality. I experience her as my mother. When I am with Mary, I am a child with my mother. This relationship is not just for myself; she has explained to me that she is the mother of each single person in the whole world. She loves each of us as her own dear child. And she is calling us all to come back to God. The way is faith, peace, prayer, fasting and conversion. But what I want to emphasize is: she is not far away from any of us here below. The Virgin Mary is very much part of our life on earth, very close to us, very concerned about each one of us."

On 27 June 1982 the Blessed Virgin Mary in answer to a request that she do something to prove to the crowds that she really was present, replied: "Those who cannot see me should believe as though they did see me." For many, the effect on the visionaries was sufcient. During their encounter with the Virgin Mary they were as if in another world, where the happenings of this world couldn't reach them. Neither bright lights nor noise, nor touching, could distract their attention, riveted as it appeared to be on somehing above thir heads... They listened and they replied, their lips moving

Peace is *not* an unrealizable dream.
War is *not* an inevitable reality.

soundlessly, their expressions on their faces changing from pure joy to great sadness, depending on the conversation with Mary.

Mary's voice has been described as sounding like music or a song. She has been touched and embraced. She has said: "I am your Mother" and "I have come to tell the world that God exists (she had to start from scratch). He is the fullness of life, and to enjoy this fullness and obtain peace, you must return to God." She has been giving her message of peace for twenty-eight years to the whole world. Many cardinals, archbishops and bishops, plus Pope John Paul II and Pope Benedict XVI, have all given positive testimonials to Medjugorje. Almost all the candidates in the Vienna seminary have received their call to the priesthood through Medjugorje.

Then there are the testimonies from legions of pilgrims from every continent at Medjugorje; their accounts mark the beginning of a new era in the minds and hearts and lives of all people everywhere. The reports of the Six visionaries from the time when as youngsters (the 1980s) and now married with children of their own (a new century) are of such moving wonder, are shared with such profound maturity if not a luminous dignity.

I have no words for this achievement. But I know that not since the days of my childhood, when the people in books were more real than the people one saw every day, have I found myself so profoundly stirred, so deeply moved.... In what are biblical times their portraits are a biblical study of life in the midst of a war ravished world.

Endless numbers of pilgrims, thousands, have had their rosaries changed from silver to gold in color during their pilgrimage. Similar changes of heart, where rosaries have changed color, could be multiplied indefinitely. So also for the miracles of the sun. I know of one pilgrim who reported on her pilgrimage by writing, "What I went through while there could probably fill a book, but despite all the signs such as rosaries turning gold in color, the huge concrete cross atop Mount Krizevac bursting into flames, its turning, the sun spinning, or the host in front of the sun, what I came away with was the overpowering love of God, and a sort of

Peace is *not* an unrealizable dream.
War is *not* an inevitable reality.

continuous surging of spiritual energy or power that seemed to pervade the whole village."

Another pilgrim has said this: "As I watched the sun set behind the mountains and before it sank down, I witnessed it spinning, surrounded by a gold-green light, the disc turning to white, like a huge Communion host surrounded by a rim of red. Its normal color returned and it slipped down beyond sight. The next evening I saw the phenomenon of the sun again ... 7 p.m. Suddenly I was aware that the disc was quivering and the color was withdrawn, as with an mmense power ... the white disc continued to sink towards the mountain and I could easily look at it all the way down ... as it began to sink it resumed its fiery glow."

The above descriptions are rather tame when compared with the pageantries of light and color which some persons witness in the miracles of the sun. This is especially so where the heavenly phenomena last a good while and are captured at length by video cameras and with associated phenomena. The sun has been seen to spin and turn, to move about, to pulsate, to "dance," to be surrounded by varied rays and all kinds of colors, to move downwards as if coming towards the earth and then retreating, to throw colors all around the ground area, to be nearly covered as with a great host, to have circles of color around it, to appear as a monstrance; and to have in it or near it various religious symbols.. Also, light-like or white silhouettes of Mary have appeared near the sun.

At Medjugorje, besides sun miracles, numerous other luminous signs have appeared. Such include fire appearing on the mountain at night but leaving no trace behind; light appearing on dark nights around the cross on Mount Krizevac; the cross spinning like light and being replaced by a silhouette of Mary in light, or Mary standing before it. White silhouettes of Mary, made of light, have appeared in the sky or against the outside of the apparitions room of the rectory. Stars have been seen to move about at night. The word MIR (meaning PEACE) has appeared in the sky written in large letters of light.

Peace is *not* an unrealizable dream.
War is *not* an inevitable reality.

We might add that various individuals experience all sorts of signs. One priest noted that the peace of the place extended to mosquitos not biting and lizards being friendly. Other persons have found that the birds suddenly become quiet at apparition time, and that they have sung in the darkness of the night. Or a rose out of season blooms with a clear image of Mary's face in it. Still others have found themselves unhurt by thorny bushes, as one doctor in a group learned. Descending the mountain. he noticed one woman's bloodied hands and felt sure they would need treatment. But when they reached the base of the mountain, he saw that they had become perfectly normal.

What should we make about all this? I have some thoughts. We cannot agree with those who want nothing to do with signs and wonders, or who say it is better to be in church praying than looking at a miracle of the sun. One has to differentiate. Our Lord was not pleased with those who sought Him merely to witness miracles, to have a sensational experience, or as curious tourists.

But He did not stop working them until He died. Then He gave everyone the greatest sign and miracle of all; His Resurrection. He also proclaimed His miracles as proof of His divine mission. Neither did Our Lord care much for those who sought only physical cures or material bread, but He did not stop curing people.

So we can't act as if signs and wonders do not happen, nor have any good purpose. We can't, as it were, throw them back in God's face. The first Christians were convinced of the authenticity of Our Lord's mission because of the signs and wonders He worked. The early Christians saw the signs and wonders worked by the Apostles as the Acts testify. The Christians of the first centuries witnessed many miracles, which, indeed, have never ceased in the Church, including the raising of the dead.

We then should neither question nor hamper the workings of the Holy Spirit or His instruments. St. Augustine of Hippo, one of the greatest doctors of the Church, frequently presented parishioners who had experienced miracles to publicly witness to

Peace is *not* an unrealizable dream.
War is *not* an inevitable reality.

the facts in his cathedral. Augustine also wrote about miracles which occurred in the local African area.

God sends all these signs, wonders and miracles to awaken and renew our faith and to bring us back to the practice of Gospel teachings. He prods and shakes us back to the realities we have forgotten, with new examples of the original proofs authenticating our holy religion. Once again we become alive face to face with His unique wonders. We rise from the apathy of our disbelief and the sleep of mediocrity. We should thank Him and praise Him for His lavish kindness and respond with more intense Christian lives; or a true conversion.

Besides being beneficial to the individuals who experience or hear of them, the sum total of the signs, wonders and cures at Medjugorje arc, as God intended, a battery of arguments for the authenticity of the apparitions occurring there.

They call, too, for a hearty response to the messages and their implications. Never has there been such an outpouring, and in so short a time, as the endless graces, signs, wonders, miracles and cures, which have taken, place since June 1981 at Medjugorje or through its influence.

THE timing of the Medjugorje event is notable for several reasons, one of which is that it came during the pontificate of one of the most Marian popes in history, and just six weeks after he had called upon Our Lady: "Mary, come! Mary, come!" immediately following the assassination attempt on his life.

Amazingly, a little over a month after that attempt is when Mary began her apparitions at Medjugorje. Remarkable.

A little over a month later many people there including the now legendary Fra Jozo Zovko, the local pastor who has since visited here at our Welcome Mary Peace Abbey on Long Island, saw a large inscription in the sky on top of Mount Krizevac. The word "MIR" appeared in large burning letters. "MIR" is a Croatian word meaning "PEACE" . . . . and from the very beginning has been the central message of Medjugorje.

Peace is *not* an unrealizable dream.
War is *not* an inevitable reality.

In my long quest for a solution to the problem that is war and threat of war, I could not ignore it.

I remember Fra Jozo during a visit here at the abbey, our family homestead, just the two of us sitting alongside each other on our living-room couch, comfortably resting, while watching the women happily nodding and throwing smiles in our direction as they scurried back and forth arranging the dining-room table for a scrumptious mid-day meal. Jozo had been generous with a smile of kind that only he can smile coming as it does from a heart filled with love for the Gospa. A happy time. I'd never seen Adella so filled with joyful excitement. In that moment I found myself revisiting the faith journey of this quiet, soft spoken, special son of Mary. Fra Jozo had come to St. James as pastor in Medjugorje only months before the apparitions began.

He knew none of the visionaries, and only a few of the parishioners; and initially didn't believe the apparitions were real. Was it all someone's trick? Worse yet, was it the work of Satan? The government suspected some religious conspiracy concocted by this new parish priest, and being used to stir up the people to return to the old ways, days of insurrection, terror, and conflict with the (Communist) governmnt.

The authorities, certain that Fra Jozo was creating a political uprising, banned people from continuing to go up the hill where Mary was appearing. Fra Jozo's experiences through those first few months are almost beyond most of our imaginations. Not able to comply with the government's order to stop the people from going up the hill, in early August 1981 he told his assistant, "Be prepared to take over my job." Fra Jozo foresaw his fate.

Peace is *not* an unrealizable dream.
War is *not* an inevitable reality.

Subsequently he was arrested, charged with conspiracy, tortured, tried in what had been a "mock trial," and sentenced to three years in prison. "My going to prison was no accident," he'd said, "but it had nothing to do with my being stubborn or provoking the authorities. It was the logical result of the choices we all have to make at some stage of our lives."

It was on this occasion when the word "MIR" appeared in large burning letters in the sky over Mount Krizevac, that Mary said "I am the Queen of Peace." Indeed, from the earliest moments of the apparitions peace has been the plea, the prayer, the theme, the purpose, the proclamation.

One of the seers, when asked "Why do you think the Lady wants to be called the Queen of Peace?" replied, "Because the situation in the world is dreadful! Wars everywhere, tensions…! We need peace - a just and true peace - more than anything else." A second seer responded by saying, "The world has lost its way, and the Lady has come to the rescue. Merely by coming, she's put the process in motion."

It is precisely in this "process" where I believe I've found the solution to the problem that is war and threat of war, and to the problem that is slavery—of every kind. Regarding the latter, I think especially of southern Asia where many, many thousands of children are delivered into sexual slavery in an industry where girls and boys, as young as four, are bought, sold and stolen to serve this repellant trade that crosses nation's borders.

It is precisely in that "process" I realized, became convinced, where is to be found the solution to the problem that is war and threat of war. And so now "Peace, peace, you must seek peace" took on new meaning for me, new direction, new urgency, for now there was light at the end of the tunnel. And with that a compelling imperative unlike anything I'd ever imagined or experienced before.

Peace is *not* an unrealizable dream.
War is *not* an inevitable reality.

In fact, for many years I'd heard God calling, always in the still of the night, when the hour was late, always an experience as though straight out of Isaiah: chapter 6, verse 8 — "Then I heard the Voice of the Lord saying, 'Whom shall I send? And who will go for us?'" Always I'd responded with the words, "Here I am. Send me."

But this time it would be different.

My "Yes" this time would irrevocably change my life for all the rest of my days.

The Six recipients of the apparition are no longer children, they have gone beyond the years of adolescence, they are married and have children of their own. These ongoing apparitions have profoundly changed their lives as well as that of the parish and the entire region.

During the early years of the Gospa's visitations I'd made this entry in my journal: "All this has taken place in a nation where atheistic Marxism governs life with a power well-known. That these signs from heaven would take place in an atheistic environment, one that has been so well controlled for a half century, is already a sign of the times. I say this based on a vision of the whole situation: these apparitions are not an isolated phenomenon. They are part of a complex of spiritual events taking place in a country where the faith is strangled, repressed, asphyxiated.

"'They are taking place at a time when the faith in the countries of the West is becoming somnolent or is disintegrating. At a time when Christian historians are making light of the heroism of the early Church's martyrs, we see a new heroism arising in the face of a persecution which is less bloody but much more far-reaching and pervasive.

"It includes the manipulation of the human psyche in an attempt to destroy those consigned to psychiatric hospitals on the principle that faith is a psychological illness. The gifts of grace which hold these countries erect have given rise to a renewal of faith which most noteworthy is irrepressible in Poland, and less known

Peace is *not* an unrealizable dream.
War is *not* an inevitable reality.

but no less real in other countries. This new reality has shifted the Church's center of gravity, moving it to those places of courage and fidelity. The election of a Polish pope is but one more sign among others.

"Supernatural occurrences in the countries of the East are not usually known except through personal testimony, and they cannot be widely communicated without danger of fierce repression of those who are living these gifts of God in a heroic way. Through such testimony I have accumulated a working knowledge of many such examples of God's action. Thus I can have none other but a positive welcome to the events of Medjugorje as being possibly another instance of the Good News."

ONE of my most favorite memories of Medjugorje is of Ljubica (Masinica) Sivric - affectionately known as "Mama" - in whose home I stayed during my first visit. A native of Medjugorje she speaks very little English but makes herself known by way of her exuberant nature so alive with the Spirit and helped by a translator. My translator was the very articulate Franjo about whom I cannot say enough by way of gratitude for his wealth of information and generosity of service and spirituality while with me in Medjugorje.

Mama has three sons and one daughter, Ivanka, and several grandchildren. Ivanka, welcoming and delightful, plays a major part in helping Mama care for all of the pilgrims she houses since Mama lost her beloved husband, Mate, a deacon at St. James Church, the previous February. I asked Mama to describe the early apparitions that started in 1981.

". . . The first day the apparitions took place on June 24th, I did not believe it but went right to the Hill of Podbrdo to see for myself. I didn't see or feel anything but went back to the Hill for the next few days totally out of curiosity. On the third day I felt electricity going through my body during the apparition. On that day Mary told the visionaries that she came with the message of conversion for the people of Medjugorje.

Peace is *not* an unrealizable dream.
War is *not* an inevitable reality.

"On this same day, a young boy in a wheelchair was healed instantly and started to walk. Also, a blind man was healed instantly when he smeared the dirt from the Hill on his eyes." Mama feels blessed to have been in St. James Church the day the major conversion of the parish took place when the people cried out their forgiveness of each other and begged God for His forgiveness. Previously the region had been known for its strife and hatreds.

"The people now started to go to church in great numbers and one day the State police came in to nail shut the doors of St. James. They nailed wooden planks over the main entrance at least five times and each time the local people (mostly women of whom Mama was one) together with bare hands ripped the planks from the doors. Finally the police gave up." The men, long persecuted by the state for their church affiliation and thus unable to find employment, had been made to leave family and village for jobs outside the country. With an enormous smile helped by no little animation Mama exhibits great pride but mostly deep satisfaction when telling this story. They'd faced arrest, jail and worse for doing what they did, defying the authorities, especially with their men-folk absent from the scene.

It took great courage and an amazing faith to do what they did. Locals had been very cautious not to be too open about practicing their Catholic religion since Yugoslavia in those days was fiercely communistic and there were a lot of police in Medjugorje at all times. The police would watch you at all times and they didn't like Medjugorje or the people who went there. They watched them all and would keep track of all the license plates. The most important thing is that you were loyal to the communist party and communists didn't go to church.

Mama told of seeing the word "Mir" (Peace) in blazing letters across the sky. "It was a moment," she said, "I will never forget 'til the day I die." She also witnessed, along with most of the villagers, seeing an image of the Blessed Mother on the top of Mount Krizevac "...fluorescently lighting up the whole mountain."

Peace is *not* an unrealizable dream.
War is *not* an inevitable reality.

Mama was so obviously full of life, laughter and the love of God. Being her house guest was a blessed event. Mama would say, "My heart is so full of happiness. I am very blessed to be in Medjugorje now and try to help out in any way I can."

She knows all the visionaries and their families and visits them as often as possible. She is a daily church goer and often during the summer months she climbs Apparition Hill and the steep and rocky Mount Krizevac (best climbed by mountain goats) without shoes.

She greets you each morning with "hvaljen isus I Marija" (praise be Jesus and Mary) and leads you in morning prayer. In the evening before one of her sumptuous dinners, she prays Grace followed by a litany of prayers. And after dinner, perhaps, she might grace you with her heart-warming rendition of "Majci Kraljici Mira," a Croatian hymn, "To the Mother and Queen of Peace."

Peace is *not* an unrealizable dream.
War is *not* an inevitable reality.

MEDICAL SCIENCE
STUDIES

According to Msgr. Angelo Kim, president of
Catholic Bishop Conference of Korea, while he
and his bishops dined with Pope John Paul II in
November 1990, he (Kim) said to the Pope, "Thanks
to You, Poland is liberated of Communism." The
Pope retorted, "This is not I who did it. This is
the work of Virgin Mary (the Gospa), as she had
announced in Fatima and Medjugorje." *Nasa Ognjista
{Our Fireplaces}, March 1991, p 11)*

DURING the first years of the apparitions, I kept notes, wrote
articles, contributed to publications, and edited a newsletter about
the happenings at Medjugorje. Nothing of what I wrote had any
great scientific pretensions; it was based on earlier intuitions and was
intended purely to inform others about what I'd become convinced
was a sacred phenomenon of conceivably profound importance
for a world that hungered. This phenomenon I defined, as did the
researchers, in terms of the prayerful encounter of the Six children
with the Gospa...whose first message was "God exists."

Meanwhile, scientific and medical studies were already
underway to determine the authenticity of the "encounter." Some
of those studies were conducted in dialogue with theologians who
raised questions by the apparitions which, in varying degrees,
belonged to medical science. These studies — aimed at promoting
truth alone — gave my interest further stimulus.

From the very beginning it was important that the work of medical science be undertaken without pause of any kind because no one knew how long the apparitions would last; there was no way of knowing. Without such studies, their contributions would be lost forever should the apparitions suddenly cease. Without those studies, the phenomenon would remain an enigma forever, open to all kinds of objections and hypotheses.

Because medical science plays a central role in how such phenomena are evaluated, I placed a lot of weight on the approach and protocol used by the researchers to determine the validity of what both they and the Six felt to be a sacred phenomenon that transcends ordinary communications and perceptions. They asked, is it not incongruous to submit phenomena that are sacred — or presumed to be — to laboratory experiments? This objection weighed heavily on the researchers and indeed on the visionaries who were loath to become guinea pigs in an experiment.

And yet the task needed to be undertaken.

Medjugorje had awakened the almost forgotten conviction that Lord God, Christ and the Virgin Mary are real beings who are near us, converse with us and guide our lives at a personal and collective level, and that an encounter with them is capable of transforming and transfiguring us. Ecstasies, cures and other graces from Medjugorje were and continue to be the remarkable signs if not overwhelming evidence of this.

For me the fact that the event has moved and converted so many people from so many different nations in a fashion that is completely out of proportion to the unusual adventure of six young people from a tiny village hidden in the mountains of a country that was officially Marxist, is also remarkable.

Ultimately I would find myself convinced beyond doubt that this woman who speaks to us in Medjugorje as the Queen of Peace is not foreign to us, that she is the Virgin Mary — the "Gospa." From the very beginning some 2000 years ago she had been announced as the Woman through whom holiness would be brought to the world.

Peace is *not* an unrealizable dream.
War is *not* an inevitable reality.

Our Holy Mother has been appearing all over the world for centuries, and since 1981 she has been appearing in Medjugorje. One has only to discover the entire spectrum of her motherly activities — from Bethlehem to Fatima (1917)* and Medjugorje (1981 continuing) — to see and become clear about this. You will consecrate yourself to her and be ready with her to say your own "Yes" to God. It is interesting to note here that not until after the Gospa began her visits at Medjugorje had any of the six visionaries ever heard of the Blessed Mother's earlier appearances at places like Fatima (1917), Knock (1879), Lourdes (1858), LaSallete 1846), Rue du Bac (1830), or Guadalupe (1531). For them this came as a big surprise.

* An extract from the Fatima story: On 13 October 1917, with 70,000 gathered, there was this shout from Lucia: "Look at the sun!" Our Lady had promised a miracle for that day, and it was beginning. The crowds looked up to see clouds roll back and reveal the sun. The 13th had dawned rainy and windy, and yet the people came. And though soaked, they stayed.

Then, just before noon, while Jacinta, Francisco and Lucia were waiting for Our Lady, Lucia, for reasons she could not explain, told the crowd to close their umbrellas. The rain continued to come, but changed into a lighter mist.

Then, suddenly, Lucia was transformed. On their knees, the seers gazed up at the Lady who had come again to rest on the little carrasqueira. . . . . In speaking to Lucia that day, among other things Our Lady prophesied that the war (World War I) would soon end and the soldiers would be returning to their homes.

Then she opened her hands, and the light that came from them shot skyward. It was at this point precisely that Lucia shouted, "Look at the sun!" . .

Peace is *not* an unrealizable dream.
War is *not* an inevitable reality.

. . The crowds looked up to see clouds roll back and reveal the sun. But it was now like a disc of white light that all could look at without blinking. . . . . At the same time, the crowds watched in awe as the sun bobbed in the sky like a bright silver top.

Then the "dancing sun" stopped and began to spin. As it twirled, bright lights spanning every color of the spectrum shot off and washed everything on earth. Green, red, violet worlds appeared momentarily to surround the people, who shouted and praised God. . . . .

Then the 70,000 watched the sun plunge in a zigzag path toward the earth. Frightened, great numbers of people fell to their knees. But just as the sun appeared about to strike the earth, it stopped... and suddenly returned to its proper place and its proper brightness. Amazed, the crowd saw that what they were wearing, previously soaked with rain, had dried; shoes previously caked with mud were now clean; where before there'd been puddles and lakes of water, this too was dry.

Even more amazing, the "Miracle of the Sun" (as it came to be called) was seen in nearby cities. Too, there was no serious talk of mass hallucination. Portugal was convinced. . . . . Sixty-four years later — after the prophesied "more terrible war" (World War II) that would begin in the reign of "Pope Pius XI" came to pass, as did also "the scattering by Russia of her errors throughout the world, provoking wars and persecution of the Church" — the Miracle of the Sun, the "dancing sun," was seen again, but this time at Medjugorje in Yugoslavia.

Yugoslavia, crossroad between the East and the West. Yugoslavia, where the past had made the present. Yugoslavia, where it is plain that for

Peace is *not* an unrealizable dream.
War is *not* an inevitable reality.

centuries and going back a thousand years, the people there had suffered an immense amount of human pain, appalling in its unbroken continuity.

On 2 August 1981 (the Feast of Our Lady Queen of Angels and less than two months after Our Lady began appearing in Medjugorje), in late afternoon, before the sun had set, the sun was seen to spin in its orbit, then descend toward the watching people (approximately 150), then retreat — a "dance of the sun" that reminded the people of the miraculous phenomenon at Fatima.

When the people were able to look at the sun without hurting their eyes, they saw figures around the sun, as it seemed to circle, in the shape of a cross. The strange phenomena caused many to cry, or pray, or even to run away. Then six small hearts appeared in the sky, around a large heart. Then a white cloud covered the hill (Podbrdo), site of the first apparition, and the sun returned to its normal place. The people interpreted this unusual happening as the sun's witnessing to its creator. All of this happened over approximately fifteen minutes.

PERHAPS when it comes to religious themes one is accustomed to reading the works of theologians and specialists. This is understandable. Persons like myself and others who've spent time in Medjugorje have learned by multiple experiences that the Medjugorje phenomenon is carried by the laity, and most often described by the laity.

This confirms the teaching of the Second Vatican Council (1962-1963) which consigned to the laity an important role. Concerning Medjugorje, because the laity responded and gave their witness, the specialists who are the medical scientists were able to come, in this way by-passing episcopal politics and the biases of some theologians which could have seriously if not fatally delayed the onset of those studies.

Peace is *not* an unrealizable dream.
War is *not* an inevitable reality.

God's people are more sensitive to the Word, it seems, than those who hold office within the Church. First, the people accepted the Queen of Peace, and only then, the priests. Only when many groups had come without priests did the priests begin to dare to experience Medjugorje. After the priests, then came the bishops, always accompanied by the people of God. The world is hungry for the sacred, thirsty for adoration; it craves to be fully conscious of the presence of God.

DURING my exploration of the Medjugorje event, I had the privilege of spending a day in the company of Courtenay Bartholomew. He is a medical researcher of international repute who as a scientist, when writing and lecturing about the Gospa at Medjugorje, talks openly about God's work in the Blessed Virgin Mary. In his own words he says, "The call to research Mary began in Yugoslavia. I could neither pronounce nor spell 'Medjugorje' when, in 1983, I first heard about this little-known village.

In fact, it almost evoked the response: 'Can anything good come from Medjugorje?' Jesus must have smiled when Nathaniel (probably the Bartholomew of the other Gospels) made a similar remark about Him and Nazareth: 'Can anything good come from Nazareth?' (John 1:46). But there in that little village where everyone knew everyone's secrets, they did not know the greatest secret of all - that God was also living in Nazareth.

"At that time, I could not accept that the Virgin would appear every day for over two years, especially as, to my limited knowledge, there was no precedent for this. And so, I was a little skeptical, albeit not completely unbelieving. If indeed she was really appearing daily, then my logic concluded that there must be a serious reason for this extravagance in apparitions. I then read Fr. Rene Laurentin's classic book *Is The Virgin Appearing At Medjugorje?* and became more fascinated with Medjugorje after reading it. Laurentin is a French theologian acknowledged as one of the world's leading authorities on Marian theology.

"Some time later, when I was invited to a medical conference in Belgrade, Yugoslavia, beginning on October 14, 1986, I saw this

Peace is *not* an unrealizable dream.
War is *not* an inevitable reality.

as my opportunity to visit Medjugorje in route to the conference. I arrived in Medjugorje on October 13th. It was the anniversary of Mary's last apparition at Fatima in 1917. To my surprise, I was invited by Fr. Slavko Barbaric (now deceased) to be present in the Franciscan rectory for the apparition of the Virgin which was expected to take place at 5:40 p.m. Assuming that the apparitions were authentic, my first reaction to this invitation was that I was not worthy to be so close to the Holy Virgin. I articulated this to someone and the reply I received was: 'But who is worthy?'"

Subsequently, Professor Courtenay Bartholomew, M.D., penned a detailed, exhaustive report titled *A Scientist Researches MARY*, complete with references and pictures (in color) that attests to the spiritual insight of this man of science as well as to the authenticity of the Apparitions at Medjugorje.

He is a medical researcher who has published extensively in scientific journals and plays an important role in research on the AIDS virus. He's on the international committee collaborating with researchers in the United States on viruses associated not only with AIDS but, too, with cancer. In the words of Fr. Michael O'Carroll, C.S.Sp. of Blackrock College, Dublin, Ireland... Bartholomew "is in a great tradition of scientists who have an intuitive sense of the power of Mary, the Mother of God. He is a kindred spirit with the great atomic scientist Dr. J. Rand McNally, who warns of the danger of a nuclear tornado and points to Our Lady as the appropriate protectress of an imperiled world. He has a staunch faith in the miraculous which science cannot explain."

O'Carroll, who I've spent amazing time with on several occasions and much admire, hold in high esteem, is an internationally renowned authority on Marian apparitions, a reservoir of holy wisdom and fervor. One of his main achievements was the massive encyclopedic work on the Virgin Mary, *Theotokos*, which was not only widely acclaimed, but was reprinted four times in five years.

Once, while participating in a conference at Notre Dame University out in Indiana, I had occasion to meet with the aforementioned Fr. Rene Laurentin of France who, like O'Carroll, also serves as a reservoir of holy wisdom and fervor regarding Marian apparitions. He is widely and highly esteemed for his vast reservoir of knowledge concerning Mary's visits over the centuries.

He once commented in this way about Medjugorje: "In the past, I had always studied apparitions as an historian. Now, for the first time, I have found myself in the midst of one. There is no substitute for that experience and I now understand many of the things that escaped me in the past." Thus in one of his books about the apparitions at Medjugorje, he had some interesting things to say. Because it's a translation from French, the reader might encounter a little 'road-bump' in one or two places. Here goes:

". . . . This grace of God (the Medjugorje event) was born in the East like a surprising premonitory sign of the great movement which was going to free Christians from the Church of silence. It was going to (gradually) put an end to the nightmare of a watched, repressed, humiliated, and dangerous life. Undoubtedly, it is not by chance that Yugoslavia, a sensible boundary between East and West in the interior of a Marxist zone, was chosen as the place for this sign in June 1981, well ahead of perestroika (the restructuring of the Soviet economy and bureaucracy that began in the mid 1980s). During those years, how many other apparitions remained the secret of visionaries or small groups which were hunted down by the police! In Hrushiv (Ukraine), where apparitions took place daily for a year after Chernobyl, enormous crowds came, but we do not yet have any interviews of the visionary. A blurred image and uncertainties remain. . . .**

"Opposition and Constraints: The sociocultural intelligentsia looks at what comes from on high with scorn, except in the Church itself, especially in the countries of the North Atlantic where demythologization, secularism, and modernism often remain the law and the prophets. These Medjugorje apparitions, say some, rise from a basic faith, fundamental, archaic, enlightened, visionary ("road bump"). These simplistic and repetitive messages do not take into account the social and political makeup of the world which is the new objective of postconciliar (post-1963 Vatican Council II) Christians.

Peace is *not* an unrealizable dream.
War is *not* an inevitable reality.

"Once again God pokes fun at the wisdom of the wise as He did from His humble birth in the crib, then again on the cross. He ironically brings back the wise of this world to the thoughts of God, which are not those of mankind. Medjugorje is a remedy for a sterile intellectuality which polishes the faith and converts it again into human, without any intellectual pretensions, to transform the Church of the Saints into a club of experts ... or of free talking people. For the work of God is measured by faith, love, fruits (conversions, vocations, initiatives) in order to renew the world and change hearts.

"The event at Medjugorje, which has taken place under a Marxist government in a rustic small town nurtured more according to vineyards and tobacco (its crops) than universities, has created one of those great spiritual currents which restore the Church and make it, through the opening to the Holy Spirit, its spiritual force. (special note: tobacco is no longer a crop).

"One asks himself about a paradoxical contrast: why do so many intelligent, ecclesiastical, and well programmed initiatives ingeniously planted, endowed with finances and well established administrations, remain sterile and sad. void of faith; and why does the place of pilgrimage of Medjugorje, born in improvised, uncontrollable, repressed conditions, without means or infrastructures in a parish in the countryside, change so many hearts?

"It is God's secret, one of those surprises of His kindness. At times the Holy Spirit produces harvests where one does not expect them. God is surprising. Medjugorje is the grace of little David, chosen by preference over his prestigious older brothers. It is also the grace of a heroic and poor pastor who assumed from day to day the confusing event and the obstacles which had accumulated: the bishop and the government (the Church and State) as well as the unchained international intelligentsia, etcetera.

"The shepherds had been good gardeners. They cultivated the field of the Lord in spite of the bad conditions and the hail of blows received.

Peace is *not* an unrealizable dream.
War is *not* an inevitable reality.

"It is thus nine years (1990) from the time that the apparitions began."

> ** Special note: This was written in 1984. Seven years later, in 1991, the Hrushiv visionary Josyp Terelya, my friend and living in Canada as an exile, published just such an account under the title, *Josyp Terelya, WITNESS to Apparitions and Persecution in the USSR.* Terelya is a Christian mystic, a visionary, a suffering servant, a victim of Communism. WITNESS is the story of a man who spent much of his life behind bars because of his faith. He has fought for the cause of Christianity all his life and in the most hostile of circumstances. Terelya is one of the lay leaders who helped keep the Church alive through more than 40 years of persecution. It details 20 years in prisons and camps. WITNESS is his autobiography, another Alexander Solzhenitsyn crying out from deep within the Soviet prison system. It is also the story of extraordinary events - allegedly supernatural events - that are said to have occurred in Hrushiv (Ukraine).

A World Phenomenon

MEDJUGORJE, for centuries slumbering in anonymity as a small nondescript village in the mountains of the now former-Yugoslavia, had now become a world phenomenon. Word of what was happening there echoed in every corner of the world. Such was the spontaneity of the events of Medjugorje, that it took the Church and the world by surprise.

Though everything pointed to the apparitions' authenticity, the Church, traditionally cautious in these matters, not only showed lack of interest in the events, but actively opposed them. The parish pastor, Fr. Jozo Zovko and his assistant, Fr. Zrinko Cuvalo, tried every means to keep the people away from where the apparitions were taking place. In fact, both priests were purposely antagonistic although prudently open to what was happening.

It was only when they became convinced there was something serious behind it all, that they placed these extraordinary events in a pastoral and liturgical framework, leaving the rest to time and God. Fra Zovko is known for having said this: "If this is from God, neither you nor we, nobody, will be able to stop its course."

"In this place," my journal reports, "on a hillside where a weeping Madonna is calling for Peace, a meeting with God is taking place. Not on human nature is the blame, but on our behavior as humans. And so Our Lady is not here as a joke, or to perform or be mysterious, but to challenge us: we must become as little children—not like, but as.

"She is here to unlearn us. The world, stained with blood and pregnant with menacing omens, and now at a major, major crossroads, has a lot of lessons to learn. Our Lady is here to teach us anew. Dare we not listen to this Woman...whose activity at Medjugorje has been nothing less than prophetic?"

It's Beyond The Realm Of
Human Experience To Explain

IT is beyond the expertise of the scientists, the medical professionals, the academics, to explain the events at Medjugorje.

Because it is beyond the realm of human experience to explain, we must use the resources of faith, theology and Christian mysticism which have set out the boundaries of this domain.

What the six Medjugorje visionaries experience remains outside the bounds of science as do the related phenomena of light, healings, and cures.

It would be hard to find a more disparate group as these Six whose ages back in 1981, when the Gospa first appeared, ranged from 10 to 17 years. They are disparate in their sex (male and female) and in their temperaments (introvert and extrovert). And

Peace is *not* an unrealizable dream.
War is *not* an inevitable reality.

their intellectual and imaginative developments are extremely varied: Vicka, Jakov and Mirjana have lively imaginations while the imaginations of Ivan, Marija and Ivanka are somewhat duller. Indeed, little Jakov at the time was a hyperactive realist while Ivan evidenced a lack of imagination.

How do the Six see the person whom they recognize as the Gospa? It remains difficult to be precise and there is a risk of simplifying the mystery in an effort to explain this type of perception verbally. In summarizing the results of many tests, one is led to believing there is real communication from person to person, between the Six and the Gospa, and of voluntary nature. This is a communication which does not use the ordinary sensory channels (which have been suspended, disconnected, immobilized) but is achieved in a more immediate fashion at a spiritual level.

However…this communication is perfectly integrated and in direct continuity with the psychic life of the visionaries; it takes a shape just as knowledge of an ordinary, three-dimensional, concrete object does. The nerve centers of the brain are involved in this act of knowing with the difference that instead of decoding from vibrations, the visionaries' impressions are received in a more immediate fashion, the nature of which our scientists and medical professionals do not know.

The perception by the Six of the person who appears, the Gospa, is not strange for them. It provokes in them normal, coherent reactions, analogous to those aroused in us when we converse with our neighbors: expression, dialogue, surprise, smiles, answers, etcetera.

Too, the messages are coherent despite the fact that at times the visionaries - all Six - had independent and yet simultaneous conversations with the Gospa. So very absolutely remarkable!!!

There is a coherence about the secrets which they received separately according to the numbers one to ten. Even though they have not explicitly communicated them to each other, the visionaries know the object of each one of them. They refer to

Peace is *not* an unrealizable dream.
War is *not* an inevitable reality.

the secrets in code words saying, "I have received the seventh, the eighth, the tenth secret."

This coherence struck the team testers particularly when the visionaries, on the instruction of the apparition, changed their attitude towards the tests. From being vehemently opposed at first, they became completely cooperative. It is unlikely that the bare wall in front of them would have achieved this change of heart.

From the sociological point of view, Fra Slavko Barbaric established that this particular group, which of itself is disparate and has no leader, acts with paradoxical cohesion. The only plausible explanation of this is the apparition which had become their focal point.

Add to this, at the spiritual level, the great harmony that exists between their natural and supernatural growth. These then very ordinary youngsters, very like any others, "no better and no worse," says Vicka, had attained a high degree of human maturity coupled with a degree of charity and transparent holiness that causes one to marvel more and more as the months (and now years) go by. This is the real secret of Medjugorje.

Of all my most memorable impressions of the Medjugorje event, this is what has impressed me the most. I never cease to marvel at the profundity of their newfound maturity.

All the doctors who have examined or studied the ecstasy, though they may use different terms, have all arrived at the same conclusion: they reach a limit, and as one doctor states most explicitly, the best explanation is the transcendence of an object, which cannot be perceived through normal, material, scientific means, but whose existence nevertheless (transnormal, paranormal, whichever you wish) is certain.

FINALLY, to the character and virtues of the Six, we find a mixed group. As one psychologist said, while having completely different personalities and holding different opinions on various subjects, all Six were completely agreed with utter conviction that they saw the Blessed Virgin Mother, this woman they called the Gospa. And,

Peace is *not* an unrealizable dream.
War is *not* an inevitable reality.

despite ridicule, sarcasm and opposition, they have never wavered from holding to the truth of the main happenings, apparitions and messages.

That there may be slight variations of the same story is to be expected from human witnesses just as one finds apparent discrepancies in the gospel accounts. Still, throughout many trials and attacks the Six have shown patience, fortitude and charity. Of particular interest to me is that none of the six visionaries prior to their own experience with the Virgin Mary had known anything about the cycle of Mary's visits which began in the 19th century. They expressed surprise when learning about Fatima (in Portugal 1917) and Lourdes (in France 1858).

In the very beginning of the events, the Six were confused and afraid, but unshaken in their conviction. "We see!" They no longer had a private life. No one was instructing or manipulating them. They were catapulted into the focus of a monumental event without even being asked!

In some way, says one theologian, they were taken by chance. If the events were not true, after a few months and all the persecution and threats they were faced with from the Communist authorities and state police, they would have given up everything.

But no! They were steadfast and persevered. Not one of them denied the facts. While theologically illiterate and not even average among their classmates, they were used as instruments of Our Lady. God it would seem is choosing the lowly ones to put to shame the great and noble.

All Six claim to have seen Heaven. On one occasion (November 1981) Vicka and Jakov simply vanished for twenty minutes. Jakov's mother searched for him because she had seen him in the house shortly before he disappeared . . . neither Vicka nor Jakov could be found. The moment they returned, Jakov told his mother what had happened and where they had been, and both of them told her they had seen Heaven. "Now I am no longer afraid to die," said Jakov.

Peace is *not* an unrealizable dream.
War is *not* an inevitable reality.

All Six have gone about living normal lives at home, school, work, church, and now all are married with children. And this despite the abnormal pressures of constant crowds of pilgrims around them, the scientists, the press or other curious people. Under such conditions they have acquired a poise that many other persons, even professional folk, have never attained. Certainly they outmatch many in handling sly, subtle, loaded and stupid questions often aimed at them. Like the priests at Medjugorje. they have been sorely tried.

IN his book, *MEDJUGORJE: Are The Seers Telling The Truth — A Psychiatrists's Viewpoint,* Doctor Nicholas Bartulica makes this contribution: "Through the history of apparitions we have never witnessed such frequent and lengthly periods of private revelations intended for the visionaries as for the world.

"In the Medjugorje events there are supernatural interventions of such magnitude and diversity that it appears as if Heaven and earth had come together. A multiplicity of 'signs and wonders' including physical and spiritual cures, (coupled with) the extended period of apparitions, is confounding to the theologians."

ON the question of Medjugorje and an explanation for its phenomena, medical and other disciplines in the world of science have played a central role. Especially has medical science played a central role. Never before in the history of the Church has the phenomenon of ecstasy been so subjected to modern scientific tests. In Medjugorje the visionaries have undergone studies with electro-encephalographs, electro-oculographs, eye reflex tests and a study of auditory responses with the permission of the visionaries and the Gospa. They concluded that their findings were scientifically inexplicable.

The medical experts have summarized their findings in the following terms. Clinical observation of the visionaries leads us to affirm that these young people are healthy in mind and body. Detailed clinical and para-clinical studies allow us to confirm scientifically that there are no pathological modifications of the

Peace is *not* an unrealizable dream.
War is *not* an inevitable reality.

parameters studied. There is no question of hallucination in the pathological sense of that word. There is no auditory or visual hallucination. These ecstasies are absolutely authentic. During the ecstasy there is a face-to-face meeting, as it were, between the visionaries and a person whom we did not see. During the ecstasy they are in a state of prayer and interpersonal communication... The ecstasies are not pathological nor is there any element of deceit.

No scientific discipline seems to be able to describe these phenomena. We would be quite willing to define them as a state of active, intense prayer, partially disconnected from the outside world; a state of contemplation with a separate person (the Gospa) whom they alone can see, hear and touch. The conclusion of the research teams is that the children experience ecstasies which cannot be explained by contemporary science

SO very clearly then Medjugorje is not a joke. The synchronicity of the two events, John Paul II and Our Lady, Queen of Peace, together holding court on the World Stage in an era the likes of which history has never known is of enormous meaning. And consequence. One needn't be a weatherperson to know which way the wind is blowing. It is transparently clear that Our Lady has arrived at exactly the right moment – if not the last moment.

Peace is a supreme good, but it is also a fragile good, arising from mobile and complex factors, in which the person's will is in continual play. Therefore, peace is never completely stable and secure; it must at every moment be rethought and reconstituted. The Gospa sees how rapidly it weakens and degenerates...if it is not incessantly brought back to those principles which alone can generate and preserve it.

It is why we see today as a time of grace and mercy; it's an explanation for Medjugorje and why the Gospa has stayed for so very long. She sees that there is still obscured the sacred and inviolable character of human life. And once more men are being calculated in function of their numbers, their possible efficiency in war, and not by reason of their dignity, their needs, their common

Peace is *not* an unrealizable dream.
War is *not* an inevitable reality.

brotherhood. Sadly, women too now are being drawn if not sucked into this picture.

Once more the cycle of regrowth of divisions and oppositions between peoples, between the various races and different cultures, is taking place. This spirit of division is guided by nationalistic pride, by prestige, by politics, by perversion of religious beliefs, by the armaments by race, social and economical antagonisms. It is why the Gospa urges us to "Reconcile, reconcile, reconcile!" "Peace, peace, make peace!" "You must do everything with the heart!" "You will not have peace through the presidents, but through prayer." "A new age of peace has dawned, but not through the politicians."

"Pray, pray, pray!"

The Gospa sees that between wars there returns the illusory concept that peace can only be based on the terrifying power of homicidal weapons. And while on the one hand noble but weak discussion and efforts are made to limit and abolish armaments, on the other the destructive capacity of military apparatus is being continually developed and perfected. "You cannot simultaneously prevent and prepare for war," counseled Albert Einstein.

The Gospa from the very beginning - when choosing to say "Yes" - has been and remains a strong woman who changes the course of human history, even reverses the nature of spirituality, as well as immerses herself in the Divine. As history's most important woman, at Medjugorje she must be taken seriously.

Fra Ivan Dugandzic, a Franciscan priest at Medjugorje says that "Medjugorje isn't some sort of passing fancy. Medjugorje doesn't exist simply to wet our human curiosity. Critical things are happening here for all humanity. We're called to a specific goal if we want peace within ourselves, and peace in the world. Peace can't exist without God, or without our conversion or turning to God. It can't exist if we stray from the path. Thus, may we never forget, we are not alone."

Dugandzic is remembered for saying these things during the early period of the Gospa's visits, years ago. And yet the terror

Peace is *not* an unrealizable dream.
War is *not* an inevitable reality.

and loathing of war grows less as in various parts of the world episodes of war continue to explode in fearful flame, exhausting the mediating capacity of the organizations instituted to maintain peace in security.

The beloved Fra Svetozar Kraljevic, my dear friend and brother ever since collaborating in the work of war relief efforts during the Balkan Wars of the 1990's, is a Franciscan priest stationed at St. James Church in Medjugorje. Having been able to partake in the ongoing experience of the life that has surrounded these apparitions almost nightly since 24 June 1981, he brings a wealth of historical data as well as early verbatim transcripts of his interviews with the Six visionaries that can readily support what I report on these pages.

Indeed, Fra Kraljevic was a spiritual adviser to the visionaries and knows everything there is to know about Medjugorje. Relatedly, he makes this pertinent critique: "I would say that to be indifferent is worse than to be atheistic. Atheists believe there is no God. But those who are indifferent, they say: 'There is a God, but I don't need him.' And this is worse than to be an atheist."

Here it is important to communicate something of the culture and way of life in that part of the world; I explain it best by sharing something of Fra Kraljevic's life. Better known as Father "Svet" to English speaking pilgrims and one of Medjugorje's legendary friars, the mountains of Hercegovina were the first reality of his childhood. His parents and neighbors farmed their slopes and dwelt in their hollows. And when they had to go somewhere, they did not go around, they went over. It would never have occurred to them to do otherwise, and they expected their children to do the same.

From Fra Svet's earliest recollection, the mountains were a central feature in their lives. They did not give much of a living, but they did not need much. The mountains taught them to be satisfied with what they had. In a way, they were like parents, they shaped their lives. And their outlook on life. The Croatians of Hercegovina, those who lived for generations hundreds of meters above the sea,

Peace is *not* an unrealizable dream.
War is *not* an inevitable reality.

have taken on the characteristics of the mountains. Calm, steady, quiet, they endure.

The other reality was God. Like the mountains, God was just there…in his parent's prayers, in their plans, so He was there for Svet, too. In the hills next to his home, in the trees, in the cows, in the two cats who were his only playmates, God was an ever present reality. Where he lived there were three houses, built by his father and his two bothers. They were typical mountain dwellings—one room with a dirt floor measuring perhaps four by four meters. Svet was the youngest child there by several years. At birth his Dad was 46 and his Mom, 41; they had already had six children, four of whom were alive, and in the mountains after the war (World War II) there was total deprivation. The Nazis and the partizani had left no crops, no livestock, nothing. All the people had was trust in God.

Fra Svet in his book, *PILGRIMAGE, Reflections of a Medjugorje Priest*, has said this about that time in his life: "It is hard to imagine circumstances less favorable into which to bring an infant, yet terminating an unwanted pregnancy was unthinkable. Each life, no matter how inconvenient or unfortunate its environment, was given by God. For His purpose and as His blessing, though the blessing was not always readily apparent. Two of my surviving four brothers and sisters (two others had died as small children) were Mongoloids. My parents loved them, and so we loved them, too. God gave them to us, but it was not always easy to care for them. Not until they died years later did we realize what special people they were.

"Some might regard such a circumstance as a suffering or a punishment. But the one who dares to live with suffering through to its completion will discover that it is actually a great gift. Some people are difficult to live with, difficult to love. Sometimes the old or the new or the genetically defective can be a trial. But instead of routinely putting them in nursing homes or institutions—or killing them before they can be born—what if we were to live with them? What if, when our love is exhausted, we were to ask God to give us His love for them? Eventually we will discover the blessing

Peace is *not* an unrealizable dream.
War is *not* an inevitable reality.

they can be. And who knows, perhaps in the process we will become more what He intended us to be—which may have been part of His purpose?"

Whenever I think of Fra Svet it's not unusual that the legendary Jean Vanier comes to mind. Like "Svet" and Mother Teresa of Calcutta, Vanier is another one of those rare human beings about whom is said they are the great living saints of our age. For just as many decades as I've given to helping in the task of healing a broken world, Vanier himself has devoted his life to living with "people difficult to live with (like Fra Svet's two siblings with special needs), difficult to love, perhaps even a "trial."

From having founded L'Arche – a community in France for the care of the mentally challenged – he has evolved a worldwide loosely affiliated network of such communities, several of which I have visited and learned during overnight stays. His words ring with a kind of prophetic authority when speaking out of his life experience as a Christian activist successfully attempting a new way of life according to Gospel values. He's been a huge influence, a terrific role model, in my own journey as a Christian activist.

From my journals, I share this marvelous story about one of Vanier's residents, Claude, who had a truly illogical mind. He would ask such questions as, "What time is orange?" or "How was tomorrow?" but still he did have a wisdom all his own. As a result of his lack of logic, he did many things wrong, so he suffered from a kind of abuse that he had to endure all his life. Yet Claude was remarkably resilient and kept bouncing back joyfully.

For those who discovered his "music," his unique way of responding to life, he was a source of much joy. Well, one day Claude was at the beach with Jean-Pierre and several others of their community. Because the ocean was at low tide, there was an immense stretch of flat, sandy beach. They began making designs in the sand.

Claude drew a big circle with a couple of marks inside that could have been facial features. "What's that?" called Jean-Pierre.

Peace is *not* an unrealizable dream.
War is *not* an inevitable reality.

With a big smile Claude replied, "It's Madame Sun." "That's good" Jean-Pierre said. "Now let's see you draw joy."

Claude took a look around him at the wide beach that stretched out in both directions as far as the eye could see, then he turned to Jean-Pierre and said with a huge smile but in all seriousness: "There's not enough room."

In God's wisdom it is especially people like Claude, people who are deeply wounded, people who have been rejected by the world of "normality" who can speak a message of hope to that world. In my own work of many years, decades, I've been witness to this on numerous occasions. Always it's been a reality check. Indeed, I've never not failed to find these experiences enormously humbling. More, each of us who has touched or been touched by the Claudes of this world has been made whole somewhere; it has been our common experience.

The Claudes keep revealing to us, over and over again and in their own clear way, that what makes us human is not primarily our minds but our hearts; it is not first of all our ability to think which gives us our particular identity in all of creation, but it is our ability to love.

Peace is *not* an unrealizable dream.
War is *not* an inevitable reality.

FOR Colm Cahill from Jersey, England, it all began in 1998 while driving home with his dad in Jersey; they'd had quite a serious car crash. After it was over, he developed seizures. The first one was a week to the day after the crash. At first it was thought to be from the shock, but over the years they developed and got worse daily.

By the time he was nine, it was to the point where he was barely conscious most of the time from the seizures and medication. He began to lose hope about what he could do with his life. At age 13 the doctors ran tests to make sure things were in order. They realized that the electrical activity from the seizures was damaging. The doctor told his family that his life would probably be over in a year.

He began to question God. What kind of God would allow this to happen? "Why me?" he asked. "Why did this happen? I had lost my hope in Jesus. I had lost all hope."

Then in May of 2004, the parish priest who was a friend of the family came to his house. Colm was between seizures at the time. The priest asked him to chat with him in the garden. Colm managed to get up to go and have a conversation with him. "I wasn't sure what he wanted to talk to me about." While he had a high regard for the priest as a family friend, he was not very interested in listening to him as a priest.

The priest told him about a place called Medjugorje. Since he had missed so much school, he did not know where Bosnia was. He told Colm that Medjugorje was a little village in Bosnia-Hercegovina where the Mother of God was appearing daily. "He told me about the apparitions and I learned that he wanted to go there and to pray for my complete healing." The priest told him, "I want you to pray when I tell you to pray and give this a last shot."

In his hopelessness, he found a sudden feeling of optimism. He wasn't really sure about this: however, he listened and said, "OK, I'll do it."

The priest left on 17 May 2004 for one week. On the 21st of May, the priest sent Colm a text message that he would be praying with Ivan (one of the six visionaries) at an apparition on Apparition Hill that day at 10 o'clock Jersey time. "Now go to the back garden, find somewhere quiet and pray," the priest said.

"I knew I had to do this. I trusted in what he said, When I got there to pray, I was still a little confused. I did not know how to do this. I had a small crucifix to put on the bench and lit some candles in front of it. I took out a rosary and a book on how to pray the rosary and began to read it."

As it approached 9 o'clock, it was windy and there was a lot of distracting traffic noise from the main road. At 9 o'clock the wind died down and the loud noise from the busy main road stopped. It became absolutely still.

He looked up to see what was happening, and saw that the candles extinguished themselves one at a time, from left to right. At this point he was absolutely petrified and gave thought about running inside.

"Then something happened at that moment which I have never experienced either before or since. It was an amazing experience of peace which I had never experienced. The constant migraine which had been part of my life and the constant pain in my muscles from the seizures just disappeared."

He did not know at that time, but at that moment he was completely healed of everything. The next day he received a text of Our Lady's message. She had prayed for the sick people present and for the intentions of the sick of those present.

As the day went on, Colm realized that the headache that had been his constant companion was no longer there and there were no more seizures. That day turned into months and the months into

Peace is *not* an unrealizable dream.
War is *not* an inevitable reality.

years. Now five years later (year 2009) and 18 years old, he is still completely healed, all Glory to God!

Peace is *not* an unrealizable dream.
War is *not* an inevitable reality.

AN OBITUARY

IT is relevant and worth noting albeit with a certain sadness and regret to say that my dear friend Josyp Jaromyr Terelya (mentioned earlier in this chapter) died at the age of 65 while I'd been putting final touches on this book. He'd spent twenty years in some of the harshest prisons known to humanity... imprisoned in the Soviet gulag for his Catholic activism in prison... where he suffered tremendous hardship as well as mystical experiences. He was released after the intervention of President Ronald Reagan. Upon his release, he met privately on several occasions with another victor over Communism—John Paul II.

I'd never met anyone quite like him. No one was tougher; he'd had nine successful prison escapes to freedom; Josyp never quite recovered from spending his youth — his twenties, his thirties, part of his early forties — in confines. Meanwhile, no one was more dedicated to the Church and his homeland of Ukraine. He was very much like any human. And not perfect. But he was a hero for our time... a hero through and through and for as long as he lived. And his death leaves a void for all who were even vaguely familiar with what he had suffered. It is hard to be perfect when you have witnessed so many killed and your youth robbed from you.

Years in camps. Months at a time in frigid prisons. Isolation in cells the size of an outhouse—not even able to stand. Beating after beating. Water thrown on him outside in the midst of a Soviet winter... left with a coating of ice because he would not remove a religious medal. Pins stuck into his arms, lamps shined in his eyes all night, and a "freeze cell" in the notorious Corpus Two unit of Vladimir Prison, where he'd later tell of a rescue by the Blessed Mother (who appeared to him in apparition, reviewed his life and the country's future, and caused the cell to turn preternaturally warm... terrifying his captors).

Here's the story as he told it in the book *WITNESS* penned by Michael H. Brown who I know and for whom I have enormous respect for his integrity in investigative journalism: "Cell 21 had been turned into a veritable freezer. It was the middle of winter and they were forcing in frigid air. The walls were covered with ice so thick that you could make it ring by tapping an object against it.

"They stripped me of my winter clothes, leaving me there in a light shirt. In half an hour I felt my jaws freeze shut. I couldn't move them. And the very roots of my hair hurt.

"My mind was working. I was aware that I was freezing, and I gathered my strength. I climbed the grate on the cell door to warm my head against the ceiling light bulb.

"The guard on duty looked through the peephole, saw this, and switched off the light. I sat on my bed and began to freeze. There was an old quilt you could see through and I wrapped myself in it, garnering what little comfort it could afford me. Too weak, I finally lay down, praying and awaiting my fate. Within another ten minutes my lips wouldn't move, and my eyelids felt like they too were freezing shut. My head was splitting, my eyes, my temples, my jaws. I could still think but I couldn't move my limbs. I was freezing to death.

"It was then that I became aware of an intense flash in the room, a very powerful light, and heard what sounded like someone walking in my cell.

"My eyes were clamped. I couldn't tell who it was. I can't explain what happened — lying there with my eyes shut, in a state approaching paralysis — but somehow I became aware that the room was illuminated. And the cell was starting to feel warmer. Against my eyelids I felt the palm of a woman's hand and smelled the soft pure fragrance of milk.

"When the hand lifted I was able to open my eyes. There before me was the young woman. *'You called to me,'* she said, *'and I have come.'*"

It was one of several major mystical experiences in prison, in this case the date was 11 February 1972. But now, thirty-seven years later, the incredible journey of this famed Ukrainian mystic

Peace is *not* an unrealizable dream.
War is *not* an inevitable reality.

and Church hero has come to an earthly end. My only real regret is that I won't be able as planned to give him a copy of my book *this book* when it's published. I'd been so very much looking forward to that moment.

Eventually, Josyp found his way to freedom, fleeing to the West in 1987. He married the very lovely Olena, a doctor who had waited years for his release, and while living in Toronto they had three children. Olena who I very much liked – humble, peasant-like, she had a delightful sense of humor - passed on to her eternal reward just several years ago. In one example of Olena's humor, I recall the moment when Josyp first introduced me to Olena but I all too quickly while offering a hand in greeting said, "So Josyp, this is your mother!" "No, no, Teddy... Olena is *my wife!*" Seeing my embarrassment she giggled and laughed as though it was very funny. Years later when meeting her again she with a great big smile happily greeted me by saying, "Teddy. You remember me? *I'm Josyp's mother!*" And then laughed...as did I. She was like that.

Peace is *not* an unrealizable dream.
War is *not* an inevitable reality.

MY ONGOING WITNESS
TO THE 'MIRACLE OF THE SUN'

MANY phenomena which science cannot explain have been witnessed in Medjugorje and which can, therefore, be classified as supernatural. In one example, although there is no electricity on Mount Krizevac, pilgrims saw its huge Cross light up on the night of 15 August 1988, the feast of the Assumption of the Gospa. It was precisely at the same moment – 10:30 p.m. - when the Gospa appeared to the visionaries on the other hill called Podbrdo. There were thousands of pilgrims on Podbrdo that night and many of them witnessed this majestic phenomenon.

I myself have marveled at the daily "miracle of the sun" when it pulsates like a beating heart and is encircled by hoops of diverse colors. I have experienced luminous phenomena and seen Rosaries, originally silver, change to gold in color and remain gold. In addition, not infrequently, I've seen photographs taken by many people in Medjugorje and elsewhere that have depicted images of religious significance which were not present at the time when the pictures were taken (there is a term for this phenomenon: photomysticism).

I once noted in a journal entry that "one cannot help realize while sitting atop Mount Krizevac, that every peak, every valley in the scene, was laid out eons ago by God. God knew the picture He was painting on earth was a scene which, in the future, would be the stage for hosting the visit of the Woman of Revelation.

At times on the mountain you feel what Moses must have felt like, and in another moment, the Apostles; and yet in another moment, you feel crushed by smallness upon realizing the magnitude of

God's plan with Our Lady . . . and the privilege of just being here in this time of grace.

For many pilgrims who have gone to Medjugorje, the "Miracle of the Sun" is a memory they've taken back home with them. In an excerpt from "The Welcome Mary House Story" about my family homestead as a peace abbey, I share my own witness:

> "We'd flown Swiss Air out of JFK in New York, changed to Croatian Airline in Zurich, flew on to Zagreb, capital of Croatia, and then on to the coastal city of Split at the Adriatic Sea just north of the port city of Dubrovnik. Here we boarded a bus for the last leg of what had been a long journey to where in Bosnia-Hercegovina the Gospa is appearing.
>
> "Before even getting off the bus after arriving in Medjugorje, excited shouts from the rear were urging everyone to look out their windows — 'Look, the sun! The sun! Look, the sun!' Just like Fatima some were saying. Because I'd been up front, quick like a bunny I hopped off, looked up, looked at the sky, and from this vast valley found myself greeted by the most unimaginable sight.
>
> "The late afternoon sun was pulsating! Pulsating like a blinking traffic light or a rapidly beating heart. At the same time and looking for all the world like a child's 'top' it was spinning. It had the effect of enthralling all of us who for long minutes stood transfixed by what we were seeing. For many minutes we watched, without difficulty and without shielding our eyes as the sun spun and danced in the sky.
>
> "I felt it to be God's so very special way of saying, 'Welcome, welcome to Medjugorje!' It spoke joy to my heart in a way I'd never before known or experienced joy. Like the sun my heart too danced."

Peace is *not* an unrealizable dream.
War is *not* an inevitable reality.

"Except for one day of overcast while in that part of the Balkans for a full week, I saw this event of the sun every day of my stay; always in the late afternoon when the Gospa was visiting with the visionaries as was her daily practice. One year later 1 returned to Medjugorje and had the same experience.

"There'd also been other remarkable experiences: One evening, after a sumptuous home-cooked dinner in the home of Mama Zivric where I'd been lodging, I took to walking the cart paths that weave through the cluster of homes in the area. At one point I happened to look over my shoulder only to see a very large amorphous luminous-cloud hovering at somewhat less than roof-top level. I stared, not knowing what to make of it; it was an entity all by itself, didn't move; its luminosity is what I found to be remarkable.

"Puzzled, I shrugged my shoulders and resumed my walk, away from it. But when I stopped to look back I saw that it had been as though following me; and when I stopped, it too stopped. I did this several times, resuming my walk and then looking back; always it would move when I moved and stop when I stopped. Now, with my interest really piqued, I decided to see what might happen if I walked toward the cloud; I did — it backed off. I repeated the exercise; again it backed off.

"Although still puzzled, I resumed my walk of original intent only to look back (it was difficult to ignore) and see it once again following me. In fact it inspired awe in me, I experienced a sense of reverence for what was happening. Sensing that this hovering cloud of peaceful presence for some reason wanted me to follow it, silly as this may seem, real silly, I once again reversed my course back toward to where I'd begun my walk. The cloud went ahead

Peace is *not* an unrealizable dream.
War is *not* an inevitable reality.

of me. It led me through the maze of clustered red-roofed homes out into the vast valley with vineyards and towers of the twin-spired church behind me, but nothing before me other than acres upon acres of small plant-life and the darkening purplish-mountains of sunset.

"There in the distant western sky was the playful pulsating-sun, dancing for all who'd been given to see; not everyone who goes to Medjugorje sees this unnatural phenomenon. With this the luminous cloud that had been so mysteriously intent on leading me, as though an escort of celestial kind, disappeared. I was then given to perceive that luminous event as having been a manifestation of God's *glory*, of his Holy Spirit, a special gift for me. Here in a land where East meets West and far from my home on Long Island, I'd been standing in the presence of God. And that in his plan for me Lord God had deemed it important that I know the 'Miracle of the Sun' with its pageantries of light and color as of great and saving meaning for our world and our hour.

"For me it was a confirmation of my vocation as a scout, an explorer, for world peace; for a solution to the problem that is war and threat of war. Also it was a moment to recall that on several occasions during her initial visits at Medjugorje, the Gospa had promised a sign, a large, permanent sign, on the place where she first appeared.

"It will be lasting, tangible, and visible for all; one will be able to take pictures of it but not touch or destroy it. When this large sign comes to pass, it will be accompanied by other miraculous signs and miraculous healings. The sign will be given for those who do not believe in the apparitions of the Gospa, but the sign will be proof that in fact her visits had

Peace is *not* an unrealizable dream.
War is *not* an inevitable reality.

been real. After the sign which will be permanent, She will no longer return. In her words, these will have been her 'last visits here on earth.'

"Standing alone in the vastness of that valley and the sun now setting, its dance done, the hills darkening, I pondered over the experience. I found it hard to fathom how anyone who has researched the evidence of the Gospa's presence as had I could do anything but believe. I had no ear for those who babble without researching the evidence.

"However, as Franz Werfel, a Jewish convert to Catholicism, on whose book was based the film The Song of Bernadette, said about Mary's apparition at Lourdes: "For those who believe, no explanation is necessary. For those who do not believe, no explanation is possible." If, then, these apparitions of the Mother of Jesus are truly authentic, why is it that the rest of the Christian world with its many divisions pay little heed to her messages? Will they be apologizing profusely to her in the heaven they hope to see?"

In that valley of setting sun, its dance done, but more so in days long after, I knew there was something important for me to have seen or grasped . . . or God's glory that was the luminius cloud would not have led me, taken me, as it did. Gradually I came to understand that it was to enlarge my vision, to make me capable of seeing more clearly into the eternal realms. It was like with Ezekiel for whom the healing of nations seemed like a lofty goal, a difficult thing to believe in or strive for, but after having seen it with his own eyes, it was not only easy to believe in, to strive for, but it also became easy for him to declare.

Thirteen months later, in August of 2003, there'd been a Youth Festival at Medjugorje, an annual event. They'd come from more than 40 countries from around the world, including for the first time Chinese young people from Hong Kong and young

Peace is *not* an unrealizable dream.
War is *not* an inevitable reality.

Palestinians from Israel, and from Ukraine. As the opening day talks commenced, it was a sea of chanting, singing, dancing, happy teenagers.

The last speaker of the morning, a highly charismatic Croatian Franciscan priest, quoted from Scripture this line: "For the windows of heaven are opened, and the foundations of earth tremble" (Isaiah 24:18b). "If you really believe in Jesus," he trumpeted after quoting the Scripture verse again, "then the earth will truly shake!" The crowd responded with a thunderous, "Yes! We believe!" Then he proclaimed, "If you believe, if you really believe, then stand up right now and shout, "I believe in Jesus! . . . and the earth will be shaken!"

The crowd of more than 30,000 young people rose as one and began to shout, "I believe in Jesus. I believe in Jesus!" They then broke for lunch, settled down for a meal, when suddenly there was a loud rumble, and the ground and the buildings began literally to shake and sway. An earthquake lasting more than four seconds shook Medjugorje and all of its inhabitants and pilgrims. "If you really believe in Jesus, then the earth will shake!" the Franciscan priest had said.

I understood in these experiences that in today's world become now a battleground for the cosmic struggle, there is a cosmic corner to turn and it's why Our Lady has come to Medjugorje: to wake us up, to unlearn us, to teach us anew! She is like a trumpet call in a battle that is raging today as never before. A terrible evil has plagued our world since around the time of the French Revolution. Like a gathering tornado or cyclone, that evil evolved into State Communism, scientific atheism, agnostic modernism, depersonalization, and a societal aloofness that with its "Dictatorship of Relativism" has turned Europe and America into cold and secular wastelands. It has been the 'Period of the Spirit of Anti-Christ'.

I understood that God is present in all the turmoil and is leading humanity to a new era and a new order. But it requires our acknowledgement and collaboration. It must be the work of

Peace is *not* an unrealizable dream.
War is *not* an inevitable reality.

Christians and Jews, Buddhists and Hindus, Muslims and Sikhs, Native Africans and Native Americans, Quakers and Bahais, Zoroastrians, Shintos and Jainists . . . the people of all religions working together, collaborating and praying together.

Humanity, constituting the active part of the universe, is the bud in which Life is concentrated and is at work, but now at Medjugorje it was at work in a new and most glorious way. Call it what you will: the next step in evolution, or God's kingdom here on earth manifesting itself in that 'new and glorious way.' It is a message of profound hope for a frantic, frightened, foolish world.

From "The Welcome Mary House Story" there is more to share:

> "In yet another experience, I was given to see a disc-like luminous cloud, fixed in position, standing on edge precisely behind the huge concrete-cross atop Mount Krizevac on every evening (except when overcast). The cross has been seen turned into light and spinning in the dark of night although there is no electricity on the mountain. Many pilgrims - from places all over the world - have witnessed to having seen a silhouette of the Gospa on her knees, before this cross, praying in the early dawn as the sun rises. She has acknowledged to the visionaries that indeed it is really her.
>
> "And then, in August of 2002, at my family homestead back in the States, here on Long Island, I began seeing the Miracle of the Sun, the sun dancing. Daily except when overcast I've seen this phenomenon for going on eight years; I still see it. Remarkable! It began on the evening of the day when two Russian monks were scheduled to arrive following a flight from Moscow for a brief stay here at our home, The Welcome Mary House. I'd met them for the first time at the foot of Podbrdo (Apparition Hill) in Medjugorje (actually in nearby

Peace is *not* an unrealizable dream.
War is *not* an inevitable reality.

Bijakovici) after evening prayer with visionary Ivan during which time the Gospa arrived and spoke with him as usual.

"When the sun is dancing I can look directly at it with no discomfort, no injury to the eye. At such moments the sun looks as though to be a flat white disc — like a Communion host; others have seen it as a flat golden disc. The host does not cover the sun completely, there is a rim whiter than white edging the host at its perimeter. Surrounding the sun are concentric circles of colored light - pinkish-red and bluish-green - emitting their own rays.

"The sun for me has become a monstrance for the host. I know of a priest, Father Joseph Pelletier (now in Heaven) who had the same experience with the sun but beheld it as a monstrance. Once when a heavy, thick white cloud sailed along the sky and threatened to come right in the path of the sun, he begged Jesus not to let the cloud block out this beautiful sight. The Cloud sailed right along in back of the sun and as it passed behind it, he could see the brilliance of the sunshine on the cloud. This was in the early days of the Gospa's visits at Medjugorje during the early 1980s. (Special note: In July of 2008, for the first and only time, and this after six years of seeing the dance of the sun at sunset, I too beheld the sun as a monstrance, modestly bejeweled and sparkling.)

"Just several days ago, it is now December 2004, from my second-floor home office in the abbey, I saw through the trees an awesome sunset in the southwest. Wanting to get a better look at the now rapidly setting sun, I raced out to where I might see better; but alas too late, for the sun had disappeared behind neighboring buildings. God must have seen my disappointment, for in the now

Peace is *not* an unrealizable dream.
War is *not* an inevitable reality.

rapidly darkening sky appeared a huge golden disc, unmoving and perfectly circular; it was not the sun but clearly it was of God, a wonder beyond human logic and experience to explain. Several days later, again while looking at the dancing sun just before sunset, a luminous cloud extended from out of the disc as if reaching for the earth, stayed for a brief spell, then withdrew back into the host.

"It was Fr. Pelletier's considered thought that the host moves within the sun or that the sun moves in back of the host, because the brilliant white rim grows wider and then narrower, wider then narrower, repetitiously and at a speed that defies the eyes to tell what is actually going on. In my own experience, I've seen the rim as though spinning clockwise and counterclockwise at the same time. While it may very well be that the host is not moving at all but that the sun itself is spinning, seemingly in both directions at once, I too now am given to think that what I see is the host — in elegant display — moving within the sun.

"Of course ... what our Creator has created, he can manipulate. Or he can give us to see what he wants us to see even if it isn't actually happening. Amazingly, at Medjugorje I've been with large groups who have all seen the same thing, but sometimes with variations. A young mother with me saw the sun spinning off hearts; others saw it spinning off hoops of color; others saw long rays of the sun reaching down, touching the earth. These phenomena were visible from many different places throughout the surrounding geographic area.

"God, we know, is in a creative process of always revealing Himself to us in the context of our daily, material existence; inclusive of the sun and the stars. Wasn't it a star that led the three wise men to Jesus

Peace is *not* an unrealizable dream.
War is *not* an inevitable reality.

at his birth. This eternal, uncreated act of love is always constant, whether in the first moment of this universe, or in the evolving development of the human race, or in the first incarnation of Christ, or in the glorified life of the risen Christ now present, immersed immanently in this universe of ours.

"In closing I must add that looking at the sun at any other time would be enough to blind me if I dared look at it. It is a well-established scientific fact that the rays of the sun are so bright that they easily damage the retina of the eye and can cause blindness when looked at continuously for a minute or so.

"However, during the miracle of the sun at Fatima - 13 October 1917 - the 70,000 people gathered there were able to look at the sun for minutes without hurting their eyes in the slightest way. Indeed, many of us have also had the same privilege on occasions in Medjugorje."

These were incredible years, the years before John Paul II's papacy and the years after his election. There'd been the exceedingly important years-long apparitions before that election, this time in Egypt, witnessed by at least a million people (more people than any supernatural event in history); and yet the Western press, hostile to spirituality in general and Christianity in particular, all but ignored it. I share notes here from one of my journals:

"From 1968 to 1973 (just before the onset of the Medjugorje event) Our Lady appeared above a church called St. Mary's in the Middle East— it was far from a Catholic setting. The church belonged to the Orthodox – the Coptic Orthodox – and was situated, of all places, in Zeitun, Egypt, a suburb of Cairo. Mary, in the center of Islam! Mary, above a church that was located near the historic and holy area known as the Mataria—where she, Joseph, and

Peace is *not* an unrealizable dream.
War is *not* an inevitable reality.

the Christ Child had come to rest after fleeing into Egypt to escape the despot Herod.

"Standing atop and walking around the dome despite its smooth, sloping surface, she was dressed as if in a bright gown of light. She'd appear several times a week or only once a week, sometimes for only minutes, but oft'times for long periods —at night. She was seen arriving with a blinding explosion of light; then making her appearance in a clear and bright luminous body. She was seen by huge throngs, at times swelling to an estimated 250,000 — Christian and Muslim. The Muslims chanted from the Quran: "Mary, God has chosen thee. And purified thee; he has chosen thee. Above all women." She became known as the "Queen of Peace," to others "Mother of Light."

"Especially unique to the Zeitun apparition was the incense. Huge billows of purplish-red smoke with a fragrant odor would rise from the church, as from a million censers. Sometimes Mary's likeness formed in the smoke. At one point members of the Church commission witnessed the apparition for eighty minutes, and on May 5th, just a month after the main phenomena began, the patriarch announced that the apparitions were authentic and of God. 'In making this statement the Patriarchate declares with every faith, with deep joy, and with overflowing thanks to the heavenly grace, that the Virgin Mary, the Mother of Light, has appeared clearly and steadily on many different nights,' said the official statement. 'May God make this a sign of peace for the world.'

"Week after week — Muslims and Christians, believers and non-believers, Orthodox and Jews — were witness to an awesome spectacle in the middle of a densely populated suburb. Just six years later,

Peace is *not* an unrealizable dream.
War is *not* an inevitable reality.

in 1979, Poland's Cardinal Karol Wojtyla would become Pope John Paul II to lead the Church into the new millennium. Just two years after that, Our Lady began her visits in Medjugorje. The Egyptian apparitions had great significance. Zeitun is too meaningful a place to have been chosen by coincidence — the place where Mary, Joseph, and Jesus had gone to escape persecution!

"Without uttering a word Mary was saying volumes about the Middle East and the future. There was even a connection to Fatima. For centuries Portugal had been occupied by the Moors, a Muslim tribe, and, in fact, Fatima itself had been named after the daughter of Mohammad. The late Archbishop Fulton J. Sheen believed Mary wanted to be known as 'Our Lady of Fatima' as a sign and a promise that the Muslims, who accept the virgin birth of Christ, would eventually accept His divinity as well. In the latter days, predicted Saint Louis Marie Grignon de Montfort, the Muslims would be converted to Christianity."

I've always firmly believed, had the conviction, that the messages of Medjugorje are for all people, no matter of what religious persuasion. The Gospa, at Medjugorje, has always stressed the fact that to God differences do not exist. My feelings are borne out by many messages given by Mary. "In God there are no religions, no divisions...but you men have made divisions."

Every person, she has said, must be respected in his or her profession of faith. "We must respect everyone in their faith. One must never despise anyone because of their convictions. Believers have separated themselves from one another. But God controls all confessions as a king his subjects, through his ministers. Jesus Christ is the only mediator of salvation. Yet," she went on to say, "the power of the Holy Spirit is not equally strong in all the churches."

Peace is *not* an unrealizable dream.
War is *not* an inevitable reality.

One of my favorite examples of this love of God for all humankind, overriding all divisions, is a story the visionaries tell. They were asked once to inquire of Mary as to what constituted holiness. The Gospa drew their attention to a woman in the village who, she said, was the most holy person there. The visionaries were amazed. This woman was a Moslem, they said to Mary. "That is for God to decide," she answered with a smile.

All of the messages, she told Marija, concerned all people in the world — conversion, prayer, peace, fasting, penance — no matter their creed or nationality. This reminds me of Mother Teresa of Calcutta who is known to have said when explaining what she meant by conversion: "If you are going to be a Buddhist, then be the best Buddhist that you can be; if a Hindu, then the best Hindu; if a Christian, then the best Christian." To love the Ways others love God, to follow Christ while collaborating joyfully with those who walk another path, is what Mary has come to say.

I must end this chapter of my report by saying Mary is the most important woman in history. By her Fiat – her "Yes" to the angel – she entered into human history and changed the course of the world. From the very beginning, she was and is involved in the most important events of history and salvation. Therefore, whenever and wherever she was or she is appearing, it has been for a special reason.

To the point... I have just now received the following report: "By 7:00 o'clock on the morning of August 2nd 2009 (yesterday) the two wide paths heading up and all the way to the top of Mount Podbrdo were completely filled with people... many of them mistakenly believing Our Lady would be appearing on top, not realizing the location was the Blue Cross midway up the climb. There were many young people sprawled out in sleeping bags having spent the night in anticipation of Our Lady's early morning apparition. Though there can be no accurate measure of the amount of people present, we are confident in saying there were 50,000 people on and surrounding what has come to be known as Apparition Hill. It was an incredible sight — a sea of faces everywhere you looked.

Peace is *not* an unrealizable dream.
War is *not* an inevitable reality.

"**Mirjana** *who with Ivanka first saw the luminous figure of shimmering light on the hill Podbrdo back in June 1981* **came around 8:35. The apparition of Our Lady special for Mirjana began at 8:45 a.m.** — and lasted approximately 4 ½ minutes. Shortly after the apparition began, cries of surprise, shock, deep emotion and awe were heard rippling through the crowd from different directions, growing in magnitude. While Mirjana was enraptured in her own vision of the Blessed Virgin Mary, something had happened. . . .

". . . .A commotion in the crowd was paralleled by something that the pilgrims could not have known, by what Mirjana had seen; and Mirjana, on the other hand, while in ecstasy could not have known what the pilgrims were seeing during the apparition. During the apparition, Mirjana herself saw the sun behind Our Lady. When she came out of ecstasy, Mirjana had to be surprised at what was taking place.

"For the pilgrims themselves had also seen a miracle. The sun became a miraculous sign for them. More and more people began looking where the first ones were pointing—at the sun. Many were seeing the sun 'dancing' or 'spinning', others saw a cross illuminated in the sun, still others saw different colors within or streaming out of the sun. Tears were streaming down many faces, others stared in wonder, others in joy. And there were those who did not look up at all, so intense in their prayer as the apparition was still taking place.

"It was very moving as the pilgrims knew what a chance of a lifetime it was to see the actions of God take place right before their eyes. To know after the apparition that Mirjana also had the sun in her apparition, the sun behind Our Lady, confirmed the pilgrims' 'vision', and the pilgrims confirmed Mirjana's vision that the miracles were wed to each other.

"The apparition was shorter than normal... and watching Mirjana's face during the apparition it was noticed that her normal, varied expressions seen in the apparitions seemed to be changing at a faster speed than what is also typical. It is possible that the apparition lasted much longer for Mirjana than what passed in

Peace is *not* an unrealizable dream.
War is *not* an inevitable reality.

our time of 4 ½ minutes, as both Mirjana and Marija have testified at times that even though from the surface it looks like a short apparition, they often experienced a much longer apparition." Mirjana revealed that she has never seen the sun in an apparition throughout these 28 years of Our Lady appearing to her. And every time Our Lady mentioned the name of Her "Son" or Jesus or in the message referred to Him, the sun in the apparition behind Our Lady shone out brightly... which is why Mirjana stated after the apparition that she believed that in the apparition the sun was Christ's love illuminating all of us. Remarkable!

For Mirjana and Ivanka, the first of the Six to see Our Lady back in June 1981, the daily visits with the Virgin Mary had a relatively short duration. Interestingly, on her last *regular* appearance with Ivanka she had asked the seer what she would like. Ivanka asked to be able to see her earthly mother now in heaven. Our Lady smiled and nodded her head. Then all of a sudden, says Ivanka, my mom appeared. She was smiling. Our Lady told me to stand. I stood up. My mom hugged me, kissed me, and said, 'I am so poud of you!' My mom kissed me and then she was gone. After that the Blessed Virgin Mary said this to me: 'My dear child, today is our last encounter. Do not be sad, because I will come to you on every anniversary [of her first appearances].

On December 25th 1982 Our Lady said to Mirjana that she would no longer appear to her daily. Here I should note that early on in the apparitions each of the Six had been entrusted with a special ongoing assignment; for Mirjana it was to 'pray for unbelievers'. Anyway, the day when the Virgin Mary said she'd no longer appear to her daily, it was for Mirjana [as she has said] "the most difficult day of my lfe. To see Our Lady every day and all of a sudden she says to you that she will no longer be with you daily, for me that was unbelievable. I thought that maybe it won't, and can't be that way, so I cried and prayed for a long time. The next day, at the same time that I had my *daily* apparitions, I was kneeling again, praying and waiting, and that is how it was for a number of days following, all up until God gave me the strength through prayer to understand

Peace is *not* an unrealizable dream.
War is *not* an inevitable reality.

that this is God's plan and this is how it must be. And only through that praying of mine did it give me the strength to continue on."

And so it happened that from August 2, 1987, on the 2nd of every month Mirjana hears the voice of Our Lady inside her [it's called an inner locution], and sometimes she sees her, and she prays with her for nonbelievers… or as Our Lady always says, those who haven't yet come to know the love of God. Mary says, "My children, when you pray for them, you are praying for yourself and for your future." Says Mirjana, Our Lady looks for us to be an example, she doesn't look for our words. She is looking for us to speak with our lives, so that the unbelievers can see in us God, and God's love.

Twenty-eight years [as of 2009] have passed since that day the children at Medjugorje testified how the Blessed Virgin Mary was appearing to them. The parish church, Krizevac (Cross Mountain), and Mount Podbrdo (Apparition Hill), are places at which hope is renewed and the courageous steps toward Jesus begin, just as Mary the Queen of Peace tirelessly calls for in her messages.

As you remember, it all began in June 1981 during an afternoon walk with Ivanka Ivankovich and Mirjana Dragicevic down a macadam road, when Ivanka saw a Woman with a child in her arms a little farther from the path and cried out: *"There is Our Lady!"* What could Mirjana say in reply but: *"What do you mean, Our Lady? Why on earth would Our Lady appear to us?"* They ran home and described everything, and then once again with other kids, returned to the same place, only this time they all saw Our Lady. Already the next day the six of them, at the same time as the previous day, fearlessly over rocks and through brambles, ran to Our Lady. They prayed with her, talked with her, asked questions… Since that day — per the testimony of the visionaries — the Queen of Peace has appeared every day in this place now written onto the map of the world as the place where Heaven has touched the earth.

Peace is *not* an unrealizable dream.
War is *not* an inevitable reality.

THE GOSPA'S VISITS AT MEDJUGORJE DICTATED BY THE CIRCUMSTANCE IN WHICH PEOPLE TODAY LIVE

THE timing and manner of the Gospa's appearances at Medjugorje have been dictated by the circumstances in which people today live. It is not only a question of troubles, but also of insidious danger that is neither clearly perceived nor taken seriously.

"In a society brutalized by a scorn for God reaching even to the destruction of human beings... God reveals the power of the motherly heart! He is sending the Most Holy Virgin Mary right into such a time and such a world to draw people anew to the only Redeemer..." (Cardinal Franjo Kuharic, Primate of Croatia)

Yet this peril taken alone is capable of: 1) destroying the human species, 2) placing in jeopardy God's creative plan, 3) usurping Christ and His work for the rescue of all peoples with the singular aim of replacing Him with a state that is final spiritual ruin.

It's a time when we've assumed control of energies of cosmic dimensions and lost control of our destiny. And, in losing, we've awakened and caused to be arrayed against ourselves the dormant, destructive forces that exist within us and nature.

The Gospa Sees All This

THE Gospa who in all her apparitions throughout history points only to Jesus, never to herself, sees all this. Drawn by her Motherhood and by the trouble in which we find ourselves, she's come to us, to her children, to lead us to a new era, a new time.

She sees the serious threats the earth faces, and the limited amount of time we have to reverse this destruction. She sees that in the very near future, if the present trend continues, one-third of the world's productive land will have turned to dust, one million species will be extinct, and the world's climate will be changed beyond repair

The verdict is not yet in on whether damage to the ozone layer in the upper atmosphere which protects all life from damaging ultraviolet rays is also beyond repair... but this is a possibility. Destruction of the world's tropical rainforests makes headlines and magazine covers every day, and this devastation shows no signs yet of slowing down. The Gospa sees all this. She sees the need to heal the planet!

Too, the Gospa sees how an obscured sense of morality has favored the exchange of good for evil, resulting in our character becoming destructive, deadly, fierce and cruel.

She sees the transference of the center of everything from God to humanity, from God to us.

She sees how the balance of the world has shifted from its pivot... and how the unity of humanity has atomized, broken down, become divided, separated, fragmented. She sees how we've begun to take ignorance for wisdom... and base our programs for life upon it.

The Voice Of God Is Speaking
With Power At Medjugorje

ALL along Pope John Paul II was well informed about the events at Medjugorje. The Auxiliary Bishop of Rome, Mgr. Paul Hnilica, S.J., in the April issue of *Madre di Dio*, stated that he had gone to Medjugorje many times in order to investigate the Apparitions.

"I wanted to examine and understand what reasons the one who talks against Medjugorje and is opposed to it had for doing so. I am convinced that this is a case of slandering. ...Upon my conscience, I must come to the conclusion that the voice of God is speaking with

Peace is *not* an unrealizable dream.
War is *not* an inevitable reality.

power at Medjugorje." Bishop Hnilica, A Czechslovak and former prisoner for the Faith, was John Paul II's confidant and informant on Russia and Eastern Europe during the Soviet Union era.

In the fall of 1986 the Bishop stated: "The more I have gone to Medjugorje and the longer I have spoken with the children, so much more am I personally convinced of the genuineness of the Apparitions . . . When signs like Medjugorje happen before our eyes, it is the obligation of every Christian to take a stance concerning them."

On 21 April 1989, Bishop Hnilica, who met privately with the Pope once a week, gave a video taped interview while on pilgrimage in Medjugorje. He said that upon recently returning from a meeting in Moscow on behalf of the Pope, John Paul II admonished him for not stopping in Medjugorje on his return trip to Rome. The Auxiliary Bishop of Rome reported that the Pope concluded his admonition with, "If I wasn't a pope, I'd be in Medjugorje already!"

Father Rene Laurentin of France, one of the most authoritative living Mariologists, in response to the question, "You are very close to the positions of the Servant of God, John Paul II (regarding Medjugorje), aren't you," said this: "I regret to have to guide the Church from the Vatican and not from Medjugorje."

Medjugorje's Main Message

ONE of the main messages of Our Lady at Medjugorje from the very beginning has been, of course, the very profound act of her just being there — her actual presence at a time when disbelief has been rampant in a world in a rut and swirling in its own confusion. . . .

A world of bitter and reckless ideological and other kinds of warfare. A world become a place where, more and more, human life is not lived in the light of something greater than itself. In the lines of T. S. Eliot (and causing us to shiver) it's as though humanity is on a voyage "in a drifting boat with a slow leakage, the silent listening

Peace is *not* an unrealizable dream.
War is *not* an inevitable reality.

to the undeniable clamor of the bell of the last annunciation." Few could discount the possibility of it.

Are we in the last times, is there no tomorrow? Does Medjugorje represent the "bell of the last annunciation," a last opportunity and mercy to save ourselves? Perhaps. But even if it doesn't, one must admit that it is saying something immensely important, of profound instruction and bidding, for ourselves and indeed for all the world.

In that world grown perilously pagan now, dangerously toxic, the Gospa's message from the very beginning has been that God exists, that he hears us, and yes he cares; enormously. In our zeal to change we ridiculed the luminous visions that for so many generations shone in the little candles of our old, poor homes. Dazzled by the lights of the metropolis, those candles were extinguished for some of us, thus helping to extinguish the light our forebears had kindled. We have bartered holiness for convenience, loyalty for success, wisdom for information, tradition for fashion.

It's as though a world has vanished. All for us that remains is a sanctuary hidden in the realm of spirit.

The message of Medjugorje is essentially a message for a world that is undergoing a critical crisis of faith. The Gospa — sometimes sad but always wisely communicative — has said that the world is now on the edge of catastrophe. So there is a sense of urgency about the Medjugorje message that sets it apart from other apparitions.

Sir William Osler (1849-1919), one of the most revered physicians in the world of medicine, once warned that "the greater the ignorance the greater the dogmatism," and at a farewell dinner in his honor in 1905 he praised the humility associated with faith: "Nothing in life," he said, "is more wonderful than faith. It is the one great moving force which we can neither weigh in the balance nor test in the crucible."

Clearly, the Gospa has become a prophetess for our time, which has lost touch with itself and with God. And so we learn the answer to the question, "Why she the Madonna has come to Medjugorje

Peace is *not* an unrealizable dream.
War is *not* an inevitable reality.

and thus to the whole world?" She wants to put us in touch again. In looking at the world situation today, if one were delivering a State of the World Address, it would have to paraphrase the Gospa's "annunciation": The accumulation of sins in the world is so intense that it has brought the Human Enterprise to the brink of self-destruction. And it is not within the means of human beings to fashion a system of protection that would save us from the fate we are preparing for ourselves.

It bears repeating: it is not within the means of human beings to fashion a system of protection that would save us from the fate we are preparing for ourselves.

It is God our Creator whose ways are different than ours who offers the only option: "conversion, but coupled with reconciliation." A change of heart and surrender to our Source. The recognition that we are brothers and sisters not just under whatever flag we wave or land we live in, but brothers and sisters by the same supranational and supra-terrestial principle.

What We Are to Hold Fast to Ourselves

ONE thinks of the good Pope John XXIII when learning of the Gospa saying "it is you who are divided on earth; the Muslims, and the Orthodox, for the same reason as Catholics, are equal before my Son and me; you are all my children; love your Serbian, Orthodox and Muslim brothers, and the atheists who persecute you." In ultimate analysis, the Gospa's words help us to understand the wisdom that John revealed when he established a new era of ecumenism, bringing not only all Christians together but also people of all religions as well.

Also, this same pope started a new era in the history of Catholicism when he exhorted Catholics not to try to convert people of other religions because, he said, they are going to heaven anyway. In meeting with one leading Hindu guru, Pope Paul VI saluted him saying: "One day both you and I will meet in Heaven." Reportedly, Mother Teresa of Calcutta also repeated this identical statement to the same guru more recently in time.

Peace is *not* an unrealizable dream.
War is *not* an inevitable reality.

Adella my beloved honey and I once spent a most delightful afternoon with this "Saint of the Gutters" about whom I never tire telling the following story: Although Mother was a fiercely Catholic woman (who embraced the Gospa's visits at Medjugorje), her brand of religion was not exclusive. Convinced that each person she ministered to was "Christ in suffering" she reached out to people of all faiths and the faithless. "I do convert," she once said, when she was accused by the Hindu right-wing of converting poor Hindus to Catholicism. "I convert you to become a better Hindu or Moslem or Buddhist or Protestant. When you have found God it is up to you to do what you want with him."

But it is to the 'Abrahamic minorities', as I name them, in my own country and throughout the world that I call, to get moving towards making their own environment more just and human. Abraham - of the Jews, the Christians, the Muslims - was the first to be called by God to set out, face hardship, arouse his brothers and sisters and encourage them to start moving. I am absolutely convinced of the fact that all over the world, among all races, languages, religions, ideologies, there are men and women ready to serve their neighbor, ready for any sacrifice for the good of humanity, ready to build a more just and more human world, a Civilization of Love.

In ultimate analysis, the Gospa's words "it is you who are divided on earth, (all) are equal before my Son and me, you are all my children," is guiding people of all religions to Heaven through holiness that generally comes through the spirituality of prayer, meditation, and the practice of virtues. Spirituality is the highest function in guiding societies on Earth. But the Gospa sees that the world is burdened with a lack of spirituality. And because of this we are killing our future, killing our hope. Thus we must effect a major shift in the world that would have us move toward a completely Spiritual Culture, a global commonwealth of compassion, when there will be no more war or threat of war; no more slavery—of any kind.

It is our inescapable assignment.

Peace is *not* an unrealizable dream.
War is *not* an inevitable reality.

Thus, this is what we are to hold fast to ourselves: the sympathy and companionship of the unseen worlds. No doubt it is best for us now that they should be unseen. It cultivates in us that higher perception that we call faith...faith that isn't abstraction but ground to walk on.

But who can say that the time will not come when, even to those who live here upon earth, the unseen worlds shall no longer be unseen? John Paul II as well as all of the world's great mystics have known that there is a very little between us and God. And that if the doors of perception were cleansed, everything would appear to us as it is, infinite.

A Reflection: "The wolf shall dwell with the lamb, the leopard shall lie down with the goat, the calf and the lion and the yearling together; and a little child shall lead them," says Scripture in the Old Testament book of Isaiah, chapter 11, verse 6. Here is the reason, clearly without debate, why God would choose young people to convey His messages to us. It is at the same time reason and example. Unless one has the spiritual heart and soul of a child, words describing a utopian peace are not easily accepted beyond platitude.... What this Scripture verse says to us is that a child is the essence of innocence; conversion (what Our Lady is calling for at Medjugorje) is a return to that innocence.

Mary's Entire Life - In Time and Outside Or
Beyond Time - Constantly Reveals Prophetic Features.

IT is not so much a vision that Gospa brings to our world as a rightful perception of Reality, reality that is the Beyond unclouded by concepts and rational thought. Gospa herself comes to us as an apparition, yes, but also as a real person, as someone the Six can touch, hug and experience as more real even than members of their own families. Thus for the Six and also for us she is neither an image or a concept, but a substance for our hopes, an answer to our doubts, and a new way of knowing and living. The Apparition's greatest harbinger of course is the dislocation we daily witness more and more in our religious beliefs, political affiliations, social

Peace is *not* an unrealizable dream.
War is *not* an inevitable reality.

structures, establishment outlooks, personal morality, and life values.

For the moment, given our modern approach to reality, this dislocation is all most of us can use to connect with what the Six report of their experience with the Gospa. After all, we have been taught not to recognize any such vision or apparition; only the self-in-us can do so. But we have learned also to deny that self's existence or to dissect it into "parts," and in any case to tune out from the Heavenly knowledge through which it alone can then afford us. Thus we unknow it — and therefore we cannot respond to what the self perceives. More, we might even deny the Apparition's existence or explain away its effects. It is what can make any authentic visionary's believability difficult when sharing it with others.

Thus they - the Six - do not argue or defend; only to present...is their mission. In conclusion, it appears that without intermediaries whose apparitional experience has been directed to their inner selves, there is no other way open to the vision of Reality.

The message of Medjugorje quite frankly is a serious warning from Heaven to our world in the process of destroying itself. Thus, the role in part of the Mother of God in Medjugorje is a prophetic one.

Indeed, Mary's entire life - in time and outside or beyond time - constantly reveals prophetic features. Clearly, her service has not yet ended. Witness how her apparitions are relevant for our times: for threatening words are heard in our world, dark clouds are rising on the horizon, dangers are planetary in scope, human dignity and values are trampled under foot, consciousness of sin and the need for rescue or redemption have faded.

The Apparitions represent God's care and concern for the human soul, a call from the heavens to earth, the Divine response to the cries of our times. The Gospa's visitations at Medjugorje offer no new revelation, but lend validity to and confirm emphatically already existing revelation.

Peace is *not* an unrealizable dream.
War is *not* an inevitable reality.

"How Could I Have Missed It?"

FROM my report back in the early pages of this document one recalls the warm, clear morning on 6 August 1945 when the Enola Gay appeared in the sky over Hiroshima, Japan. Out of her belly fell the most awesome force the world has ever seen. In a flash, almost 100,000 people were cremated and a whole city obliterated. The heat of the firestorm that swept Hiroshima left the imprint of human shadows on stone as memorials of that dreadful day, and perhaps as a foretaste of what might be ahead; nuclear oblivion, perhaps.

In those dark days, few people would have rated the chances for peace as being very high. Though the very idea chilled the blood, I remember the time for building fall-out shelters seemed to be at hand. In 1945 the power of the 1917 Fatima event and message was underscored for the whole world during that atomic bomb explosion over Hiroshima.

A German Jesuit and seven of his colleagues were living only eight blocks from the blinding center of the nuclear flash, yet all escaped while flaming death screamed around them. Until recently, all eight occupants of that building were alive and well while others living some distance away continued to die from the radiation effects of that frightful holocaust.

Over the years some two hundred scientists have examined these eight survivors, trying to discover what could have spared them from incineration or the lethal storm of radiation. Speaking on TV in the United States, the German Jesuit, Fr. Hubert Shiffner, gave the startling answer. "In that house the rosary was prayed every day. In that house, we were living the message of Fatima." Hence, in the very light of the nuclear flash that threatens us all, we can see the sign of our salvation writ large. The Woman "more brilliant than the sun" has intervened in the most critical hour of human history and promised to save the world, stamping her words with "the most obvious and colossal miracle of history" of which the Medjugorje event is its completion.

At the same time she dramatically confirmed the faith of the Church in anticipation of one of its greatest spiritual crises in 2,000 years. Fervently I pray that we will respond to her pleading message and not spurn the hand held out to rescue and save us. "Peace, peace, you must seek peace," she cries. "There must be peace on earth, you must be reconciled with God and with each other. Peace, peace, peace."

> I recall a day spent with Fr. George Zabelka, the Catholic Chaplain who served the Atomic Bomb Crews in the summer of 1945. He once got into a "dialogue" with Boston's Fr. Charlie McCarthy, a Byzantine Rite priest, who I came to meet and know not only as a married Eastern Rite cleric with a large family; but also as a theologian and lawyer. Here in part is how it went: "What about all those children destroyed at Auschwitz?" Zabelka asked in a tone that was demanding and aggressive. "What about all those children destroyed at Hiroshima and Nagasaki?" McCarthy retorted. . . . "And never forget, Father," he continued, "it was baptized Christians who were the primary executioners of Auschwitz, Hiroshima and Nagasaki."
>
> The exchange occurred in 1973 at a retreat McCarthy was conducting on Christian Nonviolence for the priests out in Michigan. At the time he was not aware of Zabelka's involvement with the A-Bomb Group. Needless to say, Fr. Zabelka was no believer in nonviolence; his friends from behind his back called him "General George" knowing that he once received a military reprimand for "excessive zeal". Yet, unbeknown to Fr. McCarthy until several years later, Zabelka left that retreat center fighting round one of what was to be a two year battle for his faith. In December 1975, McCarthy received Zabelka's annual Christmas letter the last paragraph of which announced he had reached the conclusion

Peace is *not* an unrealizable dream.
War is *not* an inevitable reality.

that Jesus taught a way of nonviolent love of friends and enemies and that, therefore, "I must do an about face."

Years later, to a European journalist, he described his ordeal through these years. "I went through a crisis of faith. I'm a practical man and those words of Jesus - 'Love your enemies, do good to those who hate you...Turn the other cheek when someone strikes you...' - were completely impractical. Impractical and unworkable. I couldn't understand it. In many ways I still don't. Yet Jesus took this course of suffering and nonviolence. His words were so clear, and there is the example of His life and death. For me, the issue was very simple. Either Jesus was God or not.

If not, then His words could be dismissed as idealism. But if He was God, then what He said He meant. He wasn't kidding. He could not be dismissed as an idealist who didn't understand reality. So, either I accept what He says as coming from God or else I forget about the whole business... Forget about Christianity. My choice was made on the basis of faith."

In 1982-83, at the age of 67, Fr. George walked 7,500 miles from the Nuclear Submarine Base of Bangor, Washington, to Bethlehem, Israel, teaching what Jesus taught about homicide and enmity. In England, a television documentary was made of his life – The Reluctant Prophet – which since has been shown throughout the world. The anniversaries of the bombings of Hiroshima and Nagasaki were always exceptional days for him. On August 6 one year, he was proclaiming Jesus' way of peace to 1,500 people in St. James Church, Medjugorje. In 1984, he returned to Hiroshima and Nagasaki as "a Christian and a priest" to ask forgiveness from the 'hibakusha'

Peace is *not* an unrealizable dream.
War is *not* an inevitable reality.

(the disfigured victims of the bombings) for his part in "bringing you death instead of the fullness of life, for bringing you misery instead of mercy."

On the morning of 6 August 1987 Fr. Zabelka made the Stations of the Cross on Mt. Krizevac at Medjugorje. Shortly before 8:13 am, the time of the Hiroshima bombing, all stopped on the side of the mountain for a moment of quiet remembrance. Then friends saw a deep and vast wound, that none had ever seen before or after. Fr. George, overwhelmed with remorse, burst out sobbing, uttering between gasping breaths, "How could I have missed it?"

Peace is *not* an unrealizable dream.
War is *not* an inevitable reality.

"PROTECT MEDJUGORJE"
SAID JOHN PAUL II

IT is extremely noteworthy that the reported apparitions at Medjugorje are the first apparitions in history to be thoroughly investigated by science.

The current attitude of the church after 28 years of scrutiny is a kind of provisional approval. Both the pope and the former Yugoslavian bishops are treating and nurturing Medjugorje as a legitimate place of pilgrimage. The Vatican is not in a hurry to make an official statement concerning the apparitions. The apparitions must first run their course, come to an end. It is the established protocol, the tradition.

And yet Pope John Paul II when alive did allow that if he were not the pope he'd have already been in Medjugorje. When speaking to Fra Jozo Zovko, pastor of the parish there, John Paul told him, "Protect Medjugorje." To a high ranking prelate from South America he said, "Affirm everything that concerns Medjugorje." Too, he'd go to Medjugorje every day as a pilgrim in his prayers, to unite in prayer with all those who pray there or receive a callng for prayer from there. Once in closing a letter to dear friends back in Poland he wrote: "And now we every day return to Medjugorje in prayer."

And Cardinal-designate Hans Urs von Balthazar, who was considered one of the greatest theologians in the 20th century, but passed away on 26 June 1988 two days before he was to receive the red hat from the Pope, had reached this conclusion: "Medjugorje's theology rings true. I'm convinced of its truth. And everything about Medjugorje is authentic, in Catholic sense. What's happening there is so evident, so convincing."

THE whole world wept when this pope died, this shepherd of titanic stature, having a better sense now of how the apostles felt after the death and Ascension of our dear Lord, Jesus the Christ. The Golgotha of John Paul II's last moments, then his silent passing away in joy and in confidence in Mary, was an incomparable sermon before the whole world. Precious hero, he'd been light and inspiration in a world that had lost its faith and hope. We mourned the loss of this great intellect, poet and mystic who spent seven hours each day in prayer and looked at all people with the eyes of Christ; this first non-Italian born pope in over 400 years...who showed us how to respect and love each other; who taught us, all the world, that there is no such thing as a disposable human being.

He would say that the greatest sickness in the world today is that we don't appreciate the value of human life. He taught us how to forgive, laugh and cry; to know at the core of our beings that we are loved unconditionally; he elevated the world to a whole new awareness if not experience of God.

This Polish pope, the holiest of renaissance men, the one who reshaped the modern world in Mary's prayerful image, is the one who kept the world from descending into moral extinction. Exclaimed one young man, a student, at this pope's funeral: "He put the flavor in the soup of the world!"

It was John Paul II more than anyone who can be credited with one of history's great events, the fall of what was the most threatening evil up to that time in history. Ancient Rome was evil. So was Genghis Khan. There was tremendous evil in Babylonian times, and in ancient Egypt. There were the great dangers of Nazism. But no evil empire ever had the capacity as the Soviets did to destroy the world with nuclear weapons, no empire was so militantly atheistic, and no empire was so close to enslaving the world.

Peace is *not* an unrealizable dream.
War is *not* an inevitable reality.

He'd been born into an era during which time Hitler was out to control the world, Communism was out to enslave the world, and Terrorism, if it couldn't have its way, was out to destroy the world. And yet those who met him described a remarkable peace. Regularly he'd meet with the world's leading scientists and listen to what they had to report. He was a good listener. When they'd finish, and all are in agreement on this, not only had he understood everything they'd said, but he would take the conversation to a whole other level - he was profound, they'd say.

Had he seen the Virgin Mary, the Blessed Mother of Jesus? By many it is believed that he did. He certainly provided exceptional guidance to both the Church and the world at large; and his exhortations often paralleled the messages of Medjugorje. Indeed, it is said that early during her visits at Medjugorje, Our Lady told one of the visionaries that she "handpicked this man to be Pope." Her visits began in June of 1981. It was just three years earlier, in 1978, that Poland's Karol Wojtyla was elected Pope

On 24 June 1977 — the same day that Mary would appear four years later at Medjugorje for the first time — in an address as a cardinal he said this: "We find ourselves in the presence of the greatest confrontation in history, the greatest mankind has ever had to confront. We are facing the final confrontation between the church and the anti-Church, between the Gospel and the anti-Gospel."

This man had the aura of a visionary, a brightness around him that was almost incandescent. I recall very well John Paul II's first visit to America and being at the entranceway to the United Nations awaiting the Pontiff's arrival where he was scheduled to give a speech.

I'll never forget how struck I was by that aura. I knew without a kernel of doubt that I was in the presence of a truly God-sent man. It was not for nothing that the Blessed Mother herself chose this man, Karol Cardinal Wojtyla, to be Pope.

Peace is *not* an unrealizable dream.
War is *not* an inevitable reality.

It was no accident or without Divine impulse that in the 19th century, the Polish poet Julius Slowacki (1809-1849) had the premonition that a Slavonic Pope would come to the See of Peter:

THE SLAVONIC POPE

In an age of discord
God rings the massive bell, a clarion call:
There is an empty throne for a Slavonic Pope.
The sun radiating from his face
Is a beacon for his followers;
Ever growing throngs and tribes will follow him
Toward the light where is God.
Listening to his prayers and his commands,
Not only will the people hear him,
But the sun will stop
Because there is power.
Because there is a miracle.

And power is indeed needed to
Raise up this world to God.
So here he comes, this Slavonic Pope-Brother
Of the peoples of all nations;
He will distribute love as generously as, today,
The leaders of the world distribute their guns.
His spiritual power will take
The whole world in his hands.
He will cleanse the wounds of the world
Of corruption, vermin and poison.
He will bring new health, he will bring light and love
And save the world.
He will sweep out the interior of the churches,
Even their very porches;
He will show the place of God
In the creation of the world as clearly as
The light of day.

Peace is *not* an unrealizable dream.
War is *not* an inevitable reality.

In 1862, shortly after Slowacki's death, it was not without Divine impulse that the "Twin Pillars of Victory" were the subject of St. John Bosco's prophetic dream. It was revealed to him that peace in the world would come only after a fierce battle in which the Pope would triumph by anchoring Peter's barque, the Church, to the secure pillars of the Eucharist and a fervent devotion to Mary. The image of that prophecy is beautifully captured on canvas showing the great Ship of Church, in stormy waters, sailing between those two pillars with the Pope standing tall over the bow, scanning the sea and its distant horizon.

Two decades later, on 13 October 1884, it was not without Divine impulse that Pope Leo XIII experienced a vision in which he heard Satan ask God for 100 years. Satan boasted that, if he were given sufficient time and power, he could destroy the Church and drag the world to hell.

A full century later history records one-hundred years of destruction the likes of which history had never before known. It also records a pope, John Paul II, who has successfully if not masterfully steered the grand Ship of Church into the Third Christian Millennium.

His courage, dignity and faith changed the course of human history as he led the Church, and the world, into the new millennium. Like Jesus 2,000 years before him, he'd been saying for all 26 years of his pontificat, "Be not afraid. Trust. Believe."

Regarding St. John Bosco's prophetic dream of the Twin Pillars of Victory, in yet another of my witnessed "miracles of the sun" from my home here on Long Island, I once saw in a sunset two luminous pillar-like clouds, one on either side of the sun. A friend saw the same pillar-like clouds from her home many miles away.

Peace is *not* an unrealizable dream.
War is *not* an inevitable reality.

AN ARRANGEMENT MADE IN HEAVEN
AND SEALED ON EARTH

On 22 October 1978 a non-Italian was invested as pope for the first time in 455 years. Not since 1846 had one so young as Wojtyla - he was 58 - sat upon St. Peter's throne. His election was an enormous surprise and a Vatican-shaking departure. The path from little Wadowice where he'd been born and raised to the most important and influential post of spiritual leadership in the world was a long and often challenging one for Karol Wojtyla. This remarkable young man had already experienced by the age of 26, more of the trials and tragedy of human experience than most popes experience in a lifetime. Not only had he lived through the horrors of a world war at its epicenter and seen his country dismembered, he had also been witness at Ground Zero to one of the most evil and calculated acts of genocide in human history; at the same time he'd seen all of his immediate family die.

With him you have an existential experience that is not learned in conferences or papers or even in theology. He was there in the worst place. They were all horrible, but Poland was especially horrible - crushed as it was in a vise-like grip between the Nazi occupiers from the West and the Russian counterforce from the East. We will never see John Paul's like again, not because the next pope can't or won't think about the Shoah, the Holocaust, but because this pope was there.

THE Wojtyla family apartment at 7 Koscielna Street was right next to the 650-year-old parish church of the Holy Virgin Mary. It is fitting that the future pope should be baptized, receive his first holy communion, and be confirmed here, for throughout what would be a long life John Paul II had made a particular devotion to Mary, our Most Holy Mother.

After the Nazis in 1939 invaded Poland and, as time went by, they deported many of Karol's Jewish childhood friends, his professors and anybody who resisted the occupation to concentration camps, including nearby Auschwitz; Karol Wojtyla himself did forced labor in a quarry and later a chemical factory.

Amid that horror, Wojtyla found a secret life, as an actor in an underground theater group, and in a budding spiritual and religious calling that drew him into illegal prayer meetings. Both vocations tugged at him. In 1942, he surprised his friends by saying that the choice had been made for him: He would be a priest. He immediately began studies in an underground seminary in Krakow. Subsequently, after a Nazis sweep of Krakow sent thousands of able-bodied Poles to the concentration camps without warning, Archbishop Adam Sapieha, Wojtyla's mentor, took all his secret seminarians into his own mansion, where they hid until the end of the war. On 1 November 1946 Karol Wojtyla was ordained a priest of the Archdiocese of Krakow.

WOJTYLA was born in 1920 and died in 2005. While he'd been born in the wake of Our Lady's 1917 Visitations at Fatima, Portugal, his years as Pope embraced the years of her Visitations at Medjugorje, beginning in 1981, and continuing even now after his death.

His life from beginning to end had pretty much spanned a century towards the end of which lights seem to be going out in the West, and in the East as well. The twilight of our civilization seems to be signaled by our fanatical embrace of the paths that lead to

Peace is *not* an unrealizable dream.
War is *not* an inevitable reality.

death; as we slay life at its very source, in the wombs of mothers; as manifold injustices cry out to heaven for vengeance; as unbridled hedonism demands ever-greater license for its exercise.

All throughout his priesthood, inclusive of his years as a seminarian, reports of the Virgin Mary's visits were coming in from places all over the world. From deep in the former Soviet Union, to the damp and windswept peat of Ireland, to a mountainside in Venezuela, to war-torn Yugoslavia, we on earth were experiencing a major supernatural episode.

Reports of unusual events, spiritual events, were coming from every habitable continent. The accounts were of an apparitional woman calling herself the Blessed Virgin Mary who appeared to visionaries and gave them inspiration, instructions, and messages, including warnings about the future of the world.

She came as a bright light in an era of spiritual darkness, a young mother calling her children away from danger and exposing the unseen.

Often there'd be a Christ-Child in her matronly arms. Our world has lost its sense of God and spirituality, she'd say. Such events as these were unlike any reported in 2,000 years, since Christ Himself appeared after death to His apostles.

Actually, the cycle of Mary's appearances began in the 19th century. Mary has appeared constantly during the past century, the 20th, in an effort to point us back in the right direction, stepping up her activity greatly since 1981. Mary's mission is to point to Christ. By the merits of her earthly faith and suffering she has gained a special place in paradise. She is to be honored, not worshipped. She was full of grace while on earth and is full of grace as a key messenger of Heaven.

She isn't here to replace Christ, but to serve as His forerunner as she was His forerunner two millennia ago. As Martin Luther once said, "Without doubt Mary is the Mother of God. And in this one word is contained all the honor which can be given to her." She's

Peace is *not* an unrealizable dream.
War is *not* an inevitable reality.

not a godhead. She's not part of the Trinity. She's the 'handmaid' of the Lord, and as such she's an instrument of the Holy Spirit.

It was neither accidental nor coincidental that Karol Wojtyla was born into this particular era, born to an obscure mother in a village soon to be the epicenter of a Second World War. It was part of an arrangement that had been made in Heaven and meant to be sealed by Karol's particular devotion of a lifetime to the Virgin Mary, the Gospa, who herself arrived in what was an obscure village in the Balkans...just three years after Karol had been elected pope. It was an arrangement made in Heaven and Sealed on Earth. . . . At a time in history when there'd been a desperate longing in the human soul for God who sometimes seems not to be there, not with answer, God presented Karol Wojtyla and Mary as though his two calling cards saying in effect, "I exist, I am not without answer."

Our Lady has explained her visits at Medjugorje as the beginning of a new time, a new era, a new path. It's as if we've been in school for our entire lives, receiving an education that teaches the exact opposite of the way the universe actually functions. We try to make things work, as we've been taught, and we may even enjoy some degree of success, but for most of us things never seem to work out as well as we had hoped. That perfect relationship never materializes, or if it does, it soon sours or fades away. Or it may seem as though there is never quite enough money; we never feel truly secure or abundant.

Thus, our first task in building the new world is to admit that our "life education" has not necessarily taught us a satisfying way to live. We must return to kindergarten and start to learn a way of life that is completely opposite of the way we approached things before.

This may not be easy for us, and it will take time, commitment, and courage. Therefore, it's very important to be compassionate with ourselves, to continually remind ourselves how tremendous this task is that we are undertaking. It is why the Gospa at Medjugorje speaks very simply, using few words, and is taking so long, years long, to get her message across to us.

Peace is *not* an unrealizable dream.
War is *not* an inevitable reality.

It is the way of a mother for her to exercise extraordinary patience when teaching her children. It is the way of a mother to use simple words, simple language, and to keep on repeating herself no matter how long it takes until the child finally understands, gets it right. This is how it is with the Gospa at Medjugorje.

Meanwhile, many in the world keep on asking, why doesn't she say more, why doesn't she explain things, why doesn't she answer our questions? They just haven't "gotten it" yet. We have become a world too swollen with words, too puffed up with our own thought intelligence. The Gospa would have us know simpler times, a deeper faith, a more hope-filled and thus brighter future. She's leading us in that direction—with little steps.

It's as though the Gospa would have us know that just as a baby learns to walk by falling down repeatedly, we must remember that we are babies in the new world. We will learn by making lots of mistakes and often we may feel ignorant, frightened, or unsure of ourselves.

But we would not get angry at a baby every time he or she fell down (if we did, they'd probably never learn to walk with full confidence and power). So we must try not to criticize ourselves if we are not able to live and express ourselves as fully as we wish immediately — a lesson I'm still grappling with.

We are now learning to live in accordance with the true laws of the universe. God who is omnipotent has made a world that runs by laws, and he does not like to break those laws. Still, because what he creates he can manipulate, God can do anything he likes. At Medjugorje we've seen a lot of that manipulation at work. "The doings of God's logic" is how some folks explain it. God's plan, from how the Gospa presents it, is to see his Human Enterprise living in harmony with the universe.

Living in harmony with the universe is living totally alive, full of vitality, joy, serenity, love, integrity — fruitfully alive in life that is the highest value. So, although letting go of the old world may seem difficult at times, it is well worth whatever it takes to make the transition into the new world.

Peace is *not* an unrealizable dream.
War is *not* an inevitable reality.

"Plato's Cave" is an allegory that speaks pointedly to our time in history: Plato pictured our world as a group of men sitting in a cave watching the shadows that the fire makes on the wall {as in a cinema}. Someone comes running in to tell them. "Hey! There's a more real world outside! It's all around us. Those are only shadows of it. Come out and see!" The illusion of this world is that by which we mistake the figures on the screen for reality. This is the sin of idolatry, for idolatry is nothing but the worship of images, the mistaking the image of truth for Truth itself.

Our Gospa comes at a time when we are still living in biblical times, still living at the cave age of establishing right human relations on this planet. We have been able to look at the stars with gigantic telescopes, but has this species honestly tried to lift its heart and soul to the universe?

Have we tried to become not only a global family but a spiritual family, a commonwealth of compassion, standing in awe before the beautiful, stupendous creation? Have we really asked ourselves the fundamental question: what is this little planet in the universe and what is our purpose and destiny on it? Must we not see ourselves as a meaningful part of total creation and of the total stream of time?

These are the great questions we must ask! It is why at Medjugorje the Gospa has come—and stays! We have to get beyond the superficial and peripheral things if we're going to get to know the true Medjugorje, the Medjugorje that makes the 'Mystery of God' approachable. It's said that almost thirty million people from all over the world have visited Medjugorje. Of those, few have left the valley unchanged or untouched in some way.

Quite remarkably, on the night of John Paul II's death, Ivan, one of the Medjugorje visionaries, reports that while "recommending intentions to Our Lady" during her Apparition, suddenly a young, radiant John Paul appeared at her left side. Smiling, he was dressed in a white robe and was draped in a gold cape. "This is my son," she told Ivan. "He is with me."

Peace is *not* an unrealizable dream.
War is *not* an inevitable reality.

This beloved pope who had unofficially embraced the apparitions as authentic, urging bishops visiting Rome to go to Medjugorje, and stating that he wished to go himself, finally now had that wish granted but in a way he probably never imagined: accompanied by his beloved Blessed Virgin Mary.

Peace is *not* an unrealizable dream.
War is *not* an inevitable reality.

THE WOMAN WITH A BROOM

I'VE always been heartened in my quest for world peace by signs of what one can only describe as life everlasting: the invincible determination of human beings to rise out of the deadly dust of war and start over again. Always the signs are little things, the gestures of little people. Yet it seems to me that those individual gestures are always bigger with promise for the future than great political events.

I recall the devouring and devastating machine of war that smashed its way across Europe in mid-20th century. From one end of the vast battlefield to the other, from the craters of London to the rubble of Budapest and Stalingrad, from the shattered port of Le Havre to the Pompeii-like desolation of Naples, the sights were terrible and filled us with despair.

But then there were the scenes - "the gestures of little people" - that inspired hope.

For example, from earlier pages in this volume we recall the story of the 1944 Cana-like miracle, of the 20,000 German war prisoners being marched through the streets of Moscow, the crowd of mostly women with clenched fists, the soldiers and police hardly able to hold them back, but then an elderly woman who took a crust of black bread and managed to thrust it into the pocket of one of the prisoners, and then women from every side running to the prisoners pushing into their hands bread, cigarettes, whatever they had. They were no longer enemies. They were people.

It was a Cana-like miracle, except it was not water but vinegar that was changed to wine. It was war shown for what it really is: a male sickness. For if it hadn't been for the women, there wouldn't have been the wine. The women whose gesture of compassion showed just how simple a thing reconciliation can really be when the heart is right. In this story, it was simply "a crust of black bread." That's all it was. But it was enough. It started the others running, with their bread and whatever else they had. It couldn't have been much, perhaps all they had, because of the war. But it was enough.

In the act of giving the bread, was revealed the hidden things of the spirit to the spirit. Something mightier than hate and hostility took over. Love was born. There was no need to judge and condemn. Instead, there was a new awareness, a new understanding. There was a certain contentment, a new freedom. God's Love, always present, was at work.

Then there is the equally powerful story of great lesson, the story of "the woman with a broom." Anne O'Hare McCormick of The New York Times in excerpts from "Bulldozer and the Woman with a Broom" (28 March 1945), tells it this way: "Every correspondent who has been near the front has seen the woman with the broom described by John MacCormac in a dispatch from the United States Ninth Army Headquarters east of the Rhine. In a devastated town two miles behind the fighting line he observed a woman emerge from a cellar and, though her house was a ruin, proceed to sweep away the dust and rubble that covered the doorstep.

"This woman happened to be German, but in every war-ravaged country the woman with a broom trying to clear away the debris that used to be her home is as familiar and monotonous a sight as ruin itself. In one flattened village in Holland after another, dazed old men were standing in wavering clusters in the shell-pocked fields, but the women were working in the dooryards that a few hours before had led to houses.

"Several were trying to tie their chrysanthemum stalks to the poles that had held them up. The chrysanthemums were still blooming, bright yellow beside piles of brick dust, and the housewives were mechanically starting to save the one whole thing that survived the wreck of the shattered cottages. . . . . .

Peace is *not* an unrealizable dream.
War is *not* an inevitable reality.

"But the woman in Evreux, in battered Normandy, was not thinking so far ahead when she appeared with her broom that bleak Sunday morning and began raising the dust in the path of General de Gaulle and the distinguished visitors from Paris. With a dash and energy as impatient as General Patton's, as he sweeps across the German plain, she was making a broomstick attack upon the crumbled stones that lay atop a tiny patch of garden. She paid no attention to the cortege skirting the shell holes in the road until a woman in the party stopped to ask her what she thought she was doing with a broom in the wake of 2,000-pound bombs. 'Who's to save the cabbages and onions if I don't? They're all that's left of all the work of all my life,' she said fiercely. 'And somebody has to begin clearing away this mess.'

"Then there was the old woman sweeping out a cowshed in the Agro Romano, near Rome. The land had been flooded by the Germans and was once more a breeding place for malarial mosquitoes, banished by the efforts of fifty years. The house was gone. In a fifty-mile radius not an animal was left. The farmer, who had lost a hand in a minefield, looked at us with hopeless eyes; but the woman kept on sweeping, clearing a little space in the wreckage to begin life anew.

"The woman with a broom is both symbol and promise. It's pretty futile to start attacking the ruins of great cities with a kitchen broom. Yet everywhere before the monster bulldozers arrive to clear paths for the armies through the debris left by the bombers, women instinctively seize their brooms in this age old gesture of cleaning up the mess the men have made.

"There's no assurance that they can clear it up this time, but today there are more women than men in Europe, widows of soldiers, widows of hostages, widows of the last war, and they are bound to try. In Paris an association of widows of men executed by the Germans is headed by a lovely girl widow. . . . 'We are the trustees of the future,' the French girl asserted. 'We cannot leave it to the next generation because they won't have seen what we have seen, and they won't understand.'

Peace is *not* an unrealizable dream.
War is *not* an inevitable reality.

"It isn't chance that women are named for the first time to a conference called to set up the framework of international order (the 1945 San Francisco conference of delegates from 50 nations that established the United Nations). There should be more of them, for they are in the wars now, and millions of them have nothing much left but a broom."

The Special Mission Of Woman

WHEN women clear away the debris of war, instinctively they are trying to restore God's order in the chaos made by the male of our species. They see that beyond the need to reconstruct economies and political forms from the crumbled structures of the past, that there is a need to restore the spiritual value of human life trampled upon by dictators and distorted by false philosophers, undervalued by national and world leaders as though having no merited place or practical end.

It is with this, the latter, that woman, as trustee, must primarily concern herself for the sake of future generations. I have concluded that the spiritual nourishment of the race is the special mission of the eternal woman whose unique position has inspired humankind for centuries.

It bears repeating: The spiritual nourishment of the race is the special mission of the eternal woman whose unique position has inspired humankind for centuries.

The Gospa, as I have come to perceive and know her, has inspired generations for centuries. It is she who has been God's special messenger in our most difficult times. God who is the source of all life; the creator of universe behind universe; of unimaginable depths of interstellar space, and of light-years without end. But he is also the indwelling life of our own little selves.

And just as a whole world full of electricity will not light a house unless the house itself is prepared to receive that electricity, so the infinite and eternal life of God cannot help us unless we are prepared to receive that life within ourselves.

Peace is *not* an unrealizable dream.
War is *not* an inevitable reality.

It is why the Gospa has come to Medjugorje, and why she has stayed for so many years, in what historically has been a totally unprecedented and unimaginable event. "The kingdom of God is within you," said Jesus. And it is the indwelling light, the secret place of the consciousness of the Most High that is the kingdom of Heaven in its present manifestation on this earth. Learning to live in the kingdom of Heaven "in its present manifestation" is learning to turn on the light of God within.

We must learn, I've found, that God is not an unreasonable and impulsive sovereign who breaks His own laws at will. As soon as we learn that God does things through us (not for us), the matter becomes as simple as breathing, as inevitable as sunrise. "But God is omnipotent!" some will say. "He can do anything he likes!" Yes, but He has made a world that runs by law, and He does not like to break those laws.

Few of us in the north would ask God to produce a full-grown rose out of doors in January. Yet He can do this very thing, if we adapt our greenhouses to His laws of heart and light, so as to provide the necessities of the rose. And He can produce a full-blown answer to prayer if we adapt our earthly tabernacles to His laws of love and faith so as to provides the necessities of answered prayer.

Some day, perhaps sooner than one might think, the world will come to understand this fact, as it is now beginning to understand the miracle of light wave; for one generation's miracles are the commonplaces of another generation.

Medjugorje and its various phenomena involving light and the luminous invites that understanding. When the Gospa first appeared at Medjugorje she was seen as a luminous figure of shimmering light. In subsequent visits her Presence was preceded by a brilliant light that flashed three times. A "light between the hills" — in this valley where the song of bird and cricket was at times the only sound to break the silence — is how the locals began speaking of her.

Peace is *not* an unrealizable dream.
War is *not* an inevitable reality.

~~ ENDNOTES ~~

THE GEORGE WASHINGTON CARVER STORY

HE'D BEEN LIKE ONE OF
A NEW SPECIES ARISING ON THE PLANET

AT THE THRESHOLD
OF THE NEXT STEP
IN HUMANITY'S EVOLUTION

ON EARTH AS IT IS IN HEAVEN

A PROPOSAL
"A Global Commonwealth
of Compassion"

THE GEORGE WASHINGTON CARVER STORY

PREFACE: In the chapter A Hinge Between Two Ages of this volume I wrote this: "How easy it is to dupe ourselves and others with exaggerated intelligence. How deep, so very deep is the dungeon that we're digging and building for ourselves as we turn our backs to God. What a lot of undirected-propelling through cloudy-space there is in too many college classrooms today. Indeed, it is one of the reasons why our brains are so foggy, why the world is foggy — perhaps even mad. If not mad, lost." I'd prefaced this telling entry from one of my journals by noting that "Today's changed perception of the human brain has important implications for education, but also for addressing the problem that is war." I said that I'd explain in my Endnotes.

I'LL begin by saying that this report would be sorely lacking if it did not include the story of a scientist who talked to flowers and the flowers talked to him revealing their secrets. Although amazingly simple in how he thought and in his habits, George Washington Carver is considered today as great a genius in his field as Edison and Burbank and Steinmetz were in theirs.

These men lived in a time, as have I, that when someone spoke of the brain the belief had been that we had but one brain; it was the general view which prevailed until fairly recently. In the 1960s a new perception of the human brain led to the belief that we have two brains, not one!

Two brains. There is no way to overstate the importance of this enormously startling revelation. The story of George Washington Carver which I'll share in just a moment will explain.

This new view was accompanied by research that greatly expanded existing theories about the nature of human consciousness. This changed perception of the human brain and why I include it in my report has important implications for addressing the problem that is war. For example, it helps explain why an excessive reliance on reason does not lead to wisdom and life, harmony and peace, a world without war or threat of war.

Yet, most all the world today operates and plans programs for life based upon the workings of the left-brain only— completely oblivious of why Creator-God gave us a right-brain, a distinctly different device than that of the left-brain.

Yes, to learn that the brain has two hemispheres a left-brain and a right-brain was a BIG surprise for most all of us. To learn that neither of the two are in any way the same in purpose or in function, but yoked together in what is the whole-brain, yoked together as a team, complementing each other in purpose and function, one needing the other, was as though a mind boggling revelation of kind. A real surprise.

Given our choice we would no more think of choosing to live blind in one eye or walking with one leg missing than we'd think of jumping off a bridge. And yet we continue building our world with only the left brain operating. It's why we stumble and fall so much in our efforts to create a sane and sustainable world; a world without war and threat of war, a world without slavery—of any kind.

Not to exhaust the reader but there is need to explain. The two hemispheres of the brain appear to duplicate each other when casually examined. Yet research shows that they are functionally distinct. The left side is normally referred to as the logical, digital side; while the right is seen as using an analogue approach. The left is sequential, and the right is wholistic. It is almost as if we had in our heads both Democritus, the reductionist, and the wholistic Aristotle.

Democritus taught us to reduce information to its basic elements and through analytical and logical sequences build up the whole.

Aristotle believed in seeing the total picture at once.

Peace is *not* an unrealizable dream.
War is *not* an inevitable reality.

We have one consciousness but two ways of processing sensory information, which gives us a more complete picture. Thus, the two sides of the brain reflect reality in complementary ways.

Remarkably, each hemisphere is neither completely independent from the other nor are they totally fused. Recent research shows that various mental functions are dispersed throughout the brain, often in a redundant manner. Still, the primary mode of functioning seems to be that each side reacts in its characteristic way in a mutual arrangement with the other side, and the arrangement changes quickly as the need arises.

In this manner, the brain is able to process information from differing aspects and angles. The right side (non-verbal, global) provides context and order, while the left (verbal, logical, computer-like) provides facts and detail. Both are needed for a balanced life, and the whole is far greater than the sum of its parts.

Now to the point: The right-brain, the creative and intuitive brain, is the brain through which God can and does speak to us most directly. The Carver story will make this abundantly clear. Without the right-brain we'd have no creative life, no imagination, no intuition; more, absent a brain-connection with God we'd have no potential for the mystical life. God, who knows us better than we know ourselves, is not content to speak simply to the rational intelligence, but informs us through imagination and intuition.

The left-brain, in contrast, is linear and logical, rational; it is the brain by which we think things through and talk to ourselves. Without the left-brain there'd be no schools, no universities. Why? Because without the left-brain there'd be nothing in our skull to process and utilize information of any kind.

So we can say - and here the point - logic and reason alone, especially an excessive reliance on reason, does not lead to wisdom and life, harmony and peace. One can become a scholar without becoming enlightened and wise. Indeed, with the help of reason people are able to organize all manner of things, even their own annihilation.

Peace is *not* an unrealizable dream.
War is *not* an inevitable reality.

If a person relies purely upon reason, that is to say the left-brain, he or she is no more than an intelligent criminal, since reason is invariably the servant of instincts. And so we humans destroy ourselves through our own brilliance.

By assuming that we are permitted to do anything and everything we are capable of, we have unintentionally set in motion an engine of self-destruction that is moving inexorably towards its terminal destination.

Even now it is not certain which poses the greater threat to humanity, misery or progress. One would sooner say that it is progress.

However, the history of humanity, especially recent history as more and more people subscribe to the notion that there is no substitute for the intellect, shows quite clearly that in moving forward we are not necessarily building ourselves a road to a better life.

There is so much to question about the reign we've given to the left-brain in how we lead, govern, solve and make sense of things. So very much!

It's as though the left-brain has uncoupled itself from the right-brain and, like a breakaway train, is taking the world to ruin—and thus the utter importance of this Endnote as taken from notes in my journals.

I'll explain: The agonizing reality of what has been most obviously creative in human history — the rational power and technical mastery, the ability intelligently to analyze and to organize experience and to shape and transform the reality that is encountered — has strangely become demonic . . . threatening not only humanity itself but the natural world on which human beings depend and in which they participate as creatures.

This is the fault neither of science nor of technology but of humanity itself which begot and has misused them. Like human reason, emotion and will, science and technology can become

Peace is *not* an unrealizable dream.
War is *not* an inevitable reality.

demonic in the hands of people, and like all human powers they must be transformed and not rejected or suppressed.

Today's colleges and universities which make up the Learning Industry were built on the male perspective, the cognitive theories of which did not consider (the right-brain) as a reliable source of knowledge.

But then, during the 1960s, neurological studies caused scientists to postulate a revised view of the relative halves of the human brain: that both hemispheres are involved in higher cognitive functioning, with each half specialized in complementary fashion for different modes of thinking—both highly complex.

This changed perception of the human brain has important implications for both education in general and for addressing the world's problems – such as war and threat of war!

This "changed perception" came along too late, of course, to change the Learning Industry such as its Ivy League schools whose roots go nearly as deep as the history of our country. Because it was built on the "male perspective" the cognitive theories of which did not and do not consider the right-brain as a source of knowledge, is precisely the reason why that industry as we know it is so very dependent upon the left-brain to stay in business.

All along our colleges and universities have been teaching from the left-brain, in the process leaving the brain's right hemisphere, a primary means by which God speaks to us to go dormant, to atrophy. Thus allowing the dominance of the left-brain to block us from discovering and expressing our most spiritual and creative selves. For this reason there's been little to encourage spiritual solutions to life's crises.

Yet the grim seriousness of today's many crises cries out for a fuller expression of both brains about which there is a real congruence between them. (The Carver story for the reader will make this convincingly clear.)

All of this helps when explaining much of why John Paul II gave seven hours each day, every day, to prayer, and thus to the right-

Peace is *not* an unrealizable dream.
War is *not* an inevitable reality.

brain through which God spoke to him most directly, most clearly (he had a power of concentration that wholly insulated him from his temporal surroundings as he slid into prayer or meditation, even when or while facing huge crowds at an outdoor Mass).

Also it recalls the research project of the great psychoanalyst, Carl Jung, which took him to the American Southwest, where he interviewed the famous Pueblo chief, Ochwraybiano. The doctor asked the Indian what he thought of white men. "Not much," replied the chief. "They're always restless, upset, looking for something more. That's why their faces are wrinkled." He went on to say that white people must be crazy because they think with their heads: "And only crazy people think with their heads." Then how do Indians think? asked Jung. "With their hearts, of course," answered the old chief.

NOW I'll talk about Carver and the peace that is confidence in God even when all the forces of the universe seem working for ends that are undivine. The son of a Negro slave woman, Carver enjoyed a felt presence of God in a world - plants, flowers and soil - that for him was absolutely transparent. Utterly remarkable!

In what is an entirely revealing account of how through the right-brain is where the Voice of God waits to be heard, this is the story of Dr. George Washington Carver who is considered today as great a genius in his field as Edison and Burbank and Steinmetz were in theirs. Carver was a Fellow of the Royal Society of Great Britain in 1916 (one of only a handful of Americans to receive that distinguished honor); and, in 1939, was awarded the Theodore Roosevelt Medal for excelling in work related to measures this great president initiated for the conservation of natural resources.

Carver was a Tuskegee University scientist who, in talking to the flowers and letting the flowers talk to him and revealing their secrets . . . was able to do this because like John Paul II in years after him through his own daily commitment to time spent in daily communion with God, didn't allow the left-brain to dominate.

Peace is *not* an unrealizable dream.
War is *not* an inevitable reality.

I preface Carver's story by noting that one of the most striking insights we have about life today is an evolving belief that we are living in a world that is absolutely transparent; thus God, the Light of Christ, is shining through it all the time. There is a conviction that God manifests Himself everywhere, in everything — in people and in things and in nature and in events. With all creation as his Signature, it is very obvious that God is everywhere and in everything and we cannot be without Him. Indeed, it's impossible. It's simply impossible.

The only thing is that we don't see it, God's Presence isn't real to us.

Why?

Because we don't care—not enough.

Unless we see all of Creation as ablaze with the glory of God, if we don't see all existence as a medium of revelation, then no particular revelation is possible.

The essential marvel of the universe is that it is a cosmos with a vast and innumerable dazzling surge of creatures. Every single creature and species is full of God, is a book about God. And nobody could read that book better than Dr. George Washington Carver, the celebrated plant scientist who, in his experiments on the farm and in the laboratory, talked to the flowers and let the flowers talk to him, literally. By listening to the flowers he would learn their secrets. Never seen without a flower in his buttonhole and the love of God in his heart, Carver was a man of deep humility. He was a man modest and seemed even timid. He was affectionate, and often chuckled and grinned. Sundays were sacred, Scripture was important, and his love was compounded of Joy.

A tall, slender man from the Deep South, Carver was the son of a Negro slave woman who, in having given birth to this son, was destined to play a very important but inconspicuous part in the destiny of this nation. Born a slave in Missouri, as a baby and as a young lad George Carver's life had its fill of crises.

Peace is *not* an unrealizable dream.
War is *not* an inevitable reality.

But he persevered; once he'd been warned by a doctor that he would not likely live to age 21. It was one such crisis, an attack of whooping cough that, in rendering him a sickly little boy, served a larger purpose in life in a way which reveals how one's disappointments sometimes become God's appointments. For it allowed him leisure for his unique talents and genius to find expression.

This little Black boy lived and used his freedom to wander about in the woods, where he soon got on good terms with all the insects and animals in the forest, and gained an intimate and, we might say, personal acquaintance with all the plants and flowers. Years later when he would give an address on his discoveries of the peanut, one would go to the lecture expecting to learn science and come away knowing more about prayer than could ever be learned in the theological schools.

"One of my most surprising answers to prayer," he would say, "came when I was a little boy of five or six. I had no pocket knife, and how I longed for one! I was very mechanical minded. And of all things... a boy without a pocket knife! So one night I prayed to the Father to send me a knife, and that night I had a dream. I dreamed that out in the field where the corn rows joined the tobacco rows there was a watermelon cut in halves. One half was all gouged out. The other half, plump and full, was leaning up against three stacks of corn, and out of it stuck the black handle of a pocket knife.

The next morning I could hardly wait till I got through breakfast before I scampered out to the cornfield. There where the corn rows joined the tobacco rows, I saw a watermelon cut in halves, one half was all gouged out and the other half, plump and solid, rested up against three stacks of corn. And sticking out of it was the black handle of a pocket knife."

Carver is best known for not only having discovered 300 new uses for the peanut and 100 new uses for the sweet potato, but, before he was through, for having rebuilt the agriculture of the South ... a land once planted in cotton but, because it was a single

Peace is *not* an unrealizable dream.
War is *not* an inevitable reality.

crop, was wearing out the rich soils in that part of the country, and impoverishing the debt-burdened share cropper.

And yet far greater than any miracle he had produced, was the miracle of himself. The self who held intimate conversations with his "dear Creator."

Carver believed utterly and completely in the Power of God to answer prayer and, in rising regularly at four o'clock and going into the woods and talking with God, would receive from Him his orders for the day. "After my morning's talk with God, I go into my laboratory and begin to carry out His wishes for the day." When people are asleep, he would say, is when I hear God best and learn my plan.

When people are asleep...is when I hear God best! It's been my experience also. Remarkable.

How wonderful are the ways of God, he would say. And His promises, they are real, but so few people believe that they are real. Pounding his hand on the table, he would say, "They are as real, as solid, yes infinitely more solid and substantial than this table which the materialist so thoroughly believes in. If you would only believe, 0 ye of little faith."

And what a believer he was. With an eye made quiet by the power of harmony, and the deep power of joy, he saw into the life of things and there unlocked secrets of nature and of the Infinite.

This expectancy of Carver's, this awe, found "tongues in trees, books in the running brooks, sermons in stones, and good in everything." "How do I talk to a little flower? Through it I talk to the Infinite. And what is the Infinite? It is that silent, small force. It isn't the outer physical contact. No, it isn't that. The infinite is not confined to the visible world. It is not in the earthquake, the wind or the fire. It is that still small voice that calls up the fairies. Now people will say that I am getting into words - just words. I refer to the unseen Spirit that defies the human power of reproduction, that challenges the power of human expression. Try to express it.... it can't be done.

Peace is *not* an unrealizable dream.
War is *not* an inevitable reality.

"Yet, when you look out upon God's beautiful world there it is. When you look into the heart of a rose, there you experience it. But you can't explain it. You can talk and talk, but the longer you talk the worse it gets - the further you are from the truth."

He'd say there are certain things, often very little things, like the little peanut, the little piece of clay, the little flower that cause you to look within — and then it is that you see into the soul of things. He would talk to a little flower or a peanut and make it give up its secrets to him. He would look at these things as tenderly and lovingly as a doctor would look at a sick child.

He would examine these things, caress them, study them, talk with them. And in the end, after all his discoveries were in, his genius established, he would say that it is not us little people that do the work, but our blessed Creator working through us.

Nature 'crammed with God' is our religious book, with lessons for every day. It is the living, visible garment of God. Carver was often given to say, "I love to think of nature as an unlimited broadcasting station, through which God speaks to us every hour, if we will only tune in." He was a man amazingly simple and humble in faith; faith that is not belief without proof, but trust without reservation. He was amazingly simple in how he thought and in his habits. One such habit would be to recite — through all his years of work — these immortal lines of Tennyson:

> "Flower in the crannied wall,
> I pluck you out of the crannies —
> I hold you here, root and all, in my hand,
> Little flower - but if I could understand
> What you are, root and all, and all in all,
> I should know what God and man is."

Like the great Michelangelo who taught through his sacred paintings that everything is naked and open before God's eyes, and like St. Francis of Assisi who saw relationships in everything, Carter also saw the sacred and connectedness everywhere. In diversity he saw unity. He spent his whole life exploring all that he saw. In complete surrender, he gave his whole self to what animates

Peace is *not* an unrealizable dream.
War is *not* an inevitable reality.

this vast and complex experience that is life in all its many and varied forms.

He dared to think and work with an independent freedom not permissible before, unfolding before a world's very eyes a veritable mystic maze of new and useful products from material almost or quite beneath our feet but, before his discoveries, considered of little or no value. His work was the work of a creative research chemist. Born a slave, he faced life as a master — while his Master's light shone through his eyes.

Once when nearly seventy years old, this small, frail-looking, gray-haired man with a velvet-soft voice, a visiting student asked, "How do you get your ideas?" The student recalled how much Dr. Carver had done for southern agriculture whose soil had been depleted by intensive cotton farming. Dr. Carver advocated crop rotation to replace nitrogen and other nutrients in the soil.

Most famously, he found ways to use crops, especially the lowly peanut. By 1933 he had cataloged 325 uses for peanuts alone and more than 150 for sweet potatoes, pecans and soybeans. The products ranged from glue and printer's ink to synthetic rubber and material for paving highways.

"God gave the ideas to me," he declared without missing a beat. "God speaks to all of us each and every hour, if only we will listen. I silently ask the Creator, often moment by moment, to give me wisdom, understanding and bodily strength to do his will. I am asking and receiving all the time."

"God gave the ideas to me."

"God speaks to all of us each and every hour."

"If only we will listen."

"I am asking and receiving all the time."

Another student asked, "How come you only have three patents, even though you've come up with so many other inventions?"... indeed, of the products he had devised there'd been a staggering variety. "One reason I seldom patent my products is that if I did,

Peace is *not* an unrealizable dream.
War is *not* an inevitable reality.

it would take so much time that I would get nothing else done!" He laughed, but soon turned serious. "But mainly I don't want my discoveries to benefit just a few favored persons. I want them to help everybody." His inventions were available to anyone who cared to use them, and, of course, many did.

His philosophy was simple, he explained it this way to the visiting students, "It is service that measures success."

For the same reason Carver seldom patented his products is why I never had my manuscripts published: It would take so much time that I would get nothing else done! And like Carver my philosophy has been simple. It is service that measures success. In my case it's been Global Peace Service.

Dr. Carver, who'd been through - slavery, illness, poverty - and not only persevered but had triumphed, was truly a genius, and not just in science, but in art and music too. Two of Dr. Carver's paintings were displayed in the 1893 Chicago World's Fair. And in saying once that flowers had told him some wonderful things, said also that flowers never failed to tell him the truth.

One of the things he was told was that there is going to be a great spiritual awakening in the world, and it is going to come "from people up here, from people connected with you and me, from plain, simple people who know — not merely believe — but actually know that God answers prayer. It is going to be a great revival of Christianity, not a revival of religion.

"We can have religion and still have wars. But this is to be a revival of true Christianity. It is going to rise up from the laymen, from men who are going about their work and putting God into what they do, from men who believe in prayer, and who want to make God real to mankind."

Happily, there is now incontrovertible evidence that humankind is now entering upon the greatest period of change the world has ever known. The ills and perils from which we are suffering have had their seat in the very foundation of human thought part of

Peace is *not* an unrealizable dream.
War is *not* an inevitable reality.

which has been the dumbing down, making dormant, the right brain.

Today, with that realization, and actually shaken by it, something is happening to the whole structure of human consciousness; a fresh kind of life is starting.

In a world burdened with a lack of spirituality, and because of this we are killing our future, killing our hope, we are seeing the beginnings of the spiritualization of that structure. In the face of such an upheaval, no one can remain indifferent. We are swept along by the tide of events, not the least of which is the ongoing Medjugorje drama where never, since when Christ walked here on earth, has there been such a breaking into human history by a Presence of the Divine.

IN South Carolina and Delaware along the Atlantic coast here in the United States, there are some men who spend their afternoons crabbing the low-country marshes and waters. Normally, they cook them by boiling them. Now there are two ways to boil crab. The one bound to elicit a battle with the crab is to bring the pot to a rolling boil and then put the crab in. It fights. It grabs at the pot with its large claws. Eventually it succumbs. The alternate method (crueler, one would think) is to put the crab in cool water, which it settles into gracefully, and then heat it slowly. It heats so slowly, the crab never figures out when to try to climb out of the pot. It dies calmly huddled at the bottom of the pot.

For humanity today life has become like that of the crab who never figures out when to try to climb out of the pot: a slow boil. We are like so many crabs immersed in a world culture where the environment of things has splintered around us as an almost total secularization of our public attitudes has turned hearts away from God. Thus for many of us, for nations and nation-states, the water has already gotten too hot. We are very much like that crab who dies calmly huddled at the bottom of the pot.

HERE in the West, by allowing ourselves to be educated predominantly through the left-brain, to become secularized, it

Peace is *not* an unrealizable dream.
War is *not* an inevitable reality.

is abundantly clear that we have been educated away from the soul, our very essence, the only part of us that survives death. The equivalent in nature of this closing of ourselves off from God, his Voice not coming through as it ought, would be an ecological disaster of major, major kind.

There is the story of some scientists who lived by their faith in the power of reason, but the story ends in a bad dream. They have scaled the mountains of ignorance. They are about to scale the highest peak, the steepest and most treacherous of all. As their leader pulls himself over the highest rock, he is greeted by a band of Christian mystics who have been sitting there for centuries.

Today there are indications that Christianity is moving into an era of mysticism. The old authors spoke of "the universal vocation to mysticism." Perhaps they were speaking prophetically of Christianity in the third millennium when the Church will either be a Mystical Church (as it was in the beginning) or it will disappear. The future Christian will either be a Mystical Christian or not a Christian at all

After having gone through a literary forest that's been more books written about Christ in the last fifty years than in all Christian centuries, I submit that to ignore the testimony of our Christian mystics is to miss a powerful, enlightening dimension of Jesus Christ. Christ, by his action on them, discloses a psychic potential, deep, subtle, rich on which he alone can act.

And that to ignore Mother Mary the Gospa as the world's most important woman, indeed history's most important woman, is to miss a powerful, enlightening dimension of this Woman, especially in her now role of 28 years and counting at Medjugorje . . . Medjugorje that is a reflection of Heaven, a mission station of Heaven . . . Medjugorje that is a totally mystical event the core of which is the Risen Christ.

There is no doubt that, of all life forms on our planet, humanity is the only one that can elevate itself above its condition, uncover a reality which was closed to its senses, comprehend outer space,

Peace is *not* an unrealizable dream.
War is *not* an inevitable reality.

inner space, and even larger and smaller infinites, conceive God and transcend itself continuously above its earthly abode.

This is why, the more we advance, the more we stand in awe before this miraculous, mysterious, incomprehensible, mind-boggling cosmos called a human person. Witness how from beneath all the debris of the 20th century something new is coming to birth.

How well and how poetically did John Paul II say of the 20th century: "The tears of this century have prepared the ground for a new springtime of the human spirit!" Already this springtime appears in the hunger for spiritual experience, the thirst for monastic meditation, the longing for mysticism, the compassion for the suffering, the solicitude for the helpless. The Beloved speaks and says to all humanity,

> Arise, my love, my dove, my beautiful one,
>   and come away;
> for now the winter is past,
>   the rain is over and gone;
> The flowers appear on the earth;
>   the time of singing has come,
> and the voice of the turtledove
>   is heard in our land.
>   (Song of Songs 2:10-12)

Peace is *not* an unrealizable dream.
War is *not* an inevitable reality.

HE'D BEEN LIKE ONE OF
A NEW SPECIES ARISING ON THE PLANET

GOING back now through many generations and centuries to the very origin of the human ego the left-brain, to Eden where began our drift away from our connection to God the right brain, we begin to see the why of why we are a war weary world. If we are to make sense of things, of why conflict, violence and war persist despite our best efforts to bring about peace and harmony in our unhappy world, then we have only to look no further than to our ego-based state of consciousness.

George Washington Carver had it right: He believed utterly and completely in the Power of God to answer prayer and, in rising regularly at four o'clock and going into the woods and talking with God, would receive from Him his orders for the day. "After my morning's talk with God, I go into my laboratory and begin to carry out His wishes for the day."

"When people are asleep, he would say, is when "I hear God best and learn my plan."

How wonderful are the ways of God, he would say. And His promises, they are real, but so few people believe that they are real. Pounding his hand on the table, he would say, "They are as real, as solid, yes infinitely more solid and substantial than this table which the materialist so thoroughly believes in. If you would only believe, 0 ye of little faith."

And what a believer he was. With an eye made quiet by the power of harmony, and the deep power of joy, he saw into the life of things and there unlocked secrets of nature and of the Infinite.

This expectancy of Carver's, this awe, found "tongues in trees, books in the running brooks, sermons in stones, and good in everything." "How do I talk to a little flower? Through it I talk to the Infinite. And what is the Infinite? It is that silent, small force. It isn't the outer physical contact. No, it isn't that. The infinite is not confined to the visible world. It is not in the earthquake, the wind or the fire. It is that still small voice that calls up the fairies. Now people will say that I am getting into words - just words. I refer to the unseen Spirit that defies the human power of reproduction, that challenges the power of human expression. Try to express it.... it can't be done.

"Yet, when you look out upon God's beautiful world there it is. When you look into the heart of a rose, there you experience it. But you can't explain it. You can talk and talk, but the longer you talk the worse it gets - the further you are from the truth."

It bears repeating: You can talk and talk, but the longer you talk the worse it gets - the further you are from the truth! I love it. It says it all.'

Some forty years ago a simple question — "How can we discover the sources of wholeness, healing and hope amidst a broken and suffering world?" — began my search for a solution to the problem that is war and threat of war.

A solution!

More than just being serious, I'd been excited about the whole idea of search, of quest. Indeed, I'd awakened to my life's purpose no matter how seemingly futile or foolish the challenge. It was a too powerful an idea to just toss aside and forget about.

I don't remember when exactly the story of Carver caught my attention except to say it had a way of surfacing every once in a while during my years of quest. He'd spoken with flowers, flowers talked to him, he'd never been without one in his buttonhole. Seeing beauty in a flower for him was a way of life, it was how he saw his own innermost being—his true nature. Feelings of joy and love were intrinsically connected to that recognition. Indeed

Peace is *not* an unrealizable dream.
War is *not* an inevitable reality.

he radiated that love. There'd been no amount of ego, none at all. Just joy.

The flower for Carver was an expression in form of that which is most high, most sacred, and ultimately formless within ourselves. Flowers, more fleeting, more ethereal, and more delicate than the plants out of which they emerged, were for this son of a slave woman like messengers from another realm... like a bridge between the world of physical forms and the formless. They not only had a scent that was delicate and pleasing to humans, but also brought a fragrance from the realm of spirit.

In Carver there'd been a certain degree of Presence, of still and alert attention in his perceptions, that allowed him to sense the divine life essence, the one indwelling consciousness or spirit in every creature, every life-form, recognizing it as one with his own essence and so loved it as himself.

Until this happens, however, most humans see only the outer forms, unaware of their inner essence, just as they are unaware of their own essence and identify, only with their own physical and psychological form.

In the case of a flower, a bird, or a precious whatever in nature, however, even someone with little or no Presence can occasionally sense that there is more there than the mere physical existence of that form, without knowing that this is the reason why they are drawn toward it, feels an affinity with it.

Especially do we sense this in all new-born life forms — babies, puppies, kittens, lambs, and so on. They are fragile, delicate; they radiate an innocence, a sweetness and beauty that are not of this world but still shines through them. They delight even relatively insensitive humans.

So when we are alert and contemplate a flower or bird or precious whatever without naming it mentally, it becomes a window for us into the formless. There is an inner opening, however slight, into the realm of spirit.

Peace is *not* an unrealizable dream.
War is *not* an inevitable reality.

NATURE is filled with "precious whatevers." Indeed it needs to be so. Why? Because ecologists are discovering that nature is so deeply interrelated, that the tiniest insect has its significance foe the whole, that there can be immense repercussions if just one species is destroyed or depleted.

Great scientists of today, standing on the shoulders of great scientists of the past, have hardly begun to unravel the secret of our universe. Our insights into the secrets of nature, of light and life, give us but a glimpse into the incredibly creative, wonderful intelligence and glory of God, and how intricately interwoven are all the processes of life.

Subatomic physicists are discovering that the tiniest particles, separated by thousands of miles, respond to each other, are in relationship.

Yet it is true today, our earth is marked by human beings fighting each other, and polluting and exploiting nature. We have hurt each other and the garden that has been given for our nourishment and our delight.

Most of us are out of touch with each other and with the earth of our own bodies... preoccupied with production and security and comfort, preparing armaments, building frontiers.

What a discrepancy between the joyful winging of birds and the fear in men and women, between the freedom of dolphins playing in the sea and men and women becoming slaves to comfort and pleasure.

The plan of Lord God is to heal and repair the damaged body, to bring it to a new and fuller beauty, to a new and deeper fecundity, a new and more abundant fruitfulness or fertility of the mind, of the right-brain.

Yes, God had a marvelous plan. At the center of that plan was his desire to become flesh, to take on our human condition, to put on human nature, so that our Creator would be touched and heard and loved, so that our brokenness could be healed into a new wholeness, so that we could become again one perfect body.

Peace is *not* an unrealizable dream.
War is *not* an inevitable reality.

And the fulfilling of this plan involved a woman who would mother the Word made flesh, a mother who would be the sign of the Eternal Father and in whose womb, created from the bowels of the earth, the Word would become flesh.

He would become the new Adam rejoicing in the new Eve... Jesus, rejoicing in the woman Mary. And they would lead a multitude into the knowledge of the Father, into the heart of the Trinity aflame in ecstasy, into the wedding feast. Yes, God had a marvelous plan, to reveal the love that burns within the Trinity of Father, Son and Holy Spirit, and to bring men and women to an even fuller unity and glory.

God would repair the brutal damage of the first Adam and the first Eve as they turned away from communion, wanting authority and power, refusing dependence upon their source. All along the plan of Lord God has been to heal and repair the damaged body, to bring it to a new and fuller beauty, a new fecundity.

Our human nature is so skillfully made by the unseen hand of God, that even within our brokenness lies the seed that will lad us back to wholeness.

It bears repeating: Our human nature is so skillfully made by the unseen hand of God, that even within our brokenness lies the seed that will lead us back to wholeness. Beautiful!

From the emptiness of Adam and Eve rises up a cry, a craving, a thirst to be filled. It is man and woman's incessant search to be filled that pushes us forward into the unknown. But the personal anguish is too great, the breaking point at the heart of heart of humanity is too painful. In itself, it is literally unbearable and cannot be faced without the knowledge that transcends it, without the love which redeems it.

Only Jesus, because he is the Word in whom we are created, could go to that point of ultimate emptiness, separation, the broken communion with Lord God.

Creator God watched over humanity as it grew over the earth. Through history and evolution God was preparing the future. In

Peace is *not* an unrealizable dream.
War is *not* an inevitable reality.

times of great darkness and pain, or when the forces of destruction intensified, holy men and women, prophets and philosophers of truth rose up. In my own time there's been more than just several such prophets. A few examples: certainly George Washington Carver (1864?-1943 by compelling example and evidence was just such a prophet; as was philosopher, physician and humanitarian Albert Schweitzer (1875-1965); and Mother Teresa of Calcutta (1910-1997) with whom on occasion I'd been blessed to cross paths and so very lovingly remember.

Then there's been the Mother of All Prophets, the Virgin Mary at Medjugorje, the New Eve, who has come to lead us, the world, into a new time, a new era, of healing and wholeness, harmony and wisdom.

THERE have been times when in Medjugorje, walking the fields, climbing Apparition Hill or Mount Krizevac, when I'd get to thinking about the years of journey and quest that had brought me to this place of previously unimaginable cosmic drama and genuine hope for a war-torn, war-weary, world.

Medjugorje is where everything had come together for me. Medjugorje is not magic. It isn't some sort of passing fancy. It doesn't exist simply to wet our human curiosity. Critical things are happening here for all humanity. Here we're called to a specific goal if we want peace within ourselves and peace in our world. Peace can't exist without God, it can't exist if we stray from the path.

Mary for me at Medjugorje has been a beacon of light, a luminous loving presence. She's been a mystical flower, like a lily, trumpeting her Son's glory. We must remember that out of her littleness greatness was formed. Indeed we are not alone.

In fact that's what she's come to say: we are not alone. God exists. He cares. All through her life she pointed to Jesus. Today, 2000 years later, she's still pointing to Jesus. 2000 years ago Mary brought Jesus to the world; today at Medjugorje she is bringing the world to Jesus. And she is doing this in a place whose people have, since time beyond remembering, epitomized the suffering at

Peace is *not* an unrealizable dream.
War is *not* an inevitable reality.

Golgatha and her own suffering at the foot of the cruel Cross. And she's doing this in a time when humanity has lost control of its destiny, but only now awakening to that reality.

Witness the unprecedented violence that humans are inflicting on other life-forms and the planet itself... the destruction of oxygen-producing forests and other plant and animal life; ill-treatment of animals in factory farms; and poisoning of rivers, oceans, and air. Driven by greed, ignorant of their connectedness to the whole, humans persist in behavior that, if continued unchecked, can only result in their own destruction.

At Medjugorje Mary, aware of all these things, is preparing humanity for a transformation of consciousness... through Jesus an inner flowering so radical and profound that compared to it, the flowering of plants, no matter how beautiful, is only a pale reflection.

The possibility of such a transformation has been the central message of the great wisdom teachings of human-kind. The messengers were humanity's early flowers. They were precursors, rare and precious beings. A widespread flowering was not yet possible at that time, and their message became largely misunderstood and often greatly distorted. It certainly did not transform human behavior, except in small minorities of people — where have lived the few who understood even without ever having heard the Sermon on the Mount what Jesus meant when saying, "Blessed are the meek, for they shall inherit the earth." They knew!

Who are the meek or the humble, and what does it mean that they shall inherit the earth? They meek are the egoless. They are those who have awakened to their essential true consciousness and recognize that essence in all "others," all life forms; flowers, trees, birds, and so on. They feel their oneness with the whole and the Source. Like did George Washington Carver.

He'd been like one of a new species arising on the planet. It is arising now. Slowly, incrementally, but arising!

Peace is *not* an unrealizable dream.
War is *not* an inevitable reality.

Meanwhile you are in it, I am in it, all of us are in it. We are in the wake of what history records as having been a "Century of Tears" and because of 9.11.01 continues now into a whole new century. We are in a transformative period of kind when all human beings are being called to awaken to our essential true consciousness and to recognize that essence in all "others," all life forms: chameleons, rabbits, horses, and so on.

Gently but oftentimes not so gently we are being called into the depths of our own heart before discovering that our God is a God of life and light. When God creates, it is life and light that is given. To understand the depth of our brokenness, our lostness, we need to look at the wholeness in which we were created, a wholeness that comes from total communion with God.

On one of the doorways to the Cathedral of Chartres there is a statue of God creating Adam. It is a beautiful statue. The father is symbolized through the body of Christ. He has the face of Christ. Adam has the same face, though younger and without a beard.

This statue radiates a deep serenity and silence. God is gently drawing Adam out of the mud. Adam is resting on the breast of God as John rested on the breast of Jesus. They are both smiling, filled with a profound joy; as if God the artist was saying, 'You are beautiful', and Adam was saying, "You are beautiful'. They are in communion with one another.

The statue at Chartres does not depict the creation of woman, but if there were such a statue it too would show the same smiling and the same profound joy, the same communion with one another, Eve in communion with God.

We know the story. At a particular moment Adam and Eve said 'no' to God. They turned away, blocking off this energy of love They refused to be dependent upon the energy flowing from God. They were seduced by the Spoiler who had said,
you can do it alone,
you can be like God,
you can be free,

Peace is *not* an unrealizable dream.
War is *not* an inevitable reality.

you don't have to obey and be like children,
you can be adults.
They turned away and closed themselves up from the source of life.
And then they discovered they were empty, naked, alone, and in
despair.

It is this severing act that is the source of all our experience of
inner conflict of so many kinds and the outer conflict that is war
and threat of war. When communion with God is broken, full
communion with each other - be it spouses, tribes, ethnic groups
or nations - is impossible.

Yet all is not lost.

For our human nature is so skillfully made by the unseen hand
of God, that even within our brokenness lies the seed that will lead
us back to wholeness. Our God is a compasssionate God. This is
precisely what Medjugorje is all about. Jesus through Mary, God's
special messenger to earth, is here to lead us back to wholeness.
In wholeness war and threat of war is unthinkable, and thus not
possible.

George Washington Carver lived wholeness, personified
wholeness. In communion with his Creator he'd been one with
all creation. Remarkable! But not so remarkable that if we really
wanted it we ourselves could live that same wholeness.

Peace is *not* an unrealizable dream.
War is *not* an inevitable reality.

AT THE THRESHOLD
OF THE NEXT STEP
IN HUMANITY'S EVOLUTION

THERE is a saying: "Where there is no vision, the people perish." In what is an evolving humanity, it is important that we have something to look forward to; a dream, a hope, a vision. John F. Kennedy's vision as our president was that we land a man on the moon; he gave us ten months to do it in. We did it in eight!

For some at the time it the dream had seemed preposterous, absurd, ridiculous. Years later however, because of that vision, we have an international station in outer space and a robot busily exploring Mars and sending its findings back to our space lab here on Earth.

Clearly, we stand poised at a threshold in human history. The shock and horror of terrorism continue to haunt us, reminding us of the alienation and hatred that have too often characterized human history. Yet, at the same time, we see reflections of the best in human nature, as people around the world continue to hold a vision of peace and justice, kindness and compassion, as they demonstrate the love and heroism that reflects a greater humanity. We saw a lot of that in the first responders - firemen, police officers, emergency medical folks - when those jet-fuel laden planes crashed into the Twin Towers and then into the Pentagon. We saw it in the many folks from all over America who rushed in to volunteer their services.

We are on the brink of a new understanding of who we are as human beings. An understanding that includes the depths to which we can plunge when we fail to pursue our greater potentials. In a sense, a new urgency has been declared in our search for self-awareness. During the last four-hundred years, science has opened the world to us of discoveries our ancestors could not have imagined. It has revealed the nature of distant galaxies, the structure of subatomic particles, and the evolutionary process that brought our universe from a tiny seed to this immense and still-expanding cosmos.

But the threshold we've now reached involves more than our physical existence. Irresistibly, we are called upon to join our exploration of the evolving universe with an equally daring and disciplined exploration of the Inner Life. In spite of the negative actions of a few, there has rarely existed a wider interest in mysteries of the soul nor so many experiments in personal transformation.

Such experiments are happening around the world, informed by discoveries in psychology, anthropology, and medical science as well as once-esoteric knowledge from every sacred tradition. They are increasing in number and sophistication today because there now exists more publicly available knowledge about our transformative capacities than at any time in human history. The nature of spirituality and the inner life is coming more clearly into focus, bringing us a vision of human transformation that is unprecedented in its scope and beauty.

From all of this, and in all of this, we are being called to rise from Something to Something; to a new dimension of life, a new realm of existence, where there is no more war or threat of war. It is an exciting time, indeed a privileged time, to be alive. Father Mychal Judge had an insight into this new realm, a grasp on it, and passed it on with his life and how he lived that life to all he met, including now-Detective Steven McDonald; he'd been promoted after having been shot.

Peace is *not* an unrealizable dream.
War is *not* an inevitable reality.

For many years, a new world view has been forming intuitively in the hearts and minds of people around the world. Though this emerging picture of our place in the universe has not been fully articulated, it is based on a central perception that we have capacities for a greater life than most of us have realized or even imagined ... a life that seems essentially joined with the evolution of the universe itself. We sense this connection, many believe. because we and the world are unfolding from the same transcendent source and are secretly moved to manifest more and more of our latent divinity.

Thus today we are being called to rise from Something to Something. That something being the truth of who we are. Knowing that something transcendent is inside us, a part of who we are, inspiring us, moving within us. It is a time of human awakening. For we are at the threshold of the next step in humanity's evolution.

Peace is *not* an unrealizable dream.
War is *not* an inevitable reality.

ON EARTH AS IT IS IN HEAVEN

previously titled
WE HAVE TO MAKE SENSE
OF THIS WORLD

The Universe is both Transient and Eternal;
Science leads inevitably to the Idea of God;
so the Soul will, as the Wise Ones tell us,
cast out everything that is foreign,
… both Politics and History.

THE wise man is the experienced man who lives with his heart wide open, full of reverent wonder and radical amazement. But he is not equally open to everything. He perceives a hierarchy of being, a gradation of value. He discriminates, distinguishes, and discerns the spirit. He also recognizes and confronts the demonic dimensions of being, the mystery of iniquity. He knows that life is short and he is limited…so he sifts, selects, and choose just that much of the raw material of this world that he knows he can infect with his love and transfigure with his spirit. He lives so wake-fully and expectantly that little of value escapes his notice, and whatever is worthwhile evokes his loving attention. He sees the things o this world as rare treasures or as things never seen before. William McNamara, O.C.D.

ON 20 July 1969 Ned Armstrong and Edwin Aldrin landed on the Sea of Peace (Sea of Tranquility. It was man's first step on the moon. Just two years later astronaut James Irwin would return from the moon and in an motional speech testify that he had felt the presence of God there. He then devoted the last two decades of his life to sharing his lunar experience and conversion: "God had a plan for me," he said to a journalist. "to leave earth and to share the adventure with others, so that they too can be lifted up."

The Russians were no less impressed. The book *The Horne Planet* records the remark of Aleksei Leonov. the first man to "walk" in space in 1965: "We have come to consider the planet a holy relic." In like manner, Russian cosmonaut Boris Volynov, one of the cosmonauts of the world's first Space Station in 1969, returned to earth saying: "Having seen the sun, the moon, the stars and our planet, you begin to look at things differently and with greater trepidation."

And so, as the anxieties and dilemmas of this advanced technological and scientific age heighten, as the menace of materialism, greed and human discord become more onerous, a sense of tragedy arising from the threat to human existence has set the stage for the resurgence of religious fervor, not despite science and technology but precisely because of them.

The irony is that while part of one of the most sophisticated scientific and technical enterprises yet devised by human beings, these explorers gazed back from where they had come and rediscovered the sacred.

In so doing they did a favor for humankind, especially that segment which has never appreciated the practical value of the aesthetic and religious perspective. Perhaps they found the missing link between science and religion: Faith!

In an age characterized by an awareness of problems that threaten the survival of humankind on this planet, what we must do is to make sense of this world; we have to do this. It is why Mary visits today at Medjugorje. She is here to guide and lead us into a new era of human relations when holy peace – lasting peace – can and will reign.

Peace is *not* an unrealizable dream.
War is *not* an inevitable reality.

The one thing we can do now without waiting is show how Jesus of Nazareth faced basically the same problem… even if it was on a much smaller scale. He lived in an age when it seemed that the world was about to come to an end. Despite differences of opinion about how, why and when, very many Jews at that time were convinced that the world was on the brink of apocalyptic catastrophe.

The second thing we can do is to acknowledge that there must be a serious reason for the extravagance in apparitions that have been the Virgin Mary's twenty-eight years continuing daily visitations at Medjugorje.

For myself, because I had no great virtue except perhaps the courage of my convictions, I began journaling my takes on what I perceived as a cosmic drama going on at Medjugorje. It's been an adventure. It's been a mystical journey. It's been an adventure in company with the most controversial and powerful Woman in the history of the world.

It's been a journey into the faith dimension of human life which began with Mary's "Yes!" in the story of the Virgin birth, a particularly striking example of faith. In my own journey into the faith dimension of life, I came to perceive and thus appreciate if not relish faith as not belief without proof, but trust without reservation. I went from not wanting merely to possess a faith, to wanting a faith that possessed me. And I got it.

Spiritual maturity begins when we realize that we are God's guests in this world. We are not householders, but pilgrims; not landlords, but tenants; not owners, but guests.

I'VE often thought how wonderful it would be if newly arriving children on this planet could bring with them the acquired wisdom and knowledge of those who came before them, instead of beginning all over again what has taken centuries for us to learn so far. This is the inconvenient truth of things. With each new generation it's as though we're starting all over again.

Despite that unkind reality, we humans have been blessed with a certain audacity of hope that allows us to start all over again in a

Peace is *not* an unrealizable dream.
War is *not* an inevitable reality.

learning process not unlike that of what our parents, grandparents and all others before us went through.

It is why we should care about others; because like us they, too, no matter where in the world they happen to be, are on the same journey. That's what life is, a journey. And we are in formation, being formed. We are meant to rise from something to something. We are more than we seem. We are spiritual beings. We have a destiny, a new realm of existence on earth as it is in heaven.

⁓ MEDITATION ⁓

IN this day of tremendous sophistication and advance in science and knowledge, belief in the Second Coming of Christ sounds rather ridiculous. It is – to those who don't share the Christian faith, to those who look at Christmas as nothing more than a fairy tale.

But Christ did come. And he will come again. In simple and succinct terms, that is what the season of advent (preceding Christmas day) is all about.

But I am not sure that the living of our faith in his coming is as simple as its stating. For even as we look back rejoicing in his coming in the flesh, even while we look ahead hoping in his coming in glory, we are by no means onlookers... passive contemplators of what was, or just as passive awaiters of what is to be.

In the past the Israelites looked ahead to the coming of their Messiah. He was to usher in a golden age of power, wealth, peace—the kingdom.

> He shall judge between the nations,
> and decide for many peoples;
> and they shall beat their swords into ploughshares,
> and their spears into pruning hooks;
> nation shall not lift up sword against nation,
> neither shall they learn war any more (Isaiah 2:4).

Peace is *not* an unrealizable dream.
War is *not* an inevitable reality.

That Messiah came in the person of Christ, and he did bring in the awaited kingdom. But the Israelites rejected it because it was not of this world.

We too are looking ahead to the coming of the Messiah — to his Second Coming. He will fully establish his kingdom then in all its power and glory, and peace will be ours forever. That Messiah has already come and he will come again. But it may be that we, the new Israelites, in divorcing our faith from life, are rejecting his kingdom because it is of this world.

The kingdom in its final consummation is indeed not of this world. But in its evolvement toward that consummation in eternity, it is very much of this world. It is here and now, of our time, of our history, incarnate as Christ himself became incarnate in our world to point us toward his final coming and the world to come.

This is why we can say: Our waiting is his coming. This is why we get involved in the building of his earthly city: In doing so we attain the eternal. This involvement is our waiting. His involvement is his coming. Otherwise we should not concern ourselves about justice and freedom, poverty and development, suffering and oppression and everything that makes life in this world unbearable.

"Come, let us walk in the light of the Lord." The light is the goal we strive for—a future thing. But even now we walk in that light—a present thing. For the Lord has come, and he is to come again. And only when we walk in his light can we make sense of it all.

Peace is *not* an unrealizable dream.
War is *not* an inevitable reality.

A PROPOSAL
"A GLOBAL COMMONWEALTH
OF COMPASSION"

SINCE World War II humankind has entered a totally new era of history, perhaps even of evolution. During most of that time my life has been spent searching for a solution to the problem that is war. Clearly, it's not been fortuitous or by chance that it's happened this way.

Clearly also during this period humans have advanced dramatically into the infinitely large and the infinitely small. More scientific progress has been achieved in the last fifty years than during the entire previous history of civilization.

So why are we still at war, acting like barbarians? Why in the Congo *in this war-torn country* is sexual assault used so frequently as a weapon that some perpetrators don't even consider it wrong — the Congo, where the weapon of sexual violence is so commonly used that people seem numb to it? Five million people have died, and an estimated 50,000 to 100,000 women have been raped in the past decade of tangled conflict among ethnic militias and regional militaries fighting for Congo's mineral riches.

Humans have set foot on the moon and have returned safely to earth. We have reached with our tools the abyss of the sea. Microbiology has opened new exhilarating and frightening vistas of scientific advance with the synthesis of genes. Never on this planet has there been such intensive research and discovery by so many scientists in so many lands.

So why are we still warring, destroying both humanity itself and our natural habitats along with our planet? Why?

Length of life has increased; diseases which caused great epidemics not long ago have been wiped out.

Yet, without pause, the blood-swollen god of greed and war has managed to hold centerstage in the theater of global human drama. Witness the recent "Century of Tears" with its two world wars with the threat of a third.

If war is an extension of politics by other means, and it is, then it is an enormous indictment of politics, politics that is too important to be left to 'politicians'.

And so the question: In the midst of the deafening issues and claims of so many tribes, nations and ethnic as well as other groups on the world stage, who speaks for the <u>human family</u> as did Christ two thousand years ago?

War in every case is organized chaos. What if Christ came back to earth, what attention—if any, what priority—if any, would he command? I wonder. Interesting!

I admit that all races are important; that all nations, tribes and ethnic groups are important; that all religions are important; that East, West, North and South are important; but pray tell what about <u>humanity as a whole</u>? What attention, what priority, does that supreme family of all receive in our society, in the media, in the schools, in the arts, in literature, in churches and other houses of worship, in our homes?

As for me, after long decades of searching for a solution to the problem that is war and threat of war, a solution to the problem that is slavery of every kind, I have decided long ago that the only realities that matter for me are Lord God, planet Earth, Humanity, my Family and my Self.

Without those realities in place and acknowledged there would have been little for me to offer to the Children of War to whom I've

Peace is *not* an unrealizable dream.
War is *not* an inevitable reality.

committed my life, dedicated my passion and resources, my God-given gifts and talents.

All other groups are in constant change: their borders, their priorities, their power, their allegiances change. But God, the planet, humanity, the natural family and the miracle of individual life are permanent realities in our cosmic presence and adventure. We do not do enough for the human family.

> Clearly, it bears repeating:
> We do not do enough for
> the human family.
> We don't!

To which without any further preface I propose that the time has arrived for us to take on the task of creating a Global Commonwealth of Compassion. It is the next great project. There are so many beautiful and useful things the world's peoples could do to accomplish that.

Where are the anthropologists, psychologists and philosophers who have the courage to speak out for the whole human race. If Kant were alive today he would come to the United Nations and rewrite his Project for Perpetual Peace. If Christ came back to earth, his first visit perhaps would be to the United Nations to see if his dream of human oneness and brother/sisterhood had come true.

He would be happy of course to see representatives of all nations, North and South, East and West, rich and poor, believers and non-believers, young and old, Philistines and Samaritans, trying to find answers to the perennial questions of human destiny and fulfillment,

But how many disappointments and criticisms would he have? Would he not say that, without seeing ourselves as one family and asking the fundamental questions of life and of our relationship with the Creator and the universe, we will never make it?

Peace is *not* an unrealizable dream.
War is *not* an inevitable reality.

I have observed in my lifetime, in my quest, that it is difficult to hold together any human group for long if there is not a vision, an ideal, an objective, a dream.

To bind the human family together, to foster its further ascent, to prevent it from losing ground and falling into the abyss of despair, we must have a constant vision, a dream for the human family. We will not swim forever in the present sea of complexity and chaos if we are not shown a shore.

It is why I am given to propose the creation of a Global Commonwealth of Compassion. With the blurring of national and other boundaries because of how technology has made us a smaller world owing to rapid communication and travel, such a dream makes sense.

Unfortunately, when one looks at the curricula of schools and universities, at the media and literature, one does not find any shores. The dreams of peace, of world fraternity and solidarity and of the United Nations are all too often scoffed at and ignored as childish and hopeless fantasies.

But as I meet with young people from here in the States and distant lands, the idea of a Global Commonwealth of Compassion makes sense to them. So much so that I've often witnessed a certain eruption of hope of kind rarely in my experience having seen before.

In them I've seen unparalleled thinking, perception, inspiration, elevation and love for the achievement of such a commonwealth. To them it makes sense.

Humanity has done marvels in the last few hundred years, but left humanity the human family abandoned as though a neglected orphan. The march of knowledge and intelligence will go on, uncovering a heretofore unknown reality which has existed all around us since the beginning of time. But there is no reason for downgrading the heart and the soul.

The miracles of science must be repeated now in the fields of sentiment and interiority. Human beings must again be seen as

Peace is *not* an unrealizable dream.
War is *not* an inevitable reality.

total beings, able to fulfill themselves and to act with the full capacity of the qualities deposited in us by God and evolution.

Once this is done, most problems will fall into place and become solvable.

During the last three hundred years humanity's progress has been essentially of an intellectual and material nature. The imperialism of reason the left-brain had little room or respect for sentiment and the world of the heart.

Scientists and thinkers believed that everything could be solved, explained and furthered by means of pure physical manipulation and intellect. We seem to have come to an end to that belief. How many times do we see in world forums that world problems are insolvable, without solution, because of the excessive intelligence of the antagonists?

In diplomatic and political science courses young people are being taught the intricacies of intellectualism and systemic falsehoods; lies are called "negotiating positions" and the truth is called a "fallback position." With such immorality we will go nowhere

In order to see right, to think right and to act right we must visualized our place in the total universe and in time, as all great prophets, spiritual leaders and philosophers have told us since the beginning.

We must absolutely restore the great moral forces of love, compassion, truthfulness, optimism and faith in human destiny which have always been at the root of civilization.

They alone will enable us to see the light and the great simplicity of the pattern of evolution foreseen by Lord God amidst the complexities, obscurities and anxieties of the present time.

More than a United Nations someday our planet will be a Global Commonwealth of Compassion. And when that happens then the United Nations will truly be nations united. The nations of the world united in heart, united in spirit, united in soul, united

Peace is *not* an unrealizable dream.
War is *not* an inevitable reality.

with the Lord God of all creation, united with the universe, united with eternity.

Today's international community is only an assemblage of powers. How the governors came to power is seldom questioned. But at some point in our evolution the question of the proper representation of the people in the management of our globe will certainly pose itself. As will the spiritual quest for our proper place in the universe and in the stream of time. There is urgent need to determine the cosmic or divine laws which must guide and rule our behavior on the earth.

I firmly believe that the human race will succeed someday in establishing right human relations and that such a day may not be quite as distant than we think.

I would even say more: I firmly believe that humanity will be able to elevate human life to unprecedented levels and achieve a happy, contented society on earth. We have this possibility.

We have been given by Creator God and evolution the means, the intelligence, the heart and the soul necessary for that possibility. The struggle for right human relations which started thousands of years ago on this planet will someday be won, and I think rather soon.

With the founding of the United Nations some sixty-five years ago, for the first time in evolution, the human species assumed a collective responsibility for the success of planet earth in the universe. But much more is needed. We must feel part of all space and time, of the greatness and wonder of the universe and come to know it as our home. From the infinitely large to the infinitely small it is our home. Entrenched as we are in that universe, in the cosmos, in space and time, we must stand in awe before the beauty and miracle of creation of which we are each a part, play a role.

Perhaps this will be the new spiritual ideology which will bind the human race.

Peace is *not* an unrealizable dream.
War is *not* an inevitable reality.

We must rise to concern ourselves with the deeper objectives and reasons of human life, its uniqueness, its miraculous character, our full potentials, our perceptions, sentiments and inner lives.

What is missing is a great core of political humanists, thinkers, prophets, poets and leaders of people who would concern themselves with the deeper objectives and reasons of human life, its uniqueness, its miraculous character, our full potentials, our perceptions, sentiments and inner lives. But they will come soon.

Indeed, some are here now, in growing numbers, but hidden by their manner of humility and simplicity of life. They too see the world as though from outside, as it hangs and twirls in the universe, visualizing as they do the grand journey of humanity towards oneness, convergence and unprecedented happiness. In them a new form of humanity most beautiful and most wonderful is being evolved right under our eyes—yet hidden.

I have good and sufficient reason for believing that the notion of a Global Commonwealth of Compassion is an idea ripe for reaping. Its time has come. Its shore is on the near horizon.

We remind ourselves now that there are moments in time, in the annals of history, when great dreams are shared, when ideas are carried forth, when inspiration propels humanity to greater good.

A dream or a vision is not just for the few, but for the many—to be influenced, impacted, led to higher ground. Filled with respect and appreciation, I give humble thanks for the greater good that comes from such visions. The intentions of those in the past and the foresight of generations yet to follow hold the keys to understanding and progress.

I thank Lord God for wise and insightful dreamers. I honor them for their contributions. And with divine guidance, together with my brothers and sisters in prayer, humbly I go forward, holding forth my own contribution, this proposal for the creation of a Global Commonwealth of Compassion. May it inspire the world. Amen.

Peace is *not* an unrealizable dream.
War is *not* an inevitable reality.

LOOKING DOWN

UP there you go around every hour and a half, time after time, after time, and you wake up in the morning over the mid-East, and over North Africa. You look out of your window as you're eating breakfast—and there's the whole Mediterranean area, and Greece and Rome, and the Sinai and Israel. And you realize that what you are seeing in one glance was the whole history of many for centuries; the cradle of civilization.

You go across the Atlantic Ocean, back across North Africa. You do it again and again. You identify with Houston, and then you identify with Los Angeles, and Phoenix and New Orleans. And the next thing you know, you are starting to identify with North Africa. You look forward to it. You anticipate it. And the whole process of what you indentify with begins to shift.

When you go around it every hour and a half, you begin to recognize that your identity is with the whole thing. And that makes a very powerful change inside of you . . .

As you look down you can't imagine how many borders and boundaries you cross—again and again. And you can't even see them. But you know that in the "wake-up" scene you saw before over the Mid-East, there are thousands of people fighting over some imaginary line that you can't even see. And you wish you could take each of them hand in hand, and say "Look at that! Look at that! What's important?"

Later the person sitting next to you goes out to the moon. And he sees the Earth, not as something big with all kinds of beautiful details; he sees it as a small thing out there. And the contrast between that small blue and white Christmas tree ornament and that black sky really comes through . . . and you realize that on the little blue and white spot is everything that means anything to you—all history, and music, and war, and death, and birth, and love, and tears, and joy—all of it on that little blue and white spot that you can cover with your thumb.

It comes through to you so clearly that you are a sensing point for man. You look down and see the surface of the globe that you have lived on all this time and you know that all those people down there—they are you. And somehow, you represent them and have a responsibility to them. Somehow you recognize that you are a piece of this total life. You're out there on the forefront and you have to bring your experience back somehow. It becomes a rather special responsibility, and it tells you about your relationship to this thing we call the world.

All though this I've used the word "you" because it's not me, Rusty Schweickart . . . or any of the others that have had his experience. It's not just my problem—my challenge—my joy to integrate into daily life. It's everyone's.

Rusty Schweickart
NASA Astronaut (former)

Peace is *not* an unrealizable dream.
War is *not* an inevitable reality.

And A Generation Will Yet Arise
To Sing 'How Majestic The Vision!'

It is for us the challenge to discover
the divine spark hidden in everything which,
when joined into the most august torch,
all nations will acquire a clear language
to call in the name of the Lord.
And a generation will yet arise to sing,
How Majestic the Vision!

Then will the world be built anew,
heaven and earth will kiss, and
the joy of creation will become manifest.
And a generation will yet arise to sing,
How Majestic the Vision!

For in the end the general love of humanity and
its basic goodness will overcome the evil surrounding it;
her broken vessels will be mended, the sparks of purity
that have been scattered will be gathered together, one by one,
the purity of the human ideal will be restored.
And a generation will yet arise to sing,
How Majestic the Vision!

Awakened, we will thrust aside all our dross,
and with a divine resoluteness we will gather to
ourselves all our good; from the holy heights
we will restore to life all her treasures,
and all her precious possessions will

shine with a higher illumination.
And a generation will yet arise to sing,
How Majestic the Vision!

The sounds of song, the majesty of the holy tongue,
the beauty that God scatters as he scatters flowers
 o'er the wide earth, and tells us all are ours,
and the ecstasy of heroism and holiness,
will return to the mountains and valleys.
And a generation will yet arise to sing,
How Majestic the Vision!

And so will fade away all the destructive winds
that have filled our lands, our languages, our history; and
we will be given a new heart, in us will be placed a new spirit;
and we will be His people and He will be our God.
And a generation will yet arise to sing,
How Majestic the Vision!

Radiant is the world soul, full of splendor and beauty,
full of life and delight, God's spiritual wellsprings everywhere,
thus why spend our substance on what does not nourish
and our labor on what cannot satisfy?
And a generation will yet arise to sing,
How Majestic the Vision!

All existence whispers to us a secret,
the secret of serving You, Lord, a sea of light;
You, Lord, and the hidden wisdom that opens its channels
sending that light into the broad places of the world's dark;
and so out of darkness going forth light, light, light,
revealing Lord your pleasantness, piercing heaven.
And a generation will yet arise to sing,
How Majestic the Vision!

It is for us the challenge to join the
ascending stream from our mortal self with
the descending stream from the Source of our soul,
the soul that in its hidden musings and flight
soars above walls of heart, walls of deed,
walls of logic, morality and custom,

Peace is *not* an unrealizable dream.
War is *not* an inevitable reality.

…..the soul that aspires.
And a generation will yet arise to sing,
How Majestic the Vision!

For within the soul is stored sparks
abounding in treasure of light and warmth,
of flames that would rise upward, allowing
lips to express what the heart meditates, and
the pen to expound what is hidden in thought,
….. thus revealing to us our only
vocation, our true vocation:
to raise our world from its lowly depths
and bring it to its authentic character.
And a generation will yet arise to sing,
The Vision! The Vision! The Vision!
O How Majestic the Vision!

Easter Sunday 2009

~~~~~~~~~~~~~~~

Peace is *not* an unrealizable dream.
War is *not* an inevitable reality.

ALL ARE INVITED
TO HELP WITH MY DREAM

It is my dream for *"And A Generation Will Yet Arise to Sing 'How Majestic the Vision!'"* that I might see its lines set to music in grand-manner. As in "Ode to Joy" (set to music by Beethoven in his Ninth Symphony) with voices, soloists, and chorus joining the orchestra in Schiller's hymn of universal brotherhood. On notes of joy, triumph, transcendence and dance—carried through every verse. Rousing and stirring. Joyful and transcending. Conducted by a symphony of mixed instrumentalists joined by a mixed chorus of rich and lifting voices. For this I pray. Can you help? Do you know of someone who might be interested? Do you have any ideas? Thank you. I am grateful. I love you. Hugs.

Author's Apology

I shall bring my own work to an end here...
If it is well written and to the point,
that is just what I wanted;
if it is poorly done and mediocre,
that is all I could manage.
2 Maccabees, Epilogue

WHEN WE

When we have done our best,
'Everything that happens
calls for our worship.'
This is the last word
of human wisdom
and of sanctity.
Teilhard, Peking,
9 May 1944

When we live our lives
as Missions, as Service,
we start thinking of
ourselves as people who
are in a faraway country
aware that there is a home
from which we are sent and
to which we have to return.
We sense we are here to bring
a message or work on a project,
but only for a certain amount
of time. When the message has
been delivered and the project
is finished, we want to return
home to give an account of
our mission and to rest
from our labors.
Ted Conlin, Long Island,
Easter Sunday 2009

Peace is *not* an unrealizable dream.
War is *not* an inevitable reality.

WITH GRATITUDE

ACKNOWLEDGEMENTS
- by Name and Contribution -

Nothing that is worth doing,
however virtuous or true,
beautiful or good,
can be accomplished alone,
this is why God gave us each other.

ADELLA J. CONLIN, my dearly beloved spouse of Christ-like womanhood. Without her my exploration for world peace might never have gotten to the starting gate let alone beyond it. I give enormous thanks for all her great demonstrations of bravery and stalwartness in the sometimes most difficult of circumstances invited by my years of quest. Although she never complained, it couldn't have been and in fact wasn't easy for her. I give thanks for her many decades spanning a half-century of enduring faith while keeping me believing and determined. Adella's boundless love, her constancy of unwavering and unselfish support, has made possible this volume.

Our children **JUDY HORNBECK, AMY MARIE WRIGHT** and **PETER CONLIN** couldn't have been more wonderful or lovingly supportive during all these years of quest. Indeed, Amy generously undertook to do the painstaking task of proofreading the manuscript for this book and providing comment. Also she serves as an archivist for all of my many writings: essays, poetry and book manuscripts. Aside from having been enormously helpful, she's been a great cheerleader. When looking back, having had a Dad committed to a career unlike any other, as some might say, couldn't have been easy for any one of my three children, the loves of my life. Especially when younger, not yet awake to the absolute

280

urgency of need for coming up with a solution to the problem that is war and threat of war. "To keep a lamp burning," said Mother Teresa of Calcutta, "we have to keep putting oil in it." For me, my children have been the oil that has kept my lamp burning all these many years. Such has been their loving and enormously supportive influence that without them there would be no book.

My parents, LUCY LOUISE (nee Leary) CONLIN and WALTER FRANCIS CONLIN, SR. who gave me a faith to live by. For we cannot tell what may happen to us in the strange medley of life, but we can decide what happens in us—how we can take it, what we do with it—and that is what really counts in the end. How to take the raw stuff of life and make it a thing of worth and beauty—that is the test of living. Life about which they taught me by example is an adventure of faith, if we are to be victors over it, not victims of it. Thank you, Mom and Dad. I love you!

My ANCESTORS of Leary and Conlin lineage upon whose shoulders I stand and do what I do. I live with enormous gratitude for all of their many kinds of struggle, suffering and sacrifice that have helped make my time here on earth fruitful in mission and ministry. To forget one's ancestors is to be a brook without a source; truely they've been my source. They are the rejoicing of my heart. Thank you all.

DR. LUIS E. NAVIA, college dean and department chair whose enormously generous contributions in time and knowledge when preparing critical reviews and assessments of my manuscripts will forever remain measureless. Beginning with my initial work, a tome, WAR ON TRIAL & the Celestial Messenger, he kept alive in me the courage to persevere in life that shrinks or expands in proportion to one's courage. This lettered man of numerous honors and awards, whose biographical listings include the Dictionary of International Biography, has long served as a steadfast and valued friend of the project: MOMMY...WHAT WAS WAR? Navia's embrace of how man's mind, once stretched by a new idea, never goes back to its original dimensions, never tires of new ideas, such as he has found and supported in my work, fills me with gratitude. Gratitude not only for his belief in my project but, also, for his years-long warm friendship and generous expressions of kinship and commitment.

SUE FLYNN ever joyful who served so faithfully and generously as my transatlantic courier during the Balkan Wars of the 1990's; she gave and gave and gave, she is loved. HENRY SATINSKAS who helped in keeping me upgraded, on track, at the computer end of things during the early years. CHARLES FARAONE who kept me at the helm of things when waves of computer and printing crises would threaten my patience and fortitude. God sent, his many expressions of generosity and caring spirit have been truly, truly remarkable. PETER REALI without whose enormous support my office could never have had an Annex in which to house my archives.

FRA SVETOZAR KRALJEVIC, OFM of Medjugorje who by friendship and brotherly example taught me so very much about the deeper meaning of pilgrimage and how to walk 'alone' in my quest. REV. JOHN WHITE, author of the introduction to The Wisdom of John Paul II, who always, always believed in me and never ever missed an opportunity to give expression to that belief.

REV. FRANK GAETA, my former pastor, who in many ways and with great enthusiasm regarded the Welcome Mary House (our family homestead) and its mission as an "Annex" to the work of his parish. His whole-hearted pastoral support, commitment and investment in our war relief work during the Balkan Wars of the 1990's, coupled with our promotion of the then unfolding events at Medjugorje in that same region, was beyond remarkable and much appreciated.

FRA SLAVKO SOLDO, OFM, of Mostar, Hercegovina, whose shepherding instincts, hospitality and warm friendship during the horrible years of war in his homeland, has meant more than mere words alone can express. MOTHER TERESA of CALCUTTA who taught me to be cautious that my rationality doesn't strangle impulses of the Spirit.

MSGR. FELIX MUCHADO of the Vatican's Pontifical Council for Interreligious Dialogue where he headed up the Eastern Desk under John Paul II, whose long, long years of brotherly affection and affirming support has meant so very much in my struggle to make sense of this world and find my God-intended place in it. He now serves as a bishop in his homeland of India. SISTER MARCIE PURPURA, master of the understatement, whose loving support and strength of faith over many years I shall always regard as treasure beyond measure.

BROTHER ROGER SCHUTZ, legendary founder and prior of Taize, the world's first and only ecumenical monastic Community. A unique center of inspiration and hope, especially for young people. A crossroads, where many traditions, Eastern and Western, agnostic and atheist, Jew and Christian, can meet on equal terms. With the monks and intercontinental teams of young adults, I had the opportunity to help plan and participate in the Taize sponsored four-years preparation for the first ever World Council of Youth (1984). Its success inspired Pope John Paul II, a dear friend of Brother Roger, to launch what is today's bi-annual World Youth Day that is celebrated at different places across the world.

UNO SVEDIN, of Stockholm, Sweden, world esteemed physicist and resource of note at world conferences on issues related to a globally sustainable environment... whose profound wisdom and insight, always eloquent and thought provoking, always deep seated, always humble, is an ever present reminder that the person is still not only the most extraordinary computer of all, but exists with the transcendent possibility if not promise of rising to a whole new dimension or realm of life.

JEAN VANIER, legendary founder and shepherd of the worldwide network of l'Arche communities for mentally challenged youths and adults, who has taught me that in a divided world of the poor and the rich, the helpless and the helpful, the handicapped and the able, there is enough room for Joy. Words alone are not sufficient enough to tell how deeply his words – eternal and life-giving – have stirred to hope-filled life the deep sources of grace in me over these last many years. Along with Mother Teresa of Calcutta, the two were friends, he is one of the great living saints of our age whose experiences as a Christian activist has enriched my own life as a Christian activist.

SOCIETY'S WOUNDED, the handicapped, those on the margins of everyday life, those who have been crushed and hurt, from whom I have learned more about the Gospels than I have from the wise and the prudent. Especially have I learned and indeed been enriched by people with few intellectual abilities…these wounded who are especially open to the message of Jesus the healer, Jesus the Lover. In their own way they have shown me how wounded I am, how wounded we all are.

REV. WALTER J. CISZEK, Jesuit priest and once a prisoner for five years in an execution cell of Moscow's infamous Lubianka Prison and then, without trial, shipped off to many years in a forced-labor penal camp north of the Arctic Circle, who valued and supported my involvements in the Great Social Causes and issues of our era — all the while teaching me an immense if not invaluable lot about despair and the indomitable soul.

HARRISON SALISBURY, Moscow bureau chief for The New York Times during the Soviet era and encourager in my then young life, the memories of which have helped sustain and keep brave my spirit during periods of grave doubt and uncertainty.

ROBERT MULLER, who fought with the French Resistance and was captured by the Nazis only later to become Assistant Secretary-General of the United Nations during its early decades of existence — who in our meetings encouraged and moved me to redouble my efforts on behalf of the true birthright of us all: the right to live in peace.

BROTHER BEN GARGULINSKI, Trappist monk and jelly-factory linchpin at St. Joseph Abbey in New England, whose amazing everything about him has served as ongoing cheer and rock-solid support for all I am and do. Ben Gargulinski, in choosing a life of solitude and obscurity in a Trappist monastery, albeit in the work of running a famous jelly factory, found his real place in the world of yesteryear and today, a world he's loved and prayed over, a world he's given his heart and hugs to—but most of all his jelly of awesome varieties and yummy tastes. Too, a salute for Trappist BROTHER CONRAD IRRGANG, the only person who has ever taken a fairly decent picture of me (it's up front in this book, also on back cover). Thanks, Conrad! A good man, great friend, true monk.

LEWIS RANDA, founder of the world renowned The Peace Abbey at Strawberry Fields in Sherborn, Massachusetts, who so profoundly deepened my appreciation for the "Ways Others Love God" — and for the myriad of creative ways that Randa promotes the causes of peace and justice, non-violence and love such as his abbey's "Courage of Conscience Award" serving to stir the conscience of the many. Cheers!

ROSIE (TOOMER) DENTON, whose many years of adventurous faith, whose spirit of reverence, curiosity and worship, whose power of conscience and the moral imperative, whose intimacy with God and with all of God's creation and creatures, and, finally, whose love and spiritual kinship…has given substance and direction to my now long life.

REV. ZLAVKO SUDAC of Mali Losinj, a remote island in the northern Adriatic Sea, whose open and generous sharing – through the profundity and gifts of his Christ-centered mystical life as a stigmatist priest – has served to richly confirm and support my own life in the adventures of the Christian mystical. The REV. BILL BRISOTTI, diocesan priest, who by example during the recent civil war in El Salvador and in years since, taught me so very much about those who are the most oppressed and suffering, the ones who are the civilian victims of conflict and war, as being the heart of the greater community, the universal community…a presence of Jesus—Jesus crucified and in pain.

REV. MARTIN LUTHER KING, JR. who taught me what the "Strength to Love" really, really means and what it really, really takes to "Walk the Talk."

REV. THIERRY de ROUCY, founder of the international network of "Heart's Home" missions of consoling presence to those who are suffering, spreading a culture of compassion in a world desperate for compassion; founder also of the International Center for a Culture of Compassion in the Catskill Mountains of New York... has brought great joy into my life otherwise troubled by ongoing war and threat of war. Here "Grandma Adella" and "Grandpapa Ted" are known for our support of Fr. Thierry's commitment of loving and restoring dignity to the most wounded people in the world.

REV. BOB McGUIRE, Jesuit priest, whose unbounded support and caring concern inspired and helped me break through the thought-impossible when a major health crisis threatened my mission just several years ago. A very special thank you and salute to TIM GOIN of the science research community in medical issues for help in keeping me going during that same crisis.

"ANNIE" (DELLER) BONURA, our spiritual daughter, whose animated passion as an encourager of rare gift has served to keep me focused. MAGGIE McCARTIN CASTELLANO, my spiritual director whose soul so splendidly formed makes goodness attractive, puts hope where it should be, sees opportunity in every difficulty, makes life worthwhile.

PHIL KAUTZMAN, Korean War veteran, a reconnaissance sergeant who completed two successive tours of active duty behind enemy lines before returning home. In what would be a last phone call to me just days before his death in a hospice, Phil, in uncharacteristic manner, quite abruptly ended our chat by raising his voice as though from the field of some great peril and said as though commanding me: "Ted, you *must* get your writings published! You MUST!!!" It was remarkable because at no point in our conversation - not until his "MUST" - had there been any mention of my writings; none at all. Repeating himself he then again ordered: "Ted, you must...!" and then a click. "Ted, you must...!" were Phil's last words to me.

I acknowledge my ancestors of Leary and Conlin lineage upon whose shoulders I stand and do what I do. I live with enormous gratitude for all of their many kinds of struggle, suffering and sacrifice that have helped make my time here on earth fruitful and thus possible. To forget one's ancestors is to be a brook without a source; indeed they've been my source. They are the rejoicing of my heart.

Not to be forgotten are the so many, many others, each in their own special way, especially those with prayer, who've lent support, been encouraging, along the way. They know and God knows who they are. Thank you dear friends, family, fellow pilgrims, strangers, thank you!

Finally, if any glory is to be given in all of this, and there is, in abundance, then all of that glory must go to our Lord God, Creator God—who is always good!

PLEASE...CONTRIBUTE TO

WHAT OTHERS ARE SAYING ABOUT
MOMMY...WHAT WAS WAR?

With Your Own Comments

And Commentary

For promotional purposes what You have to say can be of

enormous help in our efforts to market this book.

DO IT TODAY! THANK YOU!

Ted Conlin
Welcome Mary House
PEACE ABBEY
60 Lafayette Avenue
Westbury, New York 11590 USA

~ NOTES ~

~ NOTES ~

~ NOTES ~

~ N O T E S ~

~ NOTES ~

~ NOTES ~